Adam watched Lauren McKenna take her seat in the executive conference room as the meeting began. As the owner of the company introduced him as its newest officer, Lauren's gaze zeroed in on him for the first time . . . and froze.

Adam saw the shock flash across Lauren McKenna's face, and felt a spurt of satisfaction. At least he wasn't the only one caught off guard. Lauren's pole-axed expression exactly mirrored the disbelief that he'd felt when she had breezed into the room.

So this was Lauren McKenna. He'd heard so much about her. Adam had expected someone older, someone more . . . professorial. Not this ethereal beauty with the haunted eyes. The woman had a Ph.D., and a high-powered job. She wasn't exactly what you'd expect of someone who looked like a sea nymph. And of all the things he'd been told about her, he had clearly missed the most important thing of all. That he already knew her. . . .

She stared at Adam, oblivious to everyone else in the meeting. "You."

The single word, spoken during a lull, simmered with accusation, causing the babble of voices around them to fizzle like a doused flame. In the quiet that followed the others fidgeted and cast uncomfortable looks between Lauren and Adam. He nodded and sent her a cool smile. "Believe me, I'm just as surprised as you are."

. . . and she was just about to reconsider, if he had his way!

NO TRUER LOVE

Ginna Gray

Pinnacle Books
Kensington Publishing Corp.

http://www.pinnaclebooks.com

PINNACLE BOOKS are published by

Kensington Publishing Corp.
850 Third Avenue
New York, NY 10022

Pinnacle and the P logo Reg. U.S. Pat. & TM Off.

First Printing: November, 1996
10 9 8 7 6 5 4 3 2 1

Printed in the United States of America

To my mother, Ruby Conn

One

The woman was back.

Adam Rafferty felt his pulse quicken, and he realized that for the past hour he'd been waiting for her to appear.

With languid steps she strolled along the empty stretch of private beach. This evening the wind off the Pacific was unusually gentle. It played with her ankle-length gauzy dress, alternately billowing it out behind her and molding it to her slender body. Like a banner in the wind, her long hair lifted and fluttered around her face, the auburn strands glowing like fire in the blazing sunset. Now and then, in an absent gesture, she lifted her hand and raked the dancing tresses away from her face. Barefoot and graceful, she looked fragile, like a nymph rising from the sea.

Adam stepped out onto the deck of the beach house, his glass of iced tea in hand. In the six days since he had moved into the house, each evening the woman had passed by at about the same time. From the first moment he'd seen her she had fascinated him.

Leaning a hip on the deck railing, he took a sip of tea, his gaze fixed on the woman. She was his only neighbor on this wild stretch of shore just north of San Francisco. Otherwise, he had no idea who she was.

Adam had seen the woman coming and going from the house at the opposite end of the crescent-shaped cove. It was the only other one besides his own on this beach. Except for the private road off the coastal highway, which was gated and locked, the beach was inaccessible, protected all along its length by a sheer cliff of jagged boulders.

Adam stared at the woman, willing her to look his way, but, as she had the last five nights, she passed by without giving him so much as a glance.

She had to be aware of his presence, he thought with a touch of annoyance. She must have seen the lights on in his house the past five nights. He was also fairly certain that she'd noticed him standing on the deck each evening as she'd strolled by, but she gave no sign. He might as well be invisible, for all the notice she took of him.

Adam wondered what the woman's face looked like. His house, like hers, sat nestled beneath the craggy cliffs with several hundred yards separating them. Short of using binoculars, he couldn't make out her features at that distance. In the evenings she walked along the water's edge, too far away for him to see her clearly in the dim light. Mostly, she was just a graceful silhouette against the flaming sky and restless waters.

Still, something about the woman drew him, fascinated him. There was an aura of mystery about her that was almost palpable.

The woman piqued his curiosity to a degree Adam found both surprising and irksome. He had just extricated himself from a destructive relationship. The latest in a long line of unwise and hopeless relationships, he admitted to himself. He seemed to have a knack for attracting women with problems. But no more, he vowed, taking another sip of tea. With Delia, he'd learned his lesson, once and for all.

His gaze narrowed on the graceful silhouette. Yet, dammit, this woman was intriguing as hell.

She had reached the southern end of the beach, and he watched her climb the boulders at the point. At the summit she settled on a flat-topped slab, drew her knees up and wrapped her arms around them. Breakers pounded the rocks below where she sat, sending up plumes of foamy water and spray that glittered an iridescent pink against the setting sun. Her gauzy skirt fluttered around her and gulls swooped and squawked. The woman appeared oblivious.

It was the same routine every evening; a solitary walk along the beach to the rocky point. There she sat and stared out over the breakers, as still as one of the ancient boulders that surrounded her. Then, when the sun set, she rose and returned to her house at the other end of the cove.

The light grew dimmer, and Adam squinted. What was she thinking about, sitting up there all alone? What drove her to that rocky point each evening? Did she seek solitude? Or was she alone due to circumstance?

Maybe she had been widowed. Maybe she had no family or close friends. Maybe, like him, she was new to the area. Or maybe she was simply shy. For some people, meeting strangers was a painful ordeal.

The more Adam considered it, the more he warmed to the idea. Perhaps she was too reserved to make the first move— even one as simple and innocuous as introducing oneself to a new neighbor.

As the minutes passed, the clouds in the western sky faded from streaks of brilliant orange and hot pink to mauve and dusty blue, lined with silvery gold. Then, gentle as a sigh, the sun slipped beneath the watery horizon, leaving only a crimson glow.

Right on cue, in a single graceful move, the woman lowered her legs and stood up.

While she picked her way down the rocky slope to the beach, Adam made up his mind. Hell, a simple introduction didn't constitute romantic interest.

Setting his glass down on the deck table, he kicked off his shoes and headed for the outside stairs that led down to the beach. They shared this stretch of shore and it was high time they met. If she was too reticent to come to him then he'd do the honors. It was, after all, the neighborly thing to do.

The sand was still warm beneath his feet as he cut an

angled path across the beach to intercept her. The rosy glow had faded to a pale lavender light that was rapidly seeping away, but he could still make out her shape coming toward him through the gloaming.

He knew the instant she spotted him. Her steps faltered then slowed to a wary crawl. Not wanting to frighten her, Adam raised his arm and waved.

"Hi there. Nice evening, isn't it?"

She did not respond, other than to come to a full stop and eye him with suspicion.

"I guess by now you know that I'm your new neighbor." Coming to a halt in front of her, he gestured toward his beach house, but his gaze never left her face.

Pleasure wafted through him. Christ, she was lovely. Not merely attractive. The woman's beauty nearly took his breath away.

He found himself staring into an oval face with perfect features. He couldn't quite make out the color of her large, heavily lashed eyes, but they were crystal pale. Adam made a bet with himself that they were green. His gaze swept over her high cheekbones and wide, lush mouth—the kind of mouth made for kissing. Damn.

In that dress, with her hair whipping around her face, she looked like one of those fairy creatures his Irish grandmother used to tell him about.

"My name is Adam Rafferty."

He stuck out his hand but she didn't appear to notice, and after a moment he let it drop.

His name had not elicited so much as a flicker of recognition. That surprised him. These days a lot of women were avid football fans, but even among those who weren't, most had at least heard of him.

He observed her hands were ringless, then immediately scolded himself for noticing.

Get a grip, Rafferty. Remember the past six months with Delia. From now on you play it nice and cautious.

That lush mouth folded into a tight line. His neighbor looked out at the ocean, then back at him, and even in the dusky twilight Adam could see the chill in those pale eyes.

"Look, Mr. . . . Rafferty, was it?" At Adam's nod she continued. "It appears that we need to set some ground rules."

Her soft voice distracted him, and it was a few seconds before her words registered. When they did he blinked. "Excuse me?"

"Surely, you must have noticed that I've kept my distance."

"Well . . . yeah. As a matter of fact, I have."

"There's a reason for that. I value my privacy. That's why I live in such an isolated spot. I hope you won't be offended. I really don't wish to be rude, but you may as well know that I'm not interested in getting to know you. Just because we happen to share this beach is no reason to feel we must become friends, or even acquaintances. I prefer my own company. Therefore, you have my word that I will do my best not to intrude into your life, and in return I expect the same consideration from you. As long as we both manage that we should be able to coexist beautifully. Now if you'll excuse me . . ."

With that excruciatingly polite but frosty message delivered, she stepped around him and continued down the beach.

Adam stared after her, slack-jawed and speechless.

He couldn't believe it. He'd been snubbed. Cut cold. Hell, she hadn't even told him her name!

She was thirty yards down the beach before his shock faded. Hard on its heels came anger. Snapping his mouth shut, he stomped back toward his home, kicking up sand behind him with each furious stride.

He stormed up the steps to the deck and into the house. Adam was neat by nature, but he was too agitated to remember to rinse off his feet with the hose that he kept on the deck for that purpose, or even to notice the sand he'd tracked onto the polished oak floor of his living room.

Anger was an emotion he seldom experienced. During his twelve years as a pro quarterback for the Charleston Hurricanes he'd been a ferocious competitor—aggressive, tough and hard-hitting. He'd taken and dished out his share of hard licks, but that was the nature of football. Off the field very little got under his skin.

His friends and teammates used to tease him about his easygoing nature.

Adam didn't think of himself as particularly patient or easygoing. He simply had never seen the sense in getting riled over unimportant things. He shrugged off life's little irritations with a laugh. It took a hell of a lot to rouse him to true anger, but his lovely neighbor—whatever the hell her name was—had left him simmering.

"To hell with her." He stomped into the kitchen. "You want me to leave you alone? Fine. I'll leave you alone. Lady, hell will freeze over before I offer you my friendship again."

His conscience pricked him the instant he muttered the words. All right. So maybe for a second there, after he'd gotten a good look at her, he'd let himself anticipate something more than mere friendship. So what? He was a healthy male and when a woman looked like that it was perfectly natural for a man to experience a few lustful stirrings. That didn't mean he was going to follow through on them. He snorted. Not after that glimpse of her personality. That was for damn sure.

"It was probably her best side, too," he muttered.

The woman was antisocial, a cold fish. Maybe even a man-hater. The smartest thing for him to do was ignore her. After all, their houses were separated by several hundred yards of beach. It shouldn't be that difficult.

Too worked up to relax, he paced the floor, anger still churning inside him. He was in the middle of his second circuit when the telephone chirped.

He snatched it up and barked, "Yeah. What is it?"

A beat of stunned silence followed, then a low, "Adam? Is that you?"

Sighing as he heard his old friend's and former teammate's voice, Adam raked a hand through his hair and forced the edge from his voice. "Yeah, Tony, it's me."

"Holy shit, I don't believe it." Tony Diamatto, sounded surprised. "You're actually pissed. For a second there I thought I had the wrong number. What happened? Jeez, it must've been a real catastrophe to rile you."

"Not really. I just had an unpleasant run-in with my neighbor, that's all."

"You're kidding. You? Huh. Must be a real asshole if he can't get along with you."

"It's not a matter of can't, but of won't. The woman is the unfriendliest human I've ever met. With her it's strictly keep away. She took great pains to spell that out in terms any moron could understand."

"Whoa, whoa, whoa! Let me get this straight. Your neighbor is a woman?"

"Yeah."

"Old or young?"

"Around thirty."

"Good-looking?"

"Well . . . yeah." The understatement pricked Adam's conscience. He grimaced and raked his fingers through his hair again. Dammit! As far as he was concerned her personality canceled out her looks. As his mom was fond of saying, pretty is as pretty does.

In the past Adam had never given much credence to that particular homily, but now it made perfect sense.

"Oh, man, that's rich!" Tony hooted. "Hold on a sec. I gotta tell Kate."

"No, wait! Don't—"

Before Adam could stop him he heard Tony bellow to his wife, "Hey, honey! Wait'll you hear this! Adam is living on an isolated beach next door to a gorgeous woman and she won't give him the time of day!''

Adam closed his eyes and groaned. Next to Tony, Molly Kate O'Shea Diamatto was his best buddy in the world, and he adored her, but the woman was unmerciful when it came to ribbing him about his love life. She'd never let him hear the end of this.

In the background he heard Kate's disbelieving laughter. "What? You're kidding me!" She snatched up an extension phone. "Adam? Is it true? Please say it is, because if this is one of Tony's jokes I'm going to clobber the big lug."

"Look, Kate, it's no big deal. I've simply got an unfriendly neighbor."

"It *is* true?" she crowed. "There really is a female over the age of fourteen who refuses to swoon at your feet! Well saints preserve us!"

"Can you believe it, honey?" Tony chortled. "All through high school and college this guy had to beat the women off with a stick. After he joined the pros they lined up outside the locker room after every game."

"Hell, man, you got some nerve, lying to your wife that way. Don't pay any attention to him Kate. It was Tony who was the Don Juan on the team."

Adam spoke in a teasing voice, but it was true. Tony Diamatto was hell-on-women gorgeous—black hair, chiseled features, smoldering brown eyes. Women stopped and gaped when he walked by. Tony'd had lovesick females following him around ever since he was eleven or twelve. As a bachelor, Tony had taken full advantage, but, to his credit, from the moment he met Kate he hadn't looked at another woman.

"Anyway, those women were football groupies, and you know damned well they were after any guy in a jersey."

Adam could have saved his breath.

Tony heaved an exaggerated sigh. "Do you believe it, honey? For years the guy had his pick of women. And now this. How the mighty have fallen."

"Well, if you ask me, it was bound to happen sooner or later," Kate pronounced. "He's no young stud running up and down the field these days, you know."

"Very funny, you guys. Now that you've had your jollies, could we talk about something else?"

Tony laughed. "Okay, okay. I guess we've given you enough grief. Anyway, I wouldn't sweat it if I were you, Hoss. Your neighbor is probably just playing hard to get."

"Don't count on it."

"Aw, c'mon, man. Are you trying to tell us this woman isn't interested in getting to know Adam Rafferty, the most famous quarterback to ever play the game of football? I don't believe it."

"I don't think she's a fan of the game, Tony," Adam drawled. "Some people aren't, you know."

"If they live on Mars, maybe."

Adam chuckled, and felt the tightness in his gut ease. No one could hold onto negative feelings for long around Tony. His friend bounced through life with an upbeat attitude, oozing charm and energy. Though his own career in the pros had been cut short, Tony retained a passion for the game. As far as he was concerned, if you didn't like football, you were un-American.

"You know, you just might have something there," Adam drawled. "That could account for her cold-fish attitude and the fact that she hasn't the slightest idea who I am. She's an alien from outer space."

"Funny. Real funny," Tony grumbled, but he took the hint and changed the subject. "So . . . how's it shakin', buddy? You settling into your new place okay?"

"Yeah. It's a nice house, and the view is spectacular. It's even beginning to feel like home now that I've got all the boxes unpacked."

"When do you start your new job?"

"Tomorrow morning."

"I still can't believe it. Our ole buddy Ed must have made

you a helluva offer to get you to rejoin us working stiffs. Don't get me wrong, pal. Kate and I love having you live here in the Bay area. And with you and me and Ed together again in the same town it'll be like old times back in college. I just can't figure out why you want to jump back into the daily grind. God knows, you don't need the money."

"Yeah, I used to think lazing around sounded good, too, but after trying it for a couple of years I changed my mind. The life of the idle rich isn't what it's cracked up to be, my friend."

"Hmm. Maybe. But I'd sure as hell wouldn't mind giving it a shot."

Adam winced at that. Though he detected no bitterness behind the remark, he couldn't help but feel just a little guilty that his luck had been so phenomenal when Tony's had been so rotten.

Adam and Tony had played high school and college football together, and his friend had been one of the greatest tight ends the game had ever seen. He'd been fast, agile and graceful as a deer, and he'd had one helluva pair of hands on him.

Both he and Tony had been first-round draft picks when they graduated from college and had received lucrative contracts to play professional football. The future had looked rosy for them both.

Then Tony had taken that sledgehammer hit from a bruiser on the Raiders' defensive team. Two fractured vertebrae in his back had required extensive surgery, and had taken him out of the game forever.

After a brief bout of grieving and railing against fate, Tony, in his usual blythe fashion, had pulled himself together, accepted his lot and moved on.

He'd used the money he'd made that first year to finance his way through law school.

"Trust me, Tony, you'd hate it. With your energy and drive you'd be climbing the walls in two months, tops. As for the job, it wasn't Ed who made the offer. That came from his boss, and it wasn't a difficult decision. I'd been looking for something to get into, and this came along at exactly the right time. It's a really sweet deal."

"Mmm, sounds like it. But I'm curious. Won't it be a little . . . well . . . awkward, working for a friend?"

"Ton-nee!" Kate groaned.

"What? Wha'd I say?"

"Please, just overlook him, Adam. Tact is not exactly the big lug's middle name."

"Hey! Everybody knows that working for a friend can be sticky."

"Will you just hush and quit making such a big deal out of it? You know Adam is the most easygoing person in the world. He can get along with anyone."

"That's okay, Kate. Anyway, I won't actually be working for Ed. I'll report directly to the president. He's the major stockholder and head of the company. Ed doesn't own that many shares of Ingram and Bates stock."

"No shit? Hell, the way he talked back in college, I thought he was going to inherit his uncle's half of the company."

"I'm sure he expected to, but it turns out there was never any chance of that happening. I've had several long interviews with Mr. Ingram over the past couple of months. It seems that he and Howard Bates had a partnership agreement which stipulated that upon the death of either of them, ninety percent of the deceased partner's shares in the company went to the surviving partner."

Tony gave a low whistle. "Jeez, that must'a been a low blow for Ed."

"You mean he didn't tell you about it?"

"Yeah, well . . . actually, we don't see all that much of him. You know how it is; a single guy like Ed doesn't have much time for an old married couple like me'n Kate. We're hoping he'll come around more, now that you're here. We'd like to see him."

"I'll see what I can do," Adam said with a chuckle, but he was surprised.

He and Tony had met Ed Bates during their first year at Princeton. Ed had been just a bit too small to play football, but he'd been a staunch supporter, and the three of them had become friends. They had belonged to the same clubs and had even been roommates during their junior and senior years. Since Tony and Ed had both lived in San Francisco for the past eight years, Adam had assumed that they had remained close.

"Adam, I'm so happy you're here. Now we'll get to see you more than just two or three times a year, and the children will have a chance to really get to know their godfather."

"Thanks, Kate. Having you guys live here and my folks just a short drive away in San Jose were the biggest factors in my decision to take the job."

"Whatever the reason, we're delighted. You're part of our family, you know."

Adam smiled, and his voice roughened with emotion. "Thanks, Katydid. That goes double for me."

"All right, you two. Enough of this huggy-kissy stuff. Could we just get back on track here? That's my woman you're sweet-talkin'."

Kate made a disparaging sound, and Adam chuckled. He could almost see her rolling her eyes.

"What he's trying to say, Adam, is, he called to make sure the cookout at your place next weekend was still on."

"You bet. After dinner we'll build a bonfire on the beach and roast marshmallows."

"Great. The kids will love that. And I can't wait to taste one of your famous burgers again. We'll be there with bells on."

"Don't let her kid you, Hoss. Your cooking isn't the big draw. She's really dying to get a look at your place."

"Of course I am," Kate admitted with unabashed honesty. "But what I really want is to get a peek at this neighbor of his."

Two

Lauren McKenna burst out of the elevator the instant the doors opened. She headed for her office at a pace just under a run, dripping rainwater along the plush wine and grey carpet of the executive wing.

"Morning, Nan," she muttered as she dashed into a small outer office and made a beeline for the door on the other side. On its surface a discreet brass plaque read, L. L. Mc-Kenna, Executive Director, Spatial Design.

"Lauren, you're late."

"I know. Some idiot was driving too fast in the rain and caused a six car pileup on the freeway. On top of that, I got a run in my last pair of pantyhose and when I stopped to buy a pair I got drenched."

"Well, you'd better hurry. Mr. Ingram wants you in—"

"Not now, Nan. You know I have to check in with Sam Ewing before I do anything else."

"I already did that."

Lauren pulled up short and cast her middle-aged secretary a surprised look. "You did?"

"And I checked your E-mail, and your online bulletins, and I called the Reunite people. Sorry. I'm not trying to meddle in your business, but I thought it would save time. Mary Alice buzzed earlier. Mr. Ingram has called a meeting in his office and he wants you there right away."

"A meeting? When I left Friday there was no meeting on tap for today. What's this about?"

"She didn't say, but Mr. Ingram himself called back about ten minutes ago. He wasn't pleased that you weren't in yet. He said you were to come to his office the instant you arrived."

"I see." Lauren shed her raincoat and hung it and her umbrella on the coat rack. Tipping her head to one side, she shook her loose French braid, sending raindrops flying. "What did Sam say?"

"That he hasn't any news to report. Every avenue he explored last week turned into a dead end. He said to tell you that if you want him to continue, next week he'd extend his search into Oklahoma and Kansas."

"Of course I want him to continue. Why else would I be paying him?"

"I told him I was sure you'd say that."

"How about the others?"

"There were no phone messages for you, Reunite still hasn't come up with any leads and the only thing on your E-mail was a message from your mother. She wants you to call her tonight."

"I see." Lauren tried to keep her voice level but it came out desolate and a bit wobbly.

She ought to be used to the answer by now. It was the same every week. She always told herself to expect nothing and tried to brace for exactly that, yet each Monday morning when Sam delivered his report she experienced crushing disappointment. No matter how hard she fought it or told herself she was being foolish, that tiny kernel of hope lodged deep inside her persisted.

"Maybe, I should call him back and—"

"There isn't time. You have to get into Mr. Ingram's office right away. He's holding up the meeting for you. I'd get a move on if I were you. You know the boss doesn't like to be kept waiting."

"Okay, I'm going. Put my stuff away for me, will you?"

Dropping her purse on the corner of Nan's desk, Lauren hefted her briefcase. Outside in the wide hallway, she turned left and headed for the imposing set of mahogany double-doors at the end.

Walter Ingram's secretary looked up when she entered the outer office. Pleasure flashed in the older woman's eyes and for an instant the slightest hint of a smile flickered across her features. "Oh, good, you're here. Go right in, Lauren. Mr. Ingram and the others are waiting for you in the conference room."

"Thanks."

Two sets of doors opened off of Mary Alice's domain. One led into Walter's office and the other into the conference room. Lauren altered course, and headed toward the latter, sharing one last, quick smile with her friend.

Mary Alice Dodd had been Walter's secretary for thirty-two years and was absolutely devoted to him. Lauren was quite sure that if it came to it, the woman would take an assassin's bullet for him.

She had been a beauty in her youth. Over the years Mary Alice's chestnut hair had turned a brilliant silver and these days there were fine lines around her mouth and her vivid blue eyes, but she was still a handsome woman.

Rumor around the office held that Mary Alice had never married because for the past thirty-two years she had been in love with Walter.

Whether or not that was true no one could say, since her manner toward her boss was unfailingly crisp and professional, but Lauren suspected it was. For Mary Alice's sake she hoped not, because she was quite certain that Walter didn't have a clue. For over thirty-five years, his wife Helen had been the object of his complete devotion, and though she had passed away over two years ago he still grieved for her.

Walter was gruff and autocratic, but he was not unkind. He relied heavily on Mary Alice and he paid her handsomely, but she had been such a fixture in his life for so long that he took her for granted. Lauren doubted that he thought of her as a woman, but simply as another useful, highly dependable and efficient business machine, like the computers that sat on almost every desk at Ingram and Bates.

With a sigh Lauren reached for the handles of the wide doors to the conference room. Honestly, there were times she wanted to give Walter Ingram a good shake.

Heads swiveled in her direction the instant she stepped inside the conference room. "Sorry to keep you waiting. There was a pileup on the freeway and I got stuck in traffic."

At a glance Lauren recognized that this was a meeting for top level brass only. The long conference table, which could accommodate thirty, was more than half-empty. Occupying his usual place at the head of the table, Walter sat in his leather chair, his arms crossed over his chest in an attitude of impatience.

As Lauren settled into her seat he harumphed and fixed her with a steely look. She returned it with a smile.

At sixty-three, Walter was a commanding figure with silver-streaked dark hair and hawkish features. His six-foot frame was erect and lean, with only the slightest thickening around the middle, giving him an imposing military bearing that intimidated many of his employees.

Lauren, however, was not one of them. Walter had been her father's best friend and she had known him all her life. She found it difficult, if not downright impossible, to be intimidated by a man who had dandled her on his knee.

Walter's gavel banged, and the murmur of voices around the table ceased. "Now that we're finally all here, we can proceed," he growled, casting another look Lauren's way. "I called this meeting to introduce to you the newest member of our team. Although I'm sure he needs no introduction, since his name and face are no doubt familiar to all of you, it's my pleasure to present to you the new Vice President and

Director of Construction and Renovations for Ingram and Bates Construction, Mr. Adam Rafferty."

The name jolted through Lauren. All around the table the others began to clap and murmur. Lauren realized that they were all looking at the man seated to Walter's right, and as her gaze zeroed in on him for the first time she froze.

Adam watched shock flash across his neighbor's face, and felt a spurt of satisfaction. At least he wasn't the only one caught off guard. Her pole-axed expression exactly mirrored the disbelief that he'd felt when she had breezed into the room.

So this was Lauren McKenna. Walter had mentioned her so many times during their talks Adam wondered if perhaps there was more to their relationship than merely business.

The one thing he hadn't mentioned was that she would be his neighbor.

Adam had expected someone older, someone more . . . professorial. Not this ethereal beauty with the haunted eyes. Green eyes, he noted with satisfaction. The woman held a Ph.D. in Engineering Psychology and had been Executive Director of Spatial Design for Ingram and Bates for the past five years. Not exactly what you would expect of a sea nymph.

She stared at Adam, oblivious to everyone else. "You."

The single word, spoken during a lull in the greetings, shimmered with accusation, causing the babble of voices to fizzle like a doused flame. In the quiet that followed, the others fidgeted and cast uncomfortable looks between Lauren and Adam.

He nodded and sent her a cool smile. "Believe me, I'm just as surprised as you are."

"Ah, so you've already met Lauren. On the beach, I presume."

Lauren's gaze snapped to Walter. "How did you know

that?" Her eyes widened. "You *knew* he was staying in the Graysons' house, didn't you?"

"Of course I knew. I'm the one who told him it was for sale."

"For sale? I didn't know the Graysons were selling." Her glance shot back to Adam. "You mean . . ."

"That's right. I bought the place about a month ago." Adam leaned back in his chair, his gaze locked with hers. So stick that in your craw, lady, he thought.

It went against his nature to be less than courteous to a woman, and he did experience a twinge, but only a small one. Perhaps it was petty, even ungentlemanly of him, but in this case he could not help but feel smug as he watched dismay flicker over that perfect face.

"I see." Lifting her chin, she directed her gaze at Walter. "Since Mr. Rafferty has already purchased a home in the area, I suppose we can safely assume that this has been in the works for a while. One wonders why you haven't mentioned it before now."

Edward Bates gave a snort of laughter. "Good God, Lauren, where've you been? Adam has flown in from the East Coast twice in the past six weeks to meet with Walter."

Several of the others mumbled agreement and nodded, but Walter scowled at the head of his legal staff. "If you'll recall, Ed, Lauren was out of town during both of those meetings."

Glancing from his friend to the older man, Adam pursed his lips. So . . . Walter Ingram didn't take kindly to criticism of Ms. McKenna, not even the oblique variety. Interesting.

Equally fascinating was the panic that flickered across his friend's face. Ed was usually too clever and too polished to allow his emotions to show.

Adam watched with interest as he scrambled to smooth over the comment.

"Well, yes. You're right, of course, Walter." He sent both Lauren and his boss a guileless smile, and Adam's mouth twitched. Countless times throughout their years together at

Princeton he had seen Ed employ that exact smile on coeds and professors. Ed was a silver-tongued devil who could charm his way out of even the most awkward situation . . . or into almost any woman's bed.

Had he made it into Dr. McKenna's? Adam wondered. He couldn't imagine Ed working in the same office as a woman who looked like her—without trying . . . unless Walter had a prior claim.

"But naturally I assumed that by now she'd heard that Adam had been here," Ed turned to Lauren and spread his hands wide. "At the very least I thought your secretary would have told you. This place has been buzzing with rumors for weeks. But then, I guess I should have realized that you hadn't heard anything. You hardly ever stick your head out of your office." His smile flashed again. "You know, Lauren, you work much too hard. You ought to come up for air sometimes. Remember what they say about all work and no play."

Adam raised one eyebrow at Ed's flirty tone. If there was something going on between Walter and Dr. McKenna his friend was playing with fire. But then, it wouldn't be the first time.

Lauren responded with the same cool look she had given Adam on the beach the night before. "Office gossip doesn't interest me. Nan knows that." The rest of his comment she chose to ignore.

Walter, however, did not. "Ed does have a point. You spend most of your time either holed up in your office or in that isolated beach house. It's no secret that I've been looking for a replacement for Bill Nelson ever since that heart attack forced him into early retirement. I certainly wasn't trying to keep my negotiations with Adam from you or anyone else, but until we ironed out all the details and it was a done deal, there was nothing to announce."

"I see." Those clear green eyes fixed on Adam. "It's funny. There aren't that many construction companies like Ingram and Bates that operate worldwide, and even fewer who are willing to take on large-scale historical renovations. I'm acquainted with, or at least know of, most of the top executives in those firms, but I've never heard of you, Mr. Rafferty. If you don't mind my asking, which construction company did you work for before?"

Laughter erupted from the others, and Lauren shot a puzzled look around the table. "Did I say something funny?"

"Hell, Lauren, are you serious?" Ed asked, still chuckling. She merely blinked at him. He sobered and stared at her as though she'd suddenly sprouted another head. "Good God! You are. You really don't know."

"Know what?"

"That Adam Rafferty was a pro quarterback. Possibly *the* greatest ever. He played for the Hurricanes for a dozen years and broke damned near every record in the book."

Her blank expression held for several seconds longer. Then comprehension dawned, followed almost at once by disbelief.

"Football? You mean . . . you were a *football* player?"

"Not just a football player," Ed corrected in that long-suffering voice men use when instructing women on the finer points of a sport. "One of the best football players in the world."

"If you're worried about my qualifications, Ms. McKenna, I do have degrees in civil engineering and business." Adam fought back another smile. The woman was so appalled she looked ready to croak.

"But, still . . . you have no practical experience at all. Right?"

"That's right. Do you see that as a problem?"

"Of cour—"

"Relax, Lauren." Ed's chuckle gently chided. "What Adam lacks in experience he more than makes up for in other areas. Trust me, he'll be a great asset to the company."

"I suppose this was your idea."

Her voice held accusation and censure, but Ed looked pleased with himself.

"You could say that. Adam and I were roommates in college and we've been friends ever since. Even so, I wouldn't have recommended him for the position if I didn't think he could handle it. Actually, we're lucky to have him join us. Why, the name recognition factor alone will bring in all sorts of new business."

"You don't have to defend me, Ed. My work will speak for itself." The slight smile on Adam's lips held challenge. So did his steady gaze. "I'm looking forward to proving to Dr. McKenna that I can handle the job."

Walter, who had been sitting back in his chair shrewdly taking in the little scene, suddenly sat forward. "Good. I'm glad to hear that, because you're about to get your chance." He pushed a stack of folders toward Adam. "Those are the files on our latest projects. Read them over and familiarize yourself with every aspect of each one.

"Lauren, I want you to spend the next few weeks showing Adam the ropes."

"*What?* But I can't, Walter. I'm terribly busy right now. I have a stack of—"

"Whatever you're working on will wait," he decreed, shooting down her protest with a look that warned that the matter wasn't up for discussion. "After you've briefed Adam on office procedure, take him to all the job sites in this area. Show him what we've done and how we operate, then show him the bids and how we arrived at the numbers. And I expect you to give him whatever assistance he needs, to get settled in."

"But—"

"That about wraps our business here," Walter announced, cutting her off. The gavel rapped. "Meeting adjourned."

He stalked out of the room without another word, and Lauren bounded up and hurried after him.

The others clustered around Adam, eager to shake his hand and welcome him to the firm. Finally, when they had all filed out, Ed clapped him on the shoulder. "Welcome aboard, buddy. You're a real hit with the staff, my friend. But then, I knew you would be."

Adam shot him a sardonic look. "Not quite all the staff."

"You mean Lauren? Ah, man, don't pay any attention to her. She's distant with everyone. And just between us, personally I've always thought she takes her interior decorating too seriously. I do have to admit, though, she knows her stuff, and she's not difficult to work with."

Adam gave him a wry look as they headed out the door. "I don't know exactly what an engineering psychologist does, but I'm pretty sure there's more to it than picking out drapes and carpet."

"Yeah, so Walter keeps telling me. Anyway, don't take that frosty air of hers personally. She's really a nice person. A few years back she went through a divorce. I don't know the details, but I heard it was nasty. Probably made her bitter toward us guys. She gives us all the cold shoulder. Hell, the men around here call her the Ice Maiden."

Adam could believe that.

Three

Lauren marched into Walter's office right behind him, dogging his heels like an angry terrier.

"Go away, Lauren, I'm busy."

"No, I will not go away. We have to talk. Have you lost your mind, Walter? Everyone around here thought you would promote someone from within the company to take Bill Nelson's place. That you brought someone in from the outside is bad enough, but what in God's name possessed you to hire a man who has absolutely no work experience? And as vice president, for Pete's sake. That's crazy."

With a resigned sigh, Walter sat down at his desk and fixed her with a long-suffering look. "If you weren't my goddaughter I'd kick your little butt out of here for questioning my decisions."

"That rough talk doesn't scare me, and you know it. I realize that this is your company and you can run it as you please, but this is absurd. That man is going to be nothing but dead weight. And since I'm one of the people who will have to take up the slack, I think that gives me the right to complain."

Mary Alice was watering potted plants on the other side of the office, but neither Lauren nor Walter paid her any notice. Mary Alice knew everything that went on in the company anyway.

"To start with, none of the staff was qualified to step into Bill's shoes."

"But you felt that dumb jock *was?*"

"Adam Rafferty is anything but dumb."

"Oh, please. It hardly takes a rocket scientist to run up and down a football field and toss a ball around."

"There's a bit more to playing quarterback than that. It takes a lot more intelligence than you seem to think, to play the game at any position, particularly at the professional level."

Lauren rolled her eyes.

"Will you at least give me a little credit? I checked the man out thoroughly before I made the offer. Every major university in the country was after him when he graduated from high school, but he chose Princeton because of their academic standing. Even though he was the star of the football team throughout college he managed to graduate near the top of his class. Over the years he's made some shrewd investments with the money he earned playing pro ball. If he wanted, he could sit back and clip coupons and never work another day in his life, but the man is educated and sharp and too intelligent for that."

That surprised Lauren, but it didn't mollify her. "All right, so maybe he's not dumb. He still doesn't have any experience. He's what? Thirty-four? Thirty-five?"

"Thirty-six."

"There you go. And the only thing he's done during all the years since he left college is play a game, for which he was no doubt grossly overpaid."

"That may be, but playing pro ball also made him famous, and that is a definite asset. Ed was right about his value to the company. Adam Rafferty is a likeable guy. The fans love him, men and women alike. Hell, even his opponents have nothing but good things to say about him. Just having the guy on board will impress the hell out of customers."

"I see." Lauren's mouth tightened. "So he's just a shill to bring in the clients. Is that it?"

Walter's fist hit the top of his desk so hard the telephone jingled. Lauren flinched. On the other side of the room, Mary Alice continued to water the plants without batting an eye.

"Dammit, that is not it at all! Adam will pull his weight around here just like everyone else. *And* he'll be an asset to this firm to boot." He jabbed his forefinger at her. "Now I don't want to hear another word on the subject. He's hired and you're going to work with him. And that's all there is to it."

"Fine," she snapped. "I do have one more question, though."

Walter sighed and pulled his hand down over his face. "Anyone else would be quaking in their shoes by now," he muttered to no one in particular. He shot Lauren an exasperated look. "What now?"

"When you encouraged Mr. Rafferty to buy the Graysons' summer house were you trying your hand at matchmaking?"

"What? Hell no! What do I look like? Cupid?"

"It's a perfectly reasonable question. You've been nagging me to start dating for the past four years, ever since Gavin left."

"And what's wrong with that? You're a beautiful, intelligent and vibrant young woman. You should get out more, enjoy yourself, meet a man, fall in love, have ba—" He broke off, grimacing when he saw the look on Lauren's face. Chagrined, he cleared his throat and made a dismissive gesture. "You know what I mean."

"Yes. But I did that once. Once was enough."

"Horsefeathers! Just because you had one bad marriage, that doesn't mean all men are bad."

"I know. But it's not just Gavin's leaving. It's . . . all the rest."

She hated the quiver that had suddenly entered her voice, but there was nothing she could do about it. Biting her lower lip, she looked away. After all this time, she still couldn't talk about what had happened without getting upset. Would she ever be able to?

"I know, honey. I know," Walter said in his gruff, gentle way. "But, dammit, Lauren, you can't continue like this. It's not healthy. You've got to get on with your life."

"I can't." Tears rushed to her eyes, and she blinked and stared at the ceiling to hold them back. Finally she looked at Walter again, her chin still wobbling. "I . . . I just . . . can't."

Without a word, Mary Alice put down her watering can and came over to where Lauren stood. She looped her arm around her shoulders and gave her a squeeze. "Are you all right, dear?"

The compassion in her eyes, especially coming from Mary Alice, who was always so crisp and businesslike, was almost Lauren's undoing. She swallowed hard, and forced a wan smile. "I'm fine. Really."

"And don't think I don't recognize evasive tactics when I see them," she charged, refocusing on Walter. Somehow, taking the offensive again helped her to regain control. "We were talking about why you encouraged Adam Rafferty to buy the house next to mine. And don't pretend you didn't have an ulterior motive. I know you better than that, you wily old fox. You never make a move that's not thought out ten ways from Sunday."

"All right. I'll admit I did have a reason," he grumbled. "You know I've never been comfortable with you living out there on that isolated beach all alone."

"I haven't been alone. There were the Graysons."

"Humph! Fat lot of good they were. I doubt they spent a total of a month out of the year at that place. Which was precisely why you liked having them as neighbors."

"I don't mind being alone. In fact, I like it. Anyway, the beach is well protected. I've lived there almost three years and there's never been any trouble."

"So far you've been lucky, but that place isn't as secure as you want to believe. If some crook or pervert decides to try his luck that measly gate won't stop him. I thought Adam might provide a little protection."

Lauren raised an eyebrow. "How? If I did need help, he'd never know it. His house is three hundred yards or more down the beach from mine."

"I know, I know. It's not ideal. Nevertheless, I feel better, just knowing that he's there. Besides, someone was going to buy the place. I figured better someone I know and trust than just any psycho off the street who happened to have the purchase price. If that annoys you, too bad. I don't understand what your big objection is, anyway."

"Did it ever occur to you that it might be uncomfortable to have a co-worker living practically on your doorstep? I'll never get away from the man."

"So? You're making too much of this. Adam's not the type to intrude. And as you pointed out, your houses aren't all that close. I suggest you just accept the fact that from now on you'll be sharing that stretch of beach, then put the matter out of your mind."

Torn between affection and exasperation, Lauren sighed and shook her head. "I don't seem to have any other choice, do I? Now if you'll excuse me, I've got work to do."

Both Walter and Mary Alice watched her stride out with her head high.

"Stubborn female. I swear, I'll never know how the good Lord could pack so much tenacity and iron will into such a delicate package."

A smile hovered around Mary Alice's mouth. "Actually, she reminds me of you. If I didn't know better, I'd think she was your daughter instead of merely your goddaughter."

Walter harumphed and flashed her a scowl, but an instant later his expression softened. "Might as well be. Her father and I were closer than brothers for over fifty years. Lauren's the child that Helen and I never had. I couldn't love her any more if she'd been born to us."

The admission seemed to embarrass him. He cleared his throat and pretended to study the computer-generated report on his desk, until he noticed Mary Alice studying him.

"What's that look for?" he demanded.

"I was just wondering. *Were* you playing matchmaker when you sent Mr. Rafferty out to look at that beach house?"

"Certainly not. Although . . . now that I think about it, that's not such a bad idea. He's a good man. Lauren could do worse."

"Perhaps she truly isn't interested in getting married again."

"Nonsense. It's not natural or right for a woman to live her life single."

Reaching for the file folder on the corner of his desk, Walter missed the stricken look that flashed across his secretary's face. Without a word she walked out of the office.

"Oh, good. You're back. John Bailey in accounting has those figures you wanted, and here are your calls."

"Thanks, Nan." Lauren accepted the stack of messages and began to riffle through them.

"Oh, by the way, Mr. Rafferty is waiting for you in your office."

Lauren's head jerked up. "What?" Her gaze darted toward the closed door and her mouth tightened.

"He said you were supposed to introduce him around and show him the ropes. I told him he could wait for you inside." Nan eyed Lauren's annoyed expression. "Was that the wrong thing to do?"

"No. No, of course not. That's fine." The confrontation in Walter's office had so distracted Lauren it had slipped her mind that he had assigned his new "wonder boy" to her care. Wasn't she the lucky one.

Gritting her teeth, she headed for her office, but halfway there she stopped and cast her secretary a curious look over her shoulder. "By the way, did you know that Walter had hired Adam Rafferty?"

"I spotted him in the hallway last month when he was here, and I put two and two together, but no one mentioned it to me." Nan shrugged. "I'm sort of out of the loop where rumors are concerned. Mary Alice wouldn't divulge Walter's business under pain of death, and everyone else around here knows that you aren't interested in office gossip."

"You recognized him? You knew who he was?"

"Sure. Everybody knows who Adam Rafferty is. My Charley was always glued to the set when he played. I'm not that much of a football fan, myself, but even I know he'd won the Heisman Trophy and was the top draft pick for the pros the year he graduated from Princeton. Heavens, Lauren, the man's a legend. He's been on television a thousand times and there've been at least that many articles written about him in the newspapers. You'd have to be blind or totally out of touch with the everyday world not to recognize him."

"I see." A smile fluttered around Lauren's mouth. Apparently she had turned into more of a recluse than she'd realized.

Adam started to rise when she entered her office but she waved him back down. "Please, keep your seat, Mr. Rafferty," she said in a brisk voice. "Just let me return a few calls and we'll get started."

"Sure. And please, call me Adam. After all, we're going to be working closely together."

"As you wish."

He waited a beat, then cocked one eyebrow. "And may I call you Lauren?"

She wanted to say no, but all her co-workers at the executive level of the company called her by her first name. However, she rarely saw any of them in anything but a business situation. This man was her neighbor as well as a colleague.

Lauren had the uneasy feeling that if she did not keep some barriers in place he would invade that private part of her life that she shared with only a handful of people—her mother, Nan, Walter, Mary Alice and, to a lesser degree, Sam Ewing, the private investigator who had been working for her for the past three years.

Adam Rafferty made her nervous. Why, she couldn't say. Not for certain. Probably it was his size. By any standard he was big, but compared to her measly five feet, four inches he was a giant. He wasn't beefy or thick-necked like a lot of football players, but he had to top six-four, and his broad-shouldered physique was hard and corded with muscle. Not even his expertly tailored suit could disguise that. He was the most unrelentingly masculine man she'd ever encountered.

That, however, was hardly sufficient reason to refuse his request. "Of course, if you wish."

Lauren's hesitation had lasted only a few seconds, but that had been long enough for him to read her reluctance. She saw his jaw clench and his brown eyes narrow. "Tell me something. Do you hate all men? Or is it just me?"

The softly spoken frontal attack took her by surprise, and for a moment she could only stare at him across the width of her desk. "I don't hate you at all, Mr. Rafferty. I don't know you. Admittedly, I have doubts about your qualifications to step into a vice-presidency, but there's nothing personal in that.

"And I certainly don't hate men in general. I will admit that, with a few notable exceptions, I don't trust most of your sex, but hate doesn't enter into it."

"Is Walter Ingram one of those exceptions?"

"Yes, as a matter of fact, he is. Most of the time, anyway," she tacked on with a wry smile. "But even he can be sneaky at times." Siccing you on me without warning, for example.

"I see."

"I am sorry if my . . . reserve irritates you. It is not my intention to be rude, I assure you. However, as I believe I mentioned last night on the beach, I am a very private person. I . . . my own time is fully occupied with a matter that takes most of my focus and energy and, quite frankly, leaves me with neither the time nor the inclination to pursue other things."

"If by that you mean a personal relationship, let me assure you, Dr. McKenna, that I'm not looking for a hot romance."

Lauren felt a blush rise up her neck and flood her face, but she did not look away from that penetrating stare. "That's not what I meant at all. That thought never entered my mind. I was simply trying to explain my actions on the beach last night."

"C'mon, lady. Nobody's that busy. All I'm talking about here is a little neighborliness. Simple friendship. Surely that isn't asking too much. Especially now that you know we're colleagues."

"You will find, Mr. Raf—Uh . . . Adam," she amended when one of his dark eyebrows shot up, ". . . that during business hours I'm cooperative and easy to get along with and always cordial to my fellow workers, but I don't socialize with them after hours. On my own time I prefer to keep to myself."

"Do you socialize with anyone?" Or do you save all your time for Walter? he wondered.

She did not dignify that with a reply, but merely gave him a steady look and reached for the telephone on the corner of her desk. "If you'll excuse me, I'll make those calls and we can be on our way."

And that, apparently was that.

While she returned the most urgent of her calls Adam watched her, bemused. Lauren McKenna was one self-possessed lady, he'd give her that. He had put her on the spot, but she hadn't caved in or offered any real explanation.

A personal matter that took most of her time? What the hell did that mean? If Walter was her lover as he suspected, he sure as hell didn't spend much time with her. Lauren rarely left her house except to go to work and he'd not seen anyone else at her place since he moved in. The only times he saw her she was either walking the beach or sitting on a boulder staring off into space. Whatever it was that occupied her time, he wasn't going to learn it from her. Her whole demeanor shouted, loud and clear—back off.

Far from satisfying his curiosity, she had whetted it even more, which annoyed the living hell out of him. Why this iceberg of a woman intrigued him so he'd be damned if he knew.

The remainder of the morning was spent showing Adam around the office. Lauren led him from department to department, from the executive floor to the mailroom. In each one she explained its function and introduced him to the manager and the key personnel.

After lunch with Walter and Ed at the Blue Duck it was time to begin their tour of job sites in the Bay area.

"I'd be happy to take over for Lauren and show Adam around," Ed suggested as they left the restaurant. "I'm sure Lauren has other work that needs her attention."

She would have gladly accepted the offer, but Walter started shaking his head even before Ed got all of the words out. "The legal end of the business is your area of expertise. Lauren is more familiar with the physical sites. Besides, she and Adam might as well get acquainted. They're going to be working together a lot in the future."

Ed did not appear any more pleased with the decision than Lauren, but he didn't argue. Neither did she. Lauren dared to talk back to Walter more than anyone else in the company, but she also knew just how far she could push. He was fond of her, but Ingram and Bates was his baby. When he used that tone she accepted that his word was law.

Everywhere they went Adam attracted attention. On the

street, even in her car, stopped at traffic lights, people did double takes and stared. The more gregarious waved and shouted, "Yo, Adam! How's it goin' man?" as though they knew him personally.

Politically correct behavior toward females had not yet filtered down to the ground level of the construction industry. Normally, Lauren's inspection of a job site elicited whistles and catcalls and juvenile comments, but not this time. At every stop, the instant the workmen spotted Adam they went crazy. Had she been wearing a G-string and pasties she doubted they would have noticed.

Excited as children on Christmas morning, they abandoned their cranes, ladders, forklifts and scaffolds and crowded around Adam, slapping his back, pumping his hand, getting his autograph on everything conceivable—tools, hardhats, belts, shirts, toolboxes, pickup trucks. One man even had Adam autograph his arm, then announced proudly that he intended to go straight from work to a tattoo parlor and have the signature permanently etched into his flesh.

Reminding the site foremen that their men were still on the time clock did no good. At every site the man in charge was right in among his crew, pushing and jostling for a few seconds with his hero. All Lauren could do was stand aside and shake her head until the pandemonium subsided and the men could be persuaded back to work.

The first job site they visited was a Nob Hill mansion that had been built shortly after the San Francisco fire in 1906. Though the ground-to-roof renovation was running in the neighborhood of two million dollars, it was a small job for Ingram and Bates, one they normally would not have bothered with, but Walter was doing it as a favor for a friend.

"I was happy he agreed to take on this job," Lauren explained as she led Adam through the baroque structure. "Most of my work is done on new or renovated commercial construction. It isn't often I get to try my hand on one of these fancy old places. Which, by the way, the owners want to preserve with all the fancy details intact. That makes it a real challenge, but it's also a treat for me."

"I hope you'll pardon my ignorance, but I'm not sure exactly what it is that an engineering psychologist does."

Lauren shot him a wry look. "You're not alone. It involves a lot of things. The short version is, we focus on creating optimal relationships, among people, the machinery they operate and the environment in which they work.

"For example, engineering psychologists have helped design the lighting and cockpits of sophisticated aircraft. They've also been involved in the space program, developing optimal functional efficiency within the limited confines of spacecrafts.

"I also have a degree in interior decorating, which allows me to combine the two disciplines. The object is to give our clients a workspace, or in this case, a home, that is practical, efficient, comfortable and at the same time aesthetically pleasing."

"Mmm. Very impressive." He looked around, but the place was a shambles. Work had barely begun, and with all the rubble and plaster dust everywhere it was impossible to get an idea of how the house would eventually look. "Can you show me a finished example of what you mean?"

"I intend to, but that will be our last stop."

From Nob Hill she took him to a refinery in Rodeo, across the bay from San Francisco. There, when the excitement Adam's arrival had generated finally died down, they donned hard hats and safety goggles and inspected the re-erection of a hydrogen unit that Ingram and Bates had recently dismantled from an abandoned refinery in Colorado and shipped to the present site.

"As you can see, our work is not limited to commercial office space or residences," she yelled above the noise. "We build factories, refineries, processing plants, canneries, sawmills . . . whatever is needed."

"Mmm." Adam propped his hands on his hips and turned slowly, surveying the jumble of pipes and equipment.

He had left his suit coat in Lauren's car. The sleeves of his shirt were rolled up and the knot of his silk tie hung loose beneath the unbuttoned collar. She caught a whiff of his sun-warmed skin—a clean, musky scent that was uncompromisingly male. Her nose twitched. The sight of his brawny forearms, dusted with silky dark hair, made her feel strangely unsettled, and she quickly looked away.

It disturbed her that even here among the rough workmen in their tight jeans with toolbelts—that undisputed symbol of male sexiness—slung around their hips, Adam stood out as the dominant male.

Their last stop before returning to the office was a new fifty-story office tower near the pyramid-shaped Trans America building that was almost completed. Adam liked the architecture the instant he saw the building, but it was the interior that impressed him the most. Not an inch of space was wasted, yet the overall feeling was of one of light and spaciousness. The lines were clean, the traffic patterns flowing and functional, the colors soothing.

"The top five floors will house Cordex, Inc., the company that owns the building. The rest will be leased. I've chosen all of the office furnishings and accessories for the top five floors to function with and complement the overall design."

If Adam had had any doubts about the validity of Lauren's work they were gone. The office tower was a model of the efficient use of space and form combined with tremendous eye appeal.

"I'm impressed, Dr. McKenna. Looking at this place, no one could possibly say your work is merely window dressing."

Her head turned sharply. "Window dressing? Is that what people on the staff call it?"

"Now, I didn't say that." He wasn't about to mention that

Ed thought of her as nothing more than a glorified interior decorator.

"You didn't have to." She gave him a long, level look, her eyes like green ice. "I suppose you've also heard via the grapevine that I was hired because of Walter. And that I was made director of my department for the same reason. Well, let me set the record straight for you. Perhaps Walter did have a lot to do with my hiring. I've never denied that. However, any promotions I received, I received on my own merit."

She turned and walked away with her shoulders squared, her high heels clicking on the concrete floor.

"Well, well, well," he murmured. "Looks like I struck a nerve."

He jogged after her. "Hey! Wait up," he called, but she didn't even slow her pace. When he reached the bank of elevators she was already on her way down. "Damn."

By the time he snagged another elevator and reached the ground level, except for a couple of electricians working at a fuse box, the marble lobby was empty. Then he spotted her through the plate-glass doors, standing beside her car, which was parked in front of the building, searching through her purse for her keys.

"What is this? Were you just going to drive off and leave me?"

She spared him a quick, icy look as he came to a halt beside her, then went back to searching her purse. "Certainly not. I was merely going to start the car and wait for you. I'd be an idiot to pull something like that on our newest vice president, now wouldn't I."

"Ah, hell." Adam propped his balled fists on his hips and looked away down the street, then looked back, scowling. "Is that the problem? You're still pissed off that I came into the company at the VP level? What's the matter? Were you hoping to make vice president and I stepped in and got in your way?"

"Of course not, I've only been working for Ingram and

Bates for six years. I don't have enough experience yet to
merit that position."

The subtle barb scored a direct hit. Adam's mouth tightened. "Experience is valuable, I'll grant you, but so are other
things."

"Yes. So I've been told."

"What the hell does that mean?" Adam was slow to anger,
but this woman had a knack for getting under his skin.

"Simply that Walter expects your fame to be a terrific
asset to the company," she said with a tight smile. Her gaze
wandered over his shoulder to the pedestrians walking down
the opposite side of the street. "Evidently, playing football
has its—" She sucked in a sharp breath. "Oh, my God! It's
him!"

Frowning, Adam glanced over his shoulder, but all he saw
was the usual stream of pedestrians. "Who? What're you
talking—Hey, wait! Dammit, where're you going now?"

Stupefied, he watched her dart into the stream of traffic
and head for the opposite side.

Brakes squealed and horns blasted. Adam winced. In the
middle of the street a car screeched to a stop, but not before
his front fender grazed Lauren's hip. Her hand slapped the
car's hood and Adam heard her cry out as she was spun
around.

"Goddamned fool woman. Jesus! She's going to get herself killed." His face grim, he took a quick gauge of the
traffic and braced. "Probably me as well," he muttered and
stepped off the curb right behind a taxi.

The cacophony of horns, squealing brakes and shouted
curses grew louder. Adam ignored them and darted among
the traffic. Before he could reach Lauren she recovered her
balance and took off again, twisting and dodging her way
through the lines of moving vehicles.

"Dammit, Lauren! Will you wait!"

If she heard him she paid no attention. After another close
call, this time with a delivery van, by some miracle she

reached the sidewalk on the other side of the street. Without breaking stride, she took off at a dead run.

"Ah, hell." Using the skills honed during years of dodging three-hundred-pound linemen intent on making mincemeat out of him, Adam managed, despite a couple of brushes with certain death, to weave his way through the stream of traffic unscathed.

When he reached the sidewalk, Lauren was a half a block ahead. As though it were a matter of life or death, she tore down the street at a desperate pace, dodging obstacles, shoving and bumping people out of her way without pause or apology.

Damn. The woman had better moves than some tight ends he'd seen. Shaking his head, Adam took off after her. How in the hell did a woman run that fast in high heels, anyway?

"Lauren! Wait up!" Heads turned as people recognized him, but he ignored them and pounded after her. His longer stride allowed him to gain on her, but only gradually. "Lauren! Wait!"

She raced on, and he cursed roundly and poured on more speed. Dammit, he knew damn well she'd heard him that time.

He was within twenty feet of her when shooting pains began to stab through his bum knee, the one that had cost him his career in football. He gritted his teeth, but he was soon limping badly and losing ground.

Adam began to fear that he'd lose sight of Lauren, but suddenly, catching up with a man in a gray suit striding down the sidewalk, she grabbed him by the arm and jerked him to a halt.

"What the—"

"Damn you, where have you—Oh."

Adam limped up to the pair in time to see Lauren's fierce expression dissolve into heart-wrenching disappointment. She closed her eyes briefly and gasped for breath.

"What the hell's the matter with you, lady? Are you nuts?"

"I-I'm . . . sor . . . sorry. I tho . . . I thought . . . you w-were . . . someone e-else. I . . ." A sheen of tears filmed her eyes and she pressed her lips together and shook her head. "My mistake. I'm sorry."

"Well, you should be." The man huffed and made a show of straightening his suit coat, then shot her one last annoyed look before stomping away.

"What the hell was that all about?"

Her head snapped around. She looked surprised to see him, which irritated Adam all the more. Dammit, how could she not have known he was there. Hadn't he chased her down a public street yelling for her to wait and making a complete idiot of himself?

A shuttered look came down over her face. She drew a tissue from her bag and blotted the perspiration from her face and neck. "Nothing that would concern you."

Adam saw red. "Is that right? Lady, you nearly got yourself and me killed. To say nothing of doing God knows what kind of damage to my bum knee."

"I didn't ask you to come with me."

"Oh, yeah? Well, you'll have to pardon me. When I see a colleague turn white as a sheet, get hit by a car, and go chasing after someone on the street I naturally assume there's some sort of crisis brewing and try to help."

"Well, you were wrong. That was a personal matter. And I never asked for your help." Her face set, she started back for her car.

Adam stared after her, his jaw muscles bulging. He had to wait a moment and rein in his fury before he limped after her. Never in his life, not once, had he touched a woman in anger—not even Delia at her worst. But, damn, he wanted to throttle that woman.

Four

The light tap on the door barely registered on Lauren. She sat at the computer work station that comprised one side of her U-shaped desk, her gaze fixed on the PC monitor. A slight frown puckered her brow. In stops and starts, her slender fingers danced over the keyboard.

"Hi, gorgeous. Mind if I come in?"

"Mmm."

The distracted reply came out automatically, but a few seconds later she looked up and blinked at the man lounging in the doorway of her office. "Ed. What are you doing here?"

Her gaze darted beyond him to the outer office, but Nan wasn't at her desk.

Ed's slow smile crinkled the corners of his eyes and showed perfect white teeth. "What's the matter? Can't I drop by a colleague's office for a chat once in a while?"

"Well . . . yes. Of course you can."

Although he certainly never had before. Lauren doubted that Ed had been in her office a dozen times in the six years she had worked there. "Was there something you wanted?" She glanced at the monitor again and hoped he would take the hint.

He shrugged and strolled into the room with his hands in his trouser pockets. The jacket of his tailored suit was thrust back, exposing his manly chest, and the snowy whiteness of his Armani shirt. His blond hair dipped across his forehead in that elegantly casual way that could only be achieved with expert styling. Ed always looked as though he'd just stepped out of the pages of *GQ*.

"Nothing in particular. I was just passing by and saw your door open, so I thought I'd visit with you for a few minutes."

He hitched one leg over the corner of her desk and picked up a letter opener. Running his thumb back and forth over the point, he gave her a smoldering look from beneath his lashes. "You don't mind, do you?"

The gleam in his eyes was seductive. So was that killer smile. Lauren paid no attention to either. Ed flirted with every woman he encountered. With him, it was a reflex response as natural as blinking. He probably didn't even realize he was doing it.

"No, of course not."

The truth was, she did mind. She had too much work to do to sit and chat. Anyway, she couldn't imagine what she and Ed could possibly talk about. She had always gotten along with him okay, but it wasn't as though they'd ever really been friends.

He flipped the letter opener end over end, caught it by the tip on the third revolution, and tossed it again.

"So . . . how are you getting along with Adam?" he inquired, watching the rotating blade.

"All right, I suppose. Why? Has he complained?"

"No, no. Nothing like that. You two have been working together for a couple of weeks now. I was just curious how it was going."

"I see. From my perspective, I'd say we're managing to rub along together all right."

"Good. Good." He flipped the letter opener a few more times. "So tell me . . . what do you think of my pal, now that you've worked with him a while?"

"It's a bit early to form an opinion, but I will admit he appears to be intelligent and knowledgeable in his field. To his credit, he's not embarrassed about asking questions when he doesn't know something, either. And he seems willing to apply himself to learning the business as quickly as possible."

Narrowing her eyes, Lauren tipped her head to one side and studied him, and her expression turned wry. "Don't worry, Ed. I'm not going to poison your friend or push him off a building, if that's what you're worried about."

He laughed. "You have to admit, you two did get off to a rocky start. Still, the thought never occurred to me. Although, for Adam's sake, I'm glad to hear it," he added with a side-long wink.

To Lauren's growing annoyance, he continued to toss the letter opener without missing a beat.

"Actually . . . I was more concerned about the opposite happening. Adam seems to have something that most women find irresistible. What, exactly, I don't know. With that ugly mug of his, I've never been able to figure out what it is about him they find so attractive. Anyway, I wondered if maybe, since you're around him so much, both here and at home, you'd fallen under his spell, too."

Lauren stiffened. Her voice dropped several degrees in temperature. "To start with, at home Adam and I keep to ourselves. I hardly ever see him, and when I do it's from a distance. Secondly, I'm not, as you put it, in the habit of falling under any man's spell. I'm sorry to disappoint you."

"Oh, I'm not disappointed. Believe me, I'm not disappointed at all." He plucked the letter opener out of the air, returned it to her desk and leaned toward her. "Matter of fact, since I have some strong feelings for you, myself, I'm delighted."

Lauren exhaled an exasperated sigh and shook her head. "Would you please be serious?"

"I am serious. Very serious. I'm crazy about you, Lauren. I have been for a long time. If you'll recall, I asked you out once. It was about a year after your divorce."

She gave a scornful laugh. "Oh, right. Me, and every other passably attractive single female in the Bay area."

"What did you expect? You turned me down cold. But the others didn't mean anything to me, Lauren. You have to believe that. They were just distractions. I've been biding my time, waiting until you were ready to start dating again."

"And you think I am now, is that it?"

"Not exactly, no. But I don't have much choice. To tell you the truth, ever since Adam joined the company I've been terrified that you'd fall for him before I had a chance to let you know how I felt." He gave her a wry smile. "So . . . I decided I'd better not wait any longer."

Lauren stared. He had to be joking. But there was nothing humorous in his expression, and that familiar, flirty gleam was gone from his eyes. In its place was a smoldering heat. It seemed impossible, but she was very much afraid he meant every word.

It had been three years since her divorce. She could vaguely recall him asking her for a date sometime after that, but she had thought he was joking. As she recalled, she'd replied with a joking refusal and thought no more of it. She reached up and rubbed her throbbing temple with her fingertips. Lord, she didn't need this.

Beyond the professional respect she naturally awarded any co-worker, and a mild contempt for his playboy lifestyle, she felt nothing for Ed. Not once had she ever thought of him in any romantic way. She hardly ever thought of him, period.

She started to shake her head when he leaned closer and put his hand over one of hers.

"Have dinner with me tonight, Lauren. We'll go someplace intimate and quiet where we can talk. Get to know each other. Just give me a chance. That's all I ask."

"I'm sorry, Ed."

He sighed as she pulled her hand from beneath his. "Is it Adam? Did I wait too late to make my move?"

"No. Of course not. My relationship with Adam Rafferty is a strictly business one.

"Ed, this has nothing to do with anyone else. Certainly

not Adam. Nor you, for that matter. It's me. At present I've
neither the time nor the inclination to get involved with anyone. Please, won't you just accept that?"

He gave her a coaxing look. "You said, 'at present.' Does
that mean there's hope that sometime in the future you'll
change your mind?"

Lauren stared at him, her face blank. The future. The con-
cept seemed strange to her.

Long ago her world had narrowed to an existence of nothing but work and worry, of waiting and praying, of trying to
hold onto hope. The possibility that all her efforts were
doomed to failure, that the constant fear and longing was all
that fate had in store for her hovered in the darkest recesses
of her being, but that was too painful to contemplate. So she
took each day as it came and tried not to think about the
future.

"I . . . I honestly don't know, Ed. Though, I wouldn't
count on it, if I were you."

"Ah, but you're not me." Smiling, he reached out and
trailed his fingertips along her cheek. "As long as you're not
saying no, there's still hope. And you'll find that I'm a patient
man. Especially when I want something as much as I want
you."

Lauren frowned. "Ed, I don't think—"

"Ssh. Don't worry about it. I can wait." He pressed the
tip of his forefinger against her lips and winked. "See you,
gorgeous."

Frustrated, Lauren watched him saunter out, torn between
pity and irritation. She wanted to shout at him that he could
wait until he was ninety and it wouldn't make any difference.

Who knew why? Lauren was well aware that most women
went ga-ga over Ed. Though she wasn't interested in him, or
any other man for that matter, she wasn't blind. In a detached
way, she could appreciate his smooth sophistication and polished good looks, but he didn't raise her heart rate by so

much as a beat. Even if he did, she still wouldn't be interested. There was no room in her life for a man.

Annoyed with herself for wasting time, she shook her head and turned back to the PC monitor.

Work had always been more of a pleasure for Lauren than a task. For the past three years it had been a godsend. Only when she buried herself in her work could she escape, for a few hours, the never-ending grief and worry that ate at her heart like some vicious, sharp-toothed animal.

Her work was more than merely an escape, however. She loved the challenge of it, the creativity, the subtle intricacy and delicate balance of the practical and the aesthetic.

Gavin had always accused her of being ambitious. She was, though not in the way he had meant. Her ex-husband believed that ambition was a man's prerogative. In a woman, he saw it as a character flaw.

To Lauren, however, ambition was a strength. Each new project brought to successful completion gave her a sense of pride and accomplishment. So did each step she took up the corporate ladder. Both were validation of her intelligence, her abilities, her worth, of the knowledge she had labored so long and hard to acquire.

Gavin had never understood that.

When she realized where her thoughts had strayed, Lauren's lips compressed. That she had wasted even a moment thinking about her ex-husband irritated her.

Giving herself a mental shake, she pulled up another file and concentrated on the monitor with renewed determination.

Two hours later she was still there when Nan tapped on her door and walked in.

"I hate to interrupt, boss, but Mr. Ingram wants to see you in his office."

"Mmm." Lauren's fingers continued to tap the keyboard.

"Right away, Lauren."

She looked up and blinked at her secretary. "What?"

"I said, Mr. Ingram wants to see you in his office."

"Now? Did he say why?"

"Nope. Mary Alice just said for you to come right away."

Lauren checked her watch and made a harried sound. "Rats. Adam and I were leaving in ten minutes to inspect the work on the Nob Hill job. And I was hoping to finish this cost estimate before I left. Oh, well. I guess you'll just have to call Adam and tell him I'm running late." Resigned, she saved her work and shut off the computer.

"Mr. Rafferty is in Mr. Ingram's office."

"Really? Oh. Well, then, I guess we'll both be running late." She grabbed her purse and briefcase and headed for the door. "I'll probably leave as soon as I see what Walter wants. I just hope this doesn't take long. I want to get to the job site before the crew shuts down for the day. I won't be back in the office today, so if anyone needs me, tell them I'll get back to them first thing tomorrow morning."

"You got it, boss."

Mary Alice was talking on the telephone when Lauren entered her office. Immediately the older woman murmured something and put her palm over the mouthpiece. "Good afternoon, Dr. McKenna. Please, go right in. Mr. Ingram is expecting you."

When Lauren stepped into the office she was surprised to find not only Walter and Adam waiting for her, but Ed and their chief accountant, John Bailey, as well.

"Have a seat, Lauren," Walter growled with his usual impatience.

Adam lounged comfortably in the wine-red leather wing-back chair to the right of Walter's desk. Ed and John occupied two of the chairs arranged in a semicircle before it. When she slid into one of the two remaining chairs Walter shoved a sheaf of fan-folded papers across his desk to her. "Take a look at that."

His tone and the expressions on the faces of the other three men sent a dart of unease through her. She glanced at the heading on the top page and looked at Walter again. "This is our bid on the Cordex Tower."

"That's right. On pages thirty-two through eighty-seven are your detailed materials list for the interior work on the executive floor. Take a look at them and tell me if they're right."

"Of course they're ri—"

Walter silenced her with a raised hand. "Just humor me."

With an impatient sigh, she began to flip through the pages. "I don't know what the problem is, but this proposal is completely accurate," she said when she'd finished.

"Your proposal was based on using top-grade materials throughout the building. Right?"

"Yes. Of course. You know that."

Walter's fist hit the desk so hard Lauren jumped. "Then would you mind telling me why the hell, with the exception of the top five floors, the carpeting in the entire building is second rate?" he barked.

"What?" Lauren stared at him, dumbfounded. "But . . . that can't be. I personally saw to the work on the top five floors and my staff has closely supervised the rest from start to finish. If the supplier had tried to install inferior-grade carpet they would have caught it and stopped them. And they would have informed me of the problem."

"Well, someone sure as hell fouled up. There's shoddy carpet used all over that building. It's only a matter of time until the Cordex brass discovers that they didn't get what they paid for. We'll be lucky if they don't sue the pants off of us for breach of contract. I would, in their place. And Ed, here, agrees. Legally we don't have a leg to stand on."

"But there . . . there has to be some mistake."

"There's no mistake, Lauren," Adam said, speaking for the first time. "I went out to the site this morning myself and checked."

He glanced at John Bailey. Their chief accountant looked miserable. Sweat beaded the top of his bald head, and he squirmed in his chair as though it were hot. "John, here, brought the matter to my attention. One of his staff was on the ball and noticed that the name and stock number of the carpet listed on the suppliers' bill didn't match the ones on our bid."

She shot the accountant a sharp look. "This is a matter concerning my department. You couldn't simply come to me and point out the discrepancy? You had to go running to Mr. Rafferty? Thank you, John. Thank you very much."

"I, uh . . ." The accountant shifted in his chair, unable to meet her eyes. "Well, the thing is . . ."

"John was right to bring the matter to my attention. Let me remind you that I am Vice President of Construction." Adam spoke in his usual unruffled rumble, but beneath the deep tone his voice was unbending, like velvet-covered steel. The look in those brown eyes warned her it would be a mistake to question his authority, no matter how she felt about his qualifications.

Lauren gritted her teeth and bit back the angry words that hovered on her tongue, but she did not back down completely. "That's true. But, as in any good organization, there is a chain of command around here. As Director of Spatial Design, I'm responsible for the interior design and finish work on that project. John should have come to me if there was a problem. I don't appreciate him going over my head without giving me a chance to look into the matter first."

"You have a point," Adam conceded. "And normally I would agree. However, under the circumstances, that did not seem advisable."

"Why? What circumstances?"

Adam and Walter exchanged a long look. Finally, Walter folded his mouth in a grim line and nodded.

"Not only did we receive the wrong goods, we were charged the top quality price. And you approved the invoice." He took a piece of paper from the folder he held and handed it to her. "That is your signature on the invoice, isn't it?"

"Yes. Yes, it is. I checked the cost per square yard figure and the total and both agreed with mine. I . . . I guess I didn't think to check the merchandise number."

She looked up, and discovered Walter studying her with a guarded expression, and her discomfort increased. It was the first time he had ever looked at her with anything but pride and confidence.

"Look, Walter, I know this is a headache and a nuisance, but it's not an irreversible situation. It's obvious that the supplier made an error and ordered the wrong carpet. I have no idea why my staff didn't catch the mistake, but believe me, I'll look into that right away. And I'll personally deal with our supplier to get this straightened out.

"I'm sure they must have realized their mistake when the order arrived from the mill, but the restocking fee on that much merchandise would be prohibitive." She shrugged. "They probably decided to take a chance and install it anyway and hope no one would notice the difference. Nice try, but no deal.

"All we have to do is insist that they rip it all out and replace it with what we ordered. No doubt they'll squawk. This is going to wipe out their profit and then some, but it was their error, so they have no choice. Correcting the problem will delay the official completion by a few weeks, which the Cordex people aren't going to like, but that can't be helped either."

"The supplier didn't order the wrong carpet, Lauren."

She frowned at Adam. "Of course they did. It's right there on the invoice."

"The invoice doesn't agree with your proposal, that's true. However, it does match the purchase order you gave Southern Carpets." Reaching into the file, he withdrew another sheet of paper and handed it to her. "As you can see, you authorized them to install the cheaper grade carpet at the top grade price."

"But . . ." She stared at the damning slip of paper. She

couldn't have made a mistake like that. She *couldn't* have.
She always checked and double-checked her work. Certainly
she would never have knowingly ordered that cheap grade
of material. Cordex had made it crystal clear from the get-go
that the building was to be top quality all the way, and she'd
worked her buns off to make it so.

But it appeared that she had blundered. That was her signature at the bottom of the purchase order.

"Either the people over at Southern Carpet are laughing
up their sleeves, or they have an incredibly incompetent bill-
ing staff. Or . . ."

"Or?" Lauren looked at Adam, one eyebrow lifted in
haughty challenge. But she knew what was coming. She
knew. And her stomach knotted in anticipation of his answer.

"Or some money exchanged hands under the table."

Ed jerked forward in his seat, his face tight with outrage.
"Now wait just a damn minute! If you think I'm going to
sit by and let you accuse Lauren of taking a kickback, you're
crazy! She wouldn't do that!"

"Take it easy, Ed," Adam said in a placating voice. "No
one is accusing Lauren of anything."

"Oh, no? It sure as hell sounds like it to me. Well, let me
tell you something, ole buddy. Lauren may have made a mistake. A damned costly mistake, it's true, but that's all it was.
She wouldn't be a party to something crooked."

Lauren was surprised and touched by Ed's support, despite
the less-than-tactful way he'd phrased his objection. She
glanced at Walter, hoping for his backing as well, but he
remained unusually silent. He leaned back in his chair and
took it all in. His gaze moved from one person to the other
without ever meeting her eye.

"I'm sure you're right."

Drawing a deep breath, Lauren lifted her chin. "But that
was what you were implying. Wasn't it, Mr. Rafferty? That
I'm taking money illegally?"

With his elbows propped on the arms of his chair, Adam

steepled his fingers beneath his chin. Those chiseled lips pursed just slightly as he studied her from beneath half-closed lids. Lauren felt like a bug on a pin.

"I'm merely stating the possibilities. I have no proof that this was anything but an honest mistake, and no reason to accuse you of taking kickbacks. However, the fact remains that someone could have cut a deal with the supplier under the table. If not you, maybe someone on your staff."

"That's not possible. I trust my staff implicitly. In any case, I'm the only one in my department authorized to make such purchases."

He mulled that over, then shrugged. "Then it looks like you made a mistake."

Lauren wanted to feel relieved, but she didn't kid herself that the matter could be resolved quite that easily. Adam might be willing to reserve judgment, but he still had reservations; she could see that in his eyes. And in John Bailey's.

She glanced at Walter. Did he doubt her honesty as well? That thought made her feel even more miserable.

"Ed is right about one thing. This is a damned costly mistake," Walter grumbled. "We're going to have to absorb the cost of recarpeting that whole damned building. Maybe even cough up a late penalty. That's going to play hell with our profit margin. Dammit girl, this isn't like you. How could you have made such a colossal mistake?"

"I . . . I don't know. I could have sworn I ordered the right carpet. I remember working up the purchase order on my computer. I double-checked it, the way I always do." She shook her head, dazed. "I don't know what happened."

"Harumph! I'll tell you what happened. You didn't have your mind on business, that's what. Look, child, you know how I feel about you. And I know you've got personal problems, and I sympathize. You know I do. But dammit, when you're in this office, I expect you to put that stuff out of your mind and concentrate on your work. Is that clear?"

"Yes. Of course. I . . . I don't know what to say."

She had never been so humiliated. It was bad enough that she had made such a horrendous error, but to be called on the carpet for it in front of Adam Rafferty and the other two men was mortifying.

Walter loved her as he would a daughter. She knew that. He had bawled her out before, of course, but that had been over minor things and never so harshly. And never in front of other people.

That's what hurt. That, and the demoralizing knowledge that she had apparently screwed up. Big time.

Nevertheless, she understood Walter's position.

Ingram and Bates was his baby. To Walter, this company was the child that he and Helen never had. He had helped create it, had watched it grow and prosper. And he protected it with all the ferocity of a parent protecting its young. He was not about to put up with incompetence from one of his employees—not even her. If he ever had to make a choice between her welfare and the good of the company, Lauren knew she would run a poor second.

"Harumph. At this point there's nothing *to* say. We take our loss and go on. Just see that this sort of thing doesn't happen again."

Wretched, Lauren stared at the floor and nodded. "Yes, sir."

Walter studied her down-bent head and felt like an ogre. The last thing he wanted was to add to Lauren's troubles. But dammit! He wouldn't tolerate sloppy work. He had high hopes for her, but if she dropped the ball this way too many more times, he would have to rethink his plans.

The instant he dismissed the group Lauren shot out of her chair and scurried out of the office, avoiding eye contact with everyone. Walter sighed and shook his head.

As soon as they were gone Mary Alice came in. With her mouth compressed, she marched across the plush carpet and slammed a file down on his desk so hard it cracked like a rifle shot. Walter jumped and glowered.

"What the hell was that for?"

"You wanted the Cartier file. There it is."

Her snappish tone took him aback. In all the years she had worked for him Mary Alice had never displayed the least temper or emotionalism. Her demeanor had always been impassive and compliant. He eyed her set face and his frown deepened. "What's wrong with you? You look as though you swallowed a lemon."

"You could have talked to Lauren in private."

"I could have. But I told the girl when I hired her not to expect special treatment or coddling. She may be my godchild, but she has to pull her own weight around here, just like everyone else."

"You know as well as I that Lauren has always done that. More than done that. She has always had the best interests of this company at heart and next to you, she knows more about this business than anyone."

"True. But this kind of mistake is too serious to let slide with a slap on the wrists. Hell, I can't believe it. She's always been so sharp and on the ball. Even through that nightmare three years ago she never let her work slide. Now this. And wouldn't you know, her first real mistake would be a lulu."

Mary Alice folded her arms tight over her midriff and sniffed. "That may be, but I still say the reprimand should have come from you. In private."

Walter rolled his eyes. "Look, this whole thing got dumped in Adam's lap before I knew anything about it. And properly so, since he's now Vice President of Construction. He was right to call her on the carpet. I couldn't interfere and undermine his authority. Not even for Lauren. If she's done something wrong, she has to take the consequences."

Mary Alice sucked in a sharp breath and slammed her fists down on her hips. "Walter Ingram! Surely you don't actually believe that dear girl would take a kickback?"

Her tone nearly blistered the skin off his ears. Walter stared at his secretary. She was so outraged she was practically vibrating. Bright spots of angry color stained her cheeks and her eyes fairly shot sparks at him. He frowned. Had they always been that vivid shade of blue?

Staring at her flushed and animated face, he experienced a sudden wave of shock that left him dumbfounded. Good, God. Mary Alice was a handsome woman! Downright beautiful, actually. How the hell had he missed that all these years?

"Well?" she demanded.

"Of course I don't think she's taking kickbacks," he snapped, jerking himself back to the subject. "I trust Lauren implicitly. But the fact remains, she goofed. She has to take responsibility for that."

"All I know is that girl has been humiliated."

"Good God, Mary Alice, will you calm down. What's gotten into you? You're acting like a mother hen with just one chick."

"Did you think you were the only one who cared for Lauren? Well, just let me remind you, Walter Ingram, that I've been right here for the last thirty-two years," she declared, poking her chest with a perfectly manicured fingernail. "I, too, have watched her grow from a delightful child into a beautiful, intelligent and eminently capable young woman. You may not realize it—*she* may not even realize it—but that girl's the closest thing to a daughter that I will ever have also. If that makes me a silly doting female in your estimation that's just too bad!"

"Now, now, Mary Alice," he began, but she wasn't finished.

Bending forward, she thrust out her chin. "What did you expect, anyway? After all, I am one of those pathetic, unnatural women who has lived single all of her adult life!"

With that, she spun on her heel and stalked toward the door.

"What the hell is that supposed to mean?" Walter roared.

"You figure it out," she snapped back and slammed the door behind her so hard the pictures on the walls rattled.

Walter stared, too flabbergasted to move. "What in the living hell got into her?" He shook his head. "Women!"

Surprise flashed across Nan's face when Lauren rushed through her office. "I thought you were gone for the day."

Lauren didn't even slow down. "I have to check something," she replied in a distracted voice and hurried into her own office.

She dropped her purse and briefcase on the desk, flung herself into the chair and booted up her PC. "I know I ordered the right carpet. Dammit, I *know* I did," she muttered to herself as her fingers flew over the keyboard.

She located the Cordex directory and ran the cursor through the list of documents until she came to the file she wanted and pulled it up. With her lower lip clamped between her teeth, she studied the screen intently as she scrolled through the file. "Ah ha! There you are. Purchase Order 0783449CA1007, issued to Southern Carpets and Textiles," she murmured with hard satisfaction. "Now we'll just see . . ."

Shock rippled through her. She couldn't believe what she was seeing, but no matter how many times she read through the information on the screen it remained the same. The purchase order exactly matched the one Adam had shown her.

Her shoulders sagged and she closed her eyes. Oh, God, how could this be? Was she losing her mind? She would have sworn on her very life that she had ordered the right merchandise.

Five

"Is that her?"

Flames shot up through the grill as Adam flipped the last meat patty. The low rumble of the Houston fans and the disembodied voice of the TV announcer's play by play of the Astros/Padres game floated out from the living room. Now and then shouts and raucous suggestions from Tony and Ed and Adam's father, Joe Rafferty, punctuated the sounds.

Faye Rafferty, Adam's mother, bustled happily about his kitchen, preparing the fixings for their hamburgers.

In the shade directly beneath the high deck, where their mother could keep a watchful eye on them, six-year-old Molly Maria Diamatto patiently instructed her baby brother, Paulo Padraig, in the fine art of sand castle building.

Adam shut the lid on the grill. Wiping his hands on a towel, he looked at Kate, and a smile twisted his mouth.

Tony's wife was the most open, unaffected person he knew. Whatever Kate felt was obvious to the world. At the moment she almost crackled with curiosity.

Several trips with Walter to meet with prospective clients had forced Adam to put off their cookout by almost a month. The wait had been hard on Kate.

Leaning over the deck rail, she peered down the beach, her freckled face alight. Her wild mane of red corkscrew curls did a frenzied dance in the ocean breeze.

Squinting through the smoke, Adam followed the path of her gaze, and his smile faded. Lauren McKenna was coming down the beach.

He glanced at his watch: she was early this evening, by at least half an hour. Must have more than her normal load of personal matters to mull over, he thought sourly.

Was one of them how to skim money out of her lover's company without getting caught, he wondered.

Almost as soon as the idea flitted through his mind he dismissed it. Lauren enjoyed her work and she was good at what she did—more than just good at it, she was amazing. In the short time that he'd been with the company he'd heard nothing but accolades about her from their clients. She'd spent nine years getting her Ph.D. It didn't make sense that she would jeopardize all that by taking kickbacks.

But neither did it make sense that she would make such a careless mistake.

He stared at her, frowning. As usual, she walked along the water's edge at a languid pace, her stride fluid and unconsciously sensual. She wore white jeans, rolled up almost to her knees, and an oversized yellow shirt that caught the wind and billowed behind her like a sail. Over her shoulder she carried what appeared to be a windbreaker.

At the office she tended to wear her hair in a controlled style—a French braid or put up in an intricate bun or held back with a clip at her nape—but at home, at least when she strolled the beach, it was always loose and free, as it was now.

Her deep auburn hair was long and thick and shiny as a beaver's pelt. During the past week Adam had also discovered, much to his annoyance, that it smelled heavenly, like wildflowers. Numerous times he'd had to fight a strong and totally unwelcome urge to snatch out the pins or clips that held it in place and plunge his hands into that silken mass.

Dammit, it ought to be illegal for a standoffish woman to

have hair like that. Or skin like that. Or eyes that particular shade of clear green.

"Well?"

The sharp demand drew his attention back to Kate, but he had no idea what she wanted. "Well, what?"

"Is that your neighbor or not?"

His gaze slid back to the graceful figure. "Yeah. That's her."

"She looks like a perfectly nice woman to me."

"What were you expecting, a dragon lady? I never said she wasn't nice. Just unsociable."

"I wonder why? I mean, there has to be a reason. It's not natural for a young, attractive woman to cut herself off from other people."

"Uh-oh. I don't like that tone. Now, Kate, don't start fretting over this. The next thing we know you'll be making Lauren one of your charity projects, and frankly, sweetheart, I don't think the lady would appreciate your efforts. She seems quite . . . adjusted to her life."

He had almost said content, but his gut told him that was far off the mark. Haunted came to mind. Why, he didn't know exactly, except that now and then that was what he saw in those fathomless green eyes.

Kate O'Shea Diamatto was an Irish earth mother and a scrapper. If she liked you and thought you were hurting she didn't hesitate to offer solace. If she thought you had a problem or were in any way being wronged, she waded right in with her chin out and her dukes up.

"I love that name. Lauren." Kate tested it on her tongue and sighed. "It reminds me of moonlight and magnolias. Does it fit her?"

The question surprised Adam, but when he thought it over he realized that the name suited her perfectly. Lauren had that delicate kind of beauty and quiet personality that made you think of soft summer nights on a southern veranda, of fireflies and flowers and mint juleps and moonbeams.

The fanciful thought took him by surprise and made him chuckle. Christ, what the hell was wrong with him? Next thing you knew he'd be spouting poetry.

Nevertheless, he nodded at Kate. "Yeah. It fits."

She eyed him for a moment, then wrinkled her nose. "That pretty, huh?"

"Knock it off, Kate. She's my neighbor and my associate at work. That's all."

Tony and Kate had hooted with laughter when Adam told them about Lauren. He'd had to endure a barrage of teasing and smartass remarks before they'd let it drop. Ever since, Kate had been more curious about Lauren than ever.

"Besides, even if she weren't so standoffish I still wouldn't be interested. First of all, I'm not sure I even like the woman. Secondly, call me gun shy if you want, but the truth is, after Delia, I'm not anxious to jump back into the fire."

Kate made a face. "Delia. Now *there's* a dragon lady. Always acting as though she's so strong and in charge, when really she's nothing but a weak, clinging bitch who sucks the life out of men. And she's vicious, to boot. I never liked her. Not from the beginning. Didn't I warn you to stay away from her? But would you listen to me? Noooo."

"Yes, I know, I know. Jeez, you've made your point already, Katydid. Several times. Would it make you feel better if I promise that from now on I'd let you check out any woman I date more than twice?"

"Actually, yes, it would. And see that you do. When it comes to picking the right woman you haven't got a clue, boy-o. Saints be praised, you finally had the good sense to dump that she-devil Delia before it was too late," she murmured absently as her gaze zeroed in on Lauren again.

She had drawn even with Adam's house, but as usual, she did not glance in their direction.

"Och, would you look at that hair? Now I ask you, if I had to have red hair, why couldn't the good Lord have given me that color instead of this carrot top I'm stuck with? And

I'll bet she doesn't have so much as a freckle to her name, either."

"Nope. At least, none that I've seen. Of course, the lady and I aren't exactly on intimate terms," Adam drawled, fighting a grin when Kate rolled her eyes.

"I knew it. Life just isn't fair." Sighing, she braced her elbow on the rail, propped her chin in her hand and followed Lauren's progress down the beach. "She is a fascinating mystery, though. I wonder what her problem is?"

"Who knows," Adam said, feigning a disinterested shrug. And good luck finding out, he added silently.

That she continued to fascinate him annoyed the hell out of Adam but there didn't seem to be a thing he could do about it. She had intrigued him from the first moment he saw her, and ever since that mysterious chase outside the Cordex Tower his curiosity had grown steadily. Yet, other than the fact that she was a hard worker and damned good at what she did, he knew no more about her now than he had a month ago. She had recovered her composure quickly, and ever since that first day she'd acted as though that mad dash had never occurred.

Short of weaseling the official office dirt out of someone at Ingram and Bates—and Adam couldn't quite bring himself to stoop to that—it didn't look as though he was going to learn a whole helluva lot more about Dr. Lauren McKenna.

She certainly didn't volunteer any information.

Their relationship—if you could call it that—had started off the wrong foot and things had gone downhill from there. From that first day her attitude toward him had been cool. Since the confrontation over the Cordex Tower job, it had been downright frosty.

For the past two weeks they had been working hand in glove. From a business standpoint, he couldn't have asked for a more qualified or knowledgeable person to show him the ropes. Lauren knew the construction business inside out. On the whole she was even-tempered, easy to get along with—provided you didn't object to frostbite—and cooperative and helpful, though always in a crisp, strictly professional way.

The past week Adam had spent most of his working hours in her company. They'd had lunch together every day, sometimes with Ed or Walter, or both, but a couple of times when they had been out in the field it had been just the two of them. But, no matter how much time they spent together she remained distant. At all times, except occasionally around Walter, that cool reserve surrounded her like an invisible barrier, keeping everyone at arm's length.

Yet, though Adam told himself he was imagining things, beneath that composed surface he sensed that she was a taut ball of edginess and nerves . . . and dark despair.

His mouth twisted. Yeah, right, Rafferty. Or maybe you're just making excuses for her because you can't accept that someone who looks like Lauren could be an emotionless shell of a woman.

It seemed foolish to Adam that they drove separate cars to and from work each day, but he knew better than to suggest that they carpool.

Each morning he'd followed her into the office, and almost every evening he'd driven right behind her up the coastal highway all the way home. She hadn't waved or honked or in any way indicated that she was even aware of his presence.

The night before, when they'd arrived at the entrance to the beach and she had punched in the combination on the gate's electronic control box, he'd driven through right on her bumper, but she had merely zoomed ahead. By the time he passed by her place the automatic garage door was rumbling shut.

It was as though, once they left the office and the obligations of her job ended, he ceased to exist in her world.

At home Adam rarely saw her except in the early evening when she made her nightly visit to the point. Nor had he noticed anyone else at her place. If Walter was her lover, he sure as hell wasn't very attentive.

"Oh, for heaven's sake!" Kate muttered beside him, and Adam jumped. He'd been so lost in his thoughts he had almost forgotten she was there.

"This is ridiculous. I'm going to invite her to join us for hamburgers."

"What? Kate, no! Don't do that," Adam ordered, but he was too late. She was already halfway down the steps to the beach.

"What can it hurt?" she called over her shoulder without breaking stride. "The worse that can happen is she'll say no."

Which was exactly what Adam was worried about. He didn't want that icy woman to snub Kate, especially not now. His friend was seven months pregnant, and according to Tony her emotions were on a continuous roller-coaster ride.

The kids called out to their mother when she reached the bottom of the stairs and little Paulo jumped up to follow her.

"No, no, sweetie. You stay with your sister. Molly, darlin', look after him. I'll be right back."

"Okay, Mommy."

Paulo began to wail, but Molly, who had inherited Kate's mothering instincts, gently led the boy back to their sand sculpture, and within seconds she had distracted the three-year-old.

"Dammit." Feeling helpless, Adam watched his irrepressible friend slog across the sand with that funny duck walk that pregnant women get.

"When's dinner gonna be ready?" Tony asked, ambling out onto the deck through the open French doors. "I'm so hungry my stomach's gnawing at my backbone."

"Just about there."

"Hey. What's Kate doing down there?"

"She's—"

"Everything is ready when you are, Son." Adam's mother

bustled out of the house carrying a tray loaded with hamburger fixings and chips.

"Here, let me give you a hand with that, Mrs. Rafferty." Tony took the tray from her, and they began to transfer the items to the table.

"Isn't that Kate?" Faye asked. "Dinner is almost ready. What's she doing on the beach?"

"I just asked Adam the same thing."

"She's got the hare-brained idea into her head to invite my neighbor for dinner."

"Uh-oh. Watch out, buddy. When Kate gets the bit between her teeth there's no stopping her."

"Why, how lovely."

"No, Mom, it's not lovely at all. That woman is about as friendly as a block of ice."

"Nonsense. The poor thing is probably just lonely. And heaven knows, we have plenty of food. One more won't matter."

"That's not the point, Mom. Trust me, Lauren McKenna doesn't want to join us, and frankly, I don't want her here."

"Adam Joseph Rafferty! Shame on you. How could you be so inhospitable and rude? I raised you better than that."

"What's all the fuss about? What's going on?" Adam's father asked, stepping out onto the deck. Ed followed right behind him.

Joseph Liam Rafferty was a sprite of a man, barely five and a half feet tall, and wiry. Dressed in baggy shorts, with his shock of white hair, blue eyes twinkling beneath bushy eyebrows and that perpetual impish grin, he looked like a leprechaun. Whenever Adam, who topped six-four, introduced his father to people, they invariably did a double take. At five-one-and-a-half, his mother was even smaller.

"My wife has gone down to the beach to invite Lauren to eat with us."

Ed looked stunned. "You're kidding, right?"

"I tried to stop her," Adam grumbled. "But you know how stubborn Kate is when she gets an idea in her head."

"Tell me about it. I live with the woman," Tony said.

Adam quickly scooped up the last hamburger patty and added it to the platter of meat on the warming shelf before joining the others at the railing.

"She won't accept," Ed stated with absolute confidence.

"I don't know. My wife can be damned persuasive. Remember, she talked me into marrying her."

Adam snorted. "Oh, yeah, right. Who're you kidding? I was there, remember. You badgered the poor woman so, she had to marry you to shut you up."

"I've worked with Lauren for years, and I'm telling you guys, she'll say no."

"Sounds like the voice of experience to me. Whaddaya think, Adam? Our buddy here tried to romance the lady and she turned him down?"

Adam slanted a wry smile between his two friends. "Yeah, that'd be my guess."

If true, that would have been a new experience for him, Adam thought, amused. Ed might not have Tony's stunning handsomeness, nor his own fame as a football star, but he had more than his share of charisma. He was a nice-looking guy, in a polished, James Bond sort of way. He was a sharp dresser, he drove a BMW, lived in an elegant condo in a part of town with exactly the right cachet for the well-to-do yuppie crowd. He was witty, charming, sophisticated and successful. Women found him irresistible. Apparently, Lauren had been the exception.

If he had tried his luck with Lauren and struck out, Adam was surprised that he was as friendly to her as he was. Ed didn't take rejection well.

"Now, you two boys quit teasing poor Ed." Faye tsked. "I swear, you three are as bad as you were in college. Always razzing each other."

"Five'll get you ten she says no," Ed challenged, unfazed.

"You're on. I know my Kate. There's no nut she can't crack. Anyone who could win over my mother the way she did could sell a deep freeze to an Eskimo."

Adam chuckled. Tony had a point. Rosa Diamatto had wanted her only son to marry a nice Italian-American girl. She had been appalled when, in his senior year, Tony had announced that he loved Molly Kate O'Shea and intended to marry her.

Rosa had tried everything to break up the pair—hysterics, tantrums, threats, guilt, but Tony had stood firm. At the wedding his mother had sobbed like a grieving parent at a child's funeral. Adam wouldn't have given two cents for the chance of Kate and Rosa ever becoming friends.

Which showed how much he knew. Within weeks Kate had worked her charm and completely won over her hot-tempered mother-in-law. Now Rosa adored her. To hear her tell it, she had handpicked Kate to be Tony's wife.

Ed nudged Adam. "Look, Kate's got her attention."

"Excuse me! Yoo-hoo!"

Surprise rippled through Lauren when she heard someone hailing her. She was accustomed to being alone on the beach. Puzzled, she turned and saw a heavily pregnant woman waddling toward her.

For the briefest of moments envy flickered inside Lauren's chest, but she quickly beat back the feeling before it swelled into pain. It was a matter of survival. There would always be pregnant women around.

"Yes? Were you calling me?"

"Oh, my," the woman gasped. She came to a stop in front of Lauren and pressed one hand to her chest, the other to the swollen mound beneath her maternity smock. Her face was flushed and her breathing heavy. "Just give me a second to . . . to ca-catch . . . my breath."

"Certainly." Lauren eyed her cautiously. Tall and rawboned, the woman towered over her by at least five inches. She was no beauty, but she had friendly blue eyes and a milkmaid wholesomeness about her that was appealing.

Freckles, like splatters of pale brown paint, covered every inch of her skin that Lauren could see, and her wild hair was that unfortunate shade of orange-red that made her look as though her head were on fire.

A friend of Adam's, no doubt, Lauren decided. Or perhaps they were more than friends, she amended, darting another look at her swollen belly.

The woman flashed a broad smile and thrust out her hand. "Hi. I'm Kate Diamatto. Oh, my. You are a pretty little thing, aren't you?"

The unexpected compliment flustered Lauren, and she felt color rush to her cheeks. "Um . . . hello, and, uh . . . thank you." Lauren's hand was squeezed in a tight grip and given a firm shake. "I'm, uh . . . I'm Lauren McKenna."

"Yes, I know. Adam has told us all about you. Me and Tony, that is. Tony's my husband. He and Adam have been friends since they were boys."

"Really?" Lauren didn't know what else to say, or what to make of this affable woman.

"Oh, my, yes. Those two were inseparable all their lives. They even went to the same college and roomed together, right up to the time they both turned pro. When they were drafted by different teams was the first time they had been apart since they were toddlers."

"I see. How . . . interesting." Lauren gave her a wan smile, not sure what all this had to do with her. "Umm . . . did you want to see me about something?"

"Oh! Yes! Sorry. I get carried away sometimes. Actually, I came down here to invite you to have dinner with us." She gestured behind her toward the house. "We have plenty."

Lauren glanced at the redwood and glass house that she still thought of as the Graysons' place and saw Adam and

Ed and three others lining the deck rail, all watching her and this gregarious woman.

An automatic refusal sprang to her tongue, but to her surprise she realized that, deep down, she was tempted. The idea of spending a few hours in congenial company, sharing a meal, laughing, joking, tugged at something inside her that she had thought long dead.

"Thank you. That's very nice of you, but—"

"It's nothing fancy, mind you. Just burgers and chips on the deck. Later we're going to toast marshmallows on the beach. We really would love for you to join us."

Lauren looked into Kate Diamatto's bright eyes and pleasant face and experienced a reluctant spurt of amusement. She had the feeling this woman could charm the stars right out of the skies with her friendly manner. "I'm sor—"

"Please don't say no." She put her hand on Lauren's arm and tilted her head to one side. Her blue eyes coaxed. So did her smile. "Where's the harm? It's just a meal and a few hours of conversation. We're a friendly bunch, and I think you'll enjoy yourself. And trust me on this, until you've tasted Adam's hamburgers you haven't lived. They're the best. Guaranteed."

"Look, Mrs. . . ."

"Diamatto. But, please, call me Kate. When you say Mrs. Diamatto I think you're talking to Tony's mother."

A smile wavered about Lauren's mouth. "Very well. Kate. I appreciate the invitation. Really I do. But I don't want to intrude."

"Oh fiddlesticks. Is that all you're worried about? Don't be silly. You wouldn't be intruding. Didn't I just invite you? Besides, with us, the more the merrier." In a deft maneuver, she slipped her arm through Lauren's and began to steer her toward the house.

"Oh! No, I can't."

"Sure you can. And I promise you, having dinner with us is a lot more fun than sitting up there on those rocks all alone." Kate tugged her along, ignoring Lauren's efforts to dig in her heels.

"How did you know—?"

"That you go up there every evening? Adam told us. Now come along. I promise you we won't bite. Besides, no one should be alone on Saturday night."

"No, really, I can't," Lauren protested, but somehow her feet were moving of their own accord. She glanced up at the group on the deck. Her gaze met Adam's and guilt slashed her. "No, Kate. This isn't right. You're very sweet, but I promise you, Adam doesn't want me here. And I have to admit, he has good reason."

"Oh, pooh. If you mean because you gave him the brush-off the night you met, forget it. That's water under the bridge. You two are colleagues now.

"Besides, those three guys have been bowling over poor unsuspecting females ever since they were in their teens," she continued in that friendly, confiding way that Lauren found so disarming. "Why, back in college all us girls called them the Awesome Threesome. They were the best-looking, most popular men on campus. Though I'd bite off my tongue before I'd tell them that.

"Personally, mind you, I've always suspected that they had some sort of competition going. Between them, they probably dated every coed at Princeton who was even semi-eligible.

"Of course, I put a stop to that foolishness where Tony was concerned, but neither of the other two big lugs has ever married, and ever since Adam became so famous, not to mention stinking rich, the women have been after him more than ever. Trust me, it was good for his character to finally meet a woman who doesn't fall all over him."

Giving Lauren's arm a pat, she leaned in closer and confided wickedly, "As soon as I heard about it I had a feeling that you and I were going to be great friends."

Friends. The word seemed almost foreign. Lauren had had friends once. Or so she had thought. They had all drifted away, though, over the past three years. Only Walter and Nan and Mary Alice had remained steadfast.

"Kate, I'm still not sure this is such a good idea—"

"Mommy! Mommy! Come see the castle I maked!"

Lauren jerked to a stop and stared at the little boy who came tearing across the sand toward them. Her heart began to pound. He was around three, with a cherub face and a sturdy little body and his mother's wild hair.

Coming to an abrupt halt in front of them, he paused long enough to give Lauren an uncertain look, but he was too excited to be bothered by a strange woman. He grabbed Kate's hand and tried to drag her toward the house at a faster pace. "C'mon, Mommy. Hurwie! Hurwie! Come see!"

"I'm coming, I'm coming, you little monster." Chuckling, Kate released Lauren and gave the boy's hair an affectionate rub. "He's a rambunctious one, is our Paulo, but—Lauren, are you all right? Sweet heaven, you're white as a sheet!"

Lauren took a step back. Her chest felt as though there were a steel band tightening around it. She couldn't breathe. Shaking her head, she took another step back, then another. "No. No, I . . . I can't do this. I can't."

"Lauren, what's the matter?"

"I've got to go. I . . . I can't—" A sob hitched in her throat, and she shook her head harder. "I'm sor . . . sorry, I . . . I . . ."

She nearly stumbled, but she recovered and kept backing away, still shaking her head.

"Lauren, for pity's sake, what is it? Are you ill?"

"Is that lady gonna be sick, Mommy? She looks like she's gonna fro up."

"Oh, God." Lauren dragged her gaze from the boy and turned a desperate look on Kate. "I'm sorry. I'm sorry. I can't stay. I . . . I can't do this. I just can't." Pressing her balled fist to her mouth, she gave an anguished cry, spun on her heel and ran.

"Lauren! Wait!"

* * *

"Didn't I tell you?" Ed crowed. He turned to Tony with an insufferable smirk and held out his hand. "You owe me five bucks, sucker. Fork it over."

"Damn. She almost had her," Tony muttered in disgust, but he dug into his pocket, pulled out his money clip and peeled off a five-dollar bill.

"Oh, dear. That's too bad." Faye sighed. "I was looking forward to meeting your neighbor."

"Yeah, me, too. I wonder what made her take off that way?"

Annoyance rippled through Adam at his father's comment. He had to put up with the deep freeze treatment from that woman during the week, but he'd be damned if he'd let her spoil their evening.

"Forget about her. I told you she was unsociable." Forcing a smile, Adam looped his arms around his parents' shoulders and steered them toward the redwood table at the other end of the deck. "Burger time!" he yelled to the others. "Come and get it, you guys, before I throw it out!"

"Hey, you don't have to call me twice." Ed grabbed a chair and had a knife and fork in his hand before anyone else could sit down.

"Well, it's about time," Tony jeered, taking the seat beside him. "The service around this joint is lousy. I was beginning to think you'd brought us out here to starve us to death."

The kids came pounding up the stairs. Adam bent and caught them up in his arms and whirled them around, a move that produced squeals of glee. After a couple of turns, he set them down. "Now, go on, you munchkins, and get some grub before your dad and Uncle Ed eat it all," he said, giving each an affectionate slap on the rump that sent the giggling pair scampering toward the table.

While the others dug into the meal, Adam waited at the top of the stairs for Kate, who came plodding up the flight more slowly, holding the small of her back. "So, what happened down there?" He was prepared to go after Lauren and tear a strip out of her hide if she had upset Kate.

She frowned and wiped the perspiration from her brow with the back of her forearm. "I'm not sure. I was certain she was going to relent. She wanted to, I'm sure of it. But out of the blue she seemed to panic. She just took off."

Kate turned bewildered eyes on Adam. "This sounds crazy, but . . . I think she was trying to get away from Paulo. The minute she saw him she got a horrified look on her face. Oh, Adam. You don't think . . . could it be that she doesn't like kids?"

Adam's gaze snapped to Lauren. She was clambering up the rocky point as though the hounds of hell were nipping at her heels. To Kate the very idea that any woman would not love children was inconceivable, but Adam had no problem believing it. Not of this woman.

He stared at Lauren, his jaw tightening. You cold, unfeeling bitch.

An hour later Lauren still sat huddled on a boulder at the top of the point. She sniffed and wiped her wet cheeks with her fingertips, but tears continued to stream down her face.

Would the pain ever go away? It slashed at her like sharp talons, shredding her heart to ribbons.

Hugging her legs tighter, she rested her forehead on her updrawn knees. Oh, God, she had thought she was beyond tears. Hadn't she already shed an ocean full? For the past year she had been doing so well. She'd thought she had learned how to manage the hurt and keep it beaten back, but it had taken just one look at that adorable child, and it all came rushing back—all the anguish, all the agony.

She rolled her forehead against her knees and moaned. She couldn't bear it. Oh, God, it hurt so much.

Salty tears dripped onto her thighs, soaking her jeans. The

crash and roar of the breakers on the rocks drowned out the sobs that tore from the depths of her soul, wrenching, pitiful sounds, like an animal in pain. They racked her slender body and made her throat raw, but she was powerless to stop them.

She cried until her head began to pound and her eyes nearly swelled shut. She cried until her nose burned. She cried until, at last, the tears simply dried up, as though there was no more moisture left in her body.

Only then, as the last sobs subsided into little jerky sniffs did she raise her head. Her nose was stuffed up and she felt as though fifty pounds of wet cement sat on her chest. She wanted to curl up in a tight ball and die.

But, of course, she couldn't. With a shuddering sigh, she wiped the sleeve of her windbreaker across her wet cheeks and runny nose and looked around. She couldn't stay there. The sun had already set and the cold wind off the ocean cut through her like a knife.

Below, on the beach in front of Adam's house a bonfire still blazed. She cast a reluctant glance at the people gathered around it and pressed her swollen lips together.

It had been a mistake to come here. She should have turned around and returned to the safety of her home, but she had been too panicked to think clearly. How would she get past them without being seen?

Now and then she heard a note of laughter, the faintest snatch of voices, but it was all muted to an indistinct blur by the roar of the surf.

Evidently Ed had gone. She wasn't surprised. Roasting marshmallows on the beach was hardly Ed's style.

A man about Adam's age, whom she assumed was Kate's husband, had his back braced against a log and Kate sat between his spread legs, snuggled back against his chest. The older couple—Adam's parents, she supposed—sat side by side on the log, holding hands.

Sitting cross-legged in the sand, Adam held two sleepy

children, one perched on each knee, both cradled contentedly against his massive chest.

Lauren stared. She could not swallow around the lump in her throat. After a time she put her head down and wept some more.

"Son? Aren't you coming to bed? It's getting late."

Adam's mother joined him at the deck railing. He put his arm around her shoulders and gave her a squeeze. "In a minute, Mom," he said softly. It was after ten. Rather than drive all the way to their home in San Jose at this late hour he had insisted that his parents spend the night at his place.

His mother wore a serviceable flannel robe over her night-gown, the same kind she had worn when he'd been a kid. She smelled of violets and fresh-baked bread. Adam drew in the scents along with the salty tang of the ocean breeze and smiled in the darkness. No matter how long he lived he would always associate those comforting smells with his mother.

God, he had to be the luckiest sonufabitch in the world to have Joseph and Faye Rafferty for parents. He could have just as easily been stuck with someone like Lauren Mc-Kenna.

"What are you doing out here all alone, anyway?"

"Nothing. Just thinking." He bent and kissed his mother's forehead. "I can already hear Dad snoring. Why don't you go on to bed, too. I'll be in soon."

"All right. But don't be too long, you hear? You'll catch a chill out here."

"I won't."

The instant she disappeared into the house, Adam's expression sobered and his gaze refocused on the woman picking her way down the rocky point in the moonlight.

Damn her. She hadn't made a move to climb down from there until they'd left the beach and Tony and Kate and the kids had gone. He didn't think anyone else had noticed that she was still up there, thank God, but he had.

She had to be frozen stiff. Why the hell had she stayed up there so long? Because of Paulo and Molly? Dammit, if she'd go to those lengths to avoid a couple of sweet kids then she damn well deserved to catch pneumonia. Or to fall and break her neck.

He didn't know why he was concerned. He sure as hell didn't give a tinker's damn what happened to the Ice Maiden. And she made it crystal clear that she didn't want any help from him. He ought to go inside and leave her to her fate.

He remained where he was. Standing absolutely still, he squinted through the darkness, watching each cautious, testing step Lauren made. At last, after what seemed hours, her bare foot searched for and touched smooth sand. Only then did Adam turn and enter the darkened house.

Six

Adam spent Sunday with his parents. After attending church, he treated them to Sunday dinner at Maxwell's Plum. His mother was awed by the opulence and glitter and appalled by the prices.

"I could have cooked and saved you this expense," she protested as they were seated at a table by the tall glass wall.

"I know, Mom," he assured her, patting her hand. "But I wanted to take you out. And don't worry, I can afford it."

When Adam had been growing up his mother had always risen early on Sunday mornings and put dinner in the oven before they left for church. The heavenly smells that greeted them when they returned were some of Adam's most vivid and cherished memories of childhood.

After the sumptuous food arrived, they had a leisurely meal, and afterward they talked over coffee, his mom about her gardening and the new flowers she was going to plant next spring, his dad about fly fishing and the Hurricanes' chances of making it to the next Super Bowl without Adam.

After dinner Adam took his parents on a driving tour of the city before heading for San Jose.

At one point he thought about stopping by the Gothic renovation the company was doing and showing them around, but when he drove by the place it reminded him of Lauren, and he kept going. The woman was an enigma who niggled at him constantly. He'd be damned if he'd let thoughts of her ruin his Sunday.

At Fisherman's Wharf Adam parked the car and they walked down pier thirty-nine, poking into the shops and sniffing the salt air and the delicious aromas coming from the restaurants. After a half hour or so, Faye began to tire, and they headed for San Jose.

Adam resisted his mother's invitation to come in for homemade cookies and milk, but she wouldn't hear of him leaving without taking a tin of the baked goods with him.

On the drive home he rolled down the windows on the BMW put a jazz CD in the player and cranked up the volume.

He loved the sense of peace and freedom he felt, speeding along the sparsely traveled highway with his mind adrift. The setting sun warmed the side of his face and a cool breeze off the Pacific ruffled his dark hair. His fingers tapped the steering wheel in rhythm with the hot licks soaring from the speakers.

The weekend had been great, he decided. Good friends, family, no pressure—what could be better?

It was nice having his parents close by. During his years on the road he had missed them. Unlike many people, with the exception of a very brief, very minor teenage rebellion, he had always been close to his parents, and he wanted to be around for their golden years.

Shortly before sunset Adam arrived at the secluded cove feeling mellow and relaxed and pleasantly tired. He drove past Lauren's house with barely a glance, and congratulated himself on his restraint. After the incident the day before he was determined to squash this obsession he had with the woman and put her out of his mind.

The minute he entered the house he kicked off his shoes and headed for the kitchen. He poured a tumbler of iced tea and chug-a-lugged half the drink. As he reached for the pitcher to top off the glass again he noticed the red light blinking on his answering machine.

There were two calls. He pushed the play button, then refilled the glass and leaned a hip against the kitchen counter and waited.

"Hi. It's Kate. I forgot to tell you yesterday that Molly is having a dance recital next Sunday afternoon. I know this may be above and beyond the duties of a godfather, boy-o, but Molly really would like for you to be there. If you can make it, give us a call. By the way, we had a great time yesterday. See ya."

Grinning, Adam reached for the notepad by the telephone. While the answering machine beeped and clicked forward to the next message he scribbled a note to himself to call Kate the next day. Hell, yes, he'd be there. He wouldn't miss the munchkin's dance debut for the world.

"Hello, darling."

Adam's gaze jerked to the machine at the sound of that familiar voice. His grin collapsed, and with it his good humor.

"Are you there?" She paused and waited for him to pick up the receiver. When he didn't, she sighed. "Now don't be that way, darling. You must know that we have to talk." She waited again for a response. "Well, perhaps you really aren't there. Please, darling, call me as soon as you get in." That famous voice dropped to a husky pitch. "I'll be right here at home all evening, waiting to hear from you. You know the number. Ciao, darling."

"Don't hold your breath," Adam grumbled. He hit the erase button with more force than necessary.

He had known that sooner or later Delia would track him down. The ugly scene that had occurred when he had broken off with her had been stunning, but he had known she wouldn't let it go at that.

That night, as Adam had calmly packed his things, Delia's reactions and manipulative ploys had run the gamut—from disbelief to outrage to tearful pleading. When all of those had failed to move him, as they had done so many times in the past, she had capped off the one-sided fight with a temper tantrum the likes of which he had never witnessed before—and devoutly hoped he never would again.

Delia had gone on a rampage and trashed the apartment they had shared, turning over lamps and furniture, dumping drawers and their contents on the floor, breaking dishes, throwing anything she could heft. As he had loaded his personal belongings into his car she had still been lobbing plates and curses at him.

From the beginning he had known he couldn't just disappear. His celebrity status ruled out anonymity, and with her training and resources as a top network television reporter it had been just a matter of time before she located him and ferreted out his unlisted telephone number. But, damn, he had hoped it would take her longer than this.

Eventually, he would have to deal with her. Delia was as tenacious as a dog digging for a bone. Adam took a drink of tea and wandered out onto the deck.

He had no intention of calling her. Ever. He'd made the right decision. He couldn't stop her from drinking, and she wouldn't stop herself.

Hell, she wouldn't even admit she had a problem, he thought with disgust. Most of the time she had laughed off his complaints. "Oh, darling, don't be so stuffy. So maybe I do overindulge now and then. So what? That doesn't make me an alcoholic. I never miss work. I do my job, and I do it damned well. Does that sound like I have a problem?

"You have no idea how difficult my work is—the demands on me to always be on top of every story, to always look perfect and sound perfect and project just the right image. And then there are all those up-and-coming sweet young things just waiting for a chance to stab me in the back and take my place. The pressure is unrelenting. A drink now and then helps me relax."

But it hadn't been just "a" drink, and it hadn't been just now and then. Delia got soused every evening after work.

She kept a bottle stashed in her desk at the studio and another in her car. He'd even found a flask in her purse.

She could hold her liquor amazingly well—well enough to fool her co-workers and the network brass. At least for now. But there were signs that she was slipping over the edge.

Her behavior was becoming more erratic, her temper more volatile and irrational. Soon the dissipation would begin to take its toll on her looks. Then what would she do? he wondered.

A few times, when he'd had a gut full and she feared that he might leave, she had been remorseful and promised to stop, but she had never once admitted that her boozing was a problem.

Maybe—just maybe—if he was lucky, she'd take the hint and give up when he didn't return her calls.

"Yeah, right, Rafferty," he muttered. "And pigs fly."

Placing his glass on the deck rail, Adam breathed deeply of the ocean air and tried to shake off the unpleasant memories.

The sun had already slipped below the horizon, and the western sky was on fire. Against his will, Adam glanced up at the point. Lauren wasn't there.

He scanned the beach and spotted her walking home through the ankle deep wavelets at the water's edge, about fifty yards or so beyond his house.

His mouth twisted. Right on time.

Annoyed with himself for thinking about her again, and with her for rousing his curiosity, he started to turn away and go back inside when a movement down the beach caught his eye.

Adam tensed and narrowed his eyes.

As Lauren passed by a pile of boulders a man stepped out of the shadows and fell in step behind her.

Who the hell was that? And how did the guy get on this beach?

Adam sure as hell hadn't buzzed anyone in.

Lauren didn't appear to be aware of the man's presence. As usual, she appeared lost in her own little world.

Whoever he was, his pace was faster than Lauren's. In a few seconds he would overtake her. From where Adam stood, the man's movements appeared stealthy and sinister.

"Don't jump to conclusions, Rafferty," he chided himself. "The guy could be Lauren's guest, for all you know."

Could be he was a friend or a relative. Maybe he'd just been waiting for her, giving her some privacy while she completed her nightly ritual.

If he stormed down there and confronted the guy he'd probably just make a fool of himself. And get Lauren on his case again for butting into her life. Adam snorted. Not that it mattered. After that business over the Cordex job, he wasn't exactly her favorite person these days.

Besides, why should he be concerned about that cold fish of a woman? She'd made it more than clear that she didn't want or need any assistance of any kind from him.

The scene changed with a suddenness that made Adam start. Catching up with Lauren, the guy grabbed one of her arms and spun her around. She let out a shrill scream that even Adam could hear, and began to struggle.

Stunned, Adam stared, disbelieving, as the guy started dragging Lauren farther up onto the beach. "Dammit to hell!"

He jerked out of his stupor and took off down the stairs, loping over the steps three at a time. He hit the beach running flat out, arms and legs pumping. "Stop that! Get away from her, you bastard!" he yelled, but the wind off the ocean threw the words back in his face.

Screaming, Lauren twisted and bucked and kicked. She flailed out with her fists, but her efforts seemed to enrage her attacker. He stopped and drew back his arm to deal her a vicious backhanded blow across her face. She saw it coming and cringed away, turning her head at the last second, and his balled fist struck the side of her head.

Lauren cried out as the blow spun her around and knocked her to her knees.

Sonofabitch. Adam poured on more steam. He felt the shooting pain in his bum knee, but he didn't slacken his pace.

Before Lauren could recover her senses and scramble to her feet, the guy fell on her and tore her shirt half off of her with one yank. She screamed and tried to fight him off, but he hit her again. This time the blow sent her to the sand in a crumpled heap. Her attacker straddled her, and began to drag her jeans from her hips.

Lauren did her best to fight back but she was hurt and obviously stunned by the blows she'd taken, and her feeble attempts merely enraged the maniac. Adam was close enough now to hear her whimpers and the animal sounds of fury that came from the bastard's throat.

She managed to land at least one painful blow that caused the guy to yell out and jerk back, clutching his throat. With a roar of fury, he attacked again.

Grabbing a handful of Lauren's hair, he yanked her head back at a painful angle and slammed his fist into her stomach a split second before Adam reached him.

"You sorry scum!"

The attacker yelped in surprise and pain when Adam clamped one hand in his hair, grasped the back of his windbreaker with the other and lifted him bodily off of Lauren. He threw the man to the sand like a sack of garbage.

Before the animal could recover, Adam snatched him up again by the front of his windbreaker and slammed his fist into his face. Pain exploded in Adam's fist, but he also felt the satisfying crunch of cartilage and bone as blood spurted from the man's nose.

The guy went sprawling, but Adam picked him up again and delivered another blow, this one to his stomach. The rapist let out a loud *oomph!* and collapsed like an imploding building.

"You like to hit women, do you, tough guy? Well, how

does it feel to be on the receiving end?" Adam snatched him up again, but this time the guy hung limp as a wet rag in his grasp, with his head lolled to one side. He didn't so much as moan.

Making a disgusted sound, Adam flung him back to the sand and hurried over to Lauren.

She lay curled in a ball on her side clutching her stomach, writhing in pain and crying.

Adam dropped to his knees beside her. "Lauren? Oh, God, baby." Gently, he touched her shoulder, but she cringed and cried out. His heart clenched when she tried to scrunch herself into a tighter ball and roll away from him.

"Take it easy, sweetheart. It's okay. It's me. Adam. You're safe now. That creep's not going to hurt you anymore."

She was so hysterical he doubted that she heard him. She scrabbled in the sand in a desperate attempt to get away from him.

"Easy. Easy, Lauren. C'mon, sweetheart, let me help you," he pleaded, but he couldn't reach her. The last thing he wanted was to use force and frighten her even more, but her pitiful whimpers tore at his heart. It was more than he could bear.

"Noooo!" she screamed when he reached for her.

Adam gritted his teeth and gathered her in his arms. Ignoring her cries and flailing fists, he held her tight against his chest and rocked her.

"Ssh. Ssh. It's okay. It's okay now, baby. It's over. It's over," he soothed. "He's not going to hurt you anymore. I promise. Nobody's going to hurt you anymore. Take it easy, sweetheart. Take it easy."

She tried to twist away from him but she was hurt and exhausted. After only a moment what little strength she had left was depleted. She sagged in his arms as desolate cries of fear and pain tore from her throat.

"That's a girl. Take it easy. Relax. It's over now. You're safe with me," he crooned, stroking his hand over her hair.

He kept up the litany of soothing words, and after a few

minutes Adam sensed that he had finally broken through her hysteria. She quieted, and, except for the convulsive shudders that still racked her body, she grew still.

"A-Adam? Is th-that y-you?"

"Yeah, it's me," he said softly and rubbed his hand over her back in a slow circle. "I've got you. You're safe now."

"Oh, Adam," she wailed and pressed her face against his chest. She clutched his shirt with both hands, as though she would never let go, and wept.

The racking sobs shook her whole body. The sounds tearing from her throat were so raw and painful they brought tears to Adam's eyes. He wanted to get up and beat the crap out of the scumbag who had done this to her all over again. He had never felt so furious or so helpless in his life.

All he could do was hold her and stroke his hand over her hair and back, over and over. "That's all right, honey. You go ahead and cry. God knows, you're entitled. That's it. Let it all out. It's okay."

Adam had no idea how long they stayed that way. The front of his shirt was soaked with tears when her sobs finally tapered off to watery sniffles and erratic little hitches of breath.

"Are you all right?"

"I-Is he g-gone?"

"No, but don't worry. He's not going to hurt you again. He's out cold, right over th—" Adam tensed as he looked around in time to see Lauren's attacker lurching away down the beach. "Damn! He's getting away! To hell with that!"

He tried to put her from him and go after the guy, but Lauren clutched his shirt tighter. "No! Don't leave me! Please, don't leave me!"

"Sweetheart—"

"No, please! Oh, please! *Please!*"

Jaws clenched, Adam looked from Lauren to her attacker, then back. Every fiber in his being screamed for him to go after the creep, but he couldn't ignore the terror in her eyes.

With a sigh, he drew her back against his chest and wrapped his arms around her. "Okay. Ssh. Ssh. Calm down, Lauren. I'm not going anywhere. I'm not going to leave you."

Gritting his teeth, he rocked her and stared over her shoulder at the man, nearly bent double, limping away into the twilight.

Lauren pressed closer and buried her face against his chest. Her hands clutched his shirt in a death grip. Adam could feel her shaking. It was growing cold on the beach, but he was fairly certain her shivers were the result of shock.

Though she continued to shiver, after a while she seemed to regain a degree of composure—and with it came embarrassment.

Sniffing, she pulled back a bit, but she kept her head down and her gaze averted. "I . . . I'm s-sorry. I don't . . . don't usually fall apart like that." She raised a hand to push her hair out of her face, but it was shaking so badly she couldn't manage the simple task, and she gave up and clasped her arms tight about herself.

Except for the sleeve still covering her left arm and a lacy écru bra, she was bare from the waist up. What was left of her shirt hung in tatters about her hips, connected by only a thin strip to that one remaining sleeve.

Glancing down at herself, Lauren whimpered and tried to gather the remnants of the shirt to cover herself.

"Hold on. I'll get your windbreaker."

Adam sprinted down to the water's edge and retrieved the jacket from the sand where she'd dropped it. Pain shot through his knee with every step.

He gritted his teeth and tried to ignore the stabs. Christ. There was going to be hell to pay for this night. The trauma he'd dealt his knee this time was going to cost him.

After that wild chase outside the Cordex Tower the previous week he'd managed on his own to get the swelling down with ice packs, but he knew from experience that the knee could take only so much stress. From the way it felt, he was facing a trip to an orthopedic specialist and hours of physical therapy.

Hell, he might even have to dig out that damned cane he'd had to use right after the last surgery.

Adam clenched his jaw and pushed the thought aside. He couldn't worry about that right now.

"Here, this should help," he said, dropping to his good knee beside her. As gently as he could, he slipped her arms into the windbreaker and pulled the front edges closed. He tried to examine her face, but it had grown too dark to see the extent of her injuries. "Are you going to be all right?"

She nodded.

He pushed her hair back from her injured cheek and she flinched. "That needs some first aid. My house is closest, so I'm going to take you there. Okay?"

"Okay," she replied in a small voice.

"Right. Now then, I'm going to pick you up and—"

"Oh, no. You don't have to do that. I . . . I can walk."

Adam had his doubts about that, but he didn't argue. He didn't want to panic her again.

She wobbled when he helped her to her feet. He put his arm around her waist to support her, but her knees buckled after only one step, and he swooped her up in his arms.

"Oh, no—"

"Ssh. You're in no condition to walk."

"But you can't carry me all that way. I'm too heavy."

He slanted her a wry look. "Honey, I used to wear football gear that weighed more than you. Just relax and hang on. I'll have you there in no time."

Reluctantly, she looped her arms around his neck, but she was so tense she felt like a mannequin in his arms.

Adam's knee protested every step. By the time he climbed the outside stairs to his deck he was limping.

"You can put me down now. I'm sure I can manage on my own."

"Yeah, right." He carried her into his living room through the open French doors and lowered her onto the sofa cushions.

"Here, let's put this around you," he said, pulling from the back of the sofa the afghan his mother had knitted. After he had tucked the soft throw around her he paused and ran a cursory eye over her.

One side of her face was beginning to swell. Blood seeped from the abrasion on her cheek and a livid purple bruise was blossoming all around it. The wounds needed attention, but they, along with whatever other injuries she had sustained, would have to wait a bit.

"Just lie still for a minute. I'll be right back."

"Where are you going?"

The panicky edge to her voice stopped him before he could take a step. He took her hand and gave it a reassuring squeeze. "I'm just going to call the police."

"The police! But why?" Fear widened her eyes. They glittered like vivid green jewels in her chalky face. "I don't want to call the police. Surely you've heard how they treat women who claim they were raped or attacked. I don't need that."

"That won't happen. This isn't an uncorroborated incident. I was a witness to the whole thing."

"But—"

"Lauren, listen to me. You have to report this. That guy can't be allowed to run free to do this again. You escaped him with a few cuts and bruises, but the next woman might not be so lucky."

Blinking back a fresh rush of tears, she gave him an agonized look and fought to control her trembling chin, but after a moment she nodded. "All . . . all right. Call them."

"Good girl. Now you just relax. This won't take long. And as soon I'm done I'll get my first-aid kit. Unless you'd rather I took you to the hospital?"

She shook her head again, more emphatically this time. "No. No hospital."

Aware of the way she kept eyeing the open French doors, Adam closed and locked them before leaving the room. Not wanting to upset her more, he made the call from his bedroom.

"They're on their way," he announced a few minutes later, returning to the living room carrying first-aid supplies. "We're out of the city, so I had to call the sheriff's office."

Lauren was sitting up with the afghan wrapped around her shoulders. Adam placed a pan of warm water, a washcloth and a first-aid kit on the coffee table and sat down beside her.

After wringing out the washcloth, he cupped the uninjured side of her face and tipped her head up. "This is going to sting."

Lauren sucked in a sharp breath and flinched when the cloth touched her cheek, but after that she gritted her teeth and endured his ministrations with admirable stoicism. Adam had been prepared for tears and complaints.

"I . . . I haven't thanked you for saving me from . . ." She closed her eyes and struggled again to control her wobbling chin. ". . . for what you did."

"Hey, no problem. I'm just glad I was here."

"If you hadn't been . . ." She hugged the afghan closer and shuddered.

"Don't think about that. I was here. That's what counts." As gently as he could he smeared antibiotic cream on her abraded cheek, watching her all the while out of the corner of his eye. She was so pale he wondered if perhaps she had worse injuries that he hadn't discovered yet.

"Are you hurt anywhere else? How's your stomach?"

"It's bruised, but I don't think there's any permanent damage there. My head is throbbing like crazy, though."

"Hmm, let's have a look." Starting at her temples, Adam threaded his fingers through her hair. It flashed through his mind that he had been wanting to do exactly that for weeks. Not, however, under these circumstances.

94   *Ginna Gray*

Still, he could not help but notice that her hair was every bit as silky and thick as he'd thought it would be.

"Ow," she protested when his fingertips touched a bump over her left ear.

"Mmm. That's a real goose egg you got there. You sure you don't want to go to the hospital and have somebody take a look at that? You might have a concussion."

"No. If I do they'll just make me stay quiet and rest. I can do that at home."

The gate buzzer sounded before she finished speaking. Adam went to the intercom panel in the wall and pushed a button. "Yes?"

"Sheriff's department. You called about a rape attempt?"

Seven

A few minutes later, the front doorbell rang. Lauren shivered and huddled deeper in the afghan.

Adam opened the door to two deputies, one around forty with world-weary features, the other a spit-and-polished young man in his late twenties who looked as though he might have just been mustered out of the Marines.

"You the one called about an attempted rape?" the older of the two said in a bored voice.

"Yes. Come in. The victim's name is Lauren McKenna. She's inside."

"I'm Deputy Scott and this is Deputy Wright. We just want to ask a few . . . Saaay. I know you! You're Adam Rafferty! Well I'll be damned! Look, Norm, it's Adam Rafferty! Whaddaya know about that!"

The younger man crowded forward with a big grin on his face and his hand outstretched. "Mr. Rafferty, I can't tell you what a pleasure this is. Oh man, this is really something. Wait'll I tell my buddies."

"I'm your number one fan, Mr. Rafferty," Deputy Scott declared, elbowing his young partner out of the way. "Me'n my boy, Andy, we watched every game you played. Uh . . . do you think you could maybe sign the back of this citation form for me? That boy of mine will be over the moon if I bring him your autograph."

Adam wanted to shout at them that they were there to

investigate a crime, not get autographs, but he couldn't bring himself to be rude to a fan. Besides, he knew that kind of reaction would only anger the deputies.

"Look, officers, could we get to the case first? I've got a traumatized woman in my living room, and I think it might make her feel better if we got this over with. Afterwards, I'll sign all the autographs you want."

"Oh sure, sure. You got it. C'mon, Norm, let's go take the lady's statement."

When he led the officers into the living room, Lauren eyed them with apprehension. She looked like a lost child, huddled in the afghan. Her green eyes had a haunted look and her face was a deathly pale oval against her vibrant hair. Without hesitation, Adam sat down next to her on the sofa and took her hand.

He made the introductions then quickly and succinctly, recounted what had happened, from the moment he had returned from taking his parents home until he'd called the sheriff's office. All the while Deputy Scott scribbled on his notepad.

"Did anyone else see what happened? Another neighbor maybe?"

"Lauren's house and mine are the only two on this beach."

"I see. Had you ever seen the man before, Ms. McKenna?"

Lauren shook her head. "No. Never."

"How about you, Mr. Rafferty?"

"No."

"Did he say anything to you, Miss? Anything at all?"

"He . . . he just called me foul names when he first grabbed me. Then . . . then after I hit him in the throat with my fist he was furious, and he said . . ." She stopped and shuddered. "He said in this awful voice . . . 'I'm going to hurt you for that, you bitch. I'm going to hurt you real bad.' "

Adam felt her trembles increase, and he gave her hand a squeeze.

"Hmm." Deputy Scott scribbled faster. "You said this attack took place after sunset. I don't suppose either of you got a good look at the guy."

"It wasn't that long after sunset, deputy," Adam corrected. "There was still enough light to see. I saw his face clearly."

"How about you, miss? Would you recognize him if you saw him again?"

"Yes. I would." Lauren grimaced. "I'll never forget that face."

"What I don't understand is how he got onto the beach. You'd have to be Spider Man to climb down those boulders, and the gate is electronically controlled. Only Lauren and I have the combination."

"My guess is he either climbed over the gate or hid in the rocks until one of you drove through then scooted in behind you." Deputy Scott stopped writing long enough to cast them an admonishing look. "You shouldn't get to feeling safe just because you've installed a few security devices. A gate like that might slow a determined criminal down, but, trust me, it won't stop him."

He looked at his partner. "Norm, you go back to the gate and have a look around. I'll go examine the crime scene. Mr. Rafferty? You want to show me where the attack took place?"

Lauren tensed. Her hand tightened around Adam's. She turned to him with a desperate look. "You're not going to leave me here, are you?"

"It's okay," he said gently. "You'll be safe. I'll make sure all the doors and windows are locked. This will only take a few minutes. As soon as I've shown the deputy the spot, I'll be right back. Okay?"

Lauren swallowed hard and nodded. He could see she was terrified.

Once they were outside, the deputy shook his head and slipped his notepad back into his shirt pocket. "Man, that's one spooked lady."

"Yeah, and with good cause," Adam said through clenched teeth as they started down the steps to the beach. "She came damned close to being brutally raped. Maybe even murdered. That sorry bastard. I should have broken him in two while I had the chance."

"I know how you feel, but—Say, you're limping. Did the guy hurt you when you struggled with him?"

"Hardly. Football—you know. Hell on knees. And for the record, it wasn't a struggle. He never laid a hand on me. I pulled the bastard off of Lauren and beat the crap out of him. When you catch him you'll find he has a broken nose with my knuckle prints on it."

Deputy Scott chuckled. "Good for you. And don't you worry, Mr. Rafferty. We'll get the creep. He won't get by with roughing up your lady that way, I promise you."

Adam started to correct the man's assumption that he and Lauren were a couple, but he thought better of it. There was no point in complicating things by opening up that can of worms.

As they walked both men swept high-powered flashlight beams over the sand. They found the scene with no trouble; signs of the struggle were clear.

"Which way did he go when he took off?"

"That'a way," Adam said, pointing toward the road at the base of the boulders which led from the gate past both houses.

The deputy swung his light over the sand in that direction. A distinct trail of freshly disturbed sand led away into the darkness.

"Looks like we got plenty of footprints. I'll get somebody over here first thing to make a cast. In the meantime I want you and Ms. McKenna to stay off the beach. We don't want to contaminate our crime scene."

"No problem, deputy. I doubt I could drag Lauren back down here. Look, if you don't need me anymore, I'm going to go back. I don't want to leave her alone too long."

"Sure thing. Me'n Norm'll stop by the house when we're done and tell you what we found, if anything."

"Thanks. I'd appreciate that. And I'll have those autographs ready when you do."

As though she expected her attacker to burst through them at any moment, Lauren's gaze was fixed on the French doors when Adam let himself in. At the sight of him she let out her breath and closed her eyes. "Thank God. I heard the footsteps and I thought . . ." She bit her bottom lip and looked away. "I'm sorry. I know I'm being hysterical."

"Hey, it's okay. You have a right to be jumpy."

She tried to smile at him, but it was a pitiful effort. Her gaze met his for only an instant before darting away again. Adam remained by the door, studying her down-bent head and fidgety movements.

Now that the first urgency had passed, the wariness and strain that had marked their relationship from the first had begun to creep back.

"I . . . I really appreciate all you're doing for me. After . . . well . . . given our history and all . . ."

"Don't worry about it. I would have done the same for anyone."

She looked at him then. "Yes. I'm sure you would have. But thank you, all the same."

"No problem." He picked up the notepad he kept beside the telephone and sat down in the chair across from her. "How are you feeling?"

"Physically or emotionally?"

"Both."

She gave what was supposed to be a laugh. "Shaky."

"That's understandable. But I know just the thing for that." He finished signing four autographs and went to the portable bar in the corner of the room. When he returned he handed her a balloon glass containing a generous amount of amber liquor. "There you go. Drink that. It'll put the starch back in you."

"What is it?"

"Brandy."

"Oh, thank you, but no. I . . . I'm not much of a drinker."

At least that was one point in her favor, Adam thought. "Actually, neither am I, but this stuff will warm you up and take the edge off your nerves. Trust me," he urged when she continued to eye the drink.

Looking doubtful, Lauren held the snifter in both hands and raised it to her lips. She made a face and choked when the liquor slid down her throat.

"I told you it would warm you up."

"It will certainly . . . do that," she gasped between coughs. "It burns like fire going down. I think . . . I think it cauterized my throat."

"Could be. That's why it gets easier after the first swallow. Why don't you try another sip and see."

Cautiously, she did as he suggested. This time, though she made a face, she didn't choke. "You're right. It is easier to take. In fact it's . . . not too terrible."

Adam rolled his eyes. "What a thing to say about good Napoleon Brandy."

"Sorry. But I did warn you that I'm not a drinker."

"So you did. Hell, I should've palmed off the cheap stuff on you."

"Yes, you should have," she agreed, giving the brandy another try. "Believe me, I wouldn't have known the difference."

"That's what I get for trying to impress you."

"Why would you bother to do that?" She took another sip of the potent liquor and closed her eyes as it went down.

"Reflex, I guess. You know . . . that old machismo thing that automatically kicks in when a man is around a beautiful woman."

"I'm not sure if that's a compliment or an insult."

"Hey, would I insult a lady?"

It was foolish banter, the kind Adam never dreamed he would exchange with this particular woman. On her part, it was no doubt brandy-induced. The stuff he gave her went straight to your head with a kick like an army mule. Particu-

larly if you weren't used to it. But at least the inane chatter
filled in the awkward silences and kept her mind off of what
had happened.

"I don't know. Would you?"

"You've obviously never met my mother. She's no bigger
than a minute, but to this day she'd tear a strip off me if I
were less than courteous to any female."

"Mmm. She sounds like a good woman, your mother."

"Yeah. She's the best."

Adam didn't bother to mention that Lauren could have discovered that for herself if she hadn't so rudely rejected Kate's
invitation the day before. He could see by the flash of discomfort in her eyes that the same thought had occurred to her.

Footsteps clumping up the beach stairs interrupted the awkward moment. Lauren jumped and nearly spilled the brandy.

"Sounds like the posse has returned," Adam quipped and
rose to unlock the French doors and let them in.

"Well, it looks like I was right," Deputy Scott announced.
"Norm found a scrap of material on the gate. Looks like it
was torn off a windbreaker."

"The attacker was wearing a red windbreaker," Adam said.
"I grabbed it to pull him off of Lauren."

"It's a red scrap, alright. It was hanging on the inside of
the gate, so I'd say our man climbed over it to get in. The
question now is, how did he get out? Did you actually see
him leave the beach?"

"No. It was too dark by then."

"Hmm. Tell me, do you think he was physically able to
climb that gate again after you'd finished with him?"

"That would depend on what kind of physical shape he
was in before I hit him. But I doubt it. He practically had to
crawl off."

"You mean . . . Oh, God. You think he's still out there,
don't you?"

"Now take it easy, miss, I didn't say that. The guy's probably long gone. Perps don't usually stick around after a close

call like the one he had. Chances are he slipped out the gate when Mr. Rafferty opened it for us. Me 'n Norm searched the cove and didn't see any sign of him."

Adam frowned. That was hardly reassuring. There were hundreds of places in those boulders where a man could hide, particularly in the dark. He glanced at Lauren and saw that the same thought had occurred to her.

"Just to be on the safe side, though, I'd advise you to keep your doors and windows locked until we catch the guy."

"Thanks, officer. We'll do that. Is there anything else?"

"Not tonight. We'll go back to the jail and file this report. I'll get somebody out here to make a cast of those footprints and dust the gate for fingerprints. We'll check them against the known offenders in our files. Odds are, this guy's got a record, so it shouldn't take long to track him down."

"That's good. I'd like to thank you for responding so quickly. We appreciate it. And here are those autographs you wanted."

"Hey, thanks."

"Yeah, thanks a lot," the deputies replied in unison.

"And don't you worry, Ms. McKenna. We'll get the pervert," Deputy Scott added over his shoulder as Adam showed them to the door. "He'll be sorry he ever messed with Adam Rafferty's lady."

"What did he mean by that?" Lauren asked the instant Adam returned.

"They have the idea that you and I are lovers."

"What? Why on earth didn't you set them straight?"

"I thought about it, but it seemed smarter not to."

"What do you mean?"

"I'm sure the deputies are dedicated lawmen who do their best to solve every case they investigate. However . . . they're also avid football fans. It occurred to me that they just might approach this case with more enthusiasm if I let them believe we are more than just neighbors."

"You mean . . . just because you're a sports celebrity they'll work harder to find that man?"

"Honey, they'll bust their asses. It'll be a feather in their cap."

"But that's not right."

"Maybe not, but it's human nature. I know you don't think much of football players, but being one does have its advantages now and then. Of course, if it bothers you to make use of that, I can always call Deputy Scott and explain."

She hesitated, and he could see the panic and indecision mingled in her eyes. Adam was sorry she had been attacked. He wouldn't wish that on any woman, no matter how much he disliked her, but he wouldn't be human if he didn't feel just a bit smug over the current aspect of the situation.

Finally she shook her head. "No. I want that beast found as soon as possible. No matter what it takes."

"That's what I thought."

An awkward silence descended. Lauren twisted her hands together in her lap. "Well, I . . . I suppose I should go home."

"I don't think that's such a good idea. The cops are probably right about the guy making tracks, but I'd feel better if I knew you were safe. And you certainly don't have to leave. You're welcome to stay here. I have a couple of spare bedrooms."

"That's kind of you, but no. I've imposed on you enough already."

Adam studied her. She still looked fragile, but he could see that she meant to go. "All right. If you're sure that's what you want, I'll take you home."

She cast an apprehensive glance toward the beach. He pretended he hadn't noticed and picked up his car keys from the bowl on the entry-hall table. "Deputy Scott wants us to stay off the beach until his team has finished gathering evidence, so I'll drive you home."

She looked almost faint with relief.

As they headed for the door, she stopped abruptly. "You're limping. Oh, God, did he hurt you?"

"No. It's an old football injury. I aggravated it tonight when I ran to your rescue. It'll be okay in a few days."

"Oh, I'm sorry. I'm so sorry."

"It wasn't your fault. Don't worry about it. I did it to myself. C'mon, let's go."

"You are going to see a doctor, aren't you?" she asked anxiously as she followed him down the stairs to the garage beneath the house.

"Maybe. I don't know. I'll see how it comes along."

"Please do. And have the bill sent to me."

He stopped and looked at her over the top of the car. "Forget it. I can take care of my own medical bills."

"But after what you did for me, it's the least I can do."

"Just get in the car, Lauren."

Neither spoke on the short drive. When he parked before her house, Adam reached for the door handle. "I'm going inside with you and have a look around."

She merely nodded and opened the passenger door.

The fact that she hadn't argued spoke volumes. So did the trembling he could feel vibrating through her as he escorted her up the steps with a hand on her arm. The lady was gutsy, but she was also scared spitless.

"Give me your key."

"I don't have it with me. The door isn't locked."

He shot her a scorching look. "You go off down the beach and leave your door unlocked? Jesus Christ, woman! That's asking for trouble."

"This beach is secure . . ." She stopped and bit her lower lip, her face stricken.

"Exactly." Adam wanted to say more on the subject, but he limited himself to the pithy comment. She was already frightened enough.

"Okay, stick close. And here, take my car keys. If I tell you to run, you hotfoot it out of here and jump in my car and take off. And I mean burn rubber all the way to the highway. Got it?"

"Ye-yes. I understand."

Adam eased open the door and peered inside. Lauren pressed so close behind him he could feel her breasts brushing his back.

She had left a lamp burning in the living room. He stopped just inside the door and darted a look around.

"Stay here. I'll be right back."

Before he could move she clutched the back of his shirt with both hands. "No! I want to go with you!"

"Hey, hey. Take it easy, honey." Reaching around, Adam pried her fingers loose and turned to her. She looked so frightened and vulnerable he forgot all the reasons why he didn't like her.

He put his arms around her and hugged her, and Lauren burrowed against his chest. "You'll be okay. I promise." Rocking her from side to side, he held her close and stroked his hand over the back of her head. "But if that guy is in the house I want you out here while I deal with him. I don't want to take a chance of you getting in the way and maybe getting hurt." He grasped her upper arms and eased her back until he could look into her eyes. "Okay?"

"O-Okay."

"Good girl. Now just stay calm. I won't be but a minute."

Like his own house, her place was an open plan, with the kitchen separated from the living room by only an L-shaped counter. Adam checked it out, then he eased down the hall to the bedrooms.

He opened the first door and stepped inside. Immediately he knew he was in Lauren's bedroom. It was too dark at first to see anything, but he could smell her perfume, and that unique woman smell that belonged to her alone. He switched on the light, and saw a queen-sized bed and a neat-as-a-pin room done up in soft colors—peach and some sort of pale green. Sea foam, he thought was what they called it.

He would have liked to look around more and discover exactly what made Lauren tick, but he merely did a quick sweep of both the room and the adjoining bath. Finding nothing, he moved on to the room across the hall, which Lauren apparently used as an office, then to the other bathroom. Both were empty.

He paused outside the room next to Lauren's and listened. He heard a creaking sound coming from inside. He flattened himself against the adjacent wall. Slowly, he reached out and turned the doorknob and eased the door open a crack. Reaching inside, he flipped on the lights, threw the door open wide and charged. Two steps into the room he stopped cold and stared.

The room was a nursery, complete with crib, rocking chair, changing table, and every imaginable toy and accoutrement available for an infant. A colorful mobile hung over the crib and there were frilly curtains at the windows and Mother Goose wallpaper covering the walls.

Belatedly, Adam realized that the sound he had heard was the rocking chair gently tipping back and forth, pushed by the breeze coming through an open window.

Eight

Did Lauren have a child? No one had mentioned it if she did. And he sure as hell hadn't seen one around.

Maybe this setup was for a niece or nephew. Adam looked around and shook his head. No, it was too perfect. Too complete. Every item, every tiny detail had been chosen with care by an adoring mother.

But where was the baby? Had her ex-husband gotten custody of the kid? Or . . .

Adam's face contorted as another possibility occurred to him.

Ah, Jesus! Had Lauren had a baby who had died?

He raked his hand through his hair and cursed under his breath. That would certainly explain her reaction to Paulo. And that haunted look he'd glimpsed in her eyes.

It all made sense now. Why the hell hadn't it occurred to him that it could be grief that drove her to the point each night? That made her so distant? He'd read somewhere once that the loss of a child sometimes made a person withdraw from others, even their closest friends and family.

Adam remembered all the harsh thoughts he had about Lauren, and disgust twisted his features. "Aw, hell."

Lauren shifted from one foot to the other. Her gaze darted all around, checking the deck behind her, the windows, then

back to the door that led into the hallway. What was taking
Adam so long?

As though he had heard her, he limped back into the living
room. Her heart skipped a beat when she saw his expression.

"What's wrong?"

"Nothing," he said, but the way he looked at her made her
think otherwise.

"There's no one here. I closed and locked all your windows
and the door at the top of the stairs leading down into the
garage. By the way, are there any windows in your garage?"

"No."

"That's good." He circled the room, peering out and
checking all the locks on the windows. "You don't happen
to own a gun, do you?"

Lauren's heart gave a painful thump. "No. No, I don't."

"Well, don't worry. You probably won't need one. If you
hear anything—anything at all—just give me a call and I'll
be over here like a shot. Do you have my number?"

She shook her head. Fear clawed at her throat, making
speech impossible.

He was leaving. She was going to be here alone. If that
animal came back . . . Oh, God.

"I'll write it down for you." Adam walked into the kitchen
and scribbled the number on the pad beside the wall telephone. "You should probably keep a copy of this by the
telephone in your bedroom, too."

She crossed her arms over her midriff and held on tight.
Her insides were shaking so hard she felt as though she might
fly apart any second. On trembling legs she followed Adam
to the door.

He paused and looked at her. "Are you going to be all
right?"

She tried to choke out the lie, but she couldn't make her
throat open. Hugging herself tighter, she folded her lips together to stop their trembling and gave a jerky nod.

Adam frowned. "Look, if you want me to, I'll stay. I can sack out on your sofa."

"Y-you wouldn't mind?"

"Would it make you feel better?"

"I . . . yes." Lauren closed her eyes. "Oh, God, yes."

"Then it's settled. I'll stay."

"Are you sure? I know it's an imposition. You've already helped me more than I have any right to expect, but the thought of staying here alone, with that man still running loose—"

"Don't think about that. And it's not an imposition. I don't mind at all. Fact is, if I went home I doubt I'd get much sleep for worrying about how you were doing. This makes it easier on both of us."

She closed her eyes and exhaled a long sigh, and for the first time since they had entered the house the muscles in her back and shoulders relaxed. "Thank you, Adam. This is very kind of you."

"Quit worrying about it, okay? It's no big thing."

Lauren thought it was a very big thing, indeed, but it was apparent that he would rather they dropped the subject.

Feeling suddenly awkward, she looked around and gestured toward the sofa. "Please, make yourself comfortable. Umm . . . would you like some coffee?"

"Actually, I could use a bite to eat. I took my parents out to Sunday dinner after church, but that was over eight hours ago. Do you think we could whip something up?"

"Oh. Of course. Uh . . . what would you like?"

"Nothing big. An omelette would be fine. Or maybe a bowl of soup. How about you?"

"Me? Oh, I don't think I could eat a thing."

"Sure you can. When did you last eat?"

"Well, uh . . . around noon, I guess. But—"

"Then it's high time you had some nourishment." He snagged her hand and headed for the kitchen. "C'mon. We'll rustle up something together."

Lauren tried to hold back, but he simply towed her along

behind him. In the kitchen he put a dishtowel around his waist and slipped an apron over her head. "Okay, where do you keep your bowls?"

It was useless to resist. Adam simply overrode all her protests and put her to work making toast and setting out place mats and flatware on the breakfast bar, while he rummaged through her cabinets and drawers, dragging out bowls and utensils and a frying pan. In no time they were working side by side.

The whole while he kept up a running conversation, mostly about inconsequential things: the weather, a movie he'd seen, the pros and cons of buying a boat, how he planned to surprise his parents with cruise tickets for their anniversary. Lauren responded with nods and smiles and noncommittal murmurs.

"So, tell me, were you born in the San Francisco area?"

The direct question startled her. She looked up from slicing a mushroom and caught the challenging glint in his eye. Evidently he was tired of carrying the ball alone. He had deliberately changed tactics to draw her out.

Normally Lauren would not stand for anyone prying into her life, but she knew that Adam was merely trying to distract her with small talk. She found that touching.

She nodded and went back to slicing mushrooms. "Yes, I was."

"And do your parents still live here?"

A smile flirted about Lauren's mouth. My, he was determined. "No. My dad passed away a few years ago. Shortly after that my mother moved to a retirement development in Palm Springs. She likes the warm weather there. Plus she gets to play golf and bridge everyday. She's in heaven."

He laughed. "I know what you mean. As long as my mother has a garden to putter around in she's happy as a lark."

A few seconds of silence ticked by. He watched her, as though waiting for her to say more. When she didn't he asked,

"What made you choose a career in engineering psychology?"

Lauren put the pile of sliced mushrooms in a bowl and slid it toward him, then went to work dicing ham. "From the time I was a little girl, Uncle Walter encouraged me to become an architect, or a mechanical engineer, or a contract attorney—any profession that I could utilize in the construction business—so that I could someday join his company."

"Wait a second. *Uncle* Walter? Walter Ingram is your *uncle?*"

"Well, no. Not really. Actually, he's my godfather, but I grew up calling him Uncle Walter. He and my father were best friends all of their lives. I thought you knew that."

"Godfather. Well I'll be damned." Adam chuckled and shook his head. "No. No, I didn't know that."

"Really? It's common knowledge around the office. In fact I'm surprised that Walter didn't tell you himself. He's usually quick to provide that information to new employees."

"Hmm. I wonder why he neglected to mention it this time?" He went to the refrigerator and returned with butter and eggs. "Anyway, you were saying . . ."

"Well, when I first entered college, like most eighteen-year-olds, I had no idea what I wanted to do with my life. Then, in the last semester of my freshman year I took a few psychology courses, and I loved it. I knew right away what my major would be."

She stopped dicing ham and watched with amazement as, one-handed, he cracked a half-dozen eggs into a bowl with the expertise of a master chef, and began to beat them with a whisk.

"Six eggs? That's going to be a big omelette."

He smiled at her dubious expression. "I'm a big man. But don't worry, I'll share it with you. So, go on with your story."

"Oh. Well, as you can imagine, Dad and Uncle Walter were heartbroken when I announced that I was going for a Ph.D. in psychology. Especially Walter. He and his wife never had children of their own, and he'd pinned all his hopes on me following in his footsteps. He could see all those dreams of me joining the firm crumbling to dust.

"Then I discovered engineering psychology. It was perfect—a branch of my field that I could use in construction. Walter was over the moon."

"Mmm. I'll bet."

"At first I think a lot of people at Ingram and Bates had their doubts as to the validity of the specialty or how useful an addition I would be to the staff. Even Walter. Although he never said so. He was too happy that I was finally a part of the company. I think he was genuinely surprised to discover that I had something important to contribute."

"I don't imagine that took long," Adam murmured, as he swirled a gob of melting butter around the omelette pan. "You're terrific at your job."

She shot him a sharp look, suspecting he was merely giving lip service to placate her, but all she could see in those steady brown eyes was sincerity. A warm feeling swelled inside her, and she responded with a smile, the first genuine one she had bestowed all evening.

"Thank you. I appreciate that. Not everyone agrees with you, though. There are still some people in the company who think I'm just featherbedding."

"They obviously don't know Walter very well," Adam drawled. "I can't imagine him carrying dead weight on the payroll, no matter who it is." With a flourish, he poured the beaten eggs into the pan, and the hot butter sizzled.

Adam's support pleased her enormously, and as she watched him add the other ingredients to the pan and deftly flip the omelette, the warmth in her chest expanded. "You're absolutely right. It's true that I was hired mainly because I'm his goddaughter. I've never denied that. However, I wouldn't have been kept on the payroll two months if I hadn't been good at what I do. Certainly I never would have received promotions." She gave a caustic little chuckle. "I would have been out on my ear, that's what would have happened."

"I'm sure you're right." He slid the omelette onto a warm plate and divided it in half.

"Oh, no, please. I'm really not hungry. I couldn't possibly eat all that," she protested.

He merely grinned and added two pieces of toast to her plate.

Lauren honestly didn't think she could eat a bite after all that had happened, but when he served the meal the delicious aroma rising from the plate made her mouth water. She took a bite and closed her eyes. "Mmm, this is wonderful. Where did you learn to cook like this?"

"My mom. Her philosophy is, if you eat, you should know how to cook, and cook well. It's a skill that's come in handy over the years since I left home. Eating in restaurants is nice, but it gets old after a while."

"Does your father cook?" Lauren asked between bites.

"You bet. He takes his turn at cleaning up, too. Mom's old-fashioned in a lot of ways, but when it comes to equality of the sexes and a fair division of labor, she's a hardcore feminist."

"I think I'd like your mother."

"Oh, I guarantee it. You'd like my dad, too. He's a real character. I'll introduce you to them sometime."

Lauren gave him a weak smile and took another bite of omelette. She didn't know how to respond to that. He made the statement so casually, as though he assumed that everything had changed between them.

And, of course, he was right. Everything had.

The admission rattled Lauren and all her uneasiness came rushing back. Still, it was pointless to pretend otherwise. She didn't want to be beholden to Adam. She didn't want to be beholden to anyone. Every instinct she possessed urged her to pull back and shut him out.

That, however, was no longer an option. At almost certain

risk to himself, Adam had saved her from rape. Maybe even worse. And he was going out of his way to make her feel secure. She would never—could never—think of him in quite the same way again.

"See. What did I tell you? I knew you could eat."

Surprised, Lauren looked down at her plate and discovered that she had devoured every morsel. "Well . . . who could resist such wonderful cooking?" she said with a self-conscious chuckle.

She felt edgy and awkward as they cleaned the kitchen, and not all of the feelings were due to the attack. She wasn't accustomed to having a man in her house. This was her private domain, her retreat where she shut out the rest of the world.

In the small kitchen Adam seemed even larger somehow, more rawly masculine. She felt almost suffocated by his nearness. It was impossible to work together in such close quarters without brushing up against one another. Every time it happened Lauren's breathing became clogged.

When the counters were wiped clean and the dishwasher was chugging away, she scooted out of the kitchen, relieved to put more space between then. Adam made himself comfortable in the living room and she excused herself and went to the linen closet in the hall to get out sheets and blankets and a spare pillow.

"I don't know how comfortable that sofa is, but at least you'll be warm with these," she said, placing the bedding on a living room chair.

"I'll be fine. Don't worry."

"Yes, well, I hope so. I'll, uh . . . I'll say goodnight, then. I'm going to shower and go to bed."

"Good idea. And Lauren." She stopped and turned to him. "Remember, I'll be here. Just a few feet away. You're perfectly safe."

She met that steady gaze and an odd sensation moved through her, warm and tingly. A ghost of a smile flickered around her mouth, and she nodded. "Goodnight," she whispered and headed for her bedroom.

Alone in her bedroom Lauren was so jittery she could barely make herself strip and step into the shower. Without Adam there she would not have been able to do it at all. Just knowing that he was stretched out on the sofa in her living room was a comfort.

She hurried through the shower and the rest of her nightly rituals. Smelling of soap and bath talc, she pulled a long silk nightgown over her head and slipped into her bed.

An hour later Lauren still lay staring at the ceiling of her bedroom. Every muscle felt taut as a violin string. She'd tried every relaxation technique she new, including counting sheep, but nothing helped.

She turned onto her side, then flounced back. Rising up, she punched her pillow and then lay back down and drew her knees up. A minute later she flopped onto her back again with a sigh. It was no use. She was too wired to sleep.

Throwing back the covers, she sat up, slipped her feet into her house slippers and reached for her robe. She eased open the bedroom door and peered out. A dim puddle of light seeped into the hallway from the living room. She crept to the end of the hall and peeked around the door.

Except for the weak glow spilling from the kitchen, where Adam had left the light on over the stove, the living room was dark. Through the dimness, Lauren made out the familiar shapes of her furniture. The sofa was spread with the bedding she had put out for Adam, but he was not there.

Panic gushed through her. "Adam!" She rushed into the room, her gaze darting around in a frantic search. "Oh, God, Adam, where are you!"

"Lauren?"

She sagged with relief as he stepped from the shadows beside a window.

He straightened from switching on a lamp as light flooded

the room. Frowning, he covered the space between them in three long strides and grasped her arms. "What's wrong?"

"I . . . I didn't see you. I thought you were gone."

"No. I meant, what are you doing out here?"

"I, umm . . . I couldn't sleep."

His frown faded, and his mouth twitched. "Neither could I. Too keyed up, I guess. That's why I was looking out the window."

Only then did she notice that he was barefoot and shirtless. His unbuttoned suit pants rode low on his hips and where the waistband gaped open she caught a glimpse of deep maroon cotton briefs.

Lauren jerked her gaze upward, and found herself staring at an impossibly broad bare chest, just inches from her nose. Her eyes were on a level with the most impressive set of pectoral muscles she had ever seen. She stared at the thatch of dark curls in the center of his chest. She was growing woozy as his scent went to her head like brandy fumes.

Adam released her and stepped back, and to her relief the bizarre moment passed. It had been nothing but nerves, she decided, and silently chided herself for being so foolish.

Adam gestured toward the sofa. "Why don't you sit down. We might as well keep each other company."

She glanced at the blanket-draped couch, hesitated, then nodded. Tightening the belt on her robe, she crossed the room and curled up in the corner, tucking her legs beneath her. Adam picked up his shirt from a chair and shrugged into it before joining her. Sitting down at the opposite end of the sofa, he turned sideways and draped his left arm across the back. Picking up a towel-wrapped bundle from the floor, he placed it on his knee and shot her an apologetic look.

"I hope you don't mind. I filched some ice cubes and a plastic bag to make a cold pack for my knee."

"Of course not. I'm sorry, I forgot about your knee. I should have offered you an ice pack earlier."

"Don't worry about it. So how's your head? Does it still hurt?"

"Not much. I took some aspirin."

"Mmm." He leaned forward and grasped her chin between his thumb and forefinger and turned her head to examine her cheek. "Looks like you could use an ice pack, too. Your cheek is beginning to swell. By morning it'll be rather colorful, I'm afraid. How does it feel?"

"It throbs a little, but it's stopped stinging. I put antibiotic cream on it," she said, gingerly touching her face just below the abrasion.

"Mmm. So if you're not in pain, it must be nerves keeping you awake. Right?" God, she was lovely, he thought. Even with that angry scrape on her cheek and the bruise blossoming around it. She had scrubbed her face clean of every vestige of makeup and her hair was mussed from tossing and turning in bed, but she was still incredible to look at.

"I guess." She plucked at a nub on the upholstery and looked out the window at the waves crashing against the shore. The moon had risen, and its reflection spilled across the water like liquid gold. The scene had always had a lulling effect on her, soothing her nerves and calming her fears to a manageable level. Now her haven had been breached, and she found herself searching the beach for a predator.

She jerked her gaze away and encountered Adam's steady hazel eyes.

"Do you want to talk about it?" he asked gently.

"No. No, I just want to forget it ever happened."

"I'm not talking about the attack."

She tensed. "You're not?"

"No. And I think you know that. C'mon, Lauren, we've been dancing around the subject all night with small talk about everything under the sun. Don't you think it's time we discussed what's on both our minds."

"I . . . I don't know what you mean."

"Sure you do. You have to know that I saw the nursery."

She bit her bottom lip and looked out the window again, her expression stricken. Of course she had known. She had also known that sooner or later he would bring it up. She just didn't know if she could discuss it.

"I assume that you and your husband had a child?" he probed gently. "Is that right?"

Her head moved in the barest of nods, but her gaze remained fixed on the ocean.

"Is he visiting your ex now?"

"No."

Several seconds ticked by. The silence was taut and expectant. She could feel his gaze on her face. He was waiting for her to explain, but she couldn't seem to make the words come out.

Finally, he tired of waiting. "If he's not with your ex, and he's not with you, then you must have lost him." He reached out and placed his hand over hers, where it lay on the back of the sofa. "Am I right?"

"Yes."

"I'm so sorry, Lauren. I know the death of a child must be unspeakably painful."

She looked at him then. She felt icy cold on the outside, but the pain she struggled so hard to keep at bay was rising inside her, burning its way to the surface. Her chin wobbled, but she fought to control it. "My son isn't dead."

Surprise chased across Adam's face, leaving it blank. "He isn't? I don't understand. You just said that you'd lost him. If he isn't dead, then where is he?"

"I have no idea," she said in a lifeless voice. "Three years ago, when he was ten months old, my baby was kidnapped."

Nine

"Kidnapped!" Adam gaped at her.

"You mean snatched? How? Where?"

"He was taken from his crib one afternoon while his nanny was watching television. I was at work."

"Good God."

Lauren's eyes grew moist, and she turned her head to stare out at the moonlit ocean again. In profile, he could see her throat working and the quiver in her chin.

"Do the police have any idea who took him? Were there any clues?"

She pressed her lips together and shook her head. "At . . . at first we thought it was a ransom attempt by someone who knew of my connection to Walter." Her lips wavered again in a weak attempt at a smile. "Bless him. He was willing to pay any amount of money to get David back. Walter was— is—crazy about my son. But no ransom demand was ever made."

"Did the police offer any theories as to who could have taken him?"

"They said there were any number of possibilities. Some nut case who wanted a baby and couldn't have one. A black-market baby ring that provides infants for adoption to people with money. Maybe even a ransom attempt that . . . that went . . . sour."

Translation: her son could be dead. Adam watched her

press her fist against her mouth and fight for control, and his gut twisted with pity.

"What about your ex-husband? Do you suspect him?"

"Yes. No. I . . . I don't know." She sniffed and blinked rapidly. She turned her head and looked at Adam with such torment in her eyes it was all he could do not to reach across the sofa cushions and haul her into his arms. He'd never seen anyone in so much pain.

"At times I'm positive that it was Gavin who took my son. And at other times . . ." She waved her hand in a futile little gesture. ". . . I simply can't imagine him doing it. He never wanted the baby. He was furious when I refused to have an abortion."

"Sounds like a real charmer." Adam made no attempt to hide the disgust in his voice.

"Believe me, I would be the last one to defend Gavin, but well . . . to be fair, you have to understand that when I found out that I was pregnant we were already separated.

"At first Gavin accused me of getting pregnant on purpose to hold on to him. It wasn't true. By the time he walked out he had already hurt me too much. I didn't want him back."

Lauren stared at her fingers, which were plucking at a nub in the sofa upholstery. "But I did want my baby. Just because Gavin and I couldn't make our marriage work, I saw no reason to end the life of an innocent child. Financially, I could afford to raise a child alone. Actually, I made a lot more money than Gavin did." Her mouth twisted. "That was one of our problems.

"I filed for divorce when I was barely two months along. I just wanted it to be over so that I could get on with my life, but the judge refused to grant the decree until after the baby was born.

"Gavin was livid. It turned out, he had met someone else before he left me. He had planned to remarry as soon as he was free. The way he saw it, I was keeping the baby just to be vindictive and obstructive. So, to get even, he sought joint custody."

"Did the judge grant his petition?"

"In a way. He was granted partial custody. Summers mostly. But he never even came to see David. The divorce was granted three days after he was born. I haven't seen Gavin since."

"You went through pregnancy and childbirth alone?"

"I didn't have much choice. Besides, I wasn't totally alone. I had my mother and Walter, and of course Nan and Mary Alice. They were all wonderfully supportive throughout the whole thing."

Adam couldn't imagine it. With both Molly and Paulo, Tony had been right there for Kate every step of the way, as he was now with the new baby. Tony took childbirth classes, gave back rubs, tied Kate's shoelaces, hauled her up out of chairs and out of bed at all hours when her advancing pregnancy forced her to the bathroom several times a night. Many times Adam's friend drove around in the middle of the night in search of weird foods to satisfy his wife's cravings.

What kind of man would walk out on his pregnant wife and leave her to cope on her own?

For that matter, what kind of idiot would leave a woman like Lauren at all?

She was breathtakingly lovely, she was smart, she was talented and capable. Adam knew from experience that she was cooperative and easy to get along with, and he had not heard one word of complaint or criticism about her from her fellow workers, not even those on her staff.

"Anyway, my point is, Gavin didn't want our baby four years ago. He never even came to see David after he was born. Why would he kidnap him ten months later? It doesn't make sense."

"Maybe. But in most cases of child kidnapping it is the ex-spouse who is responsible. I assume the police questioned him."

"They tried, but he had moved out of his apartment about

a month before the kidnapping. He left no forwarding address, and they weren't able to locate him through other sources."

"I assume they're still looking for him?"

She slanted Adam a droll look. "Officially, yes, but as far as I can tell there hasn't been any work done on this case in years. Whenever I badger the police about it they say they would like to question Gavin, but since there's no evidence to indicate that he took David, they can't justify an intensive manhunt. So, I hired my own investigator."

"A private detective?"

"Yes. A retired police officer by the name of Sam Ewing. He came highly recommended. So far, though, he hasn't had any luck finding Gavin either."

She looked out the window again, and Adam's gaze narrowed on her profile. "That man you chased down the street. You thought he was your ex-husband, didn't you?"

Her chin came up, and the glance she sent him offered no apology. "Yes. He was the same height and build. He had the same sandy hair as Gavin. He even walked like him. It was a natural mistake."

"Hey, I'm not criticizing. I was just curious."

"Sorry. I guess I'm touchy. A lot of people think that I've held on to hope for too long. They believe that I should accept my loss and move on. But I can't do that."

"I wouldn't think so. How can anyone expect a parent to stop searching for a missing child?"

"You'd be surprised. But it doesn't matter. No matter what anyone says, I won't stop searching until I find my baby."

"Except he's not exactly a baby anymore, is he?" Adam pointed out gently. He was immediately sorry when she turned those pain-filled eyes on him again.

"No. He's not a baby anymore. He's almost four. Oh, God." She looked up at the night sky and widened her eyes in a vain effort to keep tears at bay. One rolled over her lower eyelid, hung from her lashes, then plopped onto her cheek and streamed downward. It was quickly followed by another. And another.

Wordlessly, Adam withdrew a clean handkerchief from his hip pocket and handed it to her.

She murmured a choked, "Thank you," and dabbed her eyes. "I've missed so much. His first steps. His first words. His first haircut. So many firsts. And no matter what happens, even if I found him tomorrow, I'll never get them back."

Adam ached for her. The weight of her grief was staggering. He didn't know how she had borne it all this time. Especially alone.

And she was definitely alone. In the time that he'd lived there she had not had a single visitor. Nor had he seen her leave her house other than to walk on the beach. Why that was, puzzled him. He couldn't resist probing for an answer.

"You know . . . what amazes me is that I've been working at Ingram and Bates for almost a month now, and no one has said a word to me about this."

She gave a sharp little laugh. "I'm not surprised. I've discovered that over the long haul, most people don't cope well when tragedy strikes someone they know. Maybe because it's too sharp a reminder that bad things can happen to good people, therefore they can happen to them, too.

"At first everyone rallied around—my friends and family, the neighbors where I used to live, all my co-workers. They were all sympathetic and supportive. After a while, though, when the days turned into weeks, then the weeks turned into months, they became increasingly uncomfortable with the whole thing. Evidently, being around me was awkward and depressing.

"By the time the first year passed most of my friends had drifted away. Even my mother retired to Palm Springs. At work people began to avoid the subject. Now everyone acts as though the whole thing never happened. I suppose it's easier for them to be around me if they just pretend that my son never existed."

And you became more and more isolated, Adam thought sadly. "Is that why you keep to yourself? Why you moved here? Why you reject any overture of friendship? Because it's less painful that way?"

She gave him a long look. He expected her to deny the suggestion, but after a moment she shrugged. "That's right. Besides, I don't have the time or energy to waste developing relationships that I know won't last."

He reached out and took her hand again. At his touch she jerked. Knowing her instinct was to pull away, he tightened his grip and held on. Smiling gently, he kept his voice low and persuasive. "Some relationships—the ones worth keeping—survive anything. Walter didn't desert you, did he?"

"Well . . . no."

"Has Nan? Or Mary Alice?"

"No."

"And I'll bet your mother's move to Palm Springs had little to do with your situation. Am I right?"

"Maybe not," she conceded grudgingly. "Mom has respiratory problems. Her doctor recommended a drier climate." She shot him a resentful look out of the corner of her eye. "But it still felt as though she was deserting me."

"Yeah. I can imagine. But, Lauren, not everyone will pull away from you just because you've had a tragedy."

"Oh, please. That's only four people out of dozens. They're the exceptions."

"So? Those exceptions are your real friends—the only ones worth having. There could be others like them that you don't know about because you pushed aside their offers of friendship." He gave her hand a little shake. "It's not healthy for someone to be alone all the time, Lauren. We all need friends."

"Are you saying you want to be my friend?"

"Yeah. I do."

"Why?"

"Why not?"

"Well . . . for one thing, I don't think you like me very much. I have to admit, I haven't given you much reason to."

"That's true." He smiled and rubbed his thumb back and forth over her knuckles. "But I like you anyway."

"It didn't seem like it when you called me on the carpet about that mix-up on the Cordex building."

"That was business. That had nothing to do with how I feel about you on a personal level." He waited a beat while her gaze probed his, then he gave her hand a tug. "So, how about it? Friends?"

"I don't know. Shouldn't friendship be based on mutual respect and knowledge? We really don't know each other all that well."

Adam rolled his eyes. "Man, you are a hard sell, aren't you? What's it going to take to crack through that wall you've built around yourself?"

"You know I'm right. I mean, I've just told you a big chunk of my history, but all I really know about you is you went to Princeton with Ed, you played professional football, and you have a lifelong friend named Tony who is married to a charming woman named Kate. I know almost nothing about you as a person."

"Well, let's see. I'm thirty-six. Never been married. I love children and dogs. My favorite color is blue. I enjoy tennis and handball, and I play golf occasionally, but I'm not very good at it. I like all kinds of music except rap and opera. I love steak and hate liver and brussels sprouts. Anything else you want to know?"

A self-conscious little laugh escaped her. "I can't just grill you like a police sergeant."

"Why not?" Adam spread his hands wide. "What would you like to know? My life's an open book. I'm serious," he urged when she still looked reluctant. "Go ahead, fire away."

"Well . . . okay. Umm . . . where are you from, originally."

"Texas. I grew up in Houston."

"Any brothers or sisters?"

"No. Not that I know of, anyway. I was adopted at birth."

Surprise flashed across her face. "Oh, I see. Did it ever bother you?"

"What? Being an only child? Or being adopted?"

"I don't know. Both I guess."

"No, on both counts. My parents are great, and I had a terrific childhood. Anyway, I never missed not having siblings because I had Tony. The Diamattos were our next-door neighbors the whole time I was growing up. There were four girls in that family, and Tony. He and I sort of gravitated to each other naturally. We've always been like brothers. Even closer, in some ways, because there was never that rivalry thing that occurs between siblings."

"Mmm. I know what you mean. That's how my father and Walter were. When Dad passed away a few years back, Walter took it hard."

"Yeah, that would be tough."

"So. You and Tony grew up together. And, according to his wife, you went to college together, played football together, then you both turned pro at the same time and went to separate teams. What happened then?"

Adam raised his eyebrows. "Kate told you all that in the short time you were together?"

A smile fluttered around Lauren's mouth. "Your friend is a very open person."

"I'll say. Well, let's see . . . I played pro ball for twelve years. Then a couple of seasons back I got my knee busted up pretty bad and had to have surgery. It had happened before, but this time I couldn't come back all the way afterwards. In fact, as you can see, it still gives me trouble if I put too much stress on it." He grimaced and shifted the ice pack on his knee.

"Like you did tonight. I'm sorry about th—"

"Hey, don't worry about it. A few ice packs and it'll be right as rain." He hoped. "Anyway, as I was saying, after this happened, I had no choice but to retire."

"Did you mind?"

"Not really. I was thinking about it anyway. The older you get the harder it is to take that kind of a beating week after week. It seemed like every year the other players got younger, bigger and a whole helluva lot tougher. It was time to hang it up. I can't complain. I had twelve good years."

"What have you been doing since you left football?"

"Not much. Just sort of lying back, waiting for the right business opportunity to present itself."

"And you think working for Ingram and Bates is right for you."

"Yeah. I do." He debated a moment, then decided to take a chance and reveal the whole truth. "Actually, I'm not working *for* Ingram and Bates. I'm investing in the company. Walter has agreed to sell me forty-four percent of the stock."

He braced for anger or resentment, but all he saw in her expression was surprise.

"You're kidding! Walter is actually going to turn loose part of the company? That's amazing."

"He said he was thinking about semi-retirement. Keeping his hand in, but maybe cutting back on his hours and taking more time to play golf, maybe travel a bit while he still can."

"Walter said *that?* Good heavens." Lauren looked stunned. "Well, I'll believe that when I see it. For the last thirty-five years he's lived and breathed the company. I can't imagine him retiring. Not even semi-retiring."

"You could be right. I think what he really wants is to make sure that when he's gone the business will be in good hands."

"That's possible. Actually . . . the more I think of it, you're probably right. Since Walter has no children to take over for him, I'm sure that's a matter of concern."

She nibbled at her bottom lip for a moment. "Does Ed know that you're buying into the company?"

"Not yet. Actually, outside of myself and Walter and his personal attorney, who drew up the agreement, no one else in the company knows but you."

"Umm. I'd be willing to bet there is one other person."

Adam frowned. "Who's that? Neither Walter nor I have told anyone until now."

"You're forgetting Mary Alice. Nothing goes on in that company that she doesn't know about."

"That's true." Adam chuckled. "Sometimes I wonder if Walter realizes what a jewel he's got there."

"I doubt it. Some people can't see what's right beneath their nose."

The asperity in Lauren's voice surprised Adam. "Now why do I get the feeling that we're talking about different things? You want to tell me about it?"

"Not really. Just forget it. Okay?"

"Sure."

She plucked at the upholstery again. "So . . . when are you going to tell Ed?"

"Soon. When I think the time is right."

"You do realize that he's not going to be happy, don't you? Ed thought he was going to inherit his uncle's share of the company. It was a real blow to him when he didn't."

"I know."

"Did you also know that ever since his uncle died he's been trying to persuade Walter to let him gradually buy up his uncle's shares. Walter has always refused him."

"I didn't until after we had already struck a deal. I don't know what Walter's reasons are for refusing him. I tried to get him to reconsider, but he won't budge. Since that's the case, I'm just hoping that I can make Ed see that he'll be better off with me buying out Walter, rather than some stranger."

"Hmm. Good luck."

"Thanks," he drawled.

Neither spoke for several minutes. Then Adam broke the silence. "So . . . are there any other questions you want to ask me?"

"You said you've never been married. Is there anyone special in your life?"

"Not at the moment. I just broke off a six-month relationship. The lady in question had a problem. I tried to help her, but when a person refuses to even admit that they have a problem that's pretty much a futile effort. I finally couldn't take it anymore and left."

"Did you love her?"

"No. But I cared for her."

"I see. I—" Lauren opened her mouth to say something more, but instead a yawn caught her unawares.

"Oh, my. Excuse me." Yawning again, she stretched her arms over her head. Adam's gaze homed in irresistibly on the rounded swell of flesh and the triangle of ecru lace exposed between the gaping lapels of her robe. "Oh, my, look at the time." Lauren's glance went from his wristwatch to the window. "It will be dawn in a few hours. No wonder I'm exhausted. I think I might actually be able to sleep now."

"Yeah, me, too."

She unfolded her legs and stood in one graceful movement, arching her back and stretching again. Watching her, Adam's blood pressure shot skyward. God, did she have any idea of how sexy that was?

She tightened the belt on her robe and smiled at him. "Thank you, Adam."

"For what?"

"For this evening. For taking my mind off what happened earlier. That was the real reason for all this conversation, wasn't it?"

"Maybe partly."

"Well, it worked. And it was sweet of you."

"Hey. What are friends for?"

She held his gaze for several seconds, then she nodded. "Good night, Adam."

"Good night, Lauren. And remember—I'll be right here if you need me."

Lauren fell asleep almost as soon as her head touched the pillow.

Not Adam.

With his hands stacked beneath his head, he lay on the sofa, staring at the ceiling long after the sky outside turned from ebony to pearly gray, to a soft buttery dawn.

He hadn't been altogether truthful with Lauren when he'd told her he liked her. What he felt was a helluva lot more than that. What, exactly, he didn't know, but *like* was too tepid a word to describe the feelings she aroused in him.

He had never been as attracted to a woman as he was to Lauren. From the moment he had first seen her she had fascinated him. It wasn't just that she was beautiful—he had met many beautiful women. A few, like Delia, he'd been involved with for a time. There was something about Lauren, though—something intangible that drew him to her as strongly, and inexorably as the moon drew the tides.

That worried him.

Dammit, he knew that he was one of life's lucky ones. He'd been adopted by wonderful people who had showered him with love and attention and nurtured his talents. He'd been blessed, not only with a natural grace and phenomenal athletic abilities, but brains as well. All of his life everything had come easy to him—grades, girls, friendships, athletics. He'd graduated from college with honors and double degrees and had immediately been drafted into the pros and given a lucrative contract.

Oh, sure, he'd suffered a knee injury that had perhaps prematurely ended his career, but he'd had twelve good years. He sure as hell couldn't complain. He'd achieved fame and fortune playing a game that he loved. That was more than most men could say.

The only thing that he'd ever wanted that had eluded him— that continued to elude him—was what Tony had: a solid marriage.

Hell, he was thirty-six. He'd always expected that by now he would have a wife and two or three kids. But it hadn't happened.

The problem was, for all his success with women, he'd never truly been in love.

Oh, yeah, he'd come close a few times. In the beginning he'd even thought that Delia might be the one, but it hadn't taken long to realize how wrong he was about that.

Over the years he'd been fond of several women, but that just wasn't good enough. He wanted the head-over-heels, bells ringing, heart-thumping, forever kind of love that his parents had. That Tony and Kate had.

With his track record, it was beginning to look hopeless.

He always found himself empathizing with people less fortunate than he was. Maybe it was guilt because things had always come so easy to him. Or maybe it was merely what Tony called it—a wounded-dove complex.

Whatever the reason, he'd always been a sucker for a hard-luck story. Over the years he'd spent a good chunk of his money helping out friends and relatives, and more than one stranger, for that matter, who had contacted him with a tale of woe.

Hell, even in his love life he seemed to be drawn to women who needed his help. Delia was the perfect example.

After months of enduring her boozing and erratic behavior he had finally realized that from the start his involvement with her had been based more on pity than affection. Even then, it had taken another few months before he'd accepted that he could not help her, that only Delia could do that.

He intended for this move to the West Coast to be a fresh start—not a repeat of the same destructive pattern. The last thing he needed was to fall for a wounded soul like Lauren McKenna. He'd had enough of needy women.

If he had an ounce of sense he'd stay as far away from her as he could.

But, hell, he couldn't do that. Not after that big pep talk about real friends sticking by her when she needed them.

He snorted. Smart move, Rafferty. You boxed yourself in good with that one.

Ten

The aroma of fresh-brewed coffee pulled Lauren from sleep. With a lazy moan, she rolled over, stretched, and lifted her heavy eyelids. She aimed a bleary look at the bedside clock. When the hands came into focus she yelped and sat straight up in the bed.

She was late!

Immediately her gaze swung to the door. Adam! Ohmygod! Had he left?

Heart pounding, she leaped out of bed and raced for the living room, dragging on her robe as she ran. She burst through the door at the end of the hall and was halfway across the living room when she spotted him in the kitchen.

At her explosive entrance he looked up and raised one dark eyebrow. "Hi. Is there a fire that I didn't know about?"

"You're still here."

The surprise in her voice brought a slight frown to his brow. "That's right. I told you I would be."

"I . . . I thought you might have gone to work. We both should already be there. Oh, God, look at the time. It's almost ten! Why didn't you wake me?"

"You needed the rest. Besides, you were sleeping so soundly I didn't have the heart."

"Oh, dear. Walter's probably having a fit."

"Relax. I've taken care of it. I called and left word with

both my secretary and yours that we were inspecting sites and wouldn't be in until this afternoon."

"You did?" Lauren's shoulders sagged. "Thank you."

She closed her eyes and ran both hands through her hair, pushing it away from her face. When she opened her eyes again Adam's gaze was fixed on her body.

Lauren glanced down and blushed as she realized that in her haste she had neglected to tie her robe. The lapels of the garment hung open all the way to her ankles. The coffee-colored satin nightgown she wore beneath the robe was opaque, but the material clung to her body, outlining every dip and curve—breasts, waist, hips, the nubs in the center of her nipples, even the shadowy indentation that marked her navel.

Adam's eyes seemed to darken from hazel to almost black as he took it all in, starting at her bare toes and skimming all the way up to her crimson face. When his gaze met hers, he smiled.

Lauren snatched the robe lapels together. "I, uh . . . I'd better go get dressed."

"There's no hurry." Gesturing with the knife he was using to butter toast, he pointed toward the barstools on the opposite side of the counter. "Sit down and have some breakfast."

Only as she slid onto a barstool did she notice that Adam was barefoot and the shirt he'd had on the evening before was unbuttoned and untucked. The wrinkled tails hung loose around his hips. Beard stubble shadowed his jaw and upper lip. Sleep marks still creased one cheek and his hair was rumpled and bore the marks of finger combing. He looked unkempt and rough around the edges . . . and, incredible as it seemed, impossibly sexy.

He poured a mug of coffee and slid it across the counter to her.

"Mmm, thanks." Cradling the steaming mug in both hands, Lauren raised it to her lips and tried to concentrate on keeping her gaze away from the strip of bare flesh between the gaping edges of the shirt. Good Lord. What was wrong with her? She was ogling the man like a hormone-crazed adolescent.

"I've already cooked sausage. What would you like to go with it?"

"Oh, uh . . . just toast for me, thanks."

He slid the plate stacked high with buttered toast across the counter. After retrieving the sausage from the oven he sat down beside her on the other barstool.

"Dig in," he said, spearing a patty.

Lauren picked up a triangle of toast and nibbled at it without tasting a bite. Her nerves skittered. The previous night she had been grateful for Adam's company. She still was. She didn't know how she would have gotten through the night without him.

However, in the clear light of day, the memory of how easy it had been to confide in him and lean on his strength, unsettled her.

She prided herself on being independent and strong and capable, able to handle anything on her own. Especially so since Gavin had walked out on her. She didn't want to lose that strength. What she ought to do was thank him politely for his help, then pull back and reestablish the distance between them.

That was what she *should* do. She knew that. Yet . . . when she allowed herself to think about the attack and that horrible man, terror overrode logical thought and turned her into a quivering lump.

Intellectually, Lauren knew that she was being irrational. This fear was just the normal, perhaps even slightly hysterical, reaction to an act of violence. But knowing didn't help. At the moment, only with Adam close by did she feel even a degree of safety.

Even more disturbing to her than this desperate reliance on his protection, was the undeniable fact that the previous night, once she had calmed a bit, she had actually enjoyed his company. She couldn't say she had actually enjoyed any-one's company in years.

"You do know, don't you, that we have to tell Walter about last night."

"What? I don't see why? There's nothing he can do to change what happened. Anyway, it's over now. Telling Walter would merely upset him."

"That may be, but how are you going to explain that doozy of a bruise on your cheek? Makeup won't cover it completely. Even if you did manage to hide your injuries, wouldn't you rather Walter learned about the incident from you instead of reading about it in the papers?"

"Why would it be in the newspapers? Attempted rape isn't that big a news story, especially in a metropolitan area. I'm sure every night there are many more sensational crimes committed in San Francisco."

"Lauren, you're forgetting that I was involved. I guarantee there will be some eager young reporter working the police beat who'll spot my name on the report. I'll be very surprised if we make just the local newspapers. I expect the wire serv-ices will pick up the story as well. Maybe even the six o'clock news."

She was so appalled all she could do was stare at him.

"I'm sorry, Lauren. But there's nothing I can do about it. Believe me, I would if I could."

"I know. I . . . Does this sort of thing happen to you often?"

He shrugged. "Now and then."

"How do you stand it? It's such an invasion of your pri-vacy. And it's so unfair."

"True, but it's part of the price of fame. Anyway, it doesn't happen as much as it did a few years back, and I'm sure interest in me will wane as time passes."

"And in the meantime you have to put up with reporters poking and prying into your life?"

"That's about it. I'm sorry to drag you into it."

"It's not your fault. You merely helped me. In fact if you hadn't—Never mind."

Lauren put down her half-eaten toast and blotted her mouth with a napkin. "If I'm going to tell Walter about all this I'd better get dressed. I prefer to confront the lion in his den rather than tell him over the phone. But first I have to call Sam. Would you hand me the telephone?"

"Sam? Who the hell is Sam?"

"Sam Ewing. I told you about him last night. He's the private investigator that I hired."

"Oh yeah. Right. I forgot about him."

"I always check in with his office on Monday morning."

"Just once a week? I'm surprised you don't call him every day."

Lauren shot Adam a rueful look. "I used to, but Sam said I was driving him crazy and threatened to quit if I didn't stop. Now we have an agreement. I call on Monday morning for a routine report, and if any sort of major breakthrough occurs he'll call me at once."

"I see." Suppressing a smile, Adam leaned over and plucked the cordless telephone from its wall mount and handed it to her.

As usual, Sam had no news on David or any solid leads. Lauren had expected as much, but that did not prevent her from experiencing crushing disappointment or stave off the ache that swelled in her chest.

"No news?" Adam asked as she switched off the cordless telephone.

"No. None." She swallowed hard around the knot in her throat and fought to control her wobbly chin. "I'm sorry. I know it's silly to let that bother me," she said in an unsteady voice, dabbing at her eyes with her napkin. "I should be used to it by now."

"Hey, it's not silly at all. You have every right to feel let down." Adam's voice was a husky caress. So was the touch of his fingers on her cheek as he turned her face toward his.

Compassion darkened his hazel eyes. "I'm sorry, Lauren," he whispered. "So sorry."

Still cupping her face, he leaned forward and placed his lips against the outside corner of her eye in the gentlest of kisses, then he repeated the same butterfly caress against the corner of her lips.

His mouth was warm against her skin, his breath moist. There was nothing threatening nor sexual about the tiny kisses, but she had never experienced anything so passionate in her life. The utter tenderness behind the act shook Lauren to the core of her being and sent a flood of hot emotions gushing through her. His warmth, his heat, his scent, the exquisite lightness of his touch, all combined to make her head swim. Lauren closed her eyes and shuddered.

When at last he drew back, her heart was galloping and she could barely breathe. Striving to appear unaffected, she smiled, but her face felt wooden. "Thank you. I appreciate that. Now I'd better go get dressed."

She was not at all confident that her legs would hold her, but she slid off the stool and started for the hall. After only a few steps, however, she stopped and looked back.

"Uh . . . will you still . . . That is . . ."

"I'll be here," he assured her. "Go on and get dressed. When you're ready we'll swing by my place so I can clean up before we head for the office. And Lauren. Just so it's clear—we'll be driving in together."

She gave him an uncertain look and nodded. "All right."

Three quarters of an hour later, with the sound of the shower running in the background, Lauren roamed Adam's living room like a caged cat.

The way people decorated their homes told a great deal about them, especially to someone like Lauren. If she hadn't been so edgy she would have enjoyed the opportunity to study the decor and personal items more thoroughly. As it was, she merely gave the room a cursory examination, and that only because it was automatic for her to do so, a reflex action of which she was barely aware.

Of course, she mused, for all she knew, Adam could have bought the place fully furnished from the Graysons and merely moved in his personal belongings. Until the night before, she had never been inside the house.

She wandered around the room, glancing idly at the books lining the shelves on either side of the fireplace, running her hand along the back of the overstuffed sofa and chairs. Every time she passed by the windows or the French doors she peered out, but all she saw was empty beach, endless sky and restless breakers pounding the shore.

The shower shut off. Lauren glanced toward the hall, glanced at her wristwatch, and resumed pacing.

In less than twenty minutes, Adam walked into the living room.

Lauren stopped short, and for an instant she forgot why she was so nervous. All her thoughts were focused on Adam.

The smells of soap, shaving cream and starched linen drifted to her, along with that heady smell of clean male flesh. Her nostrils quivered as the combination of scents made her head spin.

Ed was right, she realized. Adam wasn't a handsome man, not in the conventional sense, but Lauren had no difficulty at all understanding why women found him so attractive. His features were blunt and rough-hewn, almost craggy, but they held a strength that was powerfully expressed. So did that big, well-toned body. In the expertly tailored suit and crisp shirt he looked professional and businesslike, but the civilized veneer in no way lessened the impact of his maleness. It hit her like a shock wave from a bomb blast. Everything about him was so completely and uncompromisingly masculine it took her breath away.

Lauren couldn't remember any man having that kind of effect on her. It didn't make sense that the mere sight of

Adam would make her weak in the knees. The athletic type had never appealed to her before.

"Ready?"

"What?" Lauren jumped, and she realized that she had been staring. "Oh, yes. Of course."

She snatched up her purse and briefcase from the sofa and headed for the door, but she stopped after taking only a few steps and pointed to the telephone on the kitchen counter. "I almost forgot. There's a call on your answering machine."

"It's probably not important." Adam turned to leave but almost at once he turned back, frowning. "But then again, I'd better check, just in case it's my parents." He strode to the counter and pushed the play button on the machine.

Lauren's eyes widened when the husky female voice began to pour from the speaker. By the time the caller had completed the first sentence her jaw had dropped almost to her chest.

"Darling, you didn't return my call," the woman purred. "Come on, love, don't be tiresome. Pick up the phone and talk to me. I know you're there. It's three in the morning, your time. Darling, we have to ta—"

Adam punched the stop button and the voice cut off in midword.

Still slack-jawed, Lauren looked from the machine to Adam. "That . . . that was Delia Waters!"

"Uh-huh." He fast-forwarded the tape past the message and punched the erase button.

"The network anchor woman," Lauren continued in the same amazed voice. "That voice is unmistakable."

"That's right. C'mon, let's go."

"You actually *know* Delia Waters? Oh God, she's not calling you about what happened last night, is she?"

"No. She's not." He took her elbow and tried to steer her toward the basement stairs, but Lauren hung back.

"Then what does she wa—" She jerked to a halt and stared at him, her jaw sagging again. "Oh, my Lord! Don't tell me she's the woman you just broke up with?" His expression made her eyes widen even more and she sucked in an audible breath. "She *is!*"

"That's right. Now can we go?"

"But . . . but," she sputtered as he hustled her along with him down the stairs. "She's gorgeous!"

"Uh-hmm," he agreed as he stuffed her into the passenger seat of the BMW. He paused, bent over, and looked her right in the eyes. "So are you. What's your point?"

The compliment caught her off guard and left her speechless for an instant, long enough for him to straighten and close the door. Adam thought she was gorgeous? It was the first time he had in any way indicated that he found her attractive.

Lauren watched him skirt around the hood to the other side of the car. The instant he slid in behind the steering wheel she started in again.

"Delia Waters is not merely beautiful. She's also rich and famous."

"So am I," Adam came back dryly. "Well . . . except for the beautiful part."

"Adam, be serious. She has everything. She's . . . she's . . . every man's fantasy woman. Why in heaven's name would you break up with someone like that?"

"Several reasons." He activated the electronic opener, and when the garage door slid open he started the car and backed out. "The main one being I wasn't in love with her. However, she also happens to have a serious problem. One that would poison any relationship. I couldn't deal with it any longer. Maybe if I had loved her, I could have coped, but I didn't love her."

Curiosity gnawed at Lauren. She wanted to ask what kind of problem could someone like Delia Waters possibly have, but since Adam didn't volunteer the information she assumed it was private.

"How long did you date her?"

"About eight months. We lived together for the last six of those."

"Oh. I see."

Adam slanted her a look. "Do I detect a note of disapproval in your voice, Ms. McKenna?"

"Of course not. How you choose to live is your business." Which was true. Lauren had never lived with any man other than her husband, and not with him prior to their marriage, but she had no deep moral convictions against the practice. Why, then, she wondered, did the thought of Adam living with a woman make her feel so . . . unsettled?

Out of the corner of her eye, Lauren saw Adam's glance flicker her way but she kept her eyes averted and pretended not to notice.

"Uh . . . not to change the subject," he drawled. "But if I were you, I think I'd duck down in the seat about now. It looks like we have a few reporters hanging around the gate."

"What!" Lauren's gaze whipped forward, and her eyes widened. Several cars and vans were parked along the highway and eight or ten people, some with cameras, milled around in the drive on the other side of the gate. A few had climbed up on the rocks to look for a way down to the beach. The fact that they were on private property with a clearly posted No Trespassing sign did not seem to matter to them at all.

The instant Adam hit the electronic control and the gates began to swing open the group in the driveway surged through the gap and the others scrambled from the rocks and came running.

Lauren made a distressed sound and flung herself face down on the seat and put her hands over the sides of her face.

"Good girl. Now, hang on. I'm going to have to pick our way through this rabble, so just stay as you are until I tell you we're clear."

His matter-of-fact tone amazed Lauren. How could he take

this outrageous treatment so calmly? The group crowded around the car, shouting questions and banging on the windows and doors. She jumped with every thump, and though she shielded her face with her hands, through her fingers she could see the constant flashes of light from the cameras.

The shouted questions were muffled by the closed windows but they were nevertheless audible.

"Hey, Adam! You wanna tell your fans what happened?"

"According to the police report, you're a hero?"

"Is this the woman?"

"Is it true you nearly beat the guy senseless?"

"C'mon, miss, give us a shot."

"How long have you and Ms. McKenna been together?"

Lauren gasped and nearly sat up at that one, but Adam put his hand on the back of her head and pushed her back down.

"Are you and Ms. McKenna living together?"

"What happened to Delia?"

Adam merely waved and smiled pleasantly and continued to edge the car through the crowd at a snail's pace. When he finally reached the highway he waved to the reporters and turned south, peeling out with a squeal of tires.

"You can sit up now," he said, checking the rear-view mirror. "You're safe for the moment, unless they manage to catch us."

Cautiously, Lauren levered herself up and peered over the back of the seat. Behind them, the reporters and photographers were scrambling for their vehicles. A few were already peeling out in hot pursuit.

"Do you think they will?"

"Nope. Relax. Unless those vans are souped up to hell and gone, they don't stand a chance against this baby. I had this car built to order," Adam drawled, giving the dash an affectionate pat. To prove his point he grinned and poured on the gas and left their pursuers in his dust.

Sighing, Lauren leaned back against the seat and rested

her head on the neck guard. "That was awful. I don't know how you tolerate all that frenetic intrusion and prying."

Adam shrugged. "You get used to it."

"No, thank you."

She chewed her bottom lip and slanted him a look. "Where do you suppose they got the idea that you and I were, uh . . . well . . ."

"Lovers?" he supplied helpfully. "Don't take it personally. Any woman who is seen with me is assumed to be my latest love interest. They were just fishing for information, but don't be surprised if it shows up in print. Probably couched something like 'Our sources say . . .' or 'Rumor has it . . .' Put that way, the press can speculate on just about anything with impunity. Whether it's true or not, the public will believe it. So brace yourself."

"Thanks," she grumbled. "There's one more thing I have to explain to Walter. Which reminds me. Just how are we going to squelch that rumor around the office?"

"Why bother? People are going to believe what they want to believe no matter what you say. It'll all blow over in a few weeks. Besides, you're under no obligation to explain your personal life to anyone."

"That's true," she murmured, frowning. But she still didn't like it. Over the past few years privacy had become a matter of extreme importance to her. Perhaps because that was one of the few areas of her life over which she had any control.

"Mind if I put on some music?"

Lauren shook her head, and he slipped a rhythm and blues CD into the player. Neither spoke again until Adam brought the car to a halt in the office garage.

"I'll tell Walter what happened. Why don't you go to your office. No one will think twice about you holing up in there."

"All right."

They had barely stepped from the car when Ed drove into the garage and parked in his space beside the Lincoln.

Grabbing his briefcase, he got out of his car and eyed

them coolly. "Well, well. Look who's finally here. It's about time you two showed up."

Adam gave him a steady look. "I called in and left word that Lauren and I would be inspecting sites this morning."

"Yeah, that's what I heard. The interesting thing is, Walter had Mary Alice calling around all morning trying to locate you, but no one at any of the sites had seen you this morning. Which makes me wonder just where you two were all this time." His tone held accusal. So did the look in his eyes as his gaze switched back and forth between them. He tried to catch Lauren's eye, but she kept her face averted so he would not see her injured cheek.

"Why was Walter looking for us?" Adam asked, pointedly ignoring the innuendo.

Ed shrugged. "I think there's another problem with one of Lauren's orders, but you'll have to ask him."

"What?" Lauren's head whipped around. "What order? On which project?"

"Look, I don't know that much about——" He stopped in midsentence and gaped. "What the hell happened to your face?"

"I . . ."

"She had an accident." Adam took Lauren's arm and urged her toward the elevator.

"Hey, wait a minute! What kind of accident? Dammit, Adam, will you hold on a second!" He sprinted up behind them, and grabbed Adam's arm. "I want to know what kind of accident? That wound looks as though she walked into a fist."

"Look——"

"It's nothing, Ed," Lauren said quickly. "I fell on the rocks at the point. That's all."

"That's *all!* Jesus, honey, you could have been seriously hurt. Maybe even killed."

"But I wasn't. It was just a silly accident. It looks much worse than it is, I promise. Adam was kind enough to take me to the hospital this morning to have some X-rays taken—just as a precaution. He called and said we were looking at sites because I was trying to keep Walter from finding out. You know how he gets."

Ed nodded, somewhat mollified. "Oh, yeah, I know. Where you're concerned he's worse than a mother hen."

"But now it appears I'll have to tell him. Given the way you reacted to my bruises, there's not much chance that he won't notice them."

"Not hardly." Ed chuckled. "You'll be lucky if he doesn't come unspooled."

"Now that you're satisfied, could we go?" Adam inquired in a dry voice. "I'd like to find out what Walter wanted with us before the day is over."

"Are you sure you're okay?" Inside the elevator, Ed stepped close to Lauren. He smoothed a tendril of hair away from her face and studied her tenderly. "You look a bit pale. Maybe you should take the rest of the day off and rest."

"I'm fine. Really." Both Ed's nearness and concern made her uncomfortable. Lauren shifted her feet and edged away, avoiding his gaze.

That didn't stop him from fussing over her throughout the elevator ride. When they reached the executive floor, and he finally said good-bye and disappeared into his office, Lauren sent up a silent thanks and turned toward her own. Before she could open the door Adam stopped her.

"Hold on a second," he said, putting a hand on her arm.

"Yes?" She looked up and was surprised by his intent expression.

"Tell me one thing. Is there something going on between you and Ed?"

"Going on? What do you mean?"

"Are you romantically involved?"

"No! Certainly not."

"Then what was all that about just now?"

"I don't know. That is . . . well . . . recently Ed did indicate he was interested, but I told him he was wasting his time. Apparently he's not convinced of that yet."

"I see. So there's nothing between you two?"

"No."

He searched her face for several seconds. Then he nodded. "I'll go talk to Walter."

What on earth was that all about? Lauren wondered. She watched him walk away, and when he disappeared through the mahogany doors at the end of the hall she shook her head and went into her office.

As usual when Lauren was out of the office, Nan was catching up on her filing. She glanced up with a smile, murmured a greeting, then did a double take.

"Oh my God! Your poor face! What happened?"

Lauren grimaced and gingerly touched her injured cheek with her fingertips. "Does it look that bad?"

Nan put down the stack of filing and hurried over to her. "Bad. Honey, that looks like you went ten rounds with a gorilla. What on earth happened?"

For an instant, to buy time, Lauren considered giving her the same story she'd given Ed, but she quickly discarded that idea. Nan was a true friend, one of the few who had stood by her and continued to support her even after all these years. She deserved to hear the truth from her. Besides, by the evening news everyone would know what had happened. It was better that people who mattered heard it from her.

Lauren drew a deep breath and steeled herself. "I . . . I was attacked last night on the beach."

"What! Oh, my God!" Nan surged forward and snatched Lauren into her arms. "Oh, you poor thing. Are you all right? Are you badly hurt?" Her arms tightened around Lauren. "Oh, dear. Did he . . . ?"

"No." Lauren shook her head against Nan's shoulder. "No, he didn't. Thanks to Adam."

Lauren pulled back and as succinctly as possible she explained what had happened and the aftermath. It was the first time since talking to the police that she had repeated the story, and she hadn't realized how difficult it would be. She tried to keep her voice steady and matter-of-fact, but describing the attack brought it all rushing back—all the horror and fear and pain. By the time she finished, her voice was wobbly and she was trembling and on the verge of tears.

As she stammered out the story, Nan's expression ran the gamut from shock to horror to outrage, and finally deep concern. "Thank God Mr. Rafferty was there," she declared. "Are you sure you're all right?"

Lauren opened her mouth, but before she could answer Walter burst through the door like a cyclone. Right on his heels came Adam and Mary Alice.

Walter looked like a wild man. His face was a rigid mask of fury and concern. Without slowing he crossed the room in two long strides and grasped Lauren's upper arms. "My God," he gasped. His face darkened as his eyes ran over her. "I'll kill the bastard!"

He snatched Lauren into his embrace and held her tight. "You should have called me. When I think of that scum touching you—"

"Ssh. I'm okay." Lauren wrapped her arms around his waist and pressed her uninjured cheek against his chest. She closed her eyes and breathed in the familiar, comforting scents of pipe tobacco and citrusy cologne that she had known from childhood. "Really. It looks much worse than it is."

Mary Alice stepped forward and joined in the hug. "Oh, Lauren, you poor dear. What an awful experience."

Looking over his shoulder at Adam, Walter snapped, "What's the name of the deputy in charge? I want to talk to him. Whatever it takes, I want the animal who did this to pay." He drew back and scowled down at Lauren. "And this settles it. You're not staying alone in that beach house anymore."

"You don't have to worry about that." The uncompromising statement drew every eye to Adam. He stood with his arms crossed over his chest, leaning casually back against the closed door, but there was nothing casual about the look in his eyes or his tone. "Until they catch that creep, I'm not leaving her alone. I can either stay at her place, or she can stay at mine. The choice is hers. But I'm not letting her out of my sight."

"Oh, Adam, no," Lauren protested. "Really. I couldn't possibly impose—"

"It's not an imposition. Anyway, I insist."

"But—"

"Forget it. It's settled. I'm not going to lie awake every night worrying about you."

Lauren opened her mouth, then closed it again. Put that way, how could she refuse? In any case, she wasn't at all certain she could have mustered the courage to do so and make it stick.

For several seconds Walter studied Adam through narrowed eyes. He returned the look evenly, without so much as blinking. The telephone rang, but neither man moved as Nan hurried to her desk.

Finally Walter nodded. "All right, then. That's acceptable. But I still want to talk to that deputy."

"Excuse me, Mr. Rafferty," Nan interrupted. "Line one is for you."

While Adam took the call, Walter and the two women fussed over Lauren. She was still trying to convince them that she didn't need to see a doctor when Adam hung up the receiver

"It looks like you're going to meet the officers sooner than you thought. That was Deputy Scott. They've picked up a suspect, and they want Lauren and me to come down to the jail and see if we can pick him out of a lineup."

Eleven

"That's him. Number four." Adam stared with eyes like cold steel at the suspect on the other side of the two-way mirror.

"You're certain?"

"Positive. That's the slimebag who attacked Lauren." Adam's gaze bore into the man. He felt a surge of satisfaction as he noted the swelling and bruises around the creep's nose and left eye.

"Okay. Just wanted to be sure. The guy's name is Victor Spalding. He's had two priors for sexual assault, but so far no convictions on that charge. He's been in the joint twice, once for armed robbery and another time for assault with a deadly weapon, plus he's been arrested for a string of other crimes—most of them violent. We'd like nothing better than to put the asshole away."

"That makes two of us."

Deputy Scott motioned toward the door. "If you'll step out now, Mr. Rafferty, I'll bring Ms. McKenna in to view the line up."

"I'm staying." Adam aimed a level look at the officer that said he wasn't budging. Lauren had put on a brave front, but the whole way on the drive to the jail she'd trembled as though she were immersed in ice water. He wasn't about to leave her alone to view that creep with only the two deputies for moral support.

The officers exchanged a look. Deputy Scott, the older of the two, studied Adam's set expression. Finally he grimaced and nodded. "All right. You can stay." His forefinger stabbed the air in Adam's direction and he growled, "If you influence her choice in any way the I.D. is worthless. Now, I like you, Rafferty, and I'm a big fan of yours, but I'm warning you, if that happens, I don't give a rat's ass who you are, you'll answer to me. We want this guy. We want him real bad.

"I don't want to hear one word outta you until she's picked the guy out of the lineup. Don't go giving her any high signs or looks, either. As a matter of fact, don't you so much as twitch. Got it?"

"I understand."

Deputy Scott studied him a moment longer then glanced at his partner and jerked his head toward the door. "Bring Ms. McKenna in, Norm."

A moment later the young officer escorted Lauren into the viewing room. Adam gritted his teeth. She looked pale and fragile as thistledown, as though the least puff of wind would blow her apart. But that delicate chin was up.

Her gaze darted around the dimly lit room. Abject relief flashed in her eyes when she spotted him. Adam's heart clenched, but his demeanor remained impassive. He doubted that Lauren was aware of how easy it was to read her expressive face, or that she would be pleased to know she had revealed so much.

He could not, however, prevent himself from stepping forward and taking her hand. Deputy Scott scowled, but the look on Adam's face kept him silent.

"All right, Ms. McKenna, don't be nervous. And don't worry. None of those men can see you. Just take your time and look closely at each one and tell me if you see your attacker."

Lauren nodded, and her grip on Adam's hand tightened. He returned the pressure with a reassuring squeeze. Her fingers were cold as ice and trembling.

He knew the instant she spotted the man. She went rigid and her fingernails dug into his hand. Concerned by her pallor, Adam watched her intently as revulsion and fear flickered over her face. She opened her mouth to speak but she had to clear her throat before a sound would come out.

"That's him," she finally managed. "The third man from the right. The . . . the one with the battered face."

She barely got the words out before a shudder overtook her. With a muffled cry she turned blindly into Adam's arms and burrowed against his chest.

He held her tight. Over the top of her head, his gaze speared Deputy Scott. "Is that all you need from us?"

"Yeah, that'll do it. We knew the guy was our perp. That scrap of material we found came from his jacket, and his fingerprints are all over the gate. That evidence, along with your testimony, should be plenty to nail him. Thank you both for coming down. We'll keep you posted."

Adam nodded and urged Lauren toward the door. "Come on. Let's get out of here."

Walter was pacing just outside the door. He took one look at Lauren's face and glared at Adam. "Well?"

"They got him."

Walter's eyes narrowed. "Good. I hope they hang the bastard."

Lauren still clung to Adam's side, her head turned into his chest. Walter glanced at her again, and his fierce expression dissolved. "Are you okay?"

She pressed her lips together and nodded.

Adam's arm tightened around her. "She's a little shaken but she'll be all right. She just needs to get out of here."

"Good idea."

"I have another one."

Walter had started down the hall, but he stopped and sent Adam a quizzical look. "Which is?"

"I think Lauren needs to take a break and get away for a while."

"What? Oh, no, really. That's not necessary," she protested, drawing out of Adam's embrace. "I'll be fine now that I know they have that monster in jail."

Both men ignored her.

"That's an excellent idea. What do you have in mind?"

"Actually, I was thinking along the lines of a Caribbean island. Plenty of sun and sand and relaxation." Adam glanced at Lauren and his mouth twisted. "But since I have a hunch that's out of the question, then I think this would be a good time for Lauren and me to check out that job in Cripple Creek."

"I still don't think this is necessary," Lauren grumbled an hour later as she added another item to her suitcase. "I'm perfectly fine. I just want to forget about the whole thing and get on with my life."

"This is your life. This trip is a necessary part of your job. We would have made it soon in any case."

He leaned against the doorjamb with his arms crossed over his chest, watching her storm around the room. She was not happy about the trip, but Walter had given her no choice.

No sooner had they returned to the office than he had put Mary Alice to work making arrangements for them to leave immediately. With her usual efficiency, Walter's secretary had booked them on a flight to Denver with a connection to Colorado Springs, that very evening.

Lauren had tried every argument she could think of to get out of going. She'd even brought up the problem that Ed had mentioned earlier in the garage, but Walter had dismissed her concern with a gruff, "Forget it. The marble for the Nob Hill job didn't show up. When the project man called the supplier to complain he was told that you had canceled the order."

"What? That's absurd! Why would I do that? Which supplier was it? I'll call them right away."

"Forget it. I'm sure it was just a misunderstanding. Your staff can handle it. You've got a plane to catch."

"But—"

"You're going, Lauren," Walter had barked. And that had been that.

She was still thoroughly put out, but at least temper had returned her color to normal.

"We wouldn't have gotten into the Cripple Creek job for another week or so. You and Walter are simply being overprotective."

"Why don't you just humor us? Okay?"

When she snapped both cases shut Adam crossed to the bed and hefted them. "Is this all?"

"Yes."

"Good. I'll toss them in the car and we'll swing by my place. It won't take me long to throw my things together. Twelve years of traveling from game to game taught me the art of quick packing."

"That's another thing," Lauren groused, following along at his heels. "You didn't have to hover over me while I packed. There's no longer any reason for you to play bodyguard."

"It was no trouble."

"That's not the point. You and Walter are being plain silly. Hustling me out of town now is like closing the barn door after the horse has already escaped. I don't need cheering up, I'm no longer frightened, and I'm not in any danger. So what's the point of this trip?"

Adam had listened to her complaints throughout the drive home and suddenly, unexpectedly, he was fresh out of patience. He tossed her cases into the trunk of his car and slammed the lid. "Jesus, woman, hasn't it occurred to you yet that Mr. Spalding isn't going to be in jail for long?"

That stopped her cold. "Wh-what do you mean?"

"Haven't you ever heard of bail? Spalding was probably out on the street before we got home."

She looked as though he'd slapped her. Her complexion whitened several shades. "I . . . I hadn't thought of that."

"Well, start. According to the deputies, this guy has committed a string of violent crimes. He's a dangerous character with a short fuse."

"You mean . . . you mean you think he'll come back here?"

Adam's mouth compressed as he watched what little color was left in her face drain away. Aw, hell. He should have kept his big mouth shut. He raked a hand through his hair and exhaled a long sigh, but his eyes did not quite meet hers. "Probably not. But why take chances?"

She thought that over. "Of course. You're right," she said in a meek voice and got into the car without another word.

Over the next half hour Adam mentally kicked himself a dozen times. Lauren did not give him another minute of static, but he preferred her grousing to the fear in her eyes.

She was a bundle of raw nerves, so on edge she would not remain in his living room alone. The excuse she gave for following him into his bedroom was that she wanted to discuss the Cripple Creek job, but while Adam packed he noticed that every few minutes she circled the room, glancing out of the windows.

When the intercom buzzed she jumped as though she'd been shot. He pretended not to notice and strode to the control panel.

"Yes?"

"Federal Express," a bored male voice crackled through the speaker. "I have a package for an A. Rafferty."

"From whom?"

"Uh, let's see . . . from Pete Friedman at Friedman and Braun."

"Okay, come on in. My house is the one on the southern end of the beach."

Adam pressed the button to unlock the gate and gave

Lauren a reassuring wink. "Pete's my stockbroker. He's probably sending me another prospectus to look over."

A few minutes later the doorbell rang and Adam excused himself and headed for the front door. When he opened it the casual greeting he was about to utter died on his tongue.

"Hello, darling," Delia purred. Without waiting for a reply, she brushed by him and sauntered into the living room. Still holding the door wide, Adam stood immobile and watched her. He stuck his head outside and glanced around the deck, but there was no one else in sight.

Feeling like an idiot, he shut the door and stomped after her. "What are you doing here, Delia? And where's the Fed Ex guy?"

"Don't be silly, darling, there is no Fed Ex guy."

"Then who was that on the intercom?"

"My limo driver. He's waiting for me down the road a ways. I paid him twenty bucks to say that. I was afraid you might not open the gate if you knew it was me."

"You were right. I wouldn't have." Clenching his jaws, Adam put his hands in his pockets and rocked back on his heels, carefully keeping his expression remote. "If you thought that, then why are you here?"

"Oh, darling, how can you be so mean?" she pouted. "Especially after I've come all this way to see you."

"How did you find me?" He'd known that she would eventually. It had been merely a matter of time, but he'd hoped he would have longer.

Delia stepped close to him, smiling coyly as one long crimson fingernail toyed with a button on his shirt. "Now, love, you know how resourceful I am. We had to talk, and since you wouldn't return my calls you left me little choice."

"You could have taken the hint and stayed away."

"Darling, you know you don't mean that. You and I belong together. I've given you plenty of time to get over that silly quarrel we had. Now it's time to forget this nonsense of a job and come back to New York where you belong."

"It wasn't just a silly quarrel, Delia. I told you we're through. It's over."

Her laugh was husky and seductive and full of confidence. "Don't be absurd, darling. That's just that stubborn pride of yours talking. I want you back. Since it's so important to you, I promise I'll cut down on my drinking. And this time I really mean it. I swear."

"For your sake, I hope you do, Delia, but it's too late for us. I've moved on with my life. I suggest that you do the same."

"What's that supposed to mean?" she demanded, but before he could reply she chuckled. "Oh, please. Surely you're not trying to tell me that there's someone else?"

That was not precisely what he had meant, but he was willing to swear to almost anything if it would get her out of his life for good. Besides, he realized that it was true. Like it or not, there was another woman in his life now. Where that relationship would lead—or if it would lead anywhere at all—he had no idea, but he intended to find out. "That's right. There is someone."

"I don't believe you. You're bluffing. We love each other."

"Delia, please. What we had was tumultuous, emotionally draining, painful and destructive. No one in their right mind would call that love."

Her chin came up at a haughty angle. "I don't care. You're mine and I'm not letting you walk out on me. No one does that to Delia Waters. Do you hear me? No one."

"Delia, don't do this. I'm telling y—"

"Adam? What's taking so long? Is everything all ri—" Lauren jerked to a stop in the doorway, her eyes going wide as she spotted Delia. "Oh! I'm so sorry. I didn't realize . . . that is . . ."

"Ah, here's my love, now."

Stepping quickly to Lauren, Adam put his arm around her shoulders and hugged her close against his side. She shot him a startled look, but before she could say a word Adam bent his head and kissed her full on the lips.

The kiss packed a punch that rocked Lauren all the way to the ground. This was no tender caress of compassion between two friends. This was a man staking his claim. His lips rocked over hers, hot and firm and possessive. His tongue stabbed into her mouth and swirled in a quick mating.

Then he raised his head and smiled down into her eyes. His expression was passionate. "Very nice," he murmured in a suggestive voice. "Hold that thought for later, sweetheart. Right now, we have company."

Lauren was so stunned she was speechless. Taking full advantage, Adam lifted her sagging chin with one finger and dropped another quick kiss on her lips. Then he straightened and smiled cordially at the other woman. "Delia, I'd like you to meet Lauren McKenna."

Lauren started. For a moment she had forgotten that the famous newswoman was there, standing not three feet from her. Hot color surged up her neck and flooded her face. She was so flustered she could not think of a thing to say, but that was nothing compared to the shock she experienced when Adam added in an intimate voice, "Lauren and I are engaged to be married."

"Married!" Delia squawked.

At the same time Lauren sucked in a sharp breath. Before she could voice a protest Adam's fingers dug into her upper arm. She glanced up and found that his eyes held entreaty. A fresh wave of shock rolled through her as she realized that he was pleading with her to back him up.

The idea of pretending to be Adam's fiancée unnerved her. She wanted to tell him in no uncertain terms to forget it, but how could she? He had proven himself to be her friend, and he had already done so much for her.

As it turned out, all that was required of her was to stand there and remain silent.

"That's right," Adam confirmed. He smiled down at Lauren and gave her shoulders another squeeze, gentler this time.

"I don't believe you," Delia hissed, raking Lauren with a hate-filled gaze. "I know you, Adam. You're cautious about relationships. You haven't been here long enough to even get to know another woman, much less get engaged."

"Ah, but I was aware that Lauren was special from the first moment I saw her. When true love finally comes along, you know it."

Delia's mouth tightened. "Damn you, Adam Rafferty. I loved you."

"C'mon, Delia, you know that's not true. You love your job and your fame. And you loved having a rich football star for your lover, but that's as deep as your feelings went. I was just another trophy to you. It was over between us months ago, long before I left. We both knew it. Why don't you just wish Lauren and me happiness, and let's part friends?"

Her eyes narrowed to slits. "Fuck you, Rafferty. And as for you," she snarled, jutting her face close to Lauren's. "You're going to be sorry you ever set eyes on him."

She spat the words with so much venom that Lauren drew back. Unconsciously pressing against Adam's side, she watched, stunned, as Delia Waters—the most famous female television journalist in the country—stalked out in a rage. A moment later Lauren jumped as the front door slammed.

"Oh, my."

"Yeah, that was quite a display. I'm sorry you had to witness it. But that's Delia." Adam gave her arm another squeeze and released her. "Thanks for playing along. I probably shouldn't have involved you, but I was desperate."

Adam's words reminded Lauren of that searing kiss and her heart skipped a beat.

"That's all right. I understand. Anyway, after all you've done for me, I guess I owed you that much."

"I don't know about that, but I do appreciate you not spilling the beans."

An engine started outside, and Lauren looked out the window in time to see a white limo heading for the gate. "Adam? That problem of Ms. Waters's that you mentioned?" She turned her head and looked him in the eye. "She drinks, doesn't she?"

"How did you know?"

"I smelled whiskey on her breath. It's barely three o'clock in the afternoon."

"Yeah, you're right. Booze is her problem. Though she doesn't admit it."

"I don't understand. She's in the public eye constantly, and she always appears immaculate and in control. How does she function so well if she has an alcohol problem?"

"She holds her liquor well. I've seen her drink several good-sized men under the table. And like most closet drunks, she's good at hiding her drinking and disguising its side effects. But it's catching up with her. Her consumption is growing, and the effects are beginning to show—her looks are suffering, her temper has become unpredictable and she's missed assignments and done sloppy work. It's just a matter of time before the network brass catch on." His mouth twisted. "You figured it out quickly enough."

"Adam, I realize that you were in a sticky situation, but . . . well . . . do you think it was wise to let her think we are . . ."

"Lovers?" he furnished helpfully. "Maybe not, but that was the only thing I could think of to discourage her. You don't know Delia. She's tenacious as hell. Anything less than total commitment to another woman and she would never have let go."

"But what if she finds out we're not engaged? That we're not even a couple?"

Adam smiled and touched her cheek. The warm look in his eyes sent a frisson through her. "With any luck, that will never happen."

* * *

"This is where we're staying?" Lauren peered up through the rain-spattered windshield at the red brick building located a block off of Cripple Creek's main street. "It looks more like an old school than a hotel."

"That's what it is." Adam parked the rental car in front of the two-story structure. "Mary Alice said the clerk told her it was built around the turn of the century. It hadn't been used as a school in years. When the town legalized gambling, the new owner converted the building into a hotel."

"Aren't there any real hotels in this town?"

"Probably, but this was all we could get on short notice. I'm sure it'll be fine."

Reaching across the console, Adam opened the glove compartment and pushed the button to unlatch the trunk. The move brought him so close Lauren felt his heat against her thigh. She froze, and stared at the back of his head. The car heater hummed, and his scent floated to her on the warm air. Her heart pounded.

When he straightened he smiled at her through the gloom.

"Why don't you make a dash for the lobby while I get our luggage. This is a no-frills establishment. There aren't any doormen or bellhops. There's no point in both of us getting wet."

Lauren did as he suggested, shivering in the cold as she scampered for the door. Cripple Creek was an old mining town high in the Rocky Mountains, somewhere above nine thousand feet. Though it was July, the temperature was hovering around the freezing mark at that altitude, and the rain didn't help.

The inside of the old school was as ornate as the outside, boasting wide stairways with massive carved newel posts and banisters, high pressed-tin ceilings, and fancy woodwork.

Their rooms on the second floor were located off a short hallway that had obviously once been part of a classroom. A blackboard, complete with chalk and erasers, still lined one wall.

"Hmm. Handy if we want to leave each other messages," Adam drawled.

While not actually adjoining, the rooms were side by side and the only two off the secluded little hallway. The intimacy of the accommodations made Lauren's stomach flutter. Which was just plain silly, she told herself. Especially considering that Adam had slept in her house only the night before.

Adam deposited his bags inside the door to his room, then carried Lauren's into hers, which, to her surprise, also contained a blackboard.

Other than dividing the classroom in two with a partitioning wall, covering the oak floors with industrial grade carpet and the addition of a bathroom in each half, little had been done to change the classroom. The ceilings were at least fourteen feet high, there were transoms over the doors, triple hung windows that required a pole to raise and lower the top portions, and exposed pipe and wiring, which had undoubtedly been added years after the building had been erected.

"It's not the Ritz, but it's clean and the bed seems comfortable," Adam commented, giving the mattress an experimental poke.

"I'm sure it will be fine." Lauren sent him a feeble smile and shifted from one foot to the other. Her nerves were humming like high-voltage wires.

This was ridiculous. What was it about being in a hotel room that made everything seem so illicit?

If Adam noticed her discomfort he was gentlemanly enough not to show it. He looked around, then looked at her. "Are you going to be okay by yourself?"

"Of course. Even if Victor Spalding is out on bail, I seriously doubt that he followed us here. Don't worry. I'll be fine."

"Good. Good." He grasped her shoulders and looked into her eyes. His own were dark with concern. "But remember, if you get scared or if you need anything—anything at all—

I'll be right next door. Just knock on the wall and I'll come running. Okay?"

"Okay." Smiling, she placed her hand over his on her right shoulder. "Thank you, Adam."

"Sure. No problem." He hesitated, then bent and placed a soft kiss on her forehead. "Good night."

When the heavy door clicked shut behind him she raised her hand and touched her forehead. Her skin still tingled where his lips had pressed.

An hour later, Lauren lay in the bed staring through the darkness at the lofty ceiling, wide awake.

By all rights she should have been asleep the instant her head hit the pillow. It had been a busy and draining day, especially after the traumatic events of the previous night. She was utterly exhausted. Still, she couldn't sleep.

All because of Adam.

When he had stowed his suitcases inside his room earlier she couldn't help noticing that his bed and hers abutted the same wall. She had taken a hot shower, done stretching exercises designed to relax tense muscles. She'd tossed and turned and willed herself to sleep. She had even tried counting sheep. Nothing helped.

She couldn't stop picturing Adam lying stretched out in bed just inches away on the other side of the wall.

Was he one of those people who sprawled out in complete abandon when he slept? Or did he curl into a fetal position? Was he a heavy sleeper? Or did he wake at a pin drop? Did he sleep naked?

Moaning, Lauren flounced over onto her side and punched her pillow. What was the matter with her? For over three years she hadn't had a single sexual thought. She had assumed that that part of her had ceased to exist. Since David's kidnapping her whole being had been focused on only two things—work and getting her baby back. Beyond that, nothing else had mattered.

Now it was clear that all she'd done was repress her sexual needs, and apparently that was possible for only so long before something blew. Why else had her libido gone berserk?

Lord, she had never in her life had those kind of thoughts about any man before.

But then . . . she'd never been as aware of any man as she was of Adam.

Lauren moaned again. For God's sake, they were friends and business colleagues. That was all. He was probably snoring away at that very moment, blissfully undisturbed by any foolish fantasies of her.

Adam was hard as a rock.

Stark naked, he lay on his back with his hands stacked beneath his head and stared at the ceiling. He had turned the heat down and a chill permeated the room, still a sheen of sweat coated his body. His jaws ached from being clenched.

Dammit to hell, he had to quit thinking about Lauren, he told himself.

It was no use. Desire thrummed through him.

God, he wanted her. He wanted to strip her naked and kiss every inch of that silky skin. He wanted to bury himself deep in that delicate little body, feel her sheath him, hot and tight. He wanted to feel her moving under him, hear her soft moans of pleasure.

More than that, he wanted to protect her, to make everything right for her.

He'd give ten years off his life and every dime he had if he could wipe that sadness and pain from her eyes. He wanted to hear her laugh. To see that lovely face light up with happiness.

But for that to happen he would have to bring her son back to her, and he hadn't a clue of how to do that.

"Shit," he growled as his aching manhood stirred. He was tempted to march over there and seduce her. If her response to his kiss earlier was anything to go by, it was possible. If he swept her off her feet and didn't give her a chance to think.

"Ah, hell." He jerked to a sitting position, his back bowing as he hunched forward and ground the heels of his palms into his gritty eye sockets. "What the hell's the matter with you, asshole? The lady was just attacked, for God's sake. All she needs is another bastard pawing her. Jesus, man! All she wants from you is friendship. That's what you promised her, and by God, that's what you're going to give her."

Twelve

The next morning Adam knocked on Lauren's door a little before eight. When she opened it she sucked in her breath.

It wasn't fair that any man could look that devastating so early in the morning, especially when she felt—and probably looked—as though she'd been jerked through a knothole backwards.

Adam stood there with a warm smile on his face and a friendly twinkle in his eyes. He leaned with an arm braced against the frame, the other propped on his cocked hip. The casual stance spread wide the leather bomber jacket he wore over a pale green pullover and faded jeans and revealed narrow hips and an amazingly trim midsection for such a big man.

Sensations washed over Lauren like a tidal wave. His size alone overwhelmed her. So did his nearness, and that intense male aura he exuded. He looked wonderful and smelled even better. The scents of soap, shaving cream, minty toothpaste and clean male wafted to her.

"Morning," he greeted cheerfully. "You ready to grab a bite of breakfast before we meet with the building owners?"

Lauren jumped and pulled her gaze away from his body. She drew a deep breath and tried to steady her skittering pulse. "Yes, of course. That is . . . I think so." Self-conscious, she raised a hand and gingerly touched her injured cheek. She had covered most of the bruising with makeup, but the abrasion in the center was beginning to heal and scab over. "Does this look too awful?"

"Naw. It's looking better every day. If anyone asks what happened we'll just say you took a bad fall on the stairs at the office."

"All right," she agreed without much enthusiasm. "Just give me a second to get my purse."

She retrieved her shoulder bag and briefcase and hurried back, but at the door she stopped and looked him up and down.

Adam grinned. "What's the matter? Too casual?"

"Well . . . we are going to a business meeting."

He inspected her neat navy business suit, then laughed and took her arm. "Honey, you're the most dressed-up person in town. Almost everyone here is on vacation. They've come to play the slots and live it up for a few days. The dress code is strictly casual. If you didn't bring any, we'll have to see about getting you some jeans later."

As they walked down the stairs and out the front of the old schoolhouse, Lauren's awareness of his hand on her arm was so acute that, even through her suit sleeve she could feel his touch like a branding iron. The hair on the back of her neck and along her arms stood on end and her chest grew tight, but she managed to maintain a dignified facade.

The rain had stopped sometime during the night and the sun was out. It was still cool, but not unpleasantly so, and since Cripple Creek was only a few blocks long, Adam suggested that they walk. People turned to stare when they recognized him, but he pretended not to notice, and no one approached.

It was the same everywhere they went, but Lauren was still not accustomed to drawing so much attention. Inevitably the speculative stares spilled over onto her. She tried to ignore them, but she hadn't Adam's insouciance.

The night before, Lauren hadn't gotten a good look at the town, but as they strolled along she realized that almost every building on the main street, even the smallest shop, had been converted into a casino. Unlike Las Vegas and the other big gambling Meccas, here the casinos closed at two in the morning. Already people were gathering on the sidewalks, awaiting the nine o'clock opening.

Over breakfast Adam talked amiably, but all Lauren could manage was a nod and a weak smile or an occasional yes or no.

She didn't understand what had come over her. She and Adam had worked closely together for over a month, and while, in a remote way, she had recognized that he was an attractive man, until two nights ago she had not experienced this tingling awareness and dizzying excitement.

Now, for no reason, the smallest thing about him had a profound effect on her. The deep timbre of his voice sent goose flesh rippling over her skin. Every time his smile flashed, her heart skipped a beat.

His hands fascinated her. They were big and masculine, with broad palms and long fingers and clean, short nails. Her gaze zeroed in on the dark hair that grew in little tufts between the first and second knuckles and dusted the backs of his hands, and she experienced the strangest sensation in her chest.

The feelings confused and embarrassed her, especially so since it was evident from Adam's lighthearted manner that she did not have the least effect on his libido.

By the time they finished eating, the casinos were open again, and they walked down Main Street to the constant ding, ding, ding and clunk, clunk, clunk of the slot machines. The sound floated out through the open doors.

A few blocks down Main Street, Lauren and Adam met their prospective clients in front of the two adjacent derelict buildings which they planned to renovate.

"Well I'll just be damned!" exclaimed the shorter of the two men when Lauren and Adam walked up. "It is *the* Adam Rafferty. When that Ms. Dodd at your company called to set up this meeting I wondered, but I couldn't believe it was true. My name is Joe Remington, and this is Curtis Childs. It's a real pleasure, Mr. Rafferty. A real pleasure."

Grinning from ear to ear, the men stepped forward and pumped Adam's hand.

He introduced Lauren, and they acknowledged her politely. However, she knew that they were just being mannerly. It was evident that both men were anxious to talk to Adam. Although, Mr. Childs did do a double take when he spotted her injured cheek and asked about what had happened.

Heeding Adam's suggestion, Lauren told him she had fallen at work. After murmuring a few words of sympathy, they immediately refocused on Adam.

Both men were clearly bowled over at meeting a football legend and practically giddy at the thought of doing business with him.

As usual, Adam took the fawning and enthusiasm in stride, answering all their questions good-naturedly and discussing football at length.

With quite a bit of surprise and not a little chagrin, as Lauren listened she realized that Adam was a natural when it came to handling people. He talked with the two men about sports just long enough to satisfy them. Then, with a degree of diplomacy and tact that she would never have suspected of him, he deftly steered the conversation to the purpose of their meeting, without either of the men realizing that he'd made the switch.

They spent the entire day and most of the evening with their clients. The two buildings had been erected in the last century and there were no blueprints available anywhere, at least none that anyone knew about. All that morning the four of them walked through the buildings, inspecting every inch, from the basements to the roofs. While Joe and Curtis explained in general terms what they wanted and why, and how they envisioned their casino, both Adam and Lauren took notes and made sketches.

"I don't see any problem at all knocking out part of that adjoining wall and turning the space into one big casino. Do you, Adam?"

"None that I know of. However, Joe, you and Curtis do understand that Lauren and I are here merely to do a preliminary study and work up our suggestions? I can tell you whether or not a particular change would be feasible, but nothing will be chiseled in stone until our engineering staff has a chance to study the project in detail."

"Yeah. Sure. We understand."

"Good. After we've made our recommendations and the staff has reviewed the project, at that point we will present you with our proposal. If you like it, then we will submit to you a final bid with blueprints and sketches and detailed specifications."

"Good," Joe said, nodding. "That sounds real good."

"I'm going to warn you now, we don't come cheap. Ingram and Bates is a first-class company. We use top-quality materials and workmanship all the way. If you're looking to cut corners, we're not the firm for you."

"Oh, no, no. Curtis and I want this to be the best built, most elegant casino in town. It has to stand out from all the rest—be fancier and bigger, offer amenities no one else has. That's why we came to you."

They continued to discuss the partners' vision of the project over lunch and throughout the rest of the afternoon and again that evening at dinner. Every detail was hashed out at least twice. And, of course, interspersed with business was football talk.

Lauren suspected that their clients were deliberately drawing out the discussion. Not only did Joe and Curtis appear to enjoy rubbing elbows with a football star, they were basking in his reflected glory, enjoying to the hilt the furtive looks and murmurs cast their way by the other diners. They especially seemed to enjoy introducing Adam to everyone they knew who happened to pass by.

When they finally parted company outside the restaurant, Lauren sighed. "Thank goodness. They're nice men, and I know the client is always right, but enough is enough. One more football story and I think I would have run from the place screaming."

Adam laughed. "I know what you mean. Even I was reaching overload." He gripped her arm and steered her through a crush of people on the sidewalk. "So where to now? It's early yet. Shall we head back to the hotel, or try our luck at the machines?"

"I suppose I should at least walk through a few casinos to get an idea of how they're laid out and what is required."

"What do you mean? You don't know?"

"No, I don't. Until today, I'd never even seen one."

Adam stopped in the middle of the sidewalk and looked at her. "Well, I'll be damned. In that case, c'mon, sweetheart. It's time we furthered your education." Slipping an arm around her waist, he hustled her through the nearest set of open doors.

Between the dinging, clunking machines, the music pouring through the speakers, and the hum of voices, the noise level was horrendous. Adam had to raise his voice to be heard over the din as he took her on a tour of the casino and explained the various games.

"There are slot machines and poker machines and blackjack machines. Most of them take quarters, but there are nickel slots. For the real high-rollers, they've even got a few dollar and five-dollar machines. What's your pick?"

"I don't want to play," she shouted back. "I need to study the layout."

"Hey, relax. We've done enough work for one day. It's time for a little fun."

"You go ahead if you want," she said in an absent voice, studying the mezzanine area above them. "I'll just wander around." Pulling her notepad and pencil from her shoulder bag, she headed for the stairs.

Adam sighed and followed her.

He complained and argued, but she was completely absorbed in the task. She examined no less than five casinos before he finally convinced her to put away her notepad and try her hand at a machine.

Lauren agreed merely to humor him, but she resisted his efforts to seat her at a quarter machine and chose a nickel slot instead. Money was not a problem; it was the principle of the thing.

She dropped in her coins without much enthusiasm, but when, on the first pull of the arm, ten nickels dropped into the tray, she sent Adam a stunned look. "What happened?"

"You won fifty cents," he said with a grin.

"Really?" Perking up, she inserted more coins, then made a face when she lost them. On the third pull two more coins dropped out, on the fourth she won six. She came up dry on the next four pulls, but on the eleventh twenty nickels clanked into the tray, and she was hooked.

Sitting next to her, half-heartedly playing a nickel slot, Adam watched her, amused. He should have known that once started she would approach the game the same way she did everything—all out.

Lauren was the hardest-working, most dedicated person he had ever met. Whatever she did, she threw herself into the task with amazing intensity, whether it was her job or her tireless search for her son.

His mouth twitched at the thought. Which probably accounted for the fact that her whole life consisted of only those two things. With that kind of zeal, how would she find the time—or the energy—for anything else?

For the moment, however, he had succeeded in distracting her with the game of chance and he was enormously pleased with himself.

She played with a single-minded determination that had him biting back a chuckle. Dropping a steady stream of coins into the slot, she jerked the handle with a vengeance, muttering under her breath when she lost and hooting with glee whenever a few coins dribbled out.

After an hour, and a loss of fifteen dollars in nickels, Adam gave up. He stood up and stretched and moved to stand behind Lauren. She paid no attention to him.

"You know, you don't have to keep feeding that thing," he drawled. "You can quit anytime you want."

"No. I'm not going to let a machine beat me."

Adam rolled his eyes. "Oh, God. I've created a monster."

She ignored him and kept playing. Three pulls later, when the whirling stopped, sevens filled the screen and all hell broke loose. The light on top of the slot machine flashed and a bell clanged and a steady stream of nickels poured into the tray like water from a garden hose.

"I did it!" Lauren bounced on her seat and thrust her fists straight up in the air. "Yes! Yes! I won!"

"Well, I'll be damned."

"Oh, Adam, can you believe it? I won!" She bounded off the stool and threw her arms around his neck. "I actually won!" she crowed. Then she pulled his head down and kissed him full on the lips.

It was a spur-of-the-moment thing, a harmless salute given in a burst of excess excitement, yet the instant their lips met it was like striking spark to tinder.

Fire ignited between them. The kiss changed in an instant into something scorching and intense that no red-blooded man could resist.

Locking his arms around Lauren, Adam pulled her up tight against his chest, lifting her until her feet left the floor. His lips closed over hers in a greedy, open-mouthed kiss that was wet and hot and hungry.

Lauren responded with matching ardor, her hands clutching him, spearing into his hair to hold him close as the rapacious kiss deepened.

All sense of time and place was lost. Their mouths rocked together, desperate and devouring, as though they would absorb each other. Their hearts raced and their pulses pounded so hard the sound reverberated in their ears, drowning out the clanging bell and the jangle of coins hitting the tray—and the raucous hoots and whistles of the other patrons all around them.

It took a while, but slowly the cheers penetrated.

As the kiss ended their lips clung, then slowly parted. Dazed, Lauren lifted her heavy eyelids and found her gaze caught by a pair of hazel eyes that had darkened to almost black. In their center was a fiery glint that made her heart skip a beat.

Then the shouts and clapping and stomping feet drew her attention, and as she looked around hot color flooded her face.

"Hey, baby! I'll celebrate with you anytime."

"Way to go, man!"

"Whoo! Whoo! Whoo! Whoo! Whoo! Whoo!"

Someone started the chant and others quickly picked it up, and soon it seemed as though everyone in the casino had joined in.

"Oh, dear." Lauren pulled out of Adam's arms and took a quick step backward. She could feel the scalding heat in her face and neck. "I . . . I'm sorry. I got carried away there for a moment. Oh, this is so embarrassing."

Ducking her head, she sat down at the machine again and began to scoop up the money, trying desperately to ignore everyone.

Adam cast their audience a severe look. When they silenced, he hunkered down beside Lauren. "Here, let me help you," he said, scooping up her loot.

She had hit the top prize, and her winnings filled several plastic tubs. Adam had to help her carry them to the cashier's cage. When the coins were run through the counting machine she had won a little over two hundred and fifty dollars.

Lauren almost got excited all over again—until she reminded herself of what had happened the last time.

By silent agreement, they headed for their hotel. The two-block walk was excruciating. Neither said a word the whole way, but the air between them seemed to hum like a high voltage wire.

Out of the corner of her eye, Lauren cast Adam a furtive look. His devil-may-care attitude had vanished. He was taut and intense, his gaze fixed straight ahead. She bit her lower lip. She couldn't blame him for being angry. What in God's name had come over her, throwing herself at him that way? She had made a public spectacle of them.

Neither said a word until they stood in the little hallway outside their rooms. Lauren was so acutely aware of Adam, and so horribly embarrassed, every nerve ending in her body quivered.

With a trembling hand, she unlocked the door and opened it. She intended to wish him goodnight and escape inside, but at the last second she paused. Not quite able to look at him, she kept her gaze fixed on the door. "Adam . . . about what happened . . . I apologize. It was all my fault."

"Lauren—"

"I just got carried away when I won. If I weren't so competitive none of it would have happened."

"Lauren—"

"I don't know why it is, but I always have to win, even when I'm playing against a machine. When I did, I just got so excited—"

"Listen to me, Lauren."

He grasped her upper arms and turned her toward him, but she still couldn't bring herself to meet his gaze. She stared at the green knit covering his chest.

"Maybe the kiss started out that way, but it turned into something else, and we both know it."

"No. It was just the excitement of the moment, that's all. But you have every right to be angry."

"Angry. Why the hell would I be angry? I'm damned glad it happened."

That snapped her head up. "You are? But . . . why?"

His fierce look faded into a smile. "Why do you think?"

"But you're not interested in me that way," she blurted out.

Adam's eyes crinkled at the corners and a low chuckle rumbled from his chest. "Are you kidding? Honey, I've been wanting to kiss you ever since Sunday night. Probably weeks before that. I just didn't admit it to myself."

"What? You certainly haven't acted like you did."

"How could I? You had just been attacked and nearly raped. I didn't want to scare you. Anyway, I had promised to be your friend."

The admission sent a giddy pleasure coursing through Lauren. Before she could squelch it he slipped his arms around her.

"But all bets are off now," he murmured, drawing her against him.

Excitement fluttered through Lauren as her body conformed to his from knees to breasts. He was warm and firm, and against her belly she could feel his arousal. Her stomach went woozy. She braced her forearms against his chest and tried to gather her scattered senses. "Adam, I don't think—"

"Don't think. Just go with your feelings."

"But . . ."

"Ssh. Ssh."

The sibilant sound sent a wave of goose flesh rippling over her, and when he lowered his head her eyelids drifted shut of their own accord.

His mouth closed over hers as soft and warm as velvet. Lauren's breath caught and a giddy thrill whispered through her. Vaguely, she knew she should resist, but she couldn't seem to work up the will. It felt so good to be held in Adam's powerful embrace, and the pleasure of his kiss was too intense, too addictive to deny herself.

The most she could manage in the way of a resistance was a pathetic little moan, and even that came out more like a purr than a protest. Accepting defeat, she went up on tiptoe, and slid her hands up over his chest and shoulders, and as her hands laced together around his neck she felt the delicious stubble of hair prickle against her palms.

It had been so long since she had been held this way, since she had allowed herself this closeness. She had almost forgotten how wonderful it felt to experience a man's touch.

Encouraged by her response, Adam deepened the kiss, making a low sound in his throat as her mouth flowered open under his. His tongue plunged inside, swirling, twining with hers in a sensuous mating dance that made Lauren's knees turn to mush. She clung to him, her head spinning, her body on fire.

Adam's arms tightened around her and lifted. She hung in his arms like a rag doll, her feet dangling several inches off the floor. Thrusting her fingers through his hair, she clutched his head with both hands as the ravenous kiss went on and on.

Lauren was so enthralled she barely knew when Adam nudged the door open with his shoulder and carried her into the room. He closed the door with his foot and leaned back against it with his legs braced wide. His mouth left hers, and as he kissed a wet path across her cheek she trembled and dug her fingers deeper into his scalp.

His tongue traced the swirls of her ear, made a stabbing foray inside, and withdrew. Then his hot breath filled the delicate shell, and Lauren made an inarticulate sound and arched her neck as tingling heat shimmered through her. "Oh, Adam. Adam."

"I know, sweetheart. I know."

Leaning his head forward, he grazed the arch of her throat with his teeth. The delicate savagery sent desire ripping through Lauren. Her tingling nipples tightened into pebble hardness and her feminine core quickened and pulsed with unbearable need. Her head lolled back and her breathing became labored and raspy as she clutched desperately at Adam's shoulders.

"Look at me, sweetheart," he whispered. "Look at me."

The husky command barely penetrated the sensual fog that surrounded her. Slowly, as though weighted with lead, her eyelids opened part way and she met Adam's glittery stare. Passion darkened his face and burned from his eyes. Holding her gaze, he loosened his hold and let her slowly slide downward.

The erotic rub of their bodies took Lauren's breath away. Her breasts molded to his chest, soft to hard. Against her belly she felt the scrape of his belt buckle, then the hard ridge of his arousal. Her heart began to pump so hard, a flush spread over her, from her toes to the roots of her hair.

Lauren was shocked at the raw need that pulled at her. No man had ever made her feel this desperate, not even her husband. No one but Adam.

"Say you want me, too, Lauren," he whispered. "God, I need to hear you say it. I can see it in your eyes. I feel it here." He put the pad of his thumb against the pulse that throbbed in her neck. "And here." Her breath caught as he laid his palm over her left breast. "But I need to hear you say it, sweetheart."

Her heart went crazy beneath his touch, booming like a kettledrum as her nipple tightened and pushed against his palm. Lauren stared at him. She saw the longing and intensity, the caring in those beautiful eyes, and whatever tiny shred of sanity she had left turned to dust.

Holding his gaze, she unfastened the top button on his shirt, then the next, and the next. "I want you, Adam," she whispered. Her fingers released the button just above his belt, then began to tug his shirt free. "Make love to me."

In answer, Adam swept her up in his arms and strode to the bed. They sank down on the mattress together, their lips locked in a passionate kiss, their hands grasping and stroking, snatching at clothing with frantic haste. Within seconds they were naked, their bodies straining together. In a frenzy of pleasure, hands clutched and stroked, legs entwined, teeth nipped, mouths rubbed and kissed and explored.

"Ah, Lauren, sweet Lauren. I feel as though I've been waiting forever for you," Adam groaned against her neck. "Just you."

Lauren was lost, awhirl in a maelstrom of sensation, caught in the magnetic pull of passion and want. Rational thought was impossible. She had become a purely sensual creature. All she could do was surrender to the irresistible longing that pulled at her.

Writhing, she clutched at Adam's back, her head tossing from side to side on the pillow. "Please. Oh, please."

"Easy, sweetheart, easy," he murmured, rising above her.

Lauren barely heard him. Acting on instinct, she wrapped her legs around his hips, and when she felt his hard flesh nudge that intimate part of her that throbbed and burned for him she arched upward.

Braced up on his arms, Adam threw his head back, and with a groan he thrust into her, sinking deep with one powerful stroke.

Lauren clutched him tight, and as the rocking movement began, pleasure built, demanding, driving them both toward the pinnacle.

In a delirium of ecstasy and need and frustration she clung to Adam, meeting each thrust, reaching . . . reaching . . . reaching . . . until the shattering climax burst upon her in white-hot waves.

"Adam! Oh, God, *Ad-daaam!*"

Raised above her on stiffened arms, his face dark and rigid with passion, he drove into her, harder, faster. Then suddenly he arched his back and pressed deep with his head thrown back. He gritted his teeth and as his face contorted in ecstasy a low growl of completion tore from his throat.

Thirteen

For countless moments Lauren let her mind float—partly because of the lassitude that permeated her body, and partly because she did not want to face what had just happened.

What she had allowed to happen.

Eyes closed, she listened to Adam's labored breathing. But, dear God, it had been so long—so very long—since she'd experienced this kind of intimacy and closeness. A rueful smile curved her mouth. To be absolutely truthful, she wasn't certain she'd ever reached this level of closeness with Gavin. Certainly not emotionally. Nor had their lovemaking been this deeply satisfying and pleasurable.

Lauren sighed. She felt wonderful—boneless and sated and deliciously innervated. Her palms moved in hypnotic circles across Adam's back. His weight pushed her into the mattress. His warmth enveloped her. The smell of man and sweat . . . and sex . . . engulfed her.

Slowly, her heavy eyelids opened, and she stared at the high ceiling above the bed. Oh, God. What had she done?

Adam stirred. Lifting up, he braced on his forearms above her. His eyes were warm, his voice husky. "Hi. You okay?"

She nodded, unable to say a word. His hair was rumpled where she had run her fingers through it. The flush of passion still darkened his face and he had the languorous look of a satisfied man.

"Good. Because I feel like I've died and gone to heaven."

He smiled tenderly and stroked her cheek with his fingertips. "I knew we would be good together, but sweetheart, that was incredible."

Before Lauren could respond he rolled off of her and settled against the pillows with a satisfied sigh. "Come here."

He reached out to pull her close, but she evaded his arm and sat up. Tucking the covers up under her armpits, she drew her legs up and hugged them tight against her chest. "Adam . . . we have to talk."

She could feel his gaze burning into her back.

"All right," he agreed, but she heard the wariness in his voice. "Fire away."

"This . . . this was a mistake."

"Oh, no, sweetheart. I'm not going to let you get by with that. This was no mistake. This thing between us has been building ever since that night on the beach when we met. Don't pretend you haven't felt it. That kiss back at the casino proved it."

His fingertips trailed down her spine with a feather-light touch, all the way to the shadowy cleft at its base. Lauren shivered and hugged her legs tighter. "Sweetheart, the minute our lips touched it was like opening a floodgate. I've never felt this way about any woman before. I've never felt this kind of intensity. Or this kind of passion." From the corner of her eye she saw him tip his head to one side inquiringly. "Have you?"

"I . . ."

"Have you?"

Lauren sighed, and her shoulders sagged. "No. No, I haven't. But that really doesn't matter, does it? You know that an intimate relationship between us is impossible. For heaven's sake, Adam, we work together."

"So? That doesn't have to be a problem. We're adults. I think we're capable of keeping our personal and professional lives separate. Office romances happen all the time. Some with great success."

She darted him an uneasy glance over her shoulder. Something in his eyes made her heart lurch. She prudently decided to skirt the comment. She couldn't allow herself to think in those terms. "Even if that's true, for me it just won't work. There's no room in my life for a man."

"Why? Because you're trying to find your son?"

"Yes."

"Becoming involved with me won't interfere with that. Except in a positive way."

Clutching the covers to her, she twisted around, bristling. "What does that mean?"

"Just that outside the office you spend every waking moment grieving and waiting to hear from that detective you hired. That's not healthy, Lauren. You need to get out more, be with other people, lead a normal life."

"I can't! Don't you understand? My baby is missing! I have to find him."

"I know you do. Just don't let this thing consume you. Lauren, listen to me. If the detective is going to find your son, he'll find him whether or not you're sitting at home alone agonizing over the situation."

She shook her head. "I can't just put my worries on hold when you want me to. They're with me all the time. A relationship between a man and a woman should come first, but with me it can't. Getting my son back has to be my top priority."

"I know. And I accept that going in. Honey, I would never expect you to abandon your search. Hell, I wouldn't want you to. Just don't use that as an excuse to cut yourself off from life. From me," he added softly.

He reached out and tugged the cover out of her hands. Lauren gasped, but he merely took hold of her upper arms and hauled her in. In a blink, she found herself sprawled across his body. A delicious shock speared through her as her soft breasts flattened against his chest and the sensitive nipples pushed into the silky thatch of dark hair.

He brushed her tumbled hair away from her face and looked deep into her eyes. "Anyway, hasn't it occurred to you that I could help? If in no other way than to be there for moral support whenever you needed it."

Lauren stared at him. She knew he could read the doubt in her eyes, but it couldn't be helped. It had been a long time since she had allowed herself to trust a man. Her instinct was to draw back, slam down the barrier, but something about Adam's steady regard wouldn't let her. "You'd do that for me?"

He raised his hand and stroked her cheek, the side of her neck. A ghost of a smile played around his mouth. Tugging her higher on his chest, he bowed his neck and jutted his head forward. "That and more. Much, much, more," he whispered against her lips a fraction of a second before his mouth closed over hers.

Lauren sighed and snuggled closer to Adam. In the heady aftermath of lovemaking she could almost shut out her doubts.

Almost.

"Adam?"

"Mmm?"

At the sleepy sound, she tilted her head on his shoulder and looked up at him, and her heart gave a little thump. He looked so appealing, even boyish, lying there with his eyes closed and his hair all mussed.

"Are you awake?"

"Mmm." He opened one eye a fraction. "I am now. Something on your mind?"

She settled her head back on his shoulder and stared at her fingers, twining in his chest hair. "Do you believe I took a kickback from that carpet supplier?"

"Are you still fretting over that? No, of course I don't."

"Why not? The evidence against me is pretty strong."

"Lauren. Sweetheart. I've worked side by side with you for over a month. You're a conscientious, hard worker. By anyone's standards you pull down an impressive salary. You went to school for one helluva long time to get your Ph.D. In addition, there's the special relationship between you and Walter. He couldn't love you more if you were his daughter, and I know you feel the same. I don't for a minute believe you would jeopardize all that for a few extra dollars."

"Maybe I'm just incompetent. What about that marble order for the Nob Hill job that I supposedly canceled?"

"My guess is, the guys at the quarry misplaced the order, and to cover their own asses, they blamed the mistake on you." With his forefinger beneath her chin, he tipped her head up until their gazes locked. "Incompetent is a word that no one would apply to you. Lauren, you are one sharp lady, and you do a helluva good job. I've seen you in action, remember."

She stared into his eyes, searching deep. "Does that bother you?"

"Does what bother me?"

"That I have the position I do at Ingram and Bates. That I command a big salary. That I have a Ph.D. The whole thing."

"Why would any of that bother me? You're a valuable asset to the company."

She lowered her gaze and stared at her plucking fingers again. "I'm not asking you as an officer of the company. I meant, does it bother you on a personal level. Now that we . . . you know . . ."

"Now that we're lovers?" He tipped her head up again and chuckled at her blush, but the sound cut off abruptly when he got a good look at her expression. "Hey. You're serious, aren't you? What brought this on?"

Lauren bit her lower lip. "Gavin used to say that the only reason my career took off was because of Walter. He said if I'd gone to work anywhere else I wouldn't have been promoted to department director as soon as I was, if ever."

"What a crock. Sounds to me like he was jealous."

Lauren shrugged. "Maybe. But I think it goes deeper than that. When we first married, Gavin was supportive and proud of me. In those days he liked to think of himself as modern thinking and secure in his masculinity—all the things that society teaches us men should be. He'd convinced himself that he wanted a wife who had ambitions and goals, a woman who was strong and self-reliant and successful in her own right. It turned out that wasn't what he wanted at all.

"After he got his master's degree, Gavin went to work. While I was finishing grad school he was very good about being supportive, financially and emotionally. Our marriage might not have been made in heaven, but we were happy. Once I earned my Ph.D. and went to work at Ingram and Bates things began to go downhill for us.

"From day one, I made more money than Gavin, which was a sore spot with him. As an accountant, he knew he would never earn anywhere near as much. His resentment grew with every promotion I received. The more I succeeded, the more our arguments escalated and the more scornful and biting Gavin's criticisms became."

"Asshole," Adam muttered, and Lauren shot him a weak smile.

"Gavin's not really a bad person. I finally came to realize that he's simply one of those men who needs to feel that he's in charge, that he's the protector and provider."

"Ah, the hunter-gatherer type. The kind that goes out and clubs a mastodon and drags it back to the cave for the little woman to cook."

The pithy comment coaxed a chuckle out of Lauren. "I guess. Anyway, Gavin needs a clinging-vine type for a wife, someone who idolizes him and is completely dependent on him. I could never be that.

"In the end, his constant attempts to chip away at my abilities and self-confidence took their toll on our relationship until we were just two hostile strangers sharing the same roof. Finally, he found someone else and moved out."

"God, I'm sorry, sweetheart. That must have hurt."

"Not nearly as much as the years of constant ridicule and criticism." She raised up on one elbow and looked Adam straight in the eye. "I don't ever want to go through that again."

She saw understanding dawn in Adam's eyes. She expected anger and braced for it, but instead he bracketed her face with both of his big hands and returned her gaze with such solemn sincerity and caring her breathing became constricted.

"My God, sweetheart, your strength, that gritty determination of yours, your grace under fire—don't you know that those are all things that I admire and adore about you? I promise you, you'll never be subjected to that kind of abuse again. Not from me." He leaned forward and brushed a feather-light kiss over her mouth, her cheeks, each eyelid. "Never from me," he whispered.

They remained in Cripple Creek until the following Saturday. It took only a day and a half to complete their preliminary study. The rest of their stay, at Adam's insistence, was spent simply enjoying each other's company.

Now and then they ventured out of the hotel to eat and maybe play a few slots. Once they drove out of town to the Florescent Valley for a short sightseeing trip, but mostly they simply stayed in Lauren's room.

They talked for hours about everything imaginable. They shared childhood stories, personal triumphs and tragedies. Adam told Lauren anecdotes from his days as a pro football player. She told him about her longing for brothers and sisters, and how, when she and Gavin had first married she'd had hopes of having a large family.

By Saturday night when they arrived back in San Francisco they knew more about one another than most couples knew after years together.

Only one incident marred what had otherwise been an idyllic interlude. That had occurred the night before they left Cripple Creek, when Lauren thought she'd spotted her ex-husband in a crowded casino.

Before Adam could stop her she had taken off, barreling through the crush of people. Several people in the crowd were knocked aside, and their precious plastic tubs of coins went sailing, but Lauren was deaf to the cries of outrage that followed her or the scene she was creating. Her entire being was focused on the sandy-haired man. She finally caught up with him, only to discover that she had chased down a hapless tourist.

By that time several pit bosses, security guards and irate patrons were hot on her heels. Only Adam's intervention and his promise to make restitution had prevented the casino manager from having Lauren tossed out bodily. She was so dejected she barely registered the furor, and when he led her from the casino she walked like an automaton.

Not until they were home did it occur to Lauren that she had allowed Adam to get closer to her, emotionally and spiritually, than she had ever allowed anyone—even Gavin. Somehow they had forged an intimate bond that made them not merely lovers, but soul mates. Lauren didn't know quite how it had happened, or even how she felt about the turn of events, but she couldn't deny the relationship.

If she needed proof she had only to examine her feelings at the thought of parting from him, even temporarily.

For three years she had lived alone, and emotionally, she had survived almost completely on her own. Yet, on the drive from the San Francisco airport to the beach, she sank into silence, unbearably depressed at the thought of returning to that solitary existence.

However, when they reached her house, without a word, Adam carried her bags, as well as his own, inside.

"Until that creep is sent to prison, I'm sleeping here," he announced, shooting her a challenging look when he straightened from setting the cases down in her bedroom.

Lauren closed her eyes as relief flooded through her like a hot tide.

The first thing Monday morning, before leaving for the office, Lauren made her weekly call to Sam Ewing, but the detective had no new leads. She tried not to be despondent, nevertheless, on the drive to work Adam noticed her silence. He made one attempt to cheer her up, but when that didn't work he wisely fell silent himself and slipped a Mendelssohn CD into the player.

Almost immediately upon arriving at the office they met with Walter to discuss their findings on the Cripple Creek job. While Mary Alice took notes he listened to their recommendations and comments, occasionally adding one of his own or asking questions. When they were done he nodded.

"So, you think the project is feasible?"

"Yes, we do. It's not a big job, and we'll be operating under the strict regulations of the State Historical Board, so it'll be a headache, but I think we can turn a respectable profit. Plus, I'd like to see those two old buildings saved."

"You agree, Lauren?" Walter demanded.

"Yes. I do."

At that moment, Alice, in her usual unobtrusive way, went to the sideboard and poured three cups of coffee. When she had served each of them she went quietly about the office, straightening various items.

"Then it's settled. Put Anderson and Hauser to work on it right away." Walter shut the file with a snap and handed it across the desk to Adam.

"Sure. Anything else?"

"Yes. I don't know whether anyone has mentioned it to you, but the Hope Ball is coming up in about a month. Tick-

ets are one hundred dollars and there'll be an art auction. I
sponsor the shindig, and the money raised goes to help children with cancer. The art work is done by the kids themselves. It's a good cause, so I expect all my executive staff
to attend and bring their checkbooks."

Lauren rolled her eyes. Walter was the proverbial bull in
a china shop. Subtlety and tact were simply not in his
makeup.

Adam merely smiled at the gruff order. "Sure. No problem."

"Lauren, you be there early to help me see to the guests."

The Hope Ball had been Helen's pet project, and since his
wife's death Walter had continued to host the gala in her
honor, with Lauren filling in as his hostess. Not surprisingly,
seeing to the details and organization had fallen on Mary
Alice's capable shoulders.

"I'm sorry, Walter, but I'm afraid you'll have to find someone else to act as your hostess," Adam inserted before she
could reply. "This year Lauren will be attending the ball with
me."

"Adam!" Lauren gasped. They hadn't discussed the matter, but she had assumed that they would be discreet about
their relationship, particularly at the office.

"What? What's this?" Walter flashed a startled look back
and forth between them. Noting Lauren's blush, his eyes narrowed. "Humph. Like that is it? Well, I can't complain, I
suppose. I've been after this stubborn woman to get out and
meet someone for months. But just how the hell am I going
to manage all those people by myself?"

Lauren cast a glance at Mary Alice. "You could follow
your own advice and ask a ladyfriend to be your date."

"Date! Hell, I haven't been on a date in thirty-eight years.
I wouldn't know how to act. Besides, I don't know any
women."

"Oh, I'm sure you could think of someone."

"Mmm. There are a few women at the country club who've

hinted they were interested. I know. Chester Cosgrove's widow. She's about the right age, and a handsome woman, as I recall.

"Mary Alice, call Cynthia Cosgrove and ask her if she would like to go to the Hope Ball with me."

White-faced, Mary Alice turned from straightening the sideboard and stared at Walter. "You want *me* to make a date for you with Mrs. Cosgrove?"

"Isn't that what I said?"

Groaning, Lauren lowered her head and rested her forehead in her hand. Adam cleared his throat and shifted in his chair.

"Very well. If that's what you want." Mary Alice's voice shook with suppressed emotion but her face was set and icy cold. She turned on her heel and marched out, slamming the door behind her so hard the pictures on the wall rattled.

Walter's jaw sagged. "Now what the hell is wrong with her?"

"Oh, Walter, how could you!"

"How could I what?"

Lauren had already jumped up to follow the older woman, and the question bounced off her back. Walter turned bewildered eyes on Adam. "What did I do?"

"Oh, no. You're on your own. I'm not getting involved in this. Although . . . I will offer one small piece of advice. In the future, if I were you, I wouldn't ask one woman to make a date for me with another woman."

If anything, Walter looked even more befuddled. "But . . . it was Mary Alice. She makes all my appointments for me."

When Lauren stepped out of Walter's office Mary Alice sat at her computer, her fingers flying over the keyboard. Her face looked as though it were carved from marble.

"Mary Alice? Are you all right?"

Her fingers never slowed. "Of course. I'm fine."

"He doesn't mean to be insensitive, Mary Alice. Truly. He's just oblivious."

She glanced at Lauren. "You're not, I gather. How long have you known?"

"That you're in love with Walter? All my life, I think."

"Does everyone know?"

"No . . . well . . . I think a few have guessed."

"I see." She stopped typing, and an instant later the printer spit out a letter. Mary Alice plucked it out of the tray and signed her name to the bottom. "At least knowing that will make this easier."

"Make what easier? What is that?"

"Official notice that I intend to take my retirement. If I weren't required to give three months notice I'd leave right now."

"Mary Alice! Oh, my dear, don't do that. Please."

"No, it's time. Past time, actually. If I'd had any sense I would have left here years ago. I've wasted my life, loving that man. These last two years I've been waiting for him to notice me as a woman, but it's obviously hopeless. Now he has me making dates for him. That's too much to take, even for me."

Lauren sighed. She couldn't argue with that.

Five minutes after Lauren and Adam left, Mary Alice marched back into Walter's office and slapped her letter down on his desk. "Mrs. Cosgrove would be delighted to go to the Hope Ball with you and be your hostess," she announced in a chilly voice. "In fact, she was quite giddy at the prospect. I made arrangements for flowers to be delivered to her home that afternoon, and I told her you would pick her up that evening shortly before seven."

"Good. Good. What's this?"

"A letter. For you. If you will read it, I'm sure you'll find it self-explanatory. Now if you'll excuse me, I have work to do."

She barely made it back to her desk before the explosion. *"Retiring!"* he roared. "Dammit, Mary Alice, get back in here! Now!"

Over thirty years of working for Walter had rendered Mary Alice immune to his bellows, and this time she had the added shield of anger and hurt. Taking her time, she rose from her desk and returned to stand in the doorway to his office. "Yes?"

"What the hell is the meaning of this?" he demanded, shaking the sheet of paper at her. "And quit hovering in the doorway and get in here!"

She walked calmly to one of the chairs before his desk and sat down. Crossing her long legs, she meticulously smoothed the skirt of her rose silk suit over her knees and flicked off an imaginary speck of lint. "As you can see, it's a notice of my intention to take early retirement."

"The hell with that. You can't retire."

"I certainly can. I've worked for this company for thirty-two years. I could have retired anytime during the last two."

"That's not what I meant. Dammit, woman, I need you here!"

"I'm sorry. I've made up my mind. In three months I'm leaving."

"That's not acceptable. You—Wait! Dammit, Mary Alice, will you come back here!" he shouted, but she ignored him and went back to her desk. In seconds Walter came storming out of his office after her.

"Dammit, Mary Alice, what the hell's the matter with you? Does this have something to do with me asking you to call Cynthia Cosgrove? Adam seemed to think that was a mistake. If that's what has your nose out of joint, then I apologize. Although I don't know what was so terrible about asking you to call the woman. You've never objected to doing personal favors for me before."

Mary Alice looked up at him, her blue eyes flashing. *"That* is the problem."

"What is?" Walter raked a hand through his salt-and-pepper hair and made an exasperated sound.

"The fact that you have no idea why you shouldn't have asked me to call Cynthia Cosgrove and make a date for you. *That's* why I'm leaving. At least, it was the prod I needed to finally make me open my eyes." She stood and skirted around her desk—and Walter—with the regal dignity of a queen. "Now if you'll excuse me, I have to take these contracts to Legal."

"Dammit, Mary Alice, none of this makes any sense. Why don't you just spit out what you mean and let's get this thing cleared up so we can get back to normal."

She stopped at the door and fixed him with a cool stare. "As far as I'm concerned, the matter is cleared up. I'll be leaving in three months. When I get back from Legal I'll call personnel and let them know you'll be needing a new secretary and have them start screening applicants."

That night Adam lay propped up on a stack of pillows in Lauren's bed. When she emerged from the bathroom, dressed in a silky mint green nightgown, he caught a whiff of the heavenly smells that roiled out with her on the steamy air—a heady combination of shampoo, jasmine-scented bathsoap and matching talc.

He smiled. Was there anything more alluring than a clean, sweet-smelling woman?

He tossed back the covers on her side of the bed and held out his arm. She climbed in and snuggled against his side and lay her head on his shoulder with a sigh. He rubbed his chin against her temple. "Mmm, you smell good. And you feel even better."

"So do you." She turned her head and placed a kiss on his shoulder, but he could tell her mind was far away. He knew what lay behind her pensive mood. In a way, he was almost glad the incident at the office had happened. At least it had taken her mind off of her son for a while.

"How long have you known how Mary Alice felt about Walter?"

He felt her shrug. "Just lately for sure. Of course, there have been rumors for years." She told him about Walter's marriage, his devotion to his wife and Mary Alice's steadfast loyalty throughout the years.

"And he never even guessed? What's wrong with the man? His wife has been gone two years, and Mary Alice is a lovely woman."

"That's just it. I don't think he sees her as a woman. Just as his own personal, highly efficient assistant."

"Huh. All I can say is the man's got one helluva blind spot. And if he doesn't do something to clear it up soon, he's going to lose a fine woman."

"I know, but short of hitting him over the head and spelling it out to him I don't see any solution, and I doubt that Mary Alice would thank me for that."

"You're probably right." He rolled onto his side and scooted down in the bed until they were lying face to face, their noses just inches apart. "It looks like you're just going to have to be content to work on your own love life."

He watched her pensive look fade and a sensual heat kindle in her eyes as her gaze roamed over his face. An entrancing smile played about her mouth, and she winnowed her fingers through the short hair at his left temple. "I guess you're right." She kissed him softly. Once. Twice. "But I'm a little rusty, you know." With the tip of her tongue, she traced the shape of his lips, the seam between them, and a hard shudder rippled through Adam. She smiled—a sultry, siren's smile—and whispered against his lips, "This may take a while."

With a growl Adam clamped his mouth to hers, and rolled her to her back. A laugh bubbled from Lauren's throat as she wrapped her arms around him.

Fourteen

"Adam, she seems perfect," Kate whispered as she bent to place a plate of cheese crackers on the small wrought-iron table beside his chair.

Adam's gaze sought out Lauren. She stood at the other end of the Diamattos' patio with Tony, examining his friend's prize rosebushes and listening with a commendable show of interest as he expounded on the proper way to prune the plants. "Yeah. I know. She is, actually."

"Oh, dear. I'm not sure I approve of that look." Kate nudged his shoulder and nodded toward the house. "C'mon in the kitchen with me where we can talk."

The minute they stepped inside the house she whirled on him and gave his chest a poke. "We had an agreement, boy-o. You were not to get serious with another woman until I checked her out."

He grinned. "I know, but I couldn't help myself. Don't worry about it, Katydid. You're going to love Lauren. I promise."

"I see. So you *are* serious about her."

"Oh, very clever. Kate Diamatto, you're a sneak. If you wanted to know how I felt about her why didn't you just come out and ask?"

"Would you have told me?"

"No."

"There you have it, then." She headed for the refrigerator

and started pulling out salad makings. "Tony and I did wonder how long it would take you to melt all that ice and win Lauren over. Fact is, we had a bet going."

"Oh, yeah?" Adam filched a piece of carrot and popped it in his mouth. "Who won?"

"Why, me, of course."

"Of course."

He wandered over to the window overlooking the patio. Lauren and Tony were sitting on the lounge chairs talking. Molly and Paulo raced around the yard with their arms out stretched like airplanes, showing off for Lauren's benefit.

On the outside she looked serene and at ease, but Adam knew that she was a bundle of nerves. It had taken him weeks to talk her into meeting his friends, and even on the drive over he'd been afraid she was going to back out.

"I'm not sure this is a good idea, Adam," she had blurted out. When he'd glanced her way she had been so edgy she'd looked as though she might fly apart at any moment. "My social skills are so rusty, I'll probably embarrass you. Maybe . . . maybe we should call them and beg off. Or maybe you should go alone. I could take a cab home."

"Hey, take it easy. You'll be fine. There's no reason to be nervous. The Diamattos are down-to-earth people. You met Kate. They don't come any nicer. And Tony's great, too. You'll love them. And I guarantee they'll love you. Just relax, sweetheart.

"Besides, with the baby due in a couple of weeks, this will be Kate's last chance to entertain for a while. She'd be crushed if we didn't show up."

Lauren had given him an anemic smile and accepted defeat, but Adam knew that she was anything but relaxed.

Not for a minute was he concerned about her social skills. He'd seen Lauren in action with clients at meetings and business dinners. She was smooth and polished and could hold her own with anyone. He knew her real fear was that she might end up actually liking his friends.

Adam didn't have a doubt that deep down Lauren wanted friends. He'd seen the loneliness in her eyes, the yearning. Though he didn't think her solitary lifestyle was healthy, he understood why she had opted for it. After being abandoned by former friends at a time when she needed them most, the fear of becoming vulnerable to that kind of hurt again made her instinctively shy away from personal relationships.

Ever since the night she had been attacked and he'd gotten a glimpse into her past he'd had been chipping away at the wall she'd built around herself. He had managed to breach her defenses, and she seemed happy—though he suspected she was still not completely comfortable with their relationship—but she was leery of allowing anyone else to get close.

"I have to admit, though," Kate chattered on. "After that day at your place, I was a bit concerned that she wasn't the woman for you when she reacted to the kids they way she did."

"There's a reason for that." Keeping his eyes on Lauren, Adam explained about her past and her missing child.

"Oh, dear Lord," Kate gasped when he was done. Adam glanced over his shoulder. His friend leaned against the kitchen counter with her hand over her heart, staring at him, her face stricken. Tears swam in her vivid blue eyes.

"That poor woman. She must be in agony. Why, if anyone took one of my babies I'd die. No wonder she ran from Paulo that day. How painful it must be for her to be around other little boys close to her son's age. Or me, for that matter, what with this baby due soon," she added, patting her swollen belly.

Kate came to stand by Adam and gazed through the window at Lauren. "Three years. The poor, poor thing. I can't imagine anything worse for a mother."

Outside, three-year-old Paulo sidled up to Lauren and leaned against the arm of her chair. The little boy watched her solemnly, all the while sucking his thumb.

"Oh, dear. I'll go get him—"

Adam put a hand on Kate's arm. "No. Don't."

"But, Adam. That's cruel. You know he upsets her."

"The world is populated with small children, Kate. Half of them boys. Whether or not Lauren ever gets her son back, she's going to have to learn to deal with that."

"Maybe so, but—Oh, dear."

Kate put her hand over her mouth as she watched Lauren go rigid. She stared at the toddler, her face white.

Paulo dragged his thumb out of his mouth and said something to her. At first Lauren merely sat as though shell-shocked. Finally, with obvious effort, she mustered a wavery smile. Then, as though unable to help herself, she reached out and stroked his chubby cheek with her fingertips.

The boy, who had never met a stranger, made up his mind in an instant that he liked this new person and raised his arms for her to pick him up.

"Oh, Paulo," his mother moaned. "Why couldn't you be a shy child?"

Lauren flinched back. Even from that distance Adam could see the panic on her face. She glanced around for help, but Tony was busy pushing Molly on the backyard swing set.

Adam held his breath, watching Lauren's hands clench and unclench on the arms of the lounger. *Come on, sweetheart. Come on. You can do this.*

Finally he saw her draw a deep breath and lift the little boy onto her lap.

Paulo—being Paulo—made himself at home and curled against her. Content, he lay his head against her breast, stuck his thumb back in his mouth and watched his father and sister over his chubby fist.

During a long moment of indecision, Lauren simply stared down at the red-haired child, but slowly, hesitantly, she wrapped her arms around him and cuddled him close.

"Ahhhhh. Now, would you look at that," Kate murmured with maternal pride. "What a charmer my little Paulo is."

Adam's gaze riveted to Lauren. He felt as though his heart might burst. He knew how much the gesture had cost her.

The incident put an end to Lauren's jitters, as though having survived the worst, everything else was easy.

Once she relaxed, she and Kate hit it off like a house afire. Throughout the cookout on the patio and afterwards while they worked together side by side cleaning up, they chattered away like old friends. By the time Adam and Lauren left, the two women were making plans to get together for lunch the following week, provided the baby did not make an early entrance into the world.

On the drive home Lauren was quiet. Adam glanced at her pensive expression and smiled. "You see. They weren't so bad, were they?"

"They're very nice, just as you said," she replied, casting him a wry look.

"They liked you, too. In fact, I'd say you're in like Flynn. Come to think of it, this is a first. They've accepted most of the women I dated, but you're the only one who has earned their unqualified approval."

"I'm not sure if that's a compliment or a statement on your lousy taste in women."

"Both, probably," he admitted with a good-natured chuckle. "But my taste has definitely improved. Kate told me so herself."

The silence returned. Lauren waited a few moments, then cocked an eyebrow. "Well? Aren't you going to say it?"

"Say what?"

"I told you so. I know you're dying to."

He stared straight ahead at the road with a smug smile on his face. "Nope. Not me. It's enough that you admit you were wrong."

She cuffed his shoulder. "Don't gloat. It's very unattractive."

Chuckling, Adam turned into the beach road. When he brought the BMW to a halt in Lauren's garage beside her car he shut off the engine and turned to her. A gentle warmth replaced the teasing humor in his eyes.

"I'll tell you something else about my friends." He picked up one of her hands and massaged it, watching the movement of his dark thumb over her pale skin and delicate bones. He looked up, and met her gaze. "If you ever need them, they'll be there for you. You can count on it."

Hope and doubt warred in her eyes. Adam leaned forward and touched his mouth to hers in a soul-stirring kiss that made her tremble. When it was over, he drew back a few inches. His gaze held hers. "So will I. I love you, Lauren."

Her eyes widened. "Oh, Adam." She raised her hand and cupped the side of his face. Raw emotion filled her eyes and her lower lip trembled. "Adam, you . . . you can't mean that."

"I mean it. I've never meant anything more in my life."

"But we haven't known each other long enough for that. You can't be in love with me. Not yet. It's too soon."

"How long does it take?"

"I don't know, but—"

"Honey, listen to me. I'm thirty-six years old, and until now, not once have I said those words to a woman. That's because I've never been in love before. There were a few women I was genuinely fond of, but that doesn't come close to what I feel for you. When the real thing comes along, trust me, it's not difficult to recognize. Whether you believe me or not, I'm in love with you, Lauren.. Head-over-heels, madly in love. I always will be."

Lauren's mouth trembled as her throat worked with emotions. He felt her fingertips quiver against his temple. "Oh, Adam."

He smiled into her teary eyes. "You don't have to say anything. I didn't tell you to force a declaration out of you. I just wanted you to know how I felt. So you'd know that I'll always be here for you."

"Oh, Adam." She wrapped her arms around his neck and held him with all her might, her eyes squeezed shut against a painful ecstasy that burgeoned inside her. The welter of emotions swirled and swelled in her chest until it ached, but the feelings were too intense, too scary. She wasn't ready to examine them yet. Not yet.

"Do you get the feeling you're being stared at from all sides?" Adam asked under his breath. Taking two flutes of champagne from a passing waiter, he handed one to Lauren.

"Mmm." She took a sip while her gaze drifted casually around the ballroom. "And discussed, too. You can almost hear the whispers flying around."

Their arrival together at the Hope Ball had caused a stir among the company employees who were there. While Lauren and Adam had not tried to hide their new relationship, neither had they advertised it. Nan might have guessed that they were seeing each other, but until tonight only Walter and Mary Alice had known for certain.

"I feel like an insect on a pin," Adam murmured.

"Maybe, but we're not the only ones who are uncomfortable. Look at Walter."

Adam did and laughed out loud. Walter stood at the entrance greeting his guests and looking as though he'd like nothing better than to run for the hills.

"Yeah, well. Who can blame him? That woman acts as though she just won the grand prize, and Walter is it."

"That's probably what she thinks. Ever since Helen died, every widow and divorcée in his social set over the age of forty-five has been after him. Being the first woman he's asked out is a coup for Mrs. Cosgrove."

Beaming a smug smile, Connie Cosgrove clung to Walter's arm, barely allowing him to shake hands with his arriving guests. Her possessive attitude oozed triumph, particularly whenever any of her cronies walked in.

Adam looked around. "I wonder where Mary Alice is? I haven't seen her since we got here. She is attending, isn't she."

"I assume so. She always does. Maybe she's—Oh, my goodness."

As though their discussion had conjured her up, at that moment Mary Alice entered the ballroom—on the arm of a tall, handsome man of about sixty.

She looked stunning in a long-sleeved, ankle-length sheath of royal blue trimmed in silver. The gown showed off her slender figure and complimented her silver hair, which was swept up in an elegant chignon.

"Well, well. This ought to be interesting," Adam murmured.

Walter looked thunderstruck. By the time his secretary and her escort reached him he had recovered his composure, but his face looked as though it had been chiseled from stone.

Lauren almost laughed. Good for you, Mary Alice, she cheered silently.

With her usual grace and dignity, Mary Alice exchanged greetings and introduced her date, but she treated Walter with cool civility, and as quickly as possible she whisked her escort away to join the party.

Mary Alice was acquainted with almost everyone there, which meant that every few feet she had to stop and chat. Amused, Lauren noticed that Walter watched the pair like a hawk as they worked their way around the ballroom.

"Well, well. So you did succumb to Adam's charms, after all. Just like all the others."

"Ed!" Lauren had been so busy watching Walter watch Mary Alice that she hadn't seen him approach. "Hi. How are you this evening?"

Ed was one of those debonair men for whom formal wear had been designed. He looked stunningly handsome in his tux, but belatedly she realized that his pleasant smile didn't reach his eyes. Beneath that polished charm he exuded an aura of hostile challenge that made the hairs on Lauren's arms stand on end.

Adam shifted closer and put his arm around her waist, and she knew that he too had sensed his friend's mood.

"I was fine until I saw the two of you walk in together."

He looked Lauren up and down, and his mouth curled. "You led me to believe that you needed more time, so I played the gentleman and backed off. What an idiot I was. I should have known better than to leave the field wide open for him."

"I take it you have a problem with me seeing Lauren," Adam said quietly before she could find her tongue.

"Damn right, I have a problem with it. You think you're hot stuff, don't you? Big football hero."

Swaying slightly, Ed waved a flute of champagne in an encompassing gesture, sloshing some of the golden liquid over the rim. Lauren realized that he had already had too much to drink.

"You come waltzing in here and think you can have whatever you want. Just like when we were in college. Every girl I ever dated back then was crazy about you. All you had to do was lift your little finger and they would've been yours."

"But I never did that, did I? As I recall, you were the one who tried to steal every girl I dated."

"Tried, my ass. I got most of them. You may have been the big man on campus, but I was the one they wanted between the sheets. Everything's always so easy for you, isn't it—ole buddy?" Ed sneered. "You come out here and horn in on the business that's supposed to be mine. Our old friends welcome you as though you were some kind of friggin' hero. Now you're trying to take my woman, too."

"Let me remind you that you're the one who recommended me for this job."

Ed snorted. "The hell I did. Do I look crazy to you? That was all Walter's idea. He knew we'd been roommates in college and asked me to use my influence to get you to accept his offer. I took the credit when I realized I couldn't make him change his mind, but I never wanted you here."

They were beginning to attract attention. Lauren cast a nervous look around and saw that several people had stopped talking and were openly listening.

"Ed, stop this. You're making a scene. Walter will skin you alive."

Ignoring her, he stepped closer and jabbed Adam's chest with his forefinger. "You're not stealing Lauren out from under my nose. You got that—ole buddy?"

"Uh-uh. You knew Lauren for years before I ever met her. For the past four she's been single. As far as I'm concerned you had your chance."

"Why, you—" Ed took a threatening step forward.

"Ed! Stop it!" Lauren hissed. "Have you completely lost your mind?"

"No, I've just come to my senses. C'mon, forget about this dumb jock. Let's you and me dance."

He reached for her, but Adam blocked the move by extending his arm between them. Something dangerous and implacable flashed in his eyes. "I'm giving you just this one warning. Haven't you listened to what the lady said? She doesn't want you. Lauren is off limits to you. If I have to tell you again, that pretty face won't be quite so pretty anymore. So back off . . . ole buddy."

Ed glared, his jaw bulging. Though no match for Adam physically, for a moment Lauren was afraid he was going to start a fight.

Adam met his furious stare without so much as blinking, and after several tense seconds Ed turned on his heel and stomped off, weaving slightly as he shoved his way through the curious crowd.

"Thank heaven. I thought he was going to take a swing at you."

"There wasn't much chance of that. Ed's got a hot temper but he's not stupid."

"Should someone go after him? Try to sober him up, maybe?"

"He'll be okay once he cools down." Adam looked around at the interested onlookers and slipped his arm around her waist. "C'mon, let's dance."

"Did he really steal all your college girlfriends?" she asked as she slipped into Adam's arms and they began to move to the music.

"Quite a few of them."

"I'm surprised you remained friends. Didn't it bother you?"

"Not terribly. I wasn't in love with any of them." He looked down at her and something in his eyes made her heart give a little lurch. "Now, with you it's a whole different ball game. If he tried to steal you from me I'd have to break every bone in his body."

He made the outrageous remark in such an affable tone that Lauren chuckled, but the sound died away when she noticed the look in his eyes.

They didn't see any more of Ed that evening. Lauren assumed that he had left the ball. She only hoped that someone had either sobered him up first or they'd had the good sense to send him home in a taxi. He'd certainly been in no condition to drive.

The clash between Adam and Ed had been too brief to cause much of a stir, especially when the party-goers had a much more interesting topic to discuss.

"Mary Alice is creating quite a bit of excitement," Adam commented a couple of hours later while he and Lauren were dancing.

"Yes. No one is accustomed to seeing her with a date. Always in the past she's attended these sort of affairs solo and stayed in the background."

The reactions of the company employees who were there were almost as amusing as Walter's. People stared openly at Mary Alice and her handsome escort and speculation was rampant.

"Well, one thing about it. She's taking the heat off of us."

When the music stopped, the older couple was standing right beside Lauren and Adam, and the four of them walked off the dance floor together, talking. They had no sooner reached the sidelines when Walter came striding over. He looked as though he'd eaten something that had soured on his stomach.

"Mary Alice. You're just the person I want to see. There's some problem in the kitchen that needs handling. That damned caterer is threatening to walk out."

"Really? That's too bad. It would be a shame if your party was ruined. Perhaps you'd better have Mrs. Cosgrove speak to him. Now if you'll excuse us . . ." Smiling, she looped her arm through her date's and strolled away without a backward glance.

Walter stared after her with his mouth open. "I don't believe it. She just walked away! What the devil has gotten into that woman?"

"She *is* here as a guest, you know, Walter. It's not her responsibility to keep your party running smoothly. You really should ask Mrs. Cosgrove to handle the problem. That is a job for the hostess, after all."

"Humph. Not on your life. I'm not giving that woman any more ideas than she already has. Just because I invited her to the ball she's acting as though she's got some claim on me."

"Where is Mrs. Cosgrove, by the way?" Adam asked.

"In the ladies' room. And I hope to God she stays in there. This is the first time tonight I've been more than six inches from her. The woman's driving me batty. I should never have let you talk me into inviting her," he grumbled, scowling at Lauren.

"Me! I didn't tell you to invite Mrs. Cosgrove. I merely suggested that you ask out a lady friend. How was I to know you'd choose that leech? I had someone completely different in mind."

"Humph. Then why didn't you say so?"

Sighing, Lauren cast Adam a long-suffering look and muttered under her breath, "I thought I had."

Walter craned his neck trying to look over the crowd. "Where the devil did Mary Alice go?"

"I believe she and Mr. Tremaine are waltzing outside on the veranda," Lauren informed him gleefully. Walter's mouth tightened, and she had to fight back a laugh.

"Humph. Making a damned fool out of herself is more like it. Out there playing slap and tickle with that . . . that aging playboy. At her age she ought to know better."

"And why shouldn't she enjoy herself? She's a lovely woman. Any mature man would find her attractive. As for Mr. Tremaine, he seems very nice."

"Nice, my foot. I've seen his type before. He's a slick operator, the kind that preys on older women. He's probably out to fleece her."

"Uncle Walter! What a thing to say!"

"Oh, yeah? What do we know about this Brandon Tremaine guy? Where did he come from all of a sudden?"

"Umm, I believe he said he was an international banker." The dry amusement in Adam's voice earned him an approving look from Lauren and a glare from Walter.

"How do we know that? The man can claim to be whatever the hell he wants. Tomorrow I'm going to have him investigated."

"Walter Ingram, don't you dare!" Lauren gasped. "That's a terrible thing to do. Mary Alice would never speak to you again. And who could blame her?"

"Well, someone has to watch out for her," he grumbled. "She's been acting downright irrational lately."

"By that, I assume she's still planning to retire in a couple of weeks," Adam said wryly.

"Yes, dammit. I have no idea why. I've tried to get her to tell me, but she refuses to discuss it. Hell, she won't even talk to me except when it's absolutely necessary, and then her voice is so icy it's a wonder I don't have frostbite. I tell you, I'm seeing a whole new side of that woman's personality. I had no idea she was so mule stubborn. I'm at wits' end. I'll be dammed if I know what it'll take to get her to stay. I've tried everything. I apologized for whatever it is I'm supposed to have done. I even offered her a hefty raise in pay."

"Oh, Walter, you didn't," Lauren groaned.

"What's wrong with that?"

Thoroughly exasperated, Lauren shook her head. "You're impossible."

Two hours later, with a sigh Lauren kicked off her high heels and leaned her head back against the BMW's leather seat. "Thank goodness, that's over."

"It wasn't so bad."

"I guess. If you don't count Walter's black mood, that is. He looked like a thundercloud all evening."

"Yeah, but the art auction was a success. It raised a nice chunk of change for the Children's Cancer Foundation."

Lauren rolled her head on the seat and looked at Adam's profile. The faint glow from the dashboard cast his rough-hewn features in soft highlights and deep shadows. Her smile held a mixture of amusement and tenderness. "Thanks to you, mainly. I can't believe you opened the bidding on that awful picture at ten thousand dollars. I mean, it goes for a good cause and all, but that was the worst painting offered. That child has no artistic talent at all." The painting in question, a garish still-life in orange and purple, was currently propped up on the back seat.

"That's why I bought it. I didn't want it to be the only one that didn't sell, or for it to go for some insultingly low bid. The kid that painted it has enough to bring him down without that."

The statement turned Lauren's insides to warm mush. The gesture was typical of this man. Adam was big and tough and almost frighteningly strong, but she was beginning to learn that beneath that physically imposing exterior was a soft heart.

At first she had chalked up the attraction between them as

being merely physical, but it went much deeper than that, Lauren realized. He embodied everything she had ever wanted in a man. Sex with Adam was wonderful and deeply satisfying, but just as important, she loved simply being with him.

Women and men alike respected him. He was patient and intelligent and tender. And, at times, funny. In the past six weeks he had managed to make her smile more than she had in over three years. With Adam she could actually go several hours without thinking of her son.

"Out of curiosity, now that you've bought the thing, what are you going to do with it?"

"I don't know. Hang it in my bedroom, maybe. That way it will be a constant reminder of all those little kids with no hair and listless eyes. When you think about what they're going through it sort of puts your own problems in perspective."

"That's true," Lauren replied softly, smiling into the darkness.

Adam was the most thoughtful, caring man she had ever met. He was so patient with her and so understanding. Since the attack she had not gone to the point as much, but now and then, when sorrow overtook her and she needed solitude, he walked with her to the point and waited on his deck until she came down.

She had never had a relationship like the one she had with Adam. It was wonderful, and not just because their sex life was fantastic. They were so completely attuned and compatible. At times she felt as though she had known him forever.

"I'm glad you bought—Oh, my God!"

Lauren bolted up in the seat and stared at the black van driving a half car length ahead of them in the next lane.

"What? What's wrong?"

"It's him!"

"Who?"

"Gavin! That's my ex-husband driving that van!"

Adam's shoulders slumped. "Ah, hell, sweetheart. Not this again."

"It's him, I'm telling you!"

"Honey, listen to me—"

"No. That's him! I'm positive, this time!"

He sighed. "Okay, I believe you. Just calm down, okay?"

"Adam, hurry! He's pulling away. We're going to lose him!"

"All right, all right. Take it easy." As Adam speeded up, the van made a right turn onto a freeway access street.

"Oh, no. He's going to get away!"

Cursing, Adam whipped over into the right-hand lane to follow, cutting in front of another driver and earning himself a horn blast and an obscene gesture. By the time he'd made the turn onto the access road, the van had merged into the freeway traffic and was speeding away.

Lauren bounced on the seat. "Hurry! Hurry! Don't let him get away!"

"Hold on. And get out a pen and paper so you can write down his license number."

"Oh! That's a good idea!"

While Adam floorboarded the car she searched through her purse but the tiny evening bag held only a lipstick and compact and a twenty-dollar bill. Frantic, she popped open the glove compartment and pawed through the contents, spilling half of them onto the floorboard. "Here! I found a pen! And an envelope!"

"Good. He's just ahead. I'm going to pull in close."

Lauren sat forward, her gaze fixed on the rear of the van. When they pulled in close enough behind the vehicle she scribbled down the number.

"Got it?"

"Yes! I—What are you *doing?*" She turned in the seat and stared at him. "For God's sake! Don't slow down now! You're letting him get away! Speed up! Speed up!"

Instead of following her command, Adam took the next

exit off the freeway. "Are you crazy! Oh, no! No! Now we've really lost him! I thought you were on my side. How could you *do* this to me?" Lauren wailed. "How *could* you?"

Adam turned into a strip-center parking lot on the corner and brought the car to a halt. "Lauren, listen to me. We're going to turn this license number over to your investigator and let him check this guy out."

"But we could have caught up with him ourselves!"

"And if it turns out he's not your ex? Like all the other times you were so sure you'd spotted him? Sweetheart, you keep setting yourself up for disappointment, and it's painful to watch."

"I'm right this time. That was Gavin. I know it was Gavin."

"All right. For the sake of argument let's say we had caught up with the guy and it turned out he was your ex. Then what? If he has your son and he knows you're on to him, he'll take off again. If that happens you may never find him again. Is that what you want?"

She gazed at him across the dim interior of the car. Her face worked with conflicting emotions and there was torment in her eyes. Finally she slumped back against the seat with a sigh. "You're right. But it's just so hard. We were so close."

"I know. I know. Come here." He unfastened her seat belt and drew her into his arms. She went willingly and with a little cry she sagged against him and snuggled her face against his massive chest. He could feel the heavy beat of her heart and the tremors that vibrated through her. He cradled the back of her head with one hand and stared out into the night, his expression pained.

"Trust me, sweetheart, it's smarter to let your detective check the guy out. If it's him, you'll know soon enough."

"It's him," she mumbled against his shirt. "You'll see. That was Gavin. I know it was."

Fifteen

Lauren placed a call to Sam Ewing before seven the next morning. From her end of the conversation and the mumbling coming through the receiver, Adam was fairly certain she had woken the guy.

The detective wasn't pleased, but he had no idea how lucky he was. Though it had been almost two in the morning when they returned from the Hope Ball, it had taken a lot of persuasion on Adam's part to stop her from calling Mr. Ewing then.

After taking down the information about the guy they had spotted, he promised to get back to her as soon as he had anything to report. He warned her that he might not be able to trace the license number right away, since it was Sunday. It would depend on whether any of his buddies were on duty down at the precinct, but he'd see what he could do.

Nevertheless, Lauren prowled the house all morning, waiting to hear back from Sam.

The only call they received came around noon, and it wasn't Sam Ewing, but Tony.

"Kate's gone into labor. We're on our way to the hospital now. Can you and Lauren meet us there?"

"You bet. We'll be right there."

Over the past few weeks Lauren and Kate had grown close. She had been thrilled and flattered when Kate had requested that she and Adam be there for the birth. When Adam told

Lauren what was happening, she tossed her cellular phone into her purse, and within minutes they were on their way.

It was after midnight when Lauren and Adam returned to the beach house, exhausted but happy. After putting his mother through more than twelve hours of labor, Ryan Roberto Diamatto, a strapping eight-and-a-half-pounder, had made his entrance into the world at eleven-eighteen.

"Tired?" Adam asked, massaging Lauren's shoulders while she sat at her dressing table, brushing her hair.

"Mmm. But it's a pleasant tired. There's nothing more wonderful than the birth of a baby."

"Yeah," he agreed in a reflective voice. "That was really great."

In the mirror Lauren watched Adam shuck out of his clothes. Stark naked, and not in the least self-conscious, he stretched and arched his back before climbing into bed. A fluttery sensation tightened Lauren's chest. Lord, he was so beautifully male. She couldn't remember any man affecting her the way Adam did.

"All in all, it was an emotional day. But then, I learned years ago, growing up next door to them, that anytime you get that family together things get emotional."

Lauren chuckled. "I can imagine."

Throughout the day she had met several members of the Diamatto family. Tony's widowed mother, Rosa, who had a condo in the Bay Area, had come straight from church, bubbling over with excitement and happy tears. Two of Tony's sisters, Carmen, who lived in Fremont, and Sophia, who had driven up from Los Angeles with her husband, Angelo Scarpeze, arrived later in the day. The other two sisters, Gina and Marlo, had called from their homes in Houston several times.

Around eight that evening, Adam's parents had shown up. Their arrival set off a flurry of emotions as Tony's mother and sisters greeted their old neighbors and lifelong friends with hugs and laughter and tears.

Under normal circumstances Lauren would have been nervous about meeting Joseph and Faye Rafferty, but she had been too caught up in the excitement and anticipation of the occasion to experience more than a fleeting uneasiness.

Now, hours later, as she stripped out of her clothes and pulled her nightgown over her head, she recalled the meeting with a smile.

"So, this is Lauren." Faye had taken both of her hands and studied her with a warm smile. "My, my, aren't you a beauty."

Lauren blushed scarlet at the unexpected compliment. "Why, thank you. It's a pleasure to meet you, Mrs. Rafferty."

"We're glad to meet you, too, my dear. Adam has told us so much about you."

"Really?" When? she wondered. Except when they'd been at the office, Adam had hardly let her out of his sight for the past two months.

She shot him a look, and his mouth twisted ruefully. "I call them from work. I've mentioned you a few times."

"A *few* times!" Joseph Rafferty hooted. "Why, son, she's practically all you talk about."

Lauren turned out the bedside light and slipped into bed. Settling her head on Adam's shoulder she smiled into the darkness, recalling how Joseph had elbowed his son and added with a wink, "And who can blame you."

As she did every Monday, the next morning Lauren placed a call to Sam Ewing before leaving for work, but he was not in his office and his secretary had not heard from him.

"He's probably down at the DMV checking out that license number," Adam suggested, but Lauren's anxiety did not ease one whit. On the drive to the office she was wound as tight as an eight-day clock.

When she and Adam parted company outside her office door she insisted she was fine, but he was concerned about her. He knew that Lauren's method of dealing with stress was to bury herself in her work, but she looked so pale and on edge he hated to see her drive herself.

Adam was still thinking of her when he entered his office and didn't notice Ed standing by the windows at first—not until he turned with a sheepish expression.

Adam pulled up short and narrowed his eyes. "Ed. What're you doing here?"

"Adam . . . I . . ." Ed stopped and grimaced. "Look man, I came to tell you I'm sorry about Saturday night. Honest to God, I am. You know what I'm like when I drink too much. I always pop off with garbage I don't mean."

Adam remained silent and waited, his face impassive. He had to admit, Ed was a mean drunk. Back in college whenever he'd had too many beers he had subjected everyone around him to vicious verbal abuse. Adam and Tony had overlooked his tirades because the next morning he had always been sorry. A lot of times he hadn't even remembered what he'd said.

However, the bitter attack at the Hope Ball had seemed to spring from a deep well of resentment that had been festering for years. Adam wondered just how much of Ed's true feelings the tirade had revealed.

Ed shifted uneasily under Adam's steady regard. "Look, I know it's no excuse, but I had just butted heads with Walter. I tried to convince him to sell me my uncle's shares in the company, but he turned me down flat without even hearing me out."

Muttering a string of curses, Ed paced the width of the office, angrily jingling the change in his pockets. "The old bastard. He's doing this to infuriate me. He's never liked me. Not since I was a kid. He won't even let me buy the shares that should have been mine in the first place. You can imagine how that made me feel when he refused."

"I'd say you made that clear." For a moment, Adam considered telling Ed about his deal with Walter, but he thought better of it. Better to let him cool down first.

"But it wasn't you, Adam. It had nothing to do with you. I was just lashing out and you were handy. It wasn't personal."

"What about Lauren?"

Ed had the grace to look embarrassed. "All right, maybe I was a little jealous. But you can understand that, can't you? Hell, I've wanted her for years, even before her husband dumped her. I thought maybe I finally had a chance. Then you came waltzing in with her. Coming right after my argument with Walter, that really lit my fuse.

"But once I sobered up I realized you were right. I had my chance and I flubbed it. I don't have anyone to blame but myself. I swear to you, Adam, if I hadn't already been so angry I never would have said anything. You gotta believe that. I didn't mean any of it. Not a word. Hell, we've been good friends for too many years to let my drunken rantings come between us."

With an imploring look, Ed stepped forward and stuck his hand out. "Whaddaya say, Adam? Still friends?"

Adam hesitated, but only for a moment. "What the hell." He clasped Ed's outstretched hand. "I never could stay mad at you for long, anyway."

"Thanks man." Tightening his grip, Ed pulled Adam into a bear hug and the two exchanged slaps on the back.

That evening Sam Ewing called to say he'd run a make on the license and he planned to check it out the following day. "But look, I don't know how long this'll take. You never know, the guy might be out of town. Anything can happen. So don't panic if you don't hear from me, okay? Just relax, and I'll get back to you when I've got something concrete. And remember, this may turn out to be just another dead end. Don't go getting your hopes up too high."

The advice was sound, but hope was all Lauren had and relaxing was not an option. Victor Spalding's trial began the next day and she and Adam had to testify.

Recounting the attack was painful for her, particularly the cross-examination by the defense attorney, which was riddled with innuendos that she was somehow the guilty party. Throughout her testimony the defendant tried to intimidate her with leering looks. Determined not to be his victim again, Lauren ignored him as best she could. By the time she finished she was shaking inside, but she left the stand with her head high.

That afternoon after the lunch break Adam gave his testimony and afterward the judge dismissed them for the day. The investigating officers were slated to take the stand next, but when the trial resumed the following morning the defendant changed his plea to guilty. After a short break to deliberate, the judge sentenced him to twenty years in prison.

Lauren felt as though a weight had been lifted from her shoulders—until it occurred to her that now that Victor Spalding was in prison, there was no longer any reason for Adam to stay at her place.

On the drive home she kept expecting him to bring up the subject. The thought of him moving back to his own house depressed her. She was comfortable with Adam. She had grown used to him being there, to seeing his clothes in her closet, his shaving gear on the bathroom counter next to her talc and bath oil. She loved sleeping in his arms, having his solid warmth next to her all night.

And of course, there was their lovemaking. Until Adam, she had never known pleasure that intense, or that sex could be so deeply satisfying.

It was funny, really. She had bought the beach house and moved there for solitude, but now the thought of living there alone depressed her. The house would not seem right without Adam in it.

Lauren was braced for the worst, but when they arrived home he behaved as he always had and made a beeline for the bedroom to get out of his suit and tie and slip on a pair of worn jeans and a sweatshirt. When he noticed her watching him he grinned and gave her bottom a pat as he passed by on his way to the kitchen. There he took a soft drink from the refrigerator before settling down in the living room to read the newspaper.

Lauren tried to relax and dismiss the matter from her mind, but she couldn't. She fidgeted and prowled the living room, unable to settled. After a while, as much as she dreaded the possibility of him leaving, she couldn't take the uncertainty any longer. She had to know.

"You do realize that now that Victor Spalding is in prison, you don't have to stay here any longer," she blurted out.

Adam lowered one corner of the newspaper and looked at her over the top. "I never *had* to stay here."

"I know that. But . . . Oh, you know what I mean!" She twisted her hands together. "Protecting me was the main reason you stayed."

"Yes, that was part of it. But we both know that wasn't the only reason." Adam put down the paper and rose. He came toward Lauren with a slow, purposeful stride that sent a little flutter through her. Stopping in front of her, he cocked his head to one side and studied her for several seconds. "Why don't we cut to the chase here. Do you want me to go, Lauren?"

"I . . ."

"Do you?"

His hazel eyes drilled into her, demanding a reply. Lauren could barely breathe. She licked her lips. "Do . . . do you want to stay?"

Something flashed in Adam's eyes, something that looked very much like relief. He tipped his head back, and a low, sexy laugh rumbled from his throat. When his gaze met hers again his eyes glowed with sensual heat, but they were crinkled at the corners. "What do you think? Honey, even if that creep had been killed weeks ago resisting arrest I would still have come up with an excuse to stay. The truth is, I'm in love with you and I don't want to leave you. Ever."

Lauren's knees went weak. With a sigh, she sagged forward and put her arms around his waist. As he enfolded her in his embrace she rested her head against his chest and closed her eyes. "And I don't want you to go," she whispered. "Ever."

The next morning, Lauren, Adam and Ed were in conference with Walter in his office when his telephone rang three times without letup.

"Dammit, didn't you tell that girl at your desk to hold my calls?" Walter barked at Mary Alice. "She's certainly not a candidate for your job if she can't follow simple orders."

"Her name is Deborah Moore, as you very well know. She's going to be your secretary in a few weeks. You really should start addressing her properly." Mary Alice reached across the desk for the receiver. "And you're being much too hard on her. The call is on the interoffice line. I may have neglected to tell her to intercept those, as well as the incoming calls."

"Humph. She should have known without being told," he grumbled as Mary Alice spoke softly into the receiver.

"Just one moment." She put her hand over the mouthpiece and looked at Lauren. "This is Nan. The detective you hired is in your office. He wants to see you right away."

"Sam? Oh, my God! He must have found Gavin!" Lauren bolted to her feet, sending the file in her lap tumbling to the floor. She was so excited she couldn't think. For a few seconds she stared at the papers scattered over the carpet, unable to fathom how they'd gotten there. Then she looked around and wrung her hands. "I . . . I have to go. He . . . oh, God!"

"Sit down, child. And for God's sake, get a grip on yourself and stop that dithering."

"I . . . I'm sorry about the meeting, Walter, but this can't wait. I have to talk to Sam. In all the time he's been on this case he's never come to the office before. He wouldn't have this time if he didn't have big news."

"For heaven's sake, child, I know that. But if he's got something important to report, then I damned well want to hear it, too. Mary Alice, tell Nan to bring Mr. Ewing to my office."

"Take it easy, sweetheart," Adam murmured. He took Lauren's hand and gave it an encouraging pat as she sank back down onto her chair.

"Lauren, if this detective has found your ex-husband, you should take your attorney with you when you confront him," Ed advised.

"Good idea," Walter agreed.

"I'd go with you myself, but my expertise is in corporate law. You need someone who handles divorce and custody cases."

"I . . . I don't know who I'd get. The attorney who handled my divorce passed away a few months ago."

"Tony's specialty is family practice. He'll help you."

"Good idea, Adam. From what I hear, he's damned good," Ed concurred.

There was a tap on the door, and Lauren's heart skipped a beat as Nan ushered the detective into the office. Sam's gaze swept the room, then zeroed in on Lauren. Her grip on Adam's hand tightened.

"Is there someplace where we can talk in private, Ms. McKenna?"

"It's all right, Sam. You can speak freely in front of my friends."

Sam shrugged. "You're the boss."

The detective wasted no time getting down to business. Once the introductions were made he took the seat offered him and directed his attention to Lauren. "I'm fairly certain that the man you and Mr. Rafferty saw the other night is your ex-husband. He resembles the picture of Mr. Stone that you gave me. The only trouble is your ex was clean-shaven and the suspect has a full beard, so it's difficult to tell for certain without knowing him."

"Oh, I knew it was Gavin," Lauren exclaimed. "I *knew* it!"

"Everything fits," Sam went on. "This guy is an accountant, the same as your ex, and he and his wife have lived at that address for a little over three years—the same amount of time that your son has been missing. Also, you'll notice that his initials are the same—Gavin Stone, Gary Smith. That's a common mistake that a lot of people on the run make.

"I took several surveillance photos. Take a look at these and see if you recognize the guy."

Lauren's hands shook as she accepted the photos. The black and white pictures had been taken with a telescopic lens. The first was of a man dressed in a business suit and carrying a briefcase. It had captured him getting out of a car in the driveway of a two-story, Tudor-style home in an upper-middle-class neighborhood. In the next one he was picking up a newspaper from the yard, in the next, waving at a neighbor.

"That's Gavin," Lauren said in a taut voice.

"You're sure?"

"Yes." He was perhaps fifteen or twenty pounds heavier and a full beard covered the lower half of his face, but the man was definitely her ex-husband.

"Let me have a look at those," Walter said, and Lauren passed them across the desk to him. "Yep. That's Gavin, all right. He's gotten a little porky, but I'd recognize that profile anywhere. Always had that squint around his eyes."

"Well, I'll be damned." Sam sat back in his chair and scratched his head. "After looking for this guy for almost three years, all along he was right down the road in San Jose. Practically right under our noses. Damn clever of him."

Lauren looked at the next picture. It had been taken in the open doorway of the house. It was of Gavin kissing a woman. Lauren assumed this was his new wife, the woman for whom he had left her. She stared at the picture, taken aback.

Leaning over her shoulder, Adam looked at the photo, and Lauren felt his surprise. "She's in a wheelchair."

"Yeah. She's paralyzed from the waist down. I did some snooping around among the neighbors. They were told she had been injured in an auto accident about eighteen months before the Smiths moved to San Jose. Apparently, Mr. Smith had been driving."

Lauren looked up. That would have been four and a half years ago—around the time when Gavin was pressuring her so hard for a divorce.

She looked at the picture again. So this was why he'd been so furious when the judge had delayed the final decree until after David's birth. Lauren had known there was another woman. She had thought that maybe he had gotten his lover pregnant as well. It had never occurred to her that the woman had been injured. Or that Gavin might have felt responsible.

That he loved the woman was obvious. Even in the harsh black and white photos the adoration in his eyes when he looked at her was plain.

One corner of Lauren's mouth twitched. If she knew Gavin, his wife's infirmity had probably made him love her all the more. Gavin was a man who desperately needed to be needed. The more dependent a woman was, the more attractive he found her.

Lauren passed the last picture to Walter without comment and looked at the detective. "Thank you, Sam. Now, if you'll give me the address, I'll handle things from here."

"Uh, there is one more thing you should know."

"Yes?"

"The Smiths have a son. According to the neighbors, he's four years old."

Adam eased the BMW to a halt across the street from the two-story Tudor-style house. "That's it."

In the back, Tony propped his forearms along the top of the front seat and leaned forward. "Now remember, Lauren, at this point we're just trying to verify that this guy really is Gavin. If he is, we'll go have a conversation with him."

"A conversation? That can be handled very quickly. He has my son. I want him back. Now."

"Now, Lauren, just because they have a little boy, that doesn't mean he's your son. They could have had a child of their own. Or they could have adopted a child. Until we know, we can't start making accusations."

"The child could also be my son."

Tony exhaled slowly. "Yes, that is a possibility. When we confront Gavin, let me do the talking. If you do say anything, for God's sake, keep it civil if you can. If things escalate into a battle, it will just make this whole thing that much more difficult. Got it?"

"I understand."

"I don't see any movement over there," Adam said. "No, wait a second. Here he comes."

As they watched, Gavin came out of the house and went into the garage.

"Is that him?" Tony asked.

Lauren stared at him and clenched her jaw. "Yes. That's Gavin."

The man backed a late-model Plymouth minivan out of the garage and into the street, coming within inches of their car. He glanced their way, and Lauren jerked back, but the tinted windows prevented him from seeing inside. She, however, got an excellent look at the man behind the wheel.

"What's next, Tony?" Adam asked.

"We can either follow Mr. Smith to work and talk to him there, or come back this evening and confront him and his wife together. I'd prefer to face them both at once."

"Okay." Adam reached for the ignition key, but Lauren grabbed his forearm.

"No, wait! Look!" She stared, her heart pumping like a wild thing in her chest. A little boy came down the front steps, lugging a toy firetruck almost as big as he was.

"David," Lauren whispered. Then louder, "Oh, God, that's David. That's my baby!"

"Are you su—Wait! Lauren, come back here!"

"Lauren, don't!" Adam added his yell to Tony's and made a grab for her, but all he caught was a handful of air. Lauren did not even know he tried to stop her. She was oblivious to everything but the child.

It hadn't been a conscious decision. As her hungry gaze devoured the boy, her hand had simply reached for the door handle of its own accord. The next instant she was out of the car and running across the street toward the child, who was making engine noises and pushing his firetruck down the sidewalk.

"David." The child looked up as she dropped to her knees beside him. Lauren's breath caught as a sweet pain squeezed her chest. She was looking into wide, wary eyes, the same crystal pale green eyes that she saw in the mirror everyday.

His resemblance to her was stunning. From his auburn curls to the wide mouth and straight nose and prominent cheekbones, his face was an endearingly young, masculine version of her own face.

Her son. This was her baby. "Oh, David," she quavered as tears welled in her eyes. "David."

With a trembling hand, she reached out and touched his cheek.

He drew back and scowled. "My name ith Keith," he announced truculently with a slight lisp. He darted a look around her at the two men running toward them, and his wary expression turned to fright.

"Mommy!" he yelled over his shoulder and scooted backwards.

"No, wait! Don't go. I'm your mommy, David."

"Mommy! Mommy! Mommy!"

"No, sweetheart, listen to me." She grabbed his arm to stop him, and he let loose with an ear-piercing scream and fought to pull away, bucking and kicking. "No, David, calm down. Please, sweetheart, don't do that! I'm not going to hurt you, darling."

"Stop that! Get away from my son!"

Adam and Tony skidded to a stop beside her. At the same time Lauren looked up and saw the woman in the pictures zooming down the sidewalk in her wheelchair. "You let go of my son! I've called the police and my husband. They're on their way here now, so if you know what's good for you you'd better let him go!"

Instinctively, Lauren jerked the boy to her and wrapped her arms around him, ignoring his struggles. She glared at the woman. "He's not your son. He's mine!"

"Lauren, for God's sake, what're you doing? Let the boy go."

"No. He's mine."

"Listen to Adam, Lauren," Tony urged in a kind voice. "This isn't the way to handle the situation. Honey, you're just making this harder."

Each taking an arm, the two men lifted her to her feet, but she held on tight to the boy. Sobbing and straining against Lauren, he twisted within her grasp and held his arms out to the other woman. *"Mommieee! Mommieee!"*

The woman rammed the wheelchair into Lauren, wrapped her arms around the boy's legs and held on. Lauren cried out at the sharp pain in her shins and staggered backwards. She would have toppled if Adam and Tony had not been holding her arms.

"Let him go! You can't take my son. I won't let you take my son!"

"*Your* son? I'm his mother. Look at me and look at him. Anyone can see that he's mine!"

The woman gasped, and for an instant she looked shocked, but at once she renewed her efforts to pry the boy from Lauren. "I don't care! You can't have him back. He belongs to us now. Let *go!*"

"Ladies. Ladies. Calm down. Let's discuss this rationally," Adam urged. He might as well have spoken to the wind.

The boy's piercing screams and the raised voices of the women brought several neighbors out of their houses. When they saw the struggle some of them came running.

"Hey! What's going on here?"

"What're you doing to that boy?"

"Annette, are they trying to take Keith?"

Tony turned, lifting his hands in a placating gesture. "Don't worry, ladies. No one's going to harm the boy. Just take it easy, and we'll get this straightened out."

At that moment a police car carrying two officers screeched to a halt at the curb. Gavin's minivan pulled up right behind them. He jumped out and tore across the lawn to join the melee before the officers could climb from the squad car.

"Get away from my son! Dammit, let him go!"

Adam stepped between Lauren and her ex. "Stay away from her. Touch Lauren, and I'll break you in half. You've hurt her enough already, you bastard."

"Lauren?" Gavin's eyes widened. He tried to bulldoze his way past Adam. "Lauren! Damn you, you're not taking my son!"

"All right, all right! Break it up!" the officers yelled, pushing their way between the combatants. "Get back. Get *back!* All of you! *Now!*"

It took a while, but finally the officers had the group divided into two camps. Lauren stubbornly clutched the boy, whose screams made communication next to impossible, and glared at her ex-husband over his head. Gavin snarled threats at her and one of the officers had to keep a hand splayed on his chest to hold him back.

"All right, what's this about?" the younger of the policemen shouted over David's wails.

Gavin's wife pointed an accusing finger at Lauren. "That woman came into our yard and tried to steal our son."

"I wasn't stealing him. He's my son!"

"She didn't want him, officer. She gave him up to my husband voluntarily three years ago. Now she's changed her mind and is trying to take him back. You've got to stop her."

"Is that what he told you? It's a lie! I never gave him up!" Lauren looked at Gavin. "You stole him from me. You sneaked into my home and took him out of his bed while he was sleeping. For three years I've had no idea where he was, or even if he was alive. I've been looking for him all this time. How could you do that, Gavin? How could you take my baby from me?"

"I have as much right to him as you! I'm his father."

The woman in the wheelchair stared at her husband with horror. "Oh my, God. It's true. You took Keith without her consent!"

Gavin's jaw took on a mulish set. "I didn't need her consent. He's my son, too."

"Oh, Gary."

"Gary?" Lauren made a disparaging sound. "He lied to you about that, too. His name is Gavin. Gavin Stone. And my son's name is David, not Keith."

"I know that. We changed our names to keep you from finding us." The woman in the wheelchair looked at her husband as if seeking his agreement.

"Annette, don't say anything else until we talk to our attorney." Gary put a hand on her shoulder.

"Oh, Gary. How could you do such a horrible thing? You said she didn't want him. That she had decided motherhood wasn't for her. But you lied. You stole him away from his mother. How could you?"

Gavin dropped down beside the wheelchair and took his wife's hands. "Annette, sweetheart, don't you understand? I did it for you. You wanted a child so much and you couldn't have one. I couldn't stand seeing you pining that way, so I gave you a child. My own son. Lauren can have more children, but Keith is the only child that we will ever have."

"But . . . you *stole* him from her, Gary. Can't you see how wrong that was?"

Gavin stood, his face obdurate again. "It's perfectly legal. I'm his father and I have custody."

"Partial custody," Lauren asserted. "And you know you only sued for that to spite me. You didn't even want him." Lauren looked at the other woman. "Did he also tell you that before my son was born he tried to force me to have an abortion."

"*Gary!*"

"Don't listen to her. She'll say anything to get her hands on Keith."

"It's true, and you know it!" Lauren charged.

"Officer, I demand that you return my son to me and throw this woman off my property."

Lauren's hold on the boy tightened. "You're not taking my baby from me again, Gavin Stone."

"The hell I'm not!"

"Back off!" Adam growled, when Gary reached for the boy.

Everyone started yelling at once. The renewed hostilities sent the boy's wails up another ten decibels.

"All right! That's it!" one of the officers bellowed. "Maybe some judge can sort this out. I sure as hell can't. In the meantime, you're all gonna take a ride down to the station house."

Sixteen

"Shouldn't the judge have reached a decision by now?"
Pacing the wide hallway, Lauren cast an agonized look at
the clock above the double doors leading into the courtroom.
"It's been over an hour. It can't be a good sign that it's taking
so long."

Adam looked to Tony for an answer, and he didn't like
what he saw in his friend's eyes.

Uneasiness squeezed Adam's chest. Lauren had voiced
what was on all their minds. Her right to her child seemed
obvious and indisputable. It should have taken the judge only
a few minutes to rule in her favor.

"Not necessarily," Tony said, trying to reassure her. "We
could simply be dealing with a cautious judge."

Adam watched Lauren pace, more concerned about her
than he dared let on. Her movements were jerky and agitated,
her eyes haunted. The drawn look on her face tore at his
heart. She looked as though she were about to fall apart.

It was no wonder. So far, this had been a hellacious day,
and it wasn't over.

Their arrival at the police station had been chaos, with
everyone shouting at everyone else, Tony wrangling with the
Smiths' attorney, who arrived minutes after they had, and the
child screaming and crying. To make things worse, a reporter
had recognized Adam and started poking a microphone in
their faces and firing questions.

Because the case involved a minor, an emergency court hearing had been convened to come up with a temporary solution. David had been turned over to a social worker until after the hearing. The situation had been excruciating for Lauren. Now that she'd finally found her son, she didn't want to let him out of her sight, and she had become almost hysterical when the police had pried him out of her arms.

News of the incident and Adam's involvement in it had spread fast. By the time the emergency hearing convened, a pack of howling journalists had followed them into the courtroom.

Judge Judith Haloran had not been pleased. Immediately she had banned the press—not just from her courtroom but the entire floor—and threatened the participants in the hearing with jail time if they didn't stop arguing long enough for her to hear the case.

At the other end of the hall Gavin and his wife and their attorney got off the elevator. Lauren halted and watched them, her hands clenching and unclenching at her sides. She was about to march down there and confront Gavin when the bailiff stuck his head out of the door and announced to both groups that the judge was ready to see them.

Inside the courtroom Lauren sat between Adam and Tony at the plaintiff's table. While they waited for the judge to begin, Lauren clutched Adam's hand so tight her fingernails dug into his flesh. He could feel her shaking all over.

The Smiths and their attorney sat at the table across the aisle, their anxious gazes fixed on Judge Haloran.

"On the surface this case appears simple," she began. "However, there are complicating factors that must be considered."

Lauren made a restive movement, and Adam squeezed her hand tighter.

Judge Haloran turned a stern look on Gavin. "Mr. Smith, as an officer of the court and as a mother, I find your actions in taking the child from Ms. McKenna both cruel and reprehensible. However, since you shared custody, technically you did not commit a crime though it was a terrible violation of the terms of custody. Therefore, no charges will be brought against you.

"Both parents are now seeking permanent custody. Before I make that decision I am ordering that you both undergo a custody fitness study, which will be done by a court appointed psychologist. The process should take three to four weeks. During that time, the child will remain in the care of Mr. and Mrs. Smith."

Lauren gave a stifled cry and Tony jumped to his feet.

"Your Honor! That's not fair to my client. Ms. McKenna has already been apart from her son for over three years because of that man's actions. Now you're letting him keep the boy?"

"Temporarily, yes. I am well aware that your client has been terribly wronged, Mr. Diamatto, and believe me, my heart goes out to her. However, this court's top priority must be to do what is best for the child.

"I've talked to the boy. I cannot ignore the fact that he is being well cared for by the Smiths and appears to be happy with them. As far as he knows, they are his parents, and he loves them. And I believe that they love him. To remove him from their care before a final decision is made would cause unnecessary trauma to the child."

Across the aisle Gavin and his wife were jubilant, but the judge quickly squelched their euphoria. "Understand this, Mr. Smith. Ms. McKenna will be allowed to visit the child three times a week. For a period of two hours at a time during the weekday visits, and five on Sundays, until the court reaches a decision in this case.

"And let me emphasize that under no circumstances are either you or your wife to do or say anything to alienate that child from his mother. Do I make myself clear?"

"But Your Honor!" Gavin's attorney protested. "If Ms.

McKenna is allowed to see the child she might take off with him."

The judge moved her glasses down her nose and looked at him over the top. "That's rather a case of the pot calling the kettle black, isn't it, Mr. Nelson? Don't worry, the visits will be court supervised.

"But while we're on the subject of running, let me warn your client that if he tries to abscond with this child again he will be in serious trouble." Pointing her gavel at Gavin, she pinned him with a warning glare. "I'm not bluffing, Mr. Smith. Do I make myself clear?"

"Yes, Your Honor."

"Your Honor—"

"I've made my ruling, Mr. Diamatto. Your client will just have to live with it." Judge Haloran banged her gavel. "This hearing is over."

Adam emerged from the bathroom expecting to find Lauren in bed. Instead she stood on the deck outside the bedroom, with her back to the French doors.

The judge's ruling had been a blow. Lauren's stunned reaction had been heartrending and painful to witness. Until today, he doubted it had ever occurred to her that she might not get her son back, once she'd found him.

She realized it now, though, and she was terrified.

And the hell of it was, there wasn't a damned thing he could do to help her.

On the drive home she had been quiet. Too quiet. Several times he had tried to get her to talk, but she had sat with her arms tightly crossed, as though physically holding all the pain inside, and stared straight ahead. By the time they had arrived she had been emotionally drained and drooping with fatigue and depression. The moment they walked in the door she announced that she was going to take a warm bath and disappeared into the bathroom.

Worry gnawed at Adam as he watched her. She was barefoot and wearing a long ice blue nightgown that skimmed her body in a whisper of silk. The delicate garment and her auburn hair fluttered and lifted in the gentle breeze off the ocean. She stood with her arms crossed over her midriff and absently rubbed her elbows, gazing out at the waves washing onto the shore.

Watching her, Adam walked to the open doors, rubbing his wet hair with a towel. "Do you want me to cook an omelette? You haven't eaten since lunch."

"No, thank you. I'm not hungry. You go ahead if you want."

Her pleasant tone didn't fool him. He knew her too well for that. When he thought about it, it amazed him that they had met just a little over two months ago. The way he felt, it could just as easily have been two years, because he loved her, completely, irrevocably.

Since they had been together he had learned that Lauren was a strong, courageous, intelligent and spirited woman. He had seen her angry, loving, terrified, sad, hopeful, despairing. About the only way he hadn't seen her was joyous and carefree. By now, he could read her moods as well as his own, and he knew that she had reached a low ebb.

Wearing only a towel knotted around his hips, he stepped through the French doors and crossed the deck to stand behind her. Cupping the rounded curve of her shoulders, he kneaded gently.

He had been worried that she might pull away and freeze him out, but she leaned back against him. He rubbed his chin against her crown. The clean fragrance of her hair filled his nostrils like subtle perfume. Fine strands caught on the stubble along his jaw, and like slippery silk, they slid back and forth with each nuzzling movement.

"I'm so sorry, sweetheart," he murmured. Curving his arms around her waist, he crossed them over her midriff.

Lauren rested her arms atop his and leaned her head back

against his chest. Absently, her nails raked his forearms as her fingers threaded through the dusting of hair that covered them. "Oh, Adam, how could this be happening?"

The fear and pain in the forlorn question tore at his heart like sharp talons. "I don't know, sweetheart. I don't know."

"I . . . I thought I would be bringing my son home tonight, at last. Instead, I may lose him forever."

"Don't start thinking that way, darling. I don't want you to give up hope. You haven't lost him yet."

"But I may. There's that custody fitness thing." Making an anguished sound, she looked up at the night sky, and Adam knew she was fighting back tears. "I haven't done anything wrong, yet I have to prove that I'm fit to raise my own child."

"You're a wonderful woman and a terrific, loving mother. You don't have a thing to worry about."

"I've been thinking about that. Financially, I'm better off, but Gavin's wife doesn't work outside the home. She would be a full-time mother to David." She gave a bitter little half laugh. "As she has been all these years. I, on the other hand, would have to put him in daycare or hire a nanny, and while there's nothing wrong with that, it's far from ideal. The judge may be swayed by that. I imagine she would prefer that he have his mother's full-time care and supervision. To be perfectly honest, *I* would prefer that myself, but staying home with David is just not an option for me.

"And then there's the fact that he's been with Gavin and Annette for over three years. He doesn't remember me at all." She sniffed and dabbed at her eyes with her fingertips. "From the way he reacted today, he doesn't even like me."

"Hey, hey. Don't do this to yourself. He's just a little guy. He didn't know what was going on and he was confused and scared. That's all. It won't take him long to get used to you again. Look at the way Paulo and Molly have taken to you. Give him time. Within a couple of visits I'll bet he'll be crazy about you."

It was a prediction that Adam desperately hoped would

come true. He had an uneasy feeling about it though. The boy's reaction to Lauren had been so extreme he had a suspicion that the Smiths—or Stones, or whatever the hell their legal name was—had been afraid of Lauren tracking them down and had warned the boy all of his life about a strange lady trying to steal him away from his mommy and daddy. If that seed had been planted, the boy might never accept Lauren completely.

Adam would have given everything he owned to put her mind at ease, but there was nothing he could do, except to be there for support and offer a shoulder to cry on when she needed it. Feeling frustrated and helpless, he held her close and rocked her within his embrace as he stared over her head at the shimmering ocean and star-studded sky.

Abruptly, Lauren turned within his embrace and locked her arms around his middle, burying her face against his bare chest. "Oh, Adam, it's not fair. I carried him alone, went through his birth alone, took care of him and loved him alone. He's mine."

"I know, honey." Adam bent his head and kissed her temple, her ear, nuzzled the side of her neck. He tipped her head up, and his lips met hers in a soft, loving kiss that offered succor and solace. When he pulled back he looked at her tenderly.

"You're taut as a bowstring and dead on your feet. C'mon." He led her inside and nudged her toward the bed. "A good night's sleep is what you need. Last night you were so keyed up I doubt that you slept two hours."

Lauren didn't argue, and a moment later she lay in his arms with her head on his shoulder. Adam gazed up through the darkness at the ceiling, gritting his teeth. The feel of her, soft and yielding against his side, was pure torture. He wanted her so much he ached all over.

His timing was lousy, but he supposed it was some sort of primal male reaction to his mate being threatened. He wanted to hold her close, bury himself in her, drive her passion to a fever pitch and flood her being with so much pleasure she couldn't think of anything else.

But she was exhausted, physically and emotionally. She needed rest, and he'd promised himself that she would get it, even if it killed him.

Her hand lay curled on his chest, and he felt her breath skim across his shoulder, warm and moist and soft as a feather. One of her legs was hooked intimately over his. The sole of her foot rubbed against his shin, and the soft abrasion sent fire rushing straight to his loins. He swallowed hard and struggled to subdue his raging passion.

When she pressed her parted lips against his neck he could not stifle the low moan that shuddered from him.

"Love me, Adam," she whispered. Her tongue trailed a wet pattern over his skin. "I want you to make love to me."

Adam squeezed his eyes shut. "Sweetheart . . . you've had a rough day. You need rest." The throbbing in his loins intensified. He was so hot and hungry for her he felt ready to explode.

"I need you more." Lauren's fingers winnowed through the hair on his chest until she found a tiny nipple. She lightly scored it with her fingernail, and Adam groaned. Making a soft sound, she nipped his shoulder. "Please. I need . . . Oh, God, Adam, I need so much to feel loved."

It was more than he could take. With a guttural growl, he rolled her to her back. "I do love you. God, I love you so much it hurts."

"Oh, Adam."

Before she could say more he took her mouth in a fierce kiss that sent desire spiraling out of control.

Lauren's prolonged moan of pleasure was swallowed up in the kiss as their mouths rocked together. Her hands clutched him, her nails digging into the hard muscles that banded his shoulders and back.

Breathing hard, Adam pulled away and rose to his knees. Looming over her, his face rigid with desire in the pale moonlight pouring through the French doors, he stripped the nightgown from her body and tossed it aside. The wisp of silk fluttered, ghostlike, to the floor, settling in a pale puddle.

Stretching out on the bed, his body half covering hers, Adam cupped her breasts in his palms. He kneaded the lush mounds and gently pinched the pink tips. Then he lowered his head. Lauren gave a thin cry, her back arching as his mouth closed over her nipple and drew on her with a slow, rhythmic suction.

Their hands roamed frantically, touching everywhere. There was an urgency about their lovemaking, a desperation that drove them both. The future held frightful uncertainty, the threat of unthinkable loss and pain. They frantically tried to hold it at bay by immersing themselves in the sweet oblivion only they could give one another, and they grasped at these precious moments with frenzied need.

"God, I can't get enough of you," Adam groaned, trailing his lips over her flesh. He kissed the silky valley between her breasts; then his head slid downward. Heat and moisture filled her navel as he brushed his open mouth back and forth over it. His tongue swirled a wet circle around the tiny cavity, stabbed into it, withdrew, and circled again. Lauren shivered and moaned, driven nearly mindless by the sweet torment.

"Adam. Oh, darling." Her restless hands flexed against his shoulders and trailed down his chest, her fingers twining through the crisp hair. Adam jerked when her nails flicked the tiny nipples nestled there, then he gave a low growl as her exploring hands slid downward. The growl became a groan, and shudders racked him as her hand lovingly enfolded his velvet hardness.

Adam kissed her nipples and the undersides of her breasts, then threaded his fingers through the nest of curls at the apex of her thighs.

"Oh, Adam!" Lauren gasped at his probing touch.

He found her warm and wet and welcoming, and the discovery snapped the last tenuous thread of his control. He rose above her, moving into position between her thighs, and as their gazes locked, he made them one.

In the quiet aftermath, Lauren slept wrapped in Adam's arms while, once again, he lay awake in the darkness. He was exhausted, his body sated from their loving, but his mind would not let him rest.

He rubbed his jaw against Lauren's hair. Lord, how he loved her. More than anything in the world. More than he would have believed it was possible to love. And love, he was discovering, brought out some very primitive instincts in a man.

He felt an overwhelming need to protect her from hurt, both physical and emotional, but there wasn't a damned thing he could do. He knew, with gut-wrenching certainty, that if Lauren lost custody of her son, the effect on her would be devastating.

Damn! He hated feeling so helpless!

Lauren's first supervised visit with her son took place the following Sunday, two days after the initial court hearing. After an almost sleepless night spent tossing and turning in anticipation, she was a bundle of nerves as she dressed for the visit.

"Damn! Damn! Damn! Damn!" Her fingers shook so, she couldn't fasten the clasp on her necklace, and after several tries she hurled it across the room. It hit the wall and bounced onto the bed.

"Hey, take it easy, sweetheart. Everything's going to be fine." Adam plucked the necklace off the bedspread and looped it around her neck, effortlessly fastening the clasp on the first try.

"How can you say that? It's not going to be fine. It's going to be a disaster. David will probably scream bloody murder the whole time. He hates me." She twisted her fingers together and chewed on her lower lip. "Oh, God, I'm sure the social worker will report the whole thing to the judge."

"All right. That's enough fretting. Let's go." He stuffed her purse into her hands and hustled her down the steps to the BMW. He started the car, but before backing out of the garage he cocked an eyebrow at her. "Are you sure you want me to come with you?"

"Yes. Please, Adam. I need someone there who is on my side."

He leaned across the seat and kissed her. "You got it, sweetheart. Always."

An hour later, Adam turned the BMW onto the quiet San Jose street and immediately stepped on the brake.

"What the hell!"

The street was lined with parked cars and vans, and ahead, the Smiths' front yard overflowed with reporters and photographers. Up and down the block, neighbors had gathered in groups on their front lawns to watch.

Lauren stared, appalled. "I don't believe this. What are they doing here? How did they know?"

"Reporters are good at ferreting out information. Damn. I'm sorry, sweetheart. This is my fault. After that mob scene at the courthouse I should have realized that they'd turn up here, too."

"You mean . . . all of this is because you're a celebrity?"

"I'm afraid so. Hell, I shouldn't have come."

"Even if you hadn't, they would still be here. I would just have to get by them on my own."

"That's true. So what do you want to do? Do we stop, or do you want me to drive on?"

"No!" She looked panicked at the thought. "I only have a few hours with my son. I'm not going to lose that because of a mob of reporters."

"You sure?"

"Yes. I'll just have to get through them somehow."

It wasn't easy. The instant Adam turned into the Smiths' driveway, the reporters swooped down on the car like a swarm of killer bees. Adam had to shoulder his way through the crowd to get around the car to Lauren's side, and when he helped her out, the horde pressed closer, shoving microphones in their faces and bombarding her with shouted questions.

"What do you think your chances are of regaining custody of your son, Ms. McKenna?"

"If Judge Haloran rules against you will you take your case to a higher court?"

"Ms. McKenna! Ms. McKenna! Will you file charges against your ex-husband?"

"If you've been looking for the boy all this time, why did it take you so long to find him?"

"Hey, Adam! Private detectives don't come cheap. Are you picking up the tab? You paying your girlfriend's legal expenses, too?"

Keeping his arm around Lauren's shoulders, Adam held her anchored against his side and glowered as he shouldered a path through the crowd. Lauren clung to him and stared straight ahead with her chin high. Though some of the questions made her flinch, she did not respond to any of them— not until Delia Waters stepped into their path.

Startled, Adam and Lauren halted. Delia took advantage of their surprise and shoved a mike into Lauren's face.

"Ms. McKenna, in light of the two recent custody battles between adoptive parents and birth parents who gave them up, aren't you worried about the effect this fight will have on your son?"

Lauren paled. "I don't know what are you talking about. My son wasn't adopted, and never at any time did I give him up!"

Delia smirked. "So you say. But still, you must admit, to snatch the boy from his loving family at this point could cause irreparable emotional damage."

Grabbing his former girlfriend's arm, Adam jerked her close and demanded under his breath, "Dammit, Delia, what the hell are you doing here? Why are you doing this?"

She gave him a feline smile. "Darling, I did warn you that you'd pay. No one walks out on Delia Waters. No one."

He shoved her aside and hustled Lauren forward through the crush of people. "C'mon, honey."

"Ms. McKenna, don't you care that your actions will damage your child?"

"Ignore her, honey," Adam ground out through a clenched jaw. "You don't have to answer."

"But I must." She cast a frantic look over her shoulder at Delia as Adam towed her along. "You're wrong. I am David's mother. No one can love him like I do. Don't you understand—"

"C'mon, honey. Don't say any more."

Adam shoved aside two more reporters before finally reaching the front door. It was opened immediately by a middle-aged woman with salt-and-pepper hair and a kindly face, though her demeanor was distant. She quickly waved them inside and slammed the door shut behind them.

Shaken, Lauren held on to the newel post and tried to catch her breath. "Th-thank you. I'm Lauren McKenna. I'm here to see my son."

"Yes, I know. I'm Gladys Pindergast, Ms. McKenna. I'm a social worker with the Child's Protective Service. I will be supervising your visits."

Lauren nodded, too humiliated by the arrangement to speak.

"I've talked to Mr. and Mrs. Smith and explained that they will not be allowed to remain in the room while you are with Keith—"

"David," Lauren corrected. "My son's name is David."

"Uh, yes . . . David. Of course. Although, Miss McKenna . . . I would advise you to use the name Keith. He's forgotten his real name, and there's no point in confusing him more."

Lauren clenched her jaws. She wanted to scream, No! I gave my son the name David when he was born. No one has the right to change that. But she knew Mrs. Pindergast had a point. "Of course. You're right," she conceded, forcing the words out between her teeth.

The social worker turned her gaze on Adam. "And you're Adam Rafferty. I recognize you from television. I read in the case record that you are involved with Ms. McKenna. Still, may I ask what you are doing here? The court order states that Ms. McKenna has visitation privileges. There is no mention of you, sir."

"I'm Ms. McKenna's fiancé." Adam ignored Lauren's start. "We figured it would be easier on David if he got accustomed to having me around early on."

"Mmm, I see. You're probably right. All right. You can stay this time. But I'll have to check it out with Judge Haloran, before I allow you to visit again."

Mrs. Pindergast ushered them into the living room. "Please, make yourselves comfortable, while I go get the boy. I won't be but a moment."

The instant the door closed, Lauren whirled on Adam. "Why in heaven's name did you tell her that?"

"I presume you want me to stay?" He wandered over to the front window and twitched aside the curtain. Delia was standing on the front lawn with her film crew, taping a commentary. Adam didn't need to hear what she was saying to know that the piece would be slanted in favor of the Smiths. He had to resist the urge to go out there and throttle her.

"Of course I want you to stay. But—"

"Then we'll have to act like an engaged couple. Otherwise, the drill sergeant will boot me out of here before you can blink. She's a by-the-book type, if I ever saw one."

"I suppose you're right."

She glanced out the window at the pack of reporters and

grimaced. "Those adoption cases Delia mentioned—what happened? What was she talking about?"

"Didn't you see them on television? Or read about them? Both cases received national coverage."

"No, I didn't. Since David was taken I haven't paid much attention to the news, and I hardly ever watch television. What do they have to do with my situa—"

A commotion from the rear of the house interrupted her. They listened to the shrill cries and murmured voices and exchanged a worried look.

"That sounds like David." Lauren started for the door, but Adam moved faster and intercepted her.

"No, Lauren. Wait. If the boy needs settling let them handle it."

"But—"

The high-pitched wails grew louder, and a moment later Mrs. Pindergast entered carrying David. Crying hysterically, he struggled and kicked to get free. His face, which had turned an alarming shade of red, was screwed up in anguish and wet with tears. The pitiful sobs shook his little body.

He took one look at Lauren and his cries rose in volume and pitch until they ran together in a keening wail.

Lauren rushed forward. "It's all right, Da . . . Keith. I'm not going to hurt you. I would never hurt you, sweetheart," she crooned, stroking his back. "I love you very much. It's okay, sweetheart. Really. It's okay."

She tried to wipe away his tears, but he jerked away from her and buried his face against Mrs. Pindergast's shoulder. "Oh, darling, please don't cry. It's going to be all right."

The social worker tried to calm him, but nothing worked. The boy squirmed and struggled and strained toward the door with his arms outstretched. "Mommy! Mommy! Mommy!"

Each cry was a stab in Lauren's heart. She tried to distract him with one of the toys she had brought, but he slapped it away and kept screeching, refusing to even look at her.

Adam winced at each wail and shifted from one foot to the other.

Mrs. Pindergast looked at Lauren and raised her voice to be heard. "Normally, I wouldn't suggest this, but under the circumstances, I think perhaps we should allow Mrs. Smith to be present."

"What?" Lauren drew back, shaking her head. "No. No, this is *my* time with my son. I won't share it with her."

"Ms. McKenna, I understand how you feel, but if we can't calm the boy you're not going to have a visit at all. Perhaps, just until he gets used to you."

"She has a point, Lauren. Right now the kid's so scared you can't reason with him. You're not going to make any progress this way."

Resentment simmered in Lauren. She looked away and pressed her lips together, fighting back tears. "Very well. I don't seem to have much choice."

The older woman left the room with the boy, and gradually his cries faded, until after a few minutes they could hear nothing at all. Then they heard the wheelchair approaching, and over the whir, Gavin's furious voice.

"Wait a minute! You expect *my* wife to make this easier for *her?* Like hell! I won't have it. Lauren forced this. Let her—"

"Mr. Smith." Mrs. Pindergast cut across his tirade in an icy voice. "I'm asking your wife to do this in order to make this easier on your son."

"She's right, Gavin. If Keith doesn't calm down, he's going to make himself sick. I won't have him upset this way."

"It's Lauren's fault that he's upset. If she hadn't come here—"

"But she did come, Gavin. And she's not going to go away. We have to deal with that somehow. And I'm going to start by comforting our son."

"Fine! Do whatever you want, but you'll do it without me." Angry footsteps tapped against the terrazzo tile of the entryway, receding toward the back of the house. Then a door slammed.

The double doors opened, and Annette Smith guided her wheelchair into the room. David sat cuddled in her lap, pressed against her breasts. When he saw Lauren he buried his face against Annette and started to whimper, but she stopped him. "Ssh. Ssh. It's all right, my darling. Listen to Mommy. The nice lady's not going to hurt you. I promise."

She looked at Lauren with sad eyes. "I'm sorry. I know how difficult this must be for you."

"I doubt that." Icy bitterness frosted Lauren's voice and glittered in her eyes. She knew she was being bitchy and ungrateful, but she couldn't help it. The mere sight of Annette Smith, the woman who for three years had usurped her place in David's life, filled her with fury.

To give her credit, the woman tried her best to get David to warm to Lauren. "Remember what I told you last night, sweetheart? That you were a lucky little boy because you had two mommies? Hmm? Well, this lady is your other mommy. Won't you say hello to her?"

"Don't want 'nother mommy," he declared in a sulky voice.

"Now, sweetheart, that's not nice. She's come a long way just to see you. She's . . . she's been looking all over for you for a long time. Won't you at least give her a smile?"

"No!" To emphasize the answer, he buried his face in Annette's bosom.

For the next several hours the four adults coaxed and wheedled, but their efforts met with little success. David never left Annette's lap. The closest thing to a positive response that Lauren got was his wary acceptance of the toy truck she had brought for him. His thank-you came at Annette's insistence, but he mumbled it without looking at her. He wouldn't allow Lauren to get near to him. When she tried he fussed and whined and threatened to throw another tantrum until she backed off.

When Mrs. Pindergast announced that the visit was over, Lauren wanted to cry. She had spent five hours with her son and not once had she touched him.

After telling him good-bye and that she would be back in a few days and getting no response, she bade the two women good-bye and walked out of the living room feeling as though she had a forty-pound weight resting on her chest.

At the front door, Adam paused and looked at her with a worried expression. "Are you up to running the gauntlet again? Those reporters are still out there."

Lauren quailed at the thought. She had forgotten all about the pack of vultures outside the door. She squared her shoulders. "I don't appear to have much choice."

"Ms. McKenna, please, may I have a word with you?"

Lauren turned in time to see Annette Smith come through the door of the living room. For the first time in hours, David was not in her lap. Lauren's chin went up. "I don't think we have anything to say to one another."

"Please. I . . . I won't take but a few minutes of your time."

Lauren glanced at Adam. "It's up to you," he said in a quiet voice.

"Very well. Say what you have to say."

"I . . . I wanted to tell you how sorry I am." Lauren gave a disbelieving snort, but Annette hurried on. "Honestly, I feel terrible about all of this. I had no idea that Gavin had taken Keith from you that way. He told me that you had changed your mind about motherhood and gave him up voluntarily. You must have suffered terribly."

Lauren fixed her with a cold stare. "Suffered? That doesn't come close to describing it. I went through three years of hell."

Annette wrung her hands in her lap and wet her lips. "Then . . . then perhaps you can understand how I would feel if I lost him. Why I can't give him back to you now. Keith is the only child I'll ever have."

Lauren subjected her to a long, icy stare. "Come on, Adam. Let's get out of here."

"Please don't take him from us," Annette murmured at Lauren's back. "Please. I'm begging you."

Seventeen

Walter gazed out the window of his twentieth-story office and wondered what the hell he was going to do about Lauren.

Her mistakes were piling up at an alarming rate—cost overruns, shipments mysteriously canceled or sent to the wrong project, work orders disappearing, the wrong materials ordered.

At first the errors had been relatively minor—annoying and disappointing in someone of Lauren's ability, but fixable. He had thought the sharp reprimands he had given her would shake her up enough to keep her mind on business.

Now three major jobs were running so far over budget the company's profit margins had all but disappeared. In each case the fault had been traced back to Lauren.

This wasn't like her. It wasn't like her at all. Walter knew she was going through a rough time, what with that custody fitness nonsense and the disastrous visits with her son. Now the final hearing was coming up next week. But, dammit! Even three years ago when she'd returned to work after David was taken, she hadn't been this distracted.

He glanced at the folder on his desk. His chief accountant had brought it to him just an hour ago. It contained damming proof of yet another of her foul-ups.

With Walter's blessing, Adam was devoting a lot of time to Lauren lately, both during and after office hours. He went with her every time she visited her son, sat in on every interview with the court-appointed psychologist and every strategy session Lauren had with Tony.

Because Adam had been gone so much, for the past couple of weeks John Bailey had been bringing any problems that cropped up to Walter's attention.

Now he couldn't help but wonder if there had been errors that he hadn't heard of. Any fool could see that Adam was in love with Lauren. Perhaps he had been keeping quiet about the extent of her mistakes.

Mary Alice entered the office and headed straight for the entertainment center, discreetly concealed in the cherrywood library wall unit opposite his desk. Walter could tell by her militant stride that she was fuming. Again.

Hell, it seemed as though lately, his cool-as-a-cucumber secretary was always hopping mad at something or someone. Usually him.

He had to admit, he was kind of enjoying their sparring— or at least he would be if he didn't know that she'd be leaving soon. He had always liked spirit in a woman.

God knew, his Helen had stood toe to toe with him many a time in their years together. Walter's mouth quirked. Hell, some of their rows had been real doozies. And Lord, how he'd loved that woman.

Until now, Mary Alice had always been cool and collected and unflappable. Maybe that was why he'd never noticed how beautiful she was.

As he watched, she snatched open the doors that concealed the television set, snapped it on, then stood back to watch with her fists propped on her hips. Walter shook his head. Where the hell had all that temper come from?

"Look. Just look at that witch," Mary Alice snapped. "She's at it again. Won't she ever leave the poor girl alone?"

Walter's eyes narrowed as his gaze switched to the image on the television screen.

Delia Waters was harassing Lauren and Adam as they battled their way through the crowd in front of the Smith house.

Other reporters were also jockeying for position and shouting questions, but Delia shoved and elbowed them aside with all the politeness of an attacking shark.

When her prey escaped into Adam's car, she turned to the TV camera with a concerned expression and began her nightly crucifixion of Lauren.

"As you saw, former football star Adam Rafferty and his current lover, Ms. Lauren McKenna, refuse to discuss this case. However, this reporter has learned that because of his part in this bitter struggle, there has been a backlash of negative sentiment against Mr. Rafferty. Some are even going too far as to say he shouldn't be inducted into the Football Hall of Fame.

"From all indications, Ms. McKenna seems determined to snatch little Keith away from the only parents he has known in his young life, regardless of the trauma it will undoubtedly inflict upon him.

"Some have suggested that if that happens his distress will be temporary and that he will adjust to the change and the loss of his beloved parents. However, according to the child psychologists with whom I have consulted, there is a grave risk of scarring the boy emotionally for life.

"In recent years the American public has witnessed live coverage of two horrendous cases in which the court returned custody to a birth parent long after an adoption had been finalized. In both, the child's terror and grief at being ripped from the arms of the people he loved was heart-rending.

"Now the American people are asking just how long we are going to allow this sort of outrage to go on. While we all sympathize with Ms. McKenna . . ."

"Sympathize, my ass," Walter growled, and stabbed the off button on the remote control. "The vicious bitch would like to see Lauren burned at the stake, and she's doing her damnedest to stir up the whole country against her."

Delia Waters was clever, he'd give her that. She spread her poison subtly, with innuendo, a certain inflection in her voice, a disapproving expression, constant harping on the possible damage being done to the child's psyche. At every opportunity she implied that the whole mess was Lauren's fault for trying to regain her child in the first place.

Delia Waters was deliberately trying to turn public opinion against her. And succeeding. It was getting to the point that Lauren couldn't go out in public without being accosted and vilified by strangers.

"Dammed vicious female," Walter snarled. "What the hell is she doing here anyway? Top network anchorwomen don't do field reporting."

"She's obviously on a vendetta," Mary Alice replied. "I'm just surprised her network is airing this. If her brand of reporting isn't outright slander, it's certainly yellow journalism. Personally, I think Lauren should sue."

"Humph. She thought if she just ignored the woman she'd go away. I tried to tell her that people like that are barracudas; they smell blood and go into a feeding frenzy. Anyway, with the hearing coming up next week, Lauren has more important things on her mind."

Pursing his lips, Walter fingered the file his accountant had brought in earlier. "I just wish that work was one of them," he mumbled to himself.

Mary Alice heard the comment. She frowned when she saw what held his attention. "Walter Ingram! Surely, with all the troubles that poor girl has, you're not going to reprimand her about those projects as well? That's awful."

"What else can I do? I'm running a business here."

"Lauren is your goddaughter. I thought you loved her."

"You know damned well I love that girl! But when someone on my staff makes mistakes, particularly of this magnitude, they're going to get called on it. I can't make an exception for Lauren."

"But do you have to do it now?"

"Dammit, Mary Alice, I've already cut her more slack than I would anyone else. You know that."

"Well, I just don't see how you can be so heartless!"

"Heartless! If I really were heartless I'd have fired her weeks ago. That's what would've happened if she worked for someone else.

"And before you go making accusations about me, what about you? How can you abandon her now, when her world is in turmoil?"

"I'm not abandoning Lauren!"

"You're walking out on me and your job, aren't you? Same thing. When will you see her?"

"Whenever I like. For your information, Walter Ingram, I do exist outside this job! Just because I retire that doesn't mean that I cease to be. I have friends, a life of my own. Which, by the way, I've neglected far too long because of you."

"What does that mean?"

"It means that once this custody battle is over I intend to make some changes in my life."

"What sort of changes?"

"Well . . . travel, for one."

"You've traveled with me plenty."

"On business. All I ever saw was the inside of boardrooms and hotel suites. I've been to Paris with you I don't know how many times, but I've never so much as gotten near the Eiffel Tower. That's pathetic. And it was the same no matter where we went.

"I want to experience places and people. As a matter of fact . . ." She paused, and for an instant she looked uncertain. Then her chin tilted up. "Brandon has asked me to go on a three-month tour of Europe with him, and I'm thinking of accepting."

"What! With Tremaine? That sleaze ball!"

"Brandon is not a sleaze ball!" Mary Alice huffed. "He's a highly successful, well-respected man. Furthermore, he's a nice person."

"I don't care if he's the prince of Tasmania, you're not going! I won't have it!"

"You won't have it. You have no say in my personal life. I will go where I want, with whom I want."

She turned and headed for her own office, but Walter shot out of his chair and came after her. Before she could reach the door he blocked her way.

"Don't go, Mary Alice."

"If I decide to go, I will, and you can't stop me."

"I'm not talking about the trip. Don't leave me. Please."

Mary Alice sighed. "For heaven's sake, Walter, Deborah Moore is a very capable young woman. She'll make you a fine secretary if you'll just give her a chance."

"To hell with the damned job!" he roared. "I don't want you to walk out of my life."

"Wh-what?" Mary Alice gaped at him.

Walter didn't know who was more shocked—Mary Alice or him. The words had tumbled out of nowhere, but now that they were out, he realized they were true. He couldn't imagine his life without Mary Alice in it.

"I, uh . . ." Walter cleared his throat and stared at a point just over her left shoulder. "Look, I wasn't just feeding Adam a line when I told him that I intended to cut down on my hours and do some traveling. I want to smell some roses myself, while I still can. You could come with me."

Cocking her head to one side, she studied him. "I don't think so. I know you. Before I knew it you'd have me running errands and making calls and typing letters and sending faxes."

"I wasn't asking you to come along as my secretary, dammit!" he exploded. "I was asking you to come along as my wife!"

Mary Alice's jaw dropped. "Your . . . your wife?"

"That's right. For heaven's sake, woman, don't you know a marriage proposal when you hear one?"

His tone stiffened her spine. "Certainly, I do, but I'd hardly call that half-hearted invitation a marriage proposal."

"All right, then how's this?" Grabbing her shoulders, he hauled her up against his chest and kissed her.

The sensations that shot through Walter nearly buckled his knees. It had been so many years since he'd experienced this wild excitement, this demanding, pounding passion. He'd almost forgotten it existed. He'd almost forgotten, too, how absolutely right it felt to hold a woman. Mary Alice's slender body was soft and warm against his. God, how he'd missed this closeness.

Mary Alice hung in his arms like a rag doll. When he raised his head she gazed up at him as though in a daze. "Wa-Walter," she gasped. "You . . . I . . ."

He grinned at her confusion. "So, will you marry me?"

He thought he had her on the ropes, but Mary Alice was tougher than he thought. "Why . . . why do you want to marry me?"

"Why?" he barked. "Dammit, woman, because I'm crazy about you, and I can't stand the thought of losing you. That's why."

Her gaze turned dreamy. "Oh, Walter. If you only knew how long I've waited to hear you say that."

"Is that a yes?"

"Yes." She reached up and touched his cheek, her face glowing. "Oh, my, yes."

"Good." His expression softened, and he slipped his arms around her waist and laced his fingers together at the small of her back. "The men in my family usually live well into their nineties. I figure we have a good thirty years or more ahead of us. I want us to spend them together" He brushed her mouth with a soft kiss. "I want to grow old with you, Mary Alice."

She looked at him with a rueful half smile. "Walter, you're sixty-three and I'm fifty-six. Many people would say that we're already old."

"Humph. Young whippersnappers. What do they know?"

A devilish twinkle entered his eyes, and he reached behind him and locked the door. "There may be snow on the roof, but there's plenty of fire inside. Come here, sweetheart."

With an arm around her waist, he led Mary Alice to the leather sofa. When they were seated he kissed her again, deeply and with a gentle passion that belied his usual gruff manner. As his lips rocked over hers his hand slid upward from her waist and cupped her breast. He smiled as he felt Mary Alice quiver and deftly began to undo the buttons on her blouse.

She grasped his wrist, and when Walter broke the kiss she looked up at him with a shocked expression. "Walter, are you trying to seduce me?"

"Uh-hmm." Gazing into her eyes, he boldly flicked another button open and murmured, "How am I doing so far?"

As his big hand slipped inside her blouse Mary Alice sucked in her breath. Gradually her gaze grew dreamy and hot. Cupping her hand around his nape, she brought his head down for another kiss, and murmured against his lips, "Just fine, my love. You're doing just fine."

A few miles up the coast at Lauren's beach house, Adam walked into the living room in time to hear the tail end of Delia Waters's comments. One look at Lauren's face sent him striding across the room to snap off the television. "That's it. I've had enough," he growled, and headed for the wall phone in the kitchen.

"Adam, what are you going to do? Who are you calling?" Lauren asked in an anxious voice.

"Harve Tarrington at the network. He's an old friend of mine from my pro days."

"Adam, no. Don't—"

He waved for silence as Harve's secretary came on the line. When he identified himself she sounded reluctant to put him through but after a little wheedling on Adam's part, she put him on hold. A moment later, Adam's old friend took the call.

"Adam. How you doing? I was wondering when I'd hear from you."

"Then you know why I'm calling. Good. I want to know when you're going to put a muzzle on Delia?"

"Whoa, whoa. Hold on. You're talking about messing with freedom of speech, ole buddy."

"No, Harve, I'm talking about the lowest form of yellow journalism and character assassination. Christ, Harve, this isn't news reporting. This is a vindictive, malicious attack by a jealous woman, and we both know it."

Harve sighed. "Yeah, I know. Look, Adam, I agree with you. Hell, man, I'm a journalist. I hate this kind of sensationalism. But you gotta understand that my hands are tied. Since Delia's been covering this custody case for her weekly magazine show her ratings have jumped two and a half points. If I yanked the story now the president of the network would have my head."

"I see. What if I bought air time on your network to counter her smear campaign?"

"Holy shit, man, do you have any idea of what that would cost?"

"Yeah, I know. But it would be worth it."

"Hell, I thought this woman of yours was just another in the string. You must really love her. Even so, my advice to you is, don't do it. You'd be playing right into Delia's hands. Hell, the controversy would probably boost her ratings another couple of points. And if the boys upstairs knew I was telling you this I'd be booted outta here in a New York second.

"Look, Adam, the best thing you and your lady can do is exactly what you've been doing—tough it out. Once the case is settled it won't be news any longer and Delia will have to go away. Trust me. I'm telling you this as a friend."

"Yeah, well, thanks for your advice, Harve."

When Adam turned from hanging up the telephone Lauren

was watching him. "There's nothing your friend can do, is there?"

"Apparently not. Dammit, it's bad enough that you have to go through all this without having that bitch stirring people up and making things worse."

Just that day on their way home from the office they had stopped at a supermarket and a woman had accosted Lauren, calling her selfish and uncaring. Lauren had weathered the abuse with stoicism, but on the drive home there had been tears in her eyes.

"This is all my fault. If it weren't for me, Delia wouldn't be attacking you."

"Don't say that." Rushing forward, Lauren wrapped her arms around his waist and lay her cheek against his chest. "You're not to blame for that vicious woman. Besides, if I didn't have you here with me, I'm not sure I could survive this custody battle. Just knowing that you're on my side helps me to get through each day."

Adam held her close and rubbed her back, saying nothing, but something about his silence made her uneasy. She pulled back a little and gave him a troubled look. "You are on my side, aren't you?"

"Of course I am." Adam grimaced. "It's just that . . ."

"That what?" Lauren released him and stepped back. "What are you trying to say, Adam? That you think I'm wrong? That you agree with your friend Delia, that I'm being heartless and cruel?"

"No! No, not at all. You're a mother whose baby was taken from her. Of course you want him back, and you have every moral right in the world to take him back."

"But?"

Adam raked a hand through his hair. "But . . . I'm not sure that having the right to do something necessarily means it's the best decision to make."

"What does that mean?"

"It means that it might not be the best thing for David."

"I'm his mother!" she bristled.

"Yes. Legally and biologically you are. But in David's mind, you aren't. As far as he's concerned, Annette Smith is his mother."

Lauren made a distressed sound and backed away another step. "He's my baby. Not hers."

"I know, sweetheart. But you have to admit, you haven't made any progress with David these past weeks. He's still as leery of you now as he was the first day. He won't let you near him. He won't even be in the same room with you without Annette.

"Lauren, I hate what Gavin did. It was wrong, no matter that he did it out of love for his wife. But, sweetheart, there's no undoing it. The boy has bonded with Annette and Gavin. He loves them, and they love him. He's happy and well adjusted. Do you want to destroy that?"

She was breathing hard, on the edge of panic. "He's young. He'll adjust. In a few months he won't even remember them."

"Maybe. If he never saw them again. But I don't think that Judge Haloran will allow that to happen. I think you'd better face the probability that whichever parent loses custody will be granted visitation rights. If Gavin and Annette are around all the time, the boy won't forget them.

"And I'm afraid that no matter how much love you give him, he will always resent you for taking him from them."

Lauren made an anguished sound, and Adam took her hands in his. "Sweetheart, listen to me. I've been giving this a lot of thought. When I was young I used to wonder about my birth parents. I dreamed about maybe meeting them someday. But even if I had found them, and even if they had been nice people, I know with absolute certainty that I wouldn't have wanted them to take me away from my adoptive parents. Joe and Faye Rafferty were the people who raised me, who nurtured me and protected me from bullies and bad dreams, who got up with me in the night when I was sick, who came to my games and cheered themselves hoarse."

"But I wanted to do all those things."

"I know you did, darling, but you were cheated out of your chance, and you can't get it back. If you take David back now you'll be putting him, and yourself through a horrendous upheaval. Do you really want to do that?"

Lauren's chin began to quiver. "So. You've changed your mind. You're not on my side anymore."

"No, sweetheart! No, you're wrong! Don't ever think that. I'll always be on your side. Whatever you decide, I will understand and support you. But will you do one thing for me?"

Her eyes narrowed warily. "What?"

"I know you didn't follow those two custody cases that Delia is always harping about, but a guy I know at a local station made me a tape that shows each child being surrendered to their natural parents. Before you make a final decision, I want you to look at the tape."

"They're totally different," Lauren protested. "Those were adoptions. My son was taken from me against my will."

"That part doesn't matter. If you take David from the Smiths now, for him the result will be the same."

Releasing one of her hands, Adam stroked the side of her face and gazed at her tenderly. "Look at the tape, Lauren. Afterward, if you still think you could live with your decision, then I won't ever mention the matter again."

Indecision flickered in her eyes, but she finally clenched her jaw and nodded. "All right. If this is so important to you then I'll watch it."

"Now?"

She heaved a sigh. "All right. I'll watch it now."

Before she could change her mind, Adam retrieved the tape from his briefcase and handed it to her. "I'll leave you alone. I've got to go pick up a few things at my place, anyway."

"Fine. Just don't expect me to change my mind. If the judge rules in my favor I am going to take my son back."

Eighteen

Lauren rechecked the column of figures a third time and came up with a third different answer. In disgust, she tossed her pencil aside and rubbed her forehead. Dammit! Concentrate, she told herself. You have work to do.

Even as she silently scolded herself she knew it was hopeless. She'd been so mired down with worry and anxiety she hadn't been able to concentrate for days, not since she'd watched that news video Adam had given her. The only bright spot in the past week had been the day before, when Walter summoned her and Adam into his office and made his surprise announcement.

"Engaged! You two? I don't believe it! When did this happen? How? Oh, my goodness, this is wonderful!" Lauren had surged forward and hugged Mary Alice. "I'm so happy for you."

"Thank you, dearest." Mary Alice laughed and squeezed Lauren's hands. "I'm pretty happy myself."

"So, tell me everything. What happened?"

"Well, I'm not really certain, myself. Walter and I were having an argument, and the next thing I knew he was proposing."

"You left out the part where I kissed you." Ignoring his fiancée's blush, Walter leaned back in his desk chair with his hands laced over his middle, looking smug as an Eastern potentate in his harem. "Thirty seconds later we were engaged."

"Must've been one helluva kiss," Adam drawled.

"Damned right it was. What'd you expect?"

"When did all this happen? Where were you?"

"Right here in the office. We were working late last Friday evening and . . . it just happened," Mary Alice supplied, blushing again.

"That was four days ago. Why didn't you call me? Wait a minute." Lauren looked back and forth between Mary Alice and Walter. "Why, you sly devils. You didn't go on a business trip over the weekend. You went away together, didn't you? I should have realized when I saw how tanned you both were."

"Yep. We spent the last three days in Antigua. I wanted to elope, but Mary Alice wouldn't hear of getting married without you there, and she didn't think it would be right to ask you to stand up with her until the custody thing was settled. But I'll be damned if I was going to wait that long for a honeymoon."

"Walter! What a thing to say!"

"What's wrong with that? It's the truth."

Mary Alice had turned scarlet to the roots of her hair, and Lauren had laughed right along with Adam, but it had saddened her that her problems were spilling over onto the lives of the people she loved.

Sighing, Lauren leaned back in her desk chair and swiveled it around to look out of the window. She couldn't stop thinking about those other children, couldn't stop picturing their tears and their terror.

She'd tried. Oh, how she'd tried, but the scenes on the video tape played over and over in her mind, haunting her, squeezing her heart until it ached.

She told herself that those cases were nothing like her own. Her child had been ripped from her. She had not given him away to strangers for adoption. He was hers.

Still, no matter how much she argued that the situation

was different, she knew that if Judge Haloran ruled in her favor, taking David from Gavin and his wife would be just as horrendous and devastating for her son as it was for the other children.

Damn Adam, anyway, for insisting that she view those gut-wrenching scenes. She had been much better off not knowing how awful and frightful the parting would be for her son.

For the past three years she had been consumed with getting him back. In her mind she had pictured that happening a thousand times or more, and the rightness of it had never been in question, in her mind or her heart.

But she had been looking at the situation solely from her own perspective, projecting her feelings, her wants and needs onto her son. For her, being reunited with him was the best thing that could possibly happen, the only just and fair thing. She had always taken it for granted that it would be the best thing for David, as well.

Restless, Lauren rose and walked to the window. Fog shrouded the city—a swirling miasma, thick and gray as her emotions. In the distance she could barely see the top of the towers on the Golden Gate Bridge poking up through the mist.

Standing with her arms crossed, she absently rubbed her elbows and stared out at the gloom.

Lauren was quite certain that when David had been taken at ten months old he had suffered separation anxiety at being parted from her. She used to lie awake at night worrying about that, crying about it. Until then she had never been apart from him except for an occasional overnight business trip, and her nanny had said that he had been fretful during those short absences.

She smiled sadly, remembering how happy he had always been when she returned, how his eyes had lit up when he spotted her and how he'd kicked and squealed with glee and blown bubbles.

Her smile faded. But he had been just a baby when he'd

been taken, and he had quickly forgotten her. Now he had his father and a new mother, and their bonds had been forged strong during what was probably the most impressionable three years of anyone's life. Those first ties with her had simply faded from his memory until they no longer existed.

Could they be reestablished? Even if that were possible, could she put David through the emotional pain and upheaval those other children had suffered?

Most important of all, would that be the best thing for her son?

It was so hard . . . so hard to know what was best, but she had to decide quickly. The final hearing was scheduled for tomorrow afternoon.

Dear God, she loved her son so. He was her baby, the light of her life. How could she bear it if she lost him again?

By the time he finished reading the report Walter had handed him, Adam's jaws were clenched. He looked up at the older man and frowned. "Have you said anything to Lauren about this?"

"Not yet. I didn't want to add to her problems. But I can't put it off much longer. Too many other people know about the losses. There is already some grumbling among the staff about favoritism. You know how much that hurts Lauren."

"Yeah, I know. But if the judge rules against her at that hearing tomorrow you won't have any choice. She'll be too shattered to deal with anything for a while. I've already told personnel she'll be on indefinite leave starting tomorrow. No matter which way things go, she's going to need some time off."

"Good idea. In the meantime, what do we do about all her mistakes?" Walter said, tapping the report.

"Keep stonewalling." He looked Walter straight in the eye. "I don't give a rat's ass if every employee in this company squawks. Under no circumstances will I allow anyone to upset her right now. And I mean no one."

Scowling, Walter studied his unyielding expression for several seconds. Finally he nodded and closed the file. He leaned back in his chair with a weary sigh. "I'll be damned glad when this thing is settled and that boy is back with his mother where he belongs."

"Anxious to get to the altar, are you?"

"I won't deny it. At my age it's foolish to waste time. But I'm worried about Lauren. She's been under a strain for three years. It's a damn shame that judge didn't just throw Gavin in jail and give her the baby. She shouldn't have to be going through all this." He scowled again and shot Adam a look from beneath his bushy eyebrows. "Between you and me, what do you think her chances are?"

"According to Tony, about fifty-fifty. The only thing the custody fitness study determined was that they are both good parent material. Judge Haloran isn't especially pleased with Gavin for taking the baby from Lauren the way he did, and there's his lack of interest in the child before the kidnapping, but there's no question that he adores his son now.

"Lauren is obviously a loving and devoted mother, but so is Annette, and she's had three years to demonstrate that. Financially, Lauren is better off, but Annette would be a full-time mother. Either way, it'll be a hard call."

"Damn Gavin, anyway," Walter grumbled.

When Adam left Walter's office a few minutes later he stopped by Lauren's to check on her. The last few days she had been quiet and withdrawn, especially so after her visit with David yesterday. That had been her last visit before the hearing, and like all the others, it had been a complete failure. Despite all her efforts, the boy still treated her as though she were the Wicked Witch of the West.

Adam tried to get her to talk about it, but for once she had shut him out. On the drive in to work that morning she'd had a fragile look about her that concerned him. So far she had handled everything with admirable strength and calm, but she was strung as taut as a piano wire, and he wasn't sure how much more she could take.

Nan looked up when he entered her office. "If you're looking for Lauren, she's not here."

"Oh? Where is she?"

"She left about an hour ago to consult with her attorney."

"Tony?" Adam frowned. She hadn't said anything about having a meeting with Tony today. "Mind if I use your phone?" he asked, but he was already punching out Tony's office number before Nan had a chance to answer.

His friend wasn't in his office. When Adam pressed, Tony's secretary informed him that he was working at home that day. Adam immediately hung up and called the Diamattos' home number.

Kate answered, but Tony wasn't there, either.

"He and Lauren left about twenty minutes ago. They're on their way over to the Smiths' house. Of course, Tony wouldn't tell me anything, but I don't like it. Something is up, Adam. They both looked like they were going to a hanging when they left here."

Alarm streaked through Adam. Muttering a quick thanks to Kate, he slammed down the receiver. "Buzz my secretary and tell her I'll be gone the rest of the day," he called over his shoulder to Nan as he strode out the door.

Adam broke all speed limits on the drive to San Jose. When he brought his BMW to a screeching halt at the curb in front of the Smiths' house, Tony and Lauren had just rung the doorbell. For once the press was nowhere in sight, which meant, as Adam had suspected, this wasn't a scheduled meeting.

Lauren and Tony turned with surprised expressions as he came storming up the walk.

"Adam! What are you doing here? How did you know where to find us?"

He ignored Lauren's questions and fired some of his own. "What's going on? Why did you leave without telling me?"

"I tried to tell you. Your secretary said you were out of the office. I couldn't wait. I knew if I did—"

Gavin opened the front door, cutting off her explanation. His expression was guarded and suspicious but he stepped back and ushered them inside.

Annette was waiting for them in the living room, looking tense and apprehensive. When they were seated, Gavin sat in a chair beside his wife's wheelchair and took her hand. "When you called you said this was important. It had better be. I left two clients waiting in my office. But I'm warning you, if this is a last-ditch attempt to try and talk me into dropping my suit for full custody, you're wasting your time."

"No, that's not why we're here," Tony assured him. He looked at Lauren's pale face and raised one eyebrow. "Are you sure about this? You've got another twenty-four hours to think about it."

"No. If I don't do it now, I'm not sure I can muster the courage again."

"Okay. It's your call." Tony turned to Gavin and Annette Smith with a somber expression. "Lauren has an offer she wants to put to you."

"What sort of offer?" Suspicion and distrust sharpened Gavin's voice.

Adam sat quietly on the sofa beside Lauren, holding her hand. What the devil was going on?

Lauren pressed her lips together and closed her eyes for a moment. She looked pale as death. Finally she drew a deep breath and her grip tightened around Adam's hand. "If . . . if you will agree to certain conditions, I will drop my custody suit and allow you to keep David."

"What!" Gavin gasped.

Annette Smith clutched her husband and burst into tears. As Gavin hugged her his own eyes grew moist.

Adam had started at the announcement as though he'd received a jolt from a cattle prod. His gaze sharpened on Lauren. She looked as though she might shatter at any moment.

"Are you serious?"

"Yes. Provided you are willing to meet my conditions."

"What conditions?"

"To start with, I want generous visitation. I want to be a part of his life. Maybe all I can have is a small part, but I insist upon that. I also insist that as Dav . . . Keith grows up he be told the truth—that I am his mother, that you took him from me against my will, that I never stopped loving him or looking for him. When you speak to him of me, I expect you to treat me fairly." She fixed her ex-husband with a steady look. "I've never done anything to harm you, Gavin. I didn't deserve to lose my son. I won't lose his love and respect."

Gavin had the grace to look ashamed. "I know. You're right. I'm sorry, Lauren. I would never have taken him if I hadn't been desperate. Believe me, I didn't do it to hurt you."

"Perhaps. But you did. You hurt me in the worst way possible. However, I've come to realize that some things can't be undone."

She cleared her throat and lifted her chin. "Those are my conditions. If you agree to them, Tony has drawn up a formal agreement for all of us to sign, which he will present to Judge Haloran tomorrow."

"This is pretty straightforward, but if you want to have your attorney look it over, feel free," Tony advised, handing each of the Smiths a copy. "As long as they're signed by court time tomorrow."

Adam kept his gaze on Lauren. He hurt for her, but he was so proud of her, so choked with emotion, he felt as though his heart were about to burst. How could he ever have thought, even for a moment, that Lauren was like the other women he'd known. She was wounded, all right, deeply so, but she was no weakling. It had taken tremendous strength and courage to do what she had done. Most of all, it had taken boundless love.

"It looks fine to me," Gavin said, scanning the document. "What do you think, honey?"

"I think that Lauren is being incredibly unselfish and understanding," Annette Smith said in a shaky voice. She looked at Lauren with tears of gratitude swimming in her eyes. "You have my solemn promise that Keith will hear the unvarnished truth, and I will talk to him about you every day and make sure that he knows what a wonderful person his mother is."

"We can do even better than that," Gavin added. "If you want, we'll move back to San Francisco. That way you'll be closer to him and visits will be easier."

"Thank you. I would like that." Lauren rose stiffly, like someone recovering from a long illness. "I'm glad we've come to an agreement."

Gavin stood too and grabbed her hands. His eyes were misty and full of abject gratitude. "Thank you, Lauren. Dear God, thank you so much. I can't tell you how much this means to us."

"Yes, thank you," Annette added. "We'll always be grateful. How can we ever repay you?"

"You don't have to thank me. I'm not doing this for you, Gavin. Nor am I doing it for your wife. I'm doing it for my son. I love him too much to put him through the emotional trauma it would take for me to have him back."

Gavin nodded, shamefaced.

Lauren walked out of the room staring straight ahead, her steps stiff and jerky. Her face was an emotionless mask. Adam knew the effort it was costing her to fight back her tears.

"Lauren, wait!"

She stopped just short of the front door and turned in time to see Annette glide into the entryway with a stack of albums on her lap.

"I want you to have these. They're all the pictures of Keith we took from the time Gavin brought him home to me until just a few days ago. There are three albums, one for each year."

Adam saw Lauren's throat work as she stared at the albums. He slipped his arm around her waist, and he could feel her trembling. "But . . . they're yours."

"Please, take them. I have all the negatives. I can make new albums for us."

Gavin lifted the books from his wife's lap and handed them to Lauren. "Take them, Lauren. It's the least we can do."

"Are you going to be all right?" Tony asked once they were outside.

She didn't answer. Adam doubted that she had heard the question. Holding herself stiff, she stared straight ahead and walked jerkily down the sidewalk, clutching the albums to her.

Adam exchanged a look with Tony and slipped his arm around her waist. "I'm taking her home."

"Sure. Call later, and let us know how she's doing. Kate'll be worried sick when she finds out what happened."

Lauren did not protest when Adam led her to his car. In less than a minute he had her strapped in her seat and they were on their way.

He would have preferred hysterics to her stoic silence. Despite his coaxing, she did not utter a word all the way home. She sat with her gaze focused straight ahead, pale and lifeless and still as a statue—except for her hands. They stroked constantly over the photo albums in her lap.

Adam knew she was shattered. How could she not be? For three years she had lived on hope, and now that was gone. But Lauren was a private person; she did not lose control in public while riding down a busy freeway. By sheer strength of will she held all the grief and anguish inside.

Not until he had parked the car in her garage and come around to her side to assist her out did she break her silence.

When Adam reached for the albums to carry them for her she shot him a panicked look and clutched them tighter. "No. I'll carry them."

He didn't argue, but he stayed close beside her, watching her, worry gnawing at him.

She climbed the basement stairs like a zombie, and when she entered her house she simply stood in the middle of the kitchen looking lost, as though she had no idea what to do.

"Are you tired? Can I do anything for you?"

"No, thank you."

"How about something to eat. A bowl of soup, maybe?"

"No, I . . . I'm just going to sit for a while."

She went into the living room and sank down on the sofa. Vaguely, Lauren was aware of Adam watching her, of his concern, but she was too fragile to talk to anyone. For some time she simply stared out the window at the ocean. Numb with pain, she fought to hold back the black sorrow that was edging in on her. She tried not to look at the albums on her lap. That way lay heartache. She wasn't strong enough now to take that journey.

It was a losing fight. Like a flame drawing a moth, the photos pulled at her, called to her. After a while Lauren looked down at the albums in her lap. She stared at the top one, and the aching knot in her chest squeezed tighter. Slowly, hesitantly, she opened the album.

"Oh." The exclamation spilled from her, soft and wavery with emotion. She put her hand over her mouth and gazed at the chubby baby in the pictures—her son as she remembered him, as he'd been three years ago when he had been taken from her.

With a trembling hand she reached out and touched one of the photos. She traced her fingers over a cherub cheek, the smiling rosebud mouth, and tears filled her eyes, banking against her lower lids, blurring the picture. Her chin began to wobble. She tried to control it, but she couldn't—any more than she could hold back the sob that squeezed through her constricted throat, or stop the tears she had been holding at bay for so long from rolling down her cheeks.

In a heartbeat Adam dropped onto the sofa beside her and put his arm around her shoulders. "It's all right, honey," he crooned. "Go ahead and cry. Let it all out. Lord knows you have a right."

"Oh God, oh God, oh God." Squeezing her eyes shut, she wrapped her arms around the album and clutched it to her, and rocked back and forth as though in mortal pain. A low moan tore from her throat, raw and raspy and awful to hear. "My baby. My baby."

"I know, sweetheart. I know."

Adam wrapped both arms around her and pulled her against his chest, album and all, holding her close. Rubbing his cheek against the top of her head, he rocked her and rubbed her back, all the while crooning soft words of sympathy.

Lauren twisted her fingers into the front of his shirt and clung to him. Tears flowed in torrents from her eyes, and her shoulders heaved. She cried wretchedly, all the misery, all the longing, all the lost dreams overwhelming her.

Her sobs were harsh and choppy and they hurt her throat, but she couldn't stop them. No power on earth could have stopped them. They tore from her soul without surcease, filling the room with heart-rending sounds of anguish.

Hot tears soaked the front of Adam's shirt, melding the cloth and his chest hair to his skin. Lifting his hip, he drew a clean handkerchief from his back pocket and stuffed it into Lauren's hand, but it was soon soaked as well.

Adam simply held her and let her cry it all out. The storm of emotion lasted a long time, but gradually her sobs began to taper off. Adam kept holding her, stroking her back and hips, murmuring to her in gentle tones, and after a while the sobs turned to sniffles, then to choppy sighs, and she relaxed against him, though her hands still clutched his wet shirt.

For a long while they sat quietly. From outside came the

swish of the waves upon the shore, the occasional call of a gull. Inside, the only sounds were the hum of the refrigerator and the soft sibilance of their breathing.

She lay in his arms, spent and limp as a rag, her cheek nestled against the solid wall of his chest. The sun had dropped low on the horizon, turning the towering thunderhead clouds in the west into boiling cauldrons of vermilion and purple.

Sniffling, Lauren stared at the brilliant display, blinking wet, spiky lashes. The ache in her chest had eased a bit, and she felt safe in Adam's strong embrace. She watched a bird swoop and soar against the fiery sky, part of her wishing she could simply let her mind float and stay there forever.

"Are you okay, now?"

Sighing, Lauren sat up and swiped at her eyes with the heels of her hands. Her nose was stopped up and her head was booming. She knew she probably looked as wretched as she felt, but she didn't care. "I don't know," she whispered through quavering lips. "I'm not sure I'll ever be okay again."

Adam reached over and took her hand. "I know. You're bruised right now, and it's going to take some time to recover, but you will. Someday the sun will shine again and you'll have happiness that will last."

Lauren snorted. "Happiness? I'm not sure there is such a thing."

"Oh, yeah. There is, with the right person. Someone who truly loves you exactly as you are." Adam paused, then added softly, seriously, "The way I love you."

Lauren shot him a quick glance as a tiny frisson fluttered through her. The look in his eyes made her even more uneasy, and she wasn't sure why. "Adam—"

"Marry me, Lauren."

"*Marry* you!" She stared at him, too stunned to say more. He was serious! A panicky feeling rose inside her, suffocat-

ing her. Instinctively she started to pull away from him, but
Adam was having none of that.

He released her hand and cupped her tear-stained face between his palms. His eyes bore into hers, refusing to let her
look away.

"I hate to see you hurting like this. If I could, I'd make
everything right, but I can't. But I can make it better, if you'll
let me."

"Adam—"

"Do you love me, Lauren?"

She gave him a desperate look, silently pleading with him
to stop. "Adam, please—"

"Do you?"

"You know I do, but—"

"Then marry me."

Lauren closed her eyes as another surge of pain rose inside
her. Her lips trembled, and slowly, one by one, fresh tears
seeped from beneath her eyelids and rolled down her cheeks.
"I can't. I . . . I just can't."

"Why not? We love each other. *Really* love each other.
Together we could have it all, sweetheart—careers, a solid
marriage, a family of our own."

"Children!"

"I know our children could never replace David. No child
can replace another. But they would bring their own special
joy and love into our lives."

Panic gushed up inside Lauren. She jerked out of his hold
and bounded off the sofa, backing away. "No! No, that's
impossible. I'm not going to have any more children. I can't
risk going through this again. I can't!"

"Risk?" He looked as though she had slapped him. "You
think if we had children together I might leave and take them
away from you? God, Lauren, I thought you trusted me."

"I do. I do trust you, Adam. As much as I trust anyone.
But . . . well . . . you have to admit, there are no guarantees."

"I'll give you a guarantee. One you can take to the bank.

I'm not Gavin Stone. I would never do that to you," he ground out between clenched teeth. "Never. No matter the circumstances."

"I . . . I want to believe you."

Standing, he walked to her and took her hand. "Then prove it. Marry me, Lauren."

She pressed her lips together to stop them from trembling. "I . . . I can't."

"Can't? Or won't?"

"Oh, Adam." She raised her free hand and stroked his cheek. "I do love you. I do. Can't that be enough? Can't we go on as we have been?"

"As we have been? You mean semi-living together? Me trotting back and forth between my house and here? Not having a real home in either place?" Adam shook his head. "I don't think so. I want much more than that from you.

"I've been waiting for years to find the right woman and fall in love. Now that I have, I want the whole shooting match—marriage, family, a home in the suburbs with a white picket fence and a swing-set in the back yard. I want you to be my wife, Lauren, the mother of my children. I want to grow old with you by my side. I want all that marriage and commitment implies."

Every word he uttered felt like a knife turning in her chest. All those things were exactly what she had always wanted . . . before Gavin had sneaked into her home and stolen her baby, and her faith.

"Adam, please, try to understand. I've tried marriage once, with a man I'd known—or at least I thought I'd known—for years, and it all blew up in my face. I can't go through that again." Unable to bear his bleak expression a moment longer, she turned away and walked to the window.

When Adam spoke, he was standing behind her. His voice was soft, heavy with sadness. "Lauren, trust is part of love. If you truly loved me you wouldn't have these doubts."

Turning, she reached up and touched his cheek with the

tips of her fingers, her face tight with pain. "I *do* love you, Adam. I swear it. It's just that I . . . I can't handle marriage. Or children."

He removed her hand from his face and held it in a gentle grip. For what seemed like a long time he simply stood there, staring at her hand, brushing his thumb back and forth across her knuckles, the fine bones in the back. After a while he looked up, and his eyes held a world of sadness. "Well . . . I guess that's that."

Lauren stared at him, fear bubbling through her. "Adam, I love you."

Hurt etched his features. He edged closer and bracketed her face with his hands. He studied her anxious expression, his own heavy with regret. "I know," he said tenderly before dropping a soft kiss on her lips.

He gazed into her frightened green eyes and touched one corner of her mouth with his thumb. "Good-bye, love," he whispered, then he released her and walked away.

"Wait! Where are you going?"

"Back to my place. I'll be back tomorrow to get my things. Don't worry, you'll be all right. I'll keep a watch on the place, and if you need anything or have any problems just call me and I'll come running."

"But I don't want you to go! Don't leave me, Adam. Please."

He gazed at her sadly across the width of the room. "Lauren, don't you understand? I can't stay. Not this way. Not anymore. I'm sorry."

He opened the door and stepped out into the half-light as the sun sank beneath the watery horizon. His footsteps thudded across the deck and down the stairs.

Numb, Lauren moved to the windows. She watched him, striding away across the sand, and she was stricken with loss.

Nineteen

Lauren had thought it was impossible to hurt worse than she had when she'd walked out of Gavin's house. She was wrong.

Losing her son had broken her heart. Losing Adam just hours later had left her feeling as though her heart had been ripped right out of her chest.

After all the weeping she had done, she hadn't thought there was any moisture left in her body for tears, but she'd been wrong about that, too. When she had watched Adam disappear inside his house she had flung herself across her bed and cried inconsolably for hours.

The telephone rang off and on all evening, but she ignored it. She couldn't talk to anyone.

She must have cried herself to sleep, because sometime after midnight she awoke still sprawled across the bed in her street clothes. Her nose felt as though it were plugged with concrete and her head throbbed. When she rose up, the arm beneath her cheek was slick with tears and there was a wet circle on the patchwork bedspread.

Groaning, she dragged herself into the bathroom in search of aspirin, but one look at her blotched and puffy face and red-rimmed eyes in the mirror almost had her crying again. After taking the tablets she snatched a tissue from the box and blew her nose, then splashed her face with cold water.

When that was done, she slipped out of her wrinkled

clothes and put on her nightgown, though she knew that sleep was impossible. Listlessly, she wandered through the dark house and ended up at the windows facing Adam's place. A light was on in his living room.

Lauren folded her arms tight over her midriff and stared at the golden glow. Her throat worked, and she had to bite her bottom lip to hold back another rush of tears.

"Oh, Adam," she whispered in an aching voice. "Adam."

Lauren watched the sun come up, and later she watched Adam leave for the office, but she didn't bother to get dressed. She was in no condition to go to work.

Around eight, she called Nan to tell her she wouldn't be in, and to explain the decision she had made the day before, but she didn't mention the split with Adam.

Nan was filled with sympathy and compassion, but somehow that only made things worse, so Lauren cut the conversation short.

Next she placed a call to personnel to request sick time, only to learn that Adam had made arrangements days before for her to take an indefinite leave.

The thoughtful gesture had her snatching up another wad of tissue to blot her eyes. It was so typical of him. Adam was a giving, compassionate man who looked after those he cared about.

Within fifteen minutes of calling Nan, Walter and Mary Alice called. They were worried about her and wanted to come out to the beach house right away, but she put them off.

She had hardly hung up the receiver when it rang.

"Thank God," Kate said with heartfelt relief the instant that Lauren said hello. "Where have you been? I called last night every fifteen minutes until almost eleven. I was worried sick about you. I had visions of you throwing yourself off that rocky point."

"I'm sorry, Kate. I . . . I just didn't feel like talking to anyone."

"You mean you were there the whole time?" she squawked.

"Kate, I—"

"No, never mind. I suppose I can understand why you didn't want to talk. I probably wouldn't either, in your place. Although, Adam could have had the decency to answer the telephone." Her voice softened. "Lauren, Tony told me what you decided. I know you must be hurting like hell."

Lauren made a mirthless sound. "I've felt better."

"Would you like some company? It might help to talk about it to another woman. We could shoo Adam outta there and have a heart-to-heart, just the two of us. And the baby, of course."

"That's sweet of you, Kate, but I don't think so. Right now I just want to be alone. As for Adam . . . well . . . he's not here."

"Not there? What do you mean, he's not there? Don't tell me that after what you've just been through, that jerk went to work today and left you there alone? Ohhhh, just wait'll I get my hands on that man."

"Kate . . ." Lauren gripped the receiver tighter and closed her eyes. "It's not that. It's . . . well . . . Adam and I broke up last night."

"What! On top of everything else? All right. That's it. I'm coming over."

"Kate, no. Please . . . I'm serious. I'd really rather you didn't. Not just yet."

"Honey, I don't think you should be al—" Kate stopped and made an exasperated sound when little Ryan began to shriek.

"Look, Kate, go tend to your baby and don't worry about me. Somehow I'll get through this. I'll call you in a day or so. Okay? And don't worry."

Kate sputtered, but Lauren quickly hung up the receiver before she could argue.

The rest of the day Lauren roamed the house like a lost soul. She felt like an accident victim—bruised and battered and bleeding internally, and unable to function.

Once, she went into the nursery and ran her hands along the crib where David had slept, over the dressing table, the bureau with the clown drawer knobs, the rocking chair, the huge stuffed bear in the corner.

Later she wandered into her closet and trailed her fingers over Adam's clothes. From there she went into the bathroom, where she buried her face in his terrycloth robe hanging on the back of the door and inhaled his scent.

Each exercise brought on another flood of tears.

Around noon Tony called to say he'd had a meeting with Judge Haloran, and everything was set, although the final hearing had been postponed until the following week to give the court time to draw up the necessary documents.

Which was just as well. Lauren didn't think she had the energy or the will to dress and drag herself to the courthouse.

Around six that evening the front doorbell rang. Her heart gave a leap when she opened the door and saw Adam standing there—until she noticed his car parked in the drive and the garment bag that hung over his shoulder.

He gave her a friendly smile. "Hi. I've come for my things. I hope this isn't a bad time."

"No. It's fine." She hadn't combed her hair all day or put on a speck of makeup or even bothered to dress. She ran a self-conscious hand through her tangled mop and tightened the belt on her robe. "C'mon in."

He paused in the small entry and studied her. "Are you all right?"

"I'm fine," she lied. She had to have some pride.

"Well, that's good." He hefted his garment bag higher on his shoulder and headed for the bedroom. "This won't take long. I'll get my stuff and be out of your hair in twenty minutes."

Lauren wanted to tell him to take all the time he wanted—a week, a month, a year. Ten years, if he liked. She wanted to beg him not to go at all. She had to go into the kitchen, as far away from him as she could get, just to keep from bawling all over him again.

Thirty minutes later, she was still there, staring out the window with her arms crossed, when he returned with his garment bag bulging over one shoulder and a cardboard box balanced on the other. "Well, I think that's everything."

Turning, she nodded woodenly. She didn't dare speak or she might start crying again. Or worse, pleading, and that would be embarrassing for both of them.

"Well . . . I guess this is it." He looked at her for a long time. "You take care of yourself, Lauren. And if you need anything—anything at all—call me. I mean that."

She swallowed hard and nodded again.

"I'll see you." He headed for the front door, then stopped and looked back. "Oh, by the way. Take off as long as you want. Don't try to come back to work until you feel up to it."

"Thank you," she managed. Just barely.

"Hey, no problem. Well . . . so long."

For a long time after the door closed behind him Lauren didn't move. It had all been so calm and friendly, so . . . so civilized. Somehow that made the whole thing even more heartbreaking.

For almost a week, Lauren didn't leave the house. A couple of times she thought about climbing the point, but she had broken that habit after Adam entered her life and she didn't want to take it up again.

She had gone to the point to escape, to let the crashing waves lull her and numb her brain so that she could forget the pain for a little while. Those respites had given her the strength to continue her search, month after month, year after year. Now that was over, and she was going to have to learn to live with the pain, because David wasn't coming back.

Neither, apparently, was Adam.

With longing she watched his comings and goings every day. Several times, after returning home from work, he went out again around eight and didn't return until well after midnight. Lauren tortured herself, wondering where he spent that time. And with whom.

By the end of the week she wasn't feeling one iota better, but she knew, for the sake of her sanity, that she must do something to pull herself out of the black hole of despair she had fallen into. No matter how much she might want to curl up and die, she couldn't. She had to pick herself up and get on with the rest of her life, such as it was. To do that, she forced herself to do what proved to be the hardest thing she'd ever done.

Armed with her tool kit and a stack of empty boxes, she folded and packed away all of David's baby clothes and toys and dismantled the crib. By four that afternoon, the nursery was empty, its contents in a truck on its way to a local women's shelter.

Lauren stood at the front door and watched the van drive away with tears coursing down her face and a crushing sense of finality weighing her down like a lead shroud.

She spent the weekend ferreting out every tiny thing that had belonged to her baby—his silver spoon and cup and the plates and bowls in the kitchen with teddy bears in the bottom, a rattle she'd found under the bureau, his baby book, the unopened canisters of baby powder and wet wipes and a bottle of baby shampoo stashed under the sink of the hall bathroom.

The usable stuff she put into a plastic bag to drop off in a barrel for the needy. The keepsakes she stored away, and the rest went into the garbage.

Adam had been thorough. The only item of his she found was a cuff link that had gotten lost one night when they had stripped each other in haste and made love on the living room rug. They had searched for it later for over an hour, laughing as they crawled around on all fours.

At first Lauren dropped the cuff link into her purse and made a mental note to return it to Adam when she went back to work, but later in the day she dug it out and put it in her pocket. It was foolish, she knew, but to simply be able to touch something of his was comforting.

At the end of the second week, Lauren forced herself to do something about her appearance and reluctantly dragged herself off to the hearing.

Once again, a mob of newspeople were waiting to waylay her when she arrived at the courthouse. Without Adam to shelter her, she felt as though she were suffocating as she fought her way through the crowd. They pressed in on her, jostling, all shouting at once and shoving microphones in her face. As usual, Delia Waters was at the front of the pack. She was quick to notice Adam's absence and pounce on it.

"Ms. McKenna! Mr. Rafferty isn't with you today. Does that mean the rumor is true?"

"I don't know what you're talking about. There are a lot of rumors making the rounds. Most of them started by you, without a thread of evidence to back them up," Lauren gritted out, shoving her way through the rabble.

"Word is that Adam Rafferty has left you. And that he told friends it was because he can no longer be a part of your unconscionable efforts to rip this innocent child from his family. Would you care to comment on that?"

For an answer, Lauren kept walking. Delia smiled.

"Ms. McKenna! Ms. McKenna! What do you think your odds are of regaining your child?" another reporter shouted.

"If you lose today, will you take the case to a higher court?" still another called.

"Ms. McKenna! Will you have to pay child support if sole custody is awarded Mr. Smith?"

"Ms. McKenna, how does it feel to—"

Inside, in the lobby of the courthouse Lauren finally fought her way free of the screaming reporters and stepped into a crowded elevator. As the doors closed, the last thing she saw was Delia's face.

When she stepped off the elevator on the eleventh floor, Tony was waiting for her.

"How are you holding up?" he asked, giving her a worried once over.

"Surviving. Which, all things considered, is pretty good, I guess."

"I'm sorry about that mob out front. I should have waited downstairs to escort you up. I'm just so used to Adam being with—" He stopped and winced. "That is . . . I, uh . . . I should have remembered."

"Thanks, Tony, but that's all right. I managed to get through them."

"Are you still determined to do this?"

Lauren drew a deep breath and closed her eyes. "Yes."

"Okay. It's your call."

Throughout the hearing Tony was kind and solicitous but not once did he mention Adam. The omission was so glaring it made her all the more aware of his absence. It was the first time in months that she had faced a difficult situation without Adam by her side, and she missed him sorely.

When Judge Haloran questioned Lauren about the agreement and asked if that was what she really wanted to do, she almost laughed.

"What I want? No, it's not what I want, not at all," she said, and she could hear Gavin and Annette gasp. "But . . . I've come to the conclusion that it is the best thing for my son."

The judge nodded kindly and said something about unselfish love, but Lauren was too choked up to hear.

When the hearing was over, all she wanted to do was to escape, but she had to endure Gavin and Annette's tearful thanks, then, with Tony's help, fight her way back through the army of reporters. This time she ignored their questions. They would find out soon enough what she had done. No doubt, Delia would turn that against her, too.

When Lauren finally reached the beach house she didn't stop until she was in her bedroom. There she curled into a fetal position in the middle of her bed, still dressed in her business suit and high heels, and for hours she rocked and wailed and moaned like an animal in pain.

On Saturday, someone buzzed the gate. When Lauren pressed the intercom, Kate snapped, "You might as well go ahead and open this thing, Lauren, because I'm coming in even if I have to climb over this damned gate with my baby strapped to my back. So save your breath and don't give me any argument."

Lauren's mouth twisted, but she pushed the button. "Come on in, Kate."

Moments later, her friend came up the front steps, wagging the baby. "Sorry about this," she apologized as she maneuvered a bulging diaper bag and an infant carrier through the door. "He's breast feeding, so I have to take him with me wherever I go."

"It's no problem," Lauren replied with a wan smile. She gazed with longing at the baby, who was contentedly sucking on a pacifier, and stroked his downy cheek with her forefinger. "Where are Paulo and Molly?"

"Molly started to school this week, and Paulo is at the church's daycare for Mother's Day Out—thank God."

Kate plopped the shoulder bag down on the living room rug. She did the same with the infant carrier and set it to rocking before turning to Lauren with her hands on her hips.

"As you can see, I got tired of waiting for you to call. How are you?"

"I . . ."

"Never mind. I can see for myself. You're a mess. It's to be expected. I wanted to rush over here after the final hearing, but Tony thought I should give you time."

"He was probably right. I haven't been very good company lately. Could I get you something? Coffee? Tea? A stiff drink?"

"Iced tea, if you've got it. And I wasn't coming over for you to entertain me." Kate followed Lauren into the kitchen, and as she filled a glass with ice and poured tea from the pitcher in the refrigerator, Kate hitched herself up onto one of the barstools.

"Just tell me one thing. Why on earth would you throw out a wonderful man like Adam? Any fool can see that you two are perfect for one another. And to do it on the very day that you lost your son. That's insane. What are you? A glutton for punishment?"

Lauren halted in the act of pushing the glass across the bar to her. "Is that what Adam told you? That I threw him out?"

"No, I just assumed . . ." Kate's jaw dropped. "Ohmygod. Do you mean he dumped *you?* I'll kill him!"

"Dumped is a harsh word. Pulled away is more appropriate in this case."

"Pulled away? What the devil does that mean?"

As succinctly as possible, Lauren explained what had happened. By the time she finished Kate was staring at her as though she had taken leave of her senses.

"He asked you to *marry* him, and you turned him *down?*"

"You don't have to make me sound like a half-wit."

"Well, you must be, to turn down a man like Adam Rafferty. Do you realize that he's never even been in love before? Not once. Then when he finally does fall, and proposes, the woman he loves says no. 'Tis no wonder he pulled away, as you call it. What choice did the poor man have?"

"He didn't have to end it," Lauren said in a sulky voice. "We could have gone on as we have been. I tried to tell him that but he wouldn't listen."

"Huh. And small wonder. For heaven's sake, Lauren, the man is madly in love with you and has asked you to marry him and you rejected him. You can't expect him to just continue on as though none of that happened. It would be too heartbreaking."

"Kate, he was talking about a lifetime commitment, a home in the suburbs and . . . and children."

"Why, the filthy beast. Someone ought to take him out and horsewhip him."

"Kate, I'm serious. I can't do that again. I can't get married. I can't—I *won't* have more children. I won't risk that kind of pain again. I . . . just can't."

Kate eyed her narrowly. "I'll just be damned. You don't trust him, do you? Well, saints preserve us, no wonder Adam is hurt."

"I knew you would take his side."

"Side! This has nothing to do with taking sides. I love you both. Wasn't I ready to tear a strip off of that big lout for you? Lauren, this is about trust. About being fair. You're punishing Adam—and yourself—for what Gavin Stone did to you."

"No. I . . . I'm just trying to protect myself."

"Against what? Merciful heavens! Adam Rafferty is the kindest, most trustworthy man you will ever meet. They don't come any better, not even my Tony."

"I know that, but . . ."

Kate slid off the stool and came around the bar. She grasped Lauren's shoulders and looked straight into her eyes. "Lauren, listen to me. Adam isn't your ex-husband. He adores you. Before he'd hurt you the man would cut out his own heart. Lord, woman, don't you know that?"

Lauren's chin began to wobble. "Yes. At least . . . a part of me does. But I keep remembering that Gavin and I were once in love. Back then no one could have convinced me that he would hurt me. But he did."

"So you want guarantees, do you? Well, tough, kiddo. Look, I'm not trying to minimize what happened to you. It was horrible and excruciating. But, Lauren, life is full of risks. If you step out there and live it, now and then you're going to get knocked down. It happens to all of us. And when it does, you can either get back up and come out swinging, or you can play it safe and crawl off to the sidelines with your tail tucked between your legs and watch life pass you by."

"I . . . I don't know if I have the strength."

"Oh, you have it, all right. I've seen plenty of evidence of that. The question is, are you willing to use it?" Kate searched Lauren's teary eyes, and her expression softened. "If you're half the woman I think you are, you will," she whispered.

On Monday, two weeks after presenting her offer to Gavin and his wife, Lauren returned to work. She still felt miserable, but, as Kate had so bluntly informed her—she'd licked her wounds long enough. It was time to get on with it.

She was full of trepidation about coming face to face with Adam again, but she needn't have worried. Whenever they were together he was friendly and cordial.

The first time she met him in the hall he smiled and stopped to chat. "Hi there. Welcome back."

"Thank you." With a polite smile pasted on her face, Lauren shifted from one foot to the other, at a loss for something to say.

"How're you feeling?"

"Okay."

"How are your visits with David going? Are you making progress with him?"

Lauren shrugged. "Not so you would notice."

"Well, just hang in there. He'll come around eventually." He was carrying some rolled-up blueprints and tapped them against his leg and started easing away. "Gotta go. You take it easy."

Lauren stared after him with her throat aching. Nothing in his manner gave the least indication that there were unrequited or bitter feelings between them. He treated her with exactly the same degree of respect and distant congeniality as he did every other employee of Ingram and Bates. No one who didn't know them would ever have guessed that they had been lovers.

Lauren knew she should have been glad, but somehow Adam's impersonal friendliness wrung her heart. It hurt to see him every day knowing he was no longer hers. That he apparently had no trouble making the adjustment hurt even worse.

The attitude of the other employees did not make her return easy, either.

Lauren was not surprised that word of the outcome of her custody case had spread throughout the company. All the networks and newspapers had given the case full coverage, but none were so slanted or malicious as Delia Waters. The very next evening, she had aired their agreement, line by line, on her TV magazine show and mentioned it as well on the evening news. In that smug way she had, she implied that it had been her constant hounding that had forced Lauren into making the decision.

Apparently the news of her and Adam's split had also made the rounds of the office grapevine. Everyone tiptoed around Lauren as though they expected her to shatter into a million pieces at any moment.

With the exception of Walter, Mary Alice, and Nan, for the most part, they simply avoided her. Whenever she walked into a room all conversation ceased and gazes skittered away as everyone became suddenly busy. Even when Lauren passed people in the hallways and spoke, they muttered a quick response and hurried on by, not quite meeting her eyes.

Lauren knew that they weren't being deliberately cruel. Most people simply felt awkward and didn't know what to say, but all the same, the response added to her depression. At times she felt more isolated and alone at work than she did at home.

After two weeks back on the job, she was beginning to wonder if it wouldn't be best all around if she looked elsewhere for a job.

Hardly an hour after the thought occurred to Lauren, she was summoned to Walter's office.

Twenty

An uneasy feeling rippled through Lauren when she walked into Walter's office and found Ed and John Bailey there. Mary Alice sat in her usual place next to Walter's desk. The feeling grew worse when Lauren saw their expressions. Mary Alice looked as though she were going to be sick, and neither John nor Ed would quite meet her eyes.

She didn't like the look of this at all. Except for Adam's absence, the gathering reminded her sharply of the meeting they'd had a few months ago.

Lauren glanced at her godfather. "You sent for me, Walter?"

"Yes. Have a seat."

She complied and smoothed her skirt down over her knees. "Is something wrong?"

"You could say that." Walter plopped a thick manila folder down on the corner of the desk in front of her. "Take a look at that."

Mary Alice looked pained and shifted in her chair.

"What is it?"

"It's self-explanatory. Go ahead, read it."

"Walter, shouldn't we wait for Adam?" Ed inquired a bit uneasily, but Lauren had already started looking through the folder.

"He'll be along. He buzzed awhile ago and said he had to retrieve something first."

With every page that Lauren turned she grew sicker. "Oh, my God."

"My sentiments exactly. I didn't want to have to show you this, Lauren, but I was left with no choice. A few more mistakes of this magnitude will cripple this company."

She looked up. "Are you blaming me for these errors?"

"Those are your bids and purchase orders, aren't they?"

"Well . . . yes, but—"

"And is that your signature?"

"It appears to be. But these aren't my bids. And these aren't the orders I placed. I distinctly remember these jobs and I know these aren't mine."

"Lauren, you have been under a lot of strain lately," Ed offered kindly. "Perhaps you were distracted."

"I'm telling you, these aren't mine. You can check them against my computer files."

"Don't bother," Adam said as he walked in. "They would be the same."

"Adam!" Lauren stared at him, stricken. "You think I did this?" She felt as though she had just been kicked in the stomach.

"No, I don't. In fact, I know you didn't."

Lauren sagged with relief, but Ed gave a startled laugh.

"C'mon, Adam. You just said these documents would match the work on her computer. Even Lauren admits that the signature on those papers is hers. What other explanation could there be?"

"How about deliberate sabotage of Lauren's work?"

"What's this! What are you saying?" Walter boomed.

"C'mon, Adam," Ed chided. "That's a bit far-fetched, isn't it?"

Adam walked to Walter's desk and handed him a sheet of paper. "Those signatures are forgeries. I had a suspicion they were, so I took everything to a handwriting expert for analysis. That's his report."

"That's absurd! Who would do such a thing? And why, for God's sake?"

Adam looked at Ed. "Good questions. As to the why, I haven't quite figured that out yet. Suppose you tell me."

"*Me!* How would I know?"

"Because you're the one who falsified those papers."

"What! That's crazy."

"Not really. You see, I remembered that you were very good at forging our professors' signatures back when we were in college. As memory serves, you even filched a couple of your grade slips and substituted forged ones, and no one was ever the wiser. If you'll recall, we had a fight about it."

"That was because you were such a Boy Scout."

"I didn't like cheats then and I like them even less now. That's why I also gave the expert an example of your handwriting. He says there's no doubt those signatures are yours."

"That's a lie! Handwriting analysis isn't an exact science. It's just your guy's opinion. That's not proof of anything."

"It is when you put it with this." Adam walked to the entertainment center and inserted a video cassette into the VCR.

"What kind of nonsense is this! I don't have to sit here and listen to—"

"Shut up and sit down, Ed," Walter boomed. "Go ahead, Adam."

"I've suspected for a long time that someone had figured out Lauren's password and was breaking into her computer and altering the data on her hard disk. I worked late several nights trying to catch the culprit, but no one ever showed up.

"However, I was certain that I was right, so I set up a surveillance camera in her office."

"What! That's invasion of privacy!"

"Only of Lauren's. And given the results, I doubt that she will object. Will you, Lauren?"

She shook her head, dazed by the turn things had taken. "No. No, of course not."

Adam pressed the play button, and immediately a shot of the interior of Lauren's office filled the screen. The wall-mounted camera was aimed at her computer. For several frames there was no one there. Then Ed walked in and sat down in front of the computer and began to type. Within minutes he was retrieving files.

"As you can see on the camera's calendar/clock printout on the lower right hand corner of the screen, this was taken last Wednesday at a little after four in the morning. Very clever, Ed. The cleaning crew has left and no one had arrived yet for work. Not much chance of being caught at that hour."

Ed shot him a sullen, hate-filled glare.

Walter banged his fist down on his desk so hard the telephone jumped. "Well? What've you got to say for yourself?" he bellowed. "And don't bother denying you did it. We've all got eyes."

If looks could kill, Adam would have been incinerated on the spot. Ed was so angry he looked maniacal. "All right. Hell, yes, I did it. So what?"

"But why, Ed?" Lauren asked in a bewildered voice. "Why would you do this to me?"

"Why else? To discredit you in Walter's eyes. You're his goddaughter. I figured if he thought you were incompetent or untrustworthy he wouldn't make you his heir, not the way he feels about this company. I couldn't let you just step in and take over."

"Oh, Ed."

"Hey, it's your fault. If you hadn't given me the cold shoulder I wouldn't have had to resort to this. My original plan was to marry you. That way, if you did inherit the firm, I would have complete control."

Lauren's spine stiffened. "There was never any chance of that happening."

"Even if your plan had succeeded it has a major flaw,"

Adam added. "You obviously don't know Lauren very well if you think she would meekly turn over her share of the company to you. She'd run the business herself, and probably do one helluva job of it, too."

Lauren gazed at Adam, overwhelmed with gratitude.

"But as it turns out," Adam continued. "Whatever portion of the company Lauren does inherit, it won't amount to controlling interest. That will come to me."

"You? How do you figure into this?"

"The agreement that Walter and I made when I signed on was that I will purchase forty-four percent of the company over the next ten years, and upon his death I will inherit another seven percent."

"Is that true?" Ed demanded of Walter. When Walter nodded, Ed looked as though he were about to burst a blood vessel.

"It's not fair! Half this company should have been mine when my uncle died. Instead I ended up with a lousy five percent. Even when I tried to buy more shares Walter wouldn't sell them to me."

"Because your uncle didn't want you to have them," Walter snapped. "Howard never could stand you, not even when you were a boy. He thought you were a conniving, sneaky little snot-nosed bastard and he didn't trust you. Not an inch. And you've proved he was right not to."

"That's a lie! Uncle Howard loved me like his own son. Why . . . he even paid for me to go to Princeton."

"For your mother's sake. Before she died, he promised his sister-in-law he'd look after you. Even she was afraid that without a little help you'd end up in trouble. That's the only reason Howard gave you a job here, and left you a small amount of stock, but he never intended to leave you his share of the company. Before he died I promised him I would never let that happen."

"It's not fair. It's just not fair. I'm the heir to one of the founders of this company. Lauren isn't. Neither is Adam. *I* should get the business, not them."

Walter pointed a long, bony finger at Ed. "You listen to me, boy. *I* own this company now, and *I'm* the one who decides who gets a piece of it when I'm gone. Trust me, that won't be you. Matter of fact, I expect you to sell me the five percent share you already have or you'll be facing criminal prosecution."

"Sell? I'm not going to sell my shares."

"Oh, yes, you are. And you're going to go clean out your desk and get the hell outta here. You've got one hour before I sic the security guys on you. Now get out of my office. The sight of you makes me sick."

Ed looked to Adam for support. "Adam, do something."

"What do you expect me to do, Ed? You brought this on yourself."

"I thought you were my friend."

"I was," Adam replied in a soft voice. "Or at least I tried to be. But no more. I'm sorry, Ed."

"Fine. Who needs you." He shot to his feet so fast he knocked his chair over, but he made no effort to right it. "All right, I'm going. But don't think you've heard the end of this. You'll be hearing from my attorney." He stormed out of the room.

"Well, that's that. Good riddance," Mary Alice said when Ed slammed out. "As for you, Walter Ingram, didn't I tell you over and over that Lauren had nothing to do with those errors?"

"So you did, love," Walter conceded, reaching across the corner of the desk to give her cheek a pat.

Lauren's heart was so full it felt as though it were going to burst. She had never loved Adam more than she did at that moment. "Adam . . . I don't know how to thank you," she began, but he waved her gratitude aside.

"No problem. Don't worry about it. I'm just glad this mess is resolved. Now if you'll excuse me, I have to run."

"But, Adam, we need to talk."

"Sorry. I'm meeting a client in fifteen minutes. I'll have to catch you later."

"Oh. All right. I . . . I won't keep you then."

He executed a tiny salute of farewell and strode out. Lauren stared after him, frustrated and vaguely deflated.

The feeling stayed with her throughout the day and into the evening.

Despite his cheery parting comment, she saw nothing more of Adam at the office the rest of the day. By the time he returned to his home after eight that evening, she'd had plenty of time to mull over what had happened.

Too restless to eat, she spent the evening wandering through the house, thinking, stopping now and then to stare across the sand at the lights in Adam's house.

Dear God, how she missed him, she thought with a pang that nearly doubled her over. She was so alone—much more alone than she had ever been before Adam entered her life. The house seemed so empty, her bed so cold.

She missed everything about Adam—his warmth, his smell, the sound of his voice, that lopsided smile and the twinkle in his eyes, the way he sang off key at the top of his lungs in the shower and whistled when he worked in the kitchen. She even missed the mess he made in the bathroom.

Most of all though, she missed his touch, and his steadiness.

Without him, she felt as though her world were all topsy-turvy and out of sync.

Lauren rubbed her elbows and stared at Adam's house. Her heart hurt.

She couldn't go on like this. Smiling and nodding and making polite small talk whenever they met, as though they were merely passing acquaintances, as though they'd never been lovers. As though they'd never lain naked in each other's arms and poured out their hearts to each other. It was intolerable.

She closed her eyes, but tears seeped from between her lashes anyway and trickled down her face. She couldn't bear it any longer.

Before she could reconsider, she went to the telephone and punched out Adam's number.

"Yeah, Rafferty here," he answered on the third ring.

Lauren gripped the receiver tighter. "Adam."

"Lauren? Is that you?"

"Yes, it's me. You told me to call if I needed you."

"What's the problem?"

"The problem is . . . I need you."

A long silence followed. Then Adam said in a soft rumble, "Lauren . . . I haven't changed my mind."

She bit her lip and twined the telephone cord around her index finger. "I know."

The quiet stretched out again. She could almost feel him tensing.

"Please, Adam."

After a moment he murmured, "All right. I'll be right there."

When he knocked on her front door only minutes later she knew he had driven over. She hoped it was a sign that he was in a hurry to reach her.

When she answered the summons he stepped inside, closed the door, and leaned back against it with his arms crossed over his chest. His face was somber, his eyes brooding.

She trembled at his nearness and greedily inhaled his familiar scent.

Lauren hoped that he would make the first move. She wanted him to sweep her up in his arms and cover her face with kisses and tell her how much he loved her, but he just stood there, watching her. Waiting.

"Why did you call me, Lauren?" he said finally.

He sounded so remote, so unyielding. Lauren's lips quivered. She twisted her hands together and looked at him pleadingly. "Oh, Adam. I've missed you so. How can you be this way? So . . . so remote and unemotional?" She bowed her head and stared at her twisting hands so he wouldn't see the tears in her eyes. "For weeks you've been acting as though I were simply a casual acquaintance. Adam, what are you doing to me?"

"Giving you time to heal."

Her head snapped up. "Wha-what?"

"After you turned me down, once I'd gotten past my hurt pride, I realized that my timing had been atrocious. You needed time to grieve for your child and recover. I've been trying to give you that time."

"Oh, Adam." Lauren hurled herself against his chest and threw her arms around his neck. Burying her face against his shoulder, she held him tight and wept.

His arms enfolded her. He cupped the back of her head and tenderly stroked her hair. "Hey, take it easy. Don't cry."

"I . . . I ca-can't . . . help it." In between sobs she alternately scattered kisses along the side of his neck and gasped out her relief. "I thought I had lo-lost you. I thought . . . I thought you didn't love me anymo-more, and I cou-couldn't bear it. These past weeks without you have been mi-miserable. Oh, Adam, I love you so. Don't ever leave me again."

He rubbed her back and kissed the top of her head. "Does this mean that you're ready to accept my proposal?"

Her arms tightened around his neck. She squeezed her eyes shut and nodded. "Yes," she sniffed. "Yes."

She eased back to look at him, but he was a blur through the tears that shimmered in her eyes. Her chin wobbled and her lips trembled so she had to press them together for a moment. Emotion clogged her throat, but she forced the words past the painful lump. "I love you, Adam, and I want to be your wife."

Adam closed his eyes. "Thank God," he growled a second before he snatched her close for his kiss.

She moaned at the first touch of his lips. The kiss was

instantly wanton and fierce and sizzling with heat as each sought to make up for the long, lonely weeks apart.

Lauren clung to Adam, her restless hands caressing his back, his neck, exploring his ears, his scalp, learning anew the feel of him, the texture of his skin, the silkiness and smoothness of his hair, the warm firmness of his muscles. She had despaired of ever being in his arms again. It was heaven.

Tongues dueled in a rough caress, twisting and twining, revealing need that had grown to near desperation. Their lips rocked together in greedy passion, the kiss hot and hungry, open and wet. Their hearts thudded and their blood rushed hotly through their veins.

Adam nipped Lauren's lower lip, then drew it into his mouth and sucked gently. She made a throaty sound in the back of her throat and winnowed her fingers through the hair at his nape, telling him without words the depth of her feelings.

When at last their clinging lips parted, Adam raised his hand and cupped her jaw. Warm and intent, his gaze roamed her face, touching each feature as though trying to absorb her through his eyes. The possessive look seemed to turn Lauren's body to hot liquid, and she sagged against him. "I need you, sweetheart," Adam whispered. "I need you so much."

In answer she stepped back and took his hand in hers. With a beckoning smile on her lips, she led him through the living room and down the hall.

In the bedroom, Adam took her into his arms and kissed her again, deeply, giving full rein to the pent-up hunger that clamored in them both. His hands roamed her back, pressing her close, letting her know the strength of his need.

Looping her arms around his neck, Lauren fitted her body intimately to his and rocked her hips against him. Adam groaned and tore his mouth from hers. "Ah, sweetheart, how I love you."

He stepped back and grasped the bottom of her cotton knit top in both hands. In a single motion, he pulled the coffee-colored garment off over her head and tossed it aside, then sucked in his breath. Beneath the soft knit was only the silky, fragrant skin that had haunted his dreams for weeks.

A flame leaped in his eyes as they silently devoured her. "You're beautiful," he whispered.

With shaky hands, he lowered the zipper on her slacks and pushed them down her hips. Dropping to one knee, he pressed his face against her stomach above the tiny triangle of her panties. "So beautiful," he murmured as he kissed and licked the silky skin.

A tremor started deep inside Lauren. Clutching his head, she tunneled her fingers through his hair to hold him close and closed her eyes, awash with emotion. Her love for him was infinite, boundless. It swelled with painful sweetness in her chest and overflowed her heart to spread through her body in a warm tide.

As he continued to worship her with his mouth and tongue, Lauren glided her hands down his neck and gripped the bunched muscles in his shoulders. She tipped her head back and closed her eyes, drawing intense pleasure from the silky brush of his hair against the undersides of her breasts, the caress of his hands against her thighs.

Adam eased her panties down to her ankles, and she stepped out of them and her sandals. He stood up, and for a long moment he simply stared at her. The look in his eyes sent desire streaking through Lauren, and she quivered. The reaction caused Adam's lips to curve in a slow, sensuous smile. He bent and kissed each breast and eased her back onto the bed.

His own clothes were removed with haste, and in seconds he stretched out beside her and pulled her into his arms, and their mouths met in a searing kiss.

"Oh, Adam, I've missed you so." Her hands ran over him in a restless caress, glorying in the feel of him.

"I know sweetheart, I've missed you too," Adam gasped. "So much."

After that, neither spoke. Desperation drove them. They rolled together across the bed in a frenzy of passion and need, hands stroking and clutching, their bodies straining together in silent demand, and they came together in a blaze of desire and love so intense Lauren thought surely the heat would consume them both.

The flame burned brightly, quickly. The sweet pressure built higher and higher, and when the shattering explosion came it rocked them to the depths of their souls, and each cried out the other's name.

A long while later, lying propped on a pile of pillows with Lauren cuddled against his side, Adam gazed across the room at nothing and absently stroked her arm.

"Lauren?"

"Mmm?"

"When will you marry me?"

He felt her smile against his shoulder. "Whenever you say."

"Tomorrow?"

"Yes." She chuckled and tipped her head up to look at him. "Although I'm not sure it can be done that fast."

His gaze bore deep into her. "And children?"

Lauren stilled, and Adam's gut clenched at the flicker of fear in her eyes.

"I . . . I want that, too. I do. But . . . you'll have to be patient. It may take me a while to work up the courage."

Adam released the breath he was holding as relief poured through him. "Take as long as you want. As long as I know that you're willing to consider having a family, I can wait. I just want you to remember one thing though. You won't be alone this time. I'll be there with you."

Her eyes grew misty. "Oh, Adam." She raised her hand

and cupped his cheek. "It's scary, but I don't think there is anything I can't handle as long as I have you."

"You'll always have me, sweetheart. I promise."

"Always?"

He brought her hand to his mouth and pressed a warm kiss into her palm. Over the top his eyes caressed her. "You can count on it."

**If you liked this book, be sure to look for others
in the *Denise Little Presents* line:**